George D. Brewerton

Wars of the Western Border

New homes and a strange people - Vol. 1

George D. Brewerton

Wars of the Western Border
New homes and a strange people - Vol. 1

ISBN/EAN: 9783337345167

Printed in Europe, USA, Canada, Australia, Japan

Cover: Foto ©Andreas Hilbeck / pixelio.de

More available books at **www.hansebooks.com**

WARS

OF THE

WESTERN BORDER;

OR,

NEW HOMES AND A STRANGE PEOPLE.

BY

G. DOUGLAS BREWERTON,

AUTHOR OF "A RIDE WITH KIT CARSON," "CAMP FIRE YARNS," ETC.

———————

NEW YORK:

DERBY & JACKSON, 498 BROADWAY.

1860.

W. H. Tinson, Stereotyper.   George Russell & Co., Printers.

𝔗o

KIT CARSON,

The "Mountain-Man" and Guide, with whom we have traversed the wilds of the Rocky Mountains, and the sun-scorched sands of the American desert, this work is dedicated, as an evidence of the sincere regard which is entertained for **him**, both as a *voyageur* and as a *man*, by his old comrade

THE AUTHOR.

PREFACE.

We are about to write what nobody reads—a Preface. Did you ever, kind reader, see a young mamma in all the flutter and anxiety of adorning her "*latest* production" for its first appearance upon some public promenade? for if you have, you may the more fully appreciate our trepidation in sending *this* youngster, all unattended, into the world, to court the smiles of those crabbed old fellows, the critics, and win, if we be lucky, its "little meed of fame," from that no less difficult class to please—"our readers." But to carry out the simile, let us suppose the "infant phenomenon" aforesaid—not ours but the anxious mamma's—to be ugly by nature—in short, as peevish, squalling, ill-behaved, and unbearable a brat as ever pulled "grandpa's" hair or screamed lustily after midnight—to how great an extent *then* are our young matrons perplexities increased as she "fusses and fixes," scolds "nurse" and soothes "baby;" and where, let us ask, will you find a more ill-tempered or naturally repulsive *original* production than this very unpromising offspring of Pro-Slavery and Free Soil, which we are about to exhibit under the somewhat hackneyed title of "The War in Kansas." Yet though the words fall wearily, like a thrice-told tale, upon your ear, we flatter ourself that there are some new truths to be found upon these pages, for there is an inner life in all great events—and who shall doubt the celebrity of the Wakarusa War?—an *under-current* of adventure and character, and it is in *this* tide that we have preferred to go-a-whaling for such incidents as appeared likely to be most interesting to the reader.

Nor can we charge ourself with neglecting those more important events—with the causes which lead thereto—that have been landmarks in the progress of this much-talked-of campaign. Oh, no; we have done our duty by the "Gradgrinds" in writing up the *facts* as we present them to you, in the shape of His Excellency Governor Shannon's statement on the one side, and that of the Free Soil leader, Major-General Robinson, upon the other, with all such documents as may seem necessary to a full understanding of the same. So having been thus faithful to the *substantials* of the war, by putting in such *heavy* blocks as these, we have ventured to relieve the sternness of the whole by the *lighter*, yet no less truthful, adornments of "Squire Portly and his dame," "our friend Major Ramrod," "the Hard Shell Baptist Preacher," "Deacon Graves," and "Old Man Rhymer," for whose *peculiar* eccentricities we would respectfully refer you to the chapters of this book.

And as a *finale* to our Preface, we assure the reader that we are upon *neither* side of this unhappy quarrel, between those who, united as they are by one common bond of national brotherhood, ought to be the best of friends. On the contrary, we have gazed upon the Kansas difficulties as the old lady did when she put on her spectacles to see her husband fight the bear—on which occasion (to quote from that venerable woman's narrative of the combat just alluded to), "she allowed sometimes that she'd drather see thar old man whip, and then agin she *felt* fur thar bar; but bimeby, when they wor a goin' it strong, she didn't bother much about it, till toward thar last, an then it jest seemed as ef she didn't kear a dern *which* licked so long as she *seed thar fight*."

CONTENTS.

CHAPTER I.

OFF TO THE WAR.

CHAPTER II.

INCIDENTS BY THE WAY.

CHAPTER III.

A HARD ONE FOR THE AUTHOR.

CHAPTER IV.

OLD MAN RHYMER AND A BOONSVILLE HOTEL.

CHAPTER V.

FROM "OUR CORRESPONDENT" *en route*.

CHAPTER VI.

OUR VIRGINIAN FRIEND ON SLAVERY.

CHAPTER VII.

LEXINGTON.

CHAPTER VIII.

TREATS OF THINGS RELIGIOUS AND SECULAR.

CHAPTER IX.

OUR AUTHOR ENTERS KANSAS.

CHAPTER X.

THE SHAWNEE MANUAL LABOR SCHOOL.

CHAPTER XI.

RED-SKINS AND INDIAN YARNS.

CHAPTER XII.

NEWS-HUNTING IN WESTPORT.

CHAPTER XIII.

WE JOURNEY TO LECOMPTON.

CHAPTER XIV.

HOUSE ON THE PRAIRIE.

CHAPTER XV.

THE EXECUTIVE OFFICE AT SHAWNEE MISSION.

CHAPTER XVI.

THE PRO-SLAVERY SIDE OF THE KANSAS WAR.

CHAPTER XVII.

GOVERNOR SHANNON'S HISTORY OF THE WAKARUSA WAR.

CHAPTER XVIII.

CONTAINS A DIGRESSION BY THE GOVERNOR.

CHAPTER XIX.

THE GOVERNOR CONTINUES HIS NARRATIVE.

CHAPTER XX.

GOVERNOR'S NARRATIVE CONTINUED—THE TREATY.

CHAPTER XXI.

CHRISTMAS IN KANSAS.

CHAPTER XXII.

LIFE AT THE MISSION.

CHAPTER XXIII.

COLEMAN'S NARRATIVE.

CHAPTER XXIV.

FOR LAWRENCE DIRECT.

CHAPTER XXV.

NEW YEAR'S EVE BY A LOG-CABIN HEARTH.

CHAPTER XXVI.

OUR NEW YEAR'S CALL.

CHAPTER XXVII.

THE BALL.

CHAPTER XXVIII.

THE HEROINES OF THE WAR.

CHAPTER XXIX.

THE FREE-STATE SIDE OF THE QUESTION.

CHAPTER XXXVI.

THE SEBASTOPOL OF THE WEST.

CHAPTER XXXVII.

LAWRENCE IN A MILITARY POINT OF VIEW.

CHAPTER XXXVIII.

FREE-STATE ODDS AND ENDS.

CHAPTER XXXIX.

LAST LINES.

𝔉𝔞𝔯𝔢𝔴𝔢𝔩𝔩.

CHAPTER I.

OFF TO THE WAR.

TUESDAY, *December 4th*, 1855.—Ding—dong—ding, three o'clock by old Trinity—it rang out just as we turned into the Broadway artery of that human tide which is ever flowing through our great metropolis—three by the wintry sun—three by the Banks—three by old Trinity—and as we listened to the tones of that iron tongue, which marks the burial of the dead hours—far above the roar of Wall-street Bulls and Bears, not to mention the clatter of conflicting omnibuses—we fell into a meditative mood, and paced the sloppy pavements leisurely.

Of what we were thinking upon that memorable afternoon, we are not at this particular moment prepared to state ; but certain it is that our mental train met with an obstacle, and ran off the track instanter, to the great detriment, not to say destruction, of some four-score promising "castles in the air," exploded by the collision.

And the obstacle? most gentle reader—was a Newsboy—who had startled our ears with the curt announcement of

"Here's the New York 'Erald—second edishun—got the Great War in Kansas."

The "Great War in Kansas?" what could it mean? We had heard of the "Dorr War," the "Anti-Rent War," the "Erie Pea-nut War," and even of that stirring strife of which the poet has so beautifully sung,

"SEBASTOPOL AIN'T TAKEN YET,
Pop goes the Weasel."

But the *Kansas* War—that *was* something new! So we slackened our pace, pondered for a moment, got our mental locomotive on the track again, was "struck with an idea," but without receiving any material injury, and then halted outright, and whistled up the Newsboy, who straightway answered to the call, in the shape of a diminutive young biped, with a frosty nose, a very shrill voice, and a pair of patent ventilating pantaloons, which exhibited a suspicion of dingy-colored linen in their rear. Add to these, a huge bundle of papers under the left arm, and a brace of "specimen numbers" in the extended right hand, and you have a sketch "from the life," done at sight, of that very nondescript animal——a New York Newsboy.

"Here's the 'Erald, sir—second edishun," squeaked the shrill voice.

We satisfied ourself that there was *something* from Kansas (for we want confidence in the whole race of Newsboys—the patent-improved sort not excepted), and then, in the agitation of the moment, disbursed half a dime, at the same time grasping a paper, without asking for the change. When we recovered ourself, the vender of recent intelligence had vanished like a theatrical ghost; the dirty linen aforesaid, being the last object visible as he shot round a neighboring corner.

And now for the news, was our mental ejaculation; for if there be no compensation in the "second edishun," we are minus

five cents, federal currency, and grossly deceived to boot. So
we turned down the paper, found the " very latest by telegraph,"
pressed our beaver more firmly upon our brow, and then retreated from the vortex of a jostling crowd into the shelter of a
friendly doorway, to read, in greater quietness, the following
paragraph :—

"BY TELEGRAPH.

"Call from the Governor for United States Troops.

"*St. Louis, Dec.* 3, 1855.

"Accounts from Kansas state that Governor Shannon has telegraphed
to the President, concerning the present condition of affairs in that Territory. He says that one thousand men have arrived in Lawrence, and rescued a prisoner from the sheriff of Douglas County, and burned some
houses and other property. He asks the President to order out the troops
at Fort Leavenworth, to aid in the execution of the laws.

"Dispatches from Weston arrived here to-day by express, bringing
startling news from Atchinson. Some Free State officers had taken possession of important papers, and an attack upon Atchinson was anticipated.
A messenger had been sent to Weston for fifty armed men."

We read no more, but turned upon our heel and rammed the
" second edishun " into our great-coat pocket, with an emphasis
which bespoke a determination on our part to do " something
energetic, and that soon." And it was even so, for in that
instant of time we had made up our minds to go to Kansas,
partly because we wished to see the row, not as through a glass,
darkly (meaning the medium of printers' ink), but with our own
unspectacled eyes—yea, even as the Big Spring Free State Delegate Convention expresses it—" to a bloody issue," but most of
all because we wanted a change—the comforts of civilization
had begun to weary us—we longed for a rougher life—for
Prairie air and Border freedom ; in a word, to sum our case up
briefly, we didn't know when we were well off, and pined for an
alteration for the worse. " Westward ho !" cried our first
impulse, and we yielded—of course we did—for we always

make it a point, unless we can't help ourself, to " treat our inclinations."   Yes, we confess it, for, like Tony Lumpkin, of " the
Three Jolly Pigeons " notoriety, although we might have disappointed the dear public, and spared the book-stalls the infliction
of a new volume on Kansas—nay, have even most respectfully
declined to play historian to the far-famed Wàkarusa war—we
" couldn't bear to disappoint ourself."

But how to go ? ah ! there was the rub. It costs money to
travel, and we, alas ! so far as temporal goods are concerned,
suffer but little from taxation. It requires time, too (unless,
indeed, as the Irishman expressed it, " one could verify the revolution of the earth by sitting down upon the ground, and letting the
" counthries " come round to him in succession), and time, in
this waking world, is money. So it was with a purpose that we
turned our hasty steps towards the office of the New York
Herald, for we had a pecuniary problem to cipher out, and the
prime minister of the " Satanic Press " was just the man to lay
down its premises. What wonder then that fifteen minutes' time
found us in the editorial *sanctum sanctorum* of Bennett's paper—
where with Mr. H——, its senior editor (in big whiskers and an
arm-chair), for a *vis-à-vis*, we proceeded to unfold our wishes and
set forth our very modest expectations.

We thought there would be " wars and rumors of wars " in
Kansas   The Herald got all the news—the Herald must there-
for be posted upon Kansas—*ergo*, the Herald would require a
correspondent—a special one, in those far regions. And a " War
Correspondent " to boot. And who (we diffidently inquired),
was better fitted for this arduous position than ourself? Had
we not scribbled for the Herald, written articles for Harper,
and moreover been " a man-of-war," while in the service of that
stingy old curmudgeon—Uncle Sam. In view of all these circumstances, we made bold to talk up our stock, clinching the
whole with the insinuation, that the New York Herald *might*

do itself an injustice, by not ordering us to Kansas instanter. In fine, we retired at the expiration of a fifteen minutes' interview, with the blessed assurance that Mr. H—— would take the matter into consideration, and give us a final answer upon the morrow—at noon.

We will spare you a recital of the astonishment with which our friends received the intelligence that we *might* start next day for Kansas—to be gone for an indefinite length of time—suffice it to say that we "attended to our sleeping" that night, for it seemed just possible that it might be our last chance in bed before reaching a frontier log-cabin.

High noon of December the 5th found us again closeted with Mr. H—— of the Herald. He "didn't think the war would amount to much—he regarded it as a move to make political capital for Whitfield or Reeder at Washington. In short he believed the whole affair to be a ' Barnum '—*alias* humbug, of the most unmitigated kind. Here was a pretty state of things—if Mr. H—— didn't believe in the war, it would be no go with us —so we set to work, with a will, to correct these very erroneous impressions. Well, we argued the matter *pro* and *con*, and Mr. H—— finally asked us to reduce the thing to figures, by saying,

"How much ?"

"We mentioned a sum—it was satisfactory."

"When will you start ?"

"By the first conveyance."

"When can you get there ?"

"As soon or sooner than the mail."

"Very well ; this letter will accredit you as our correspondent. Here Mr. H—— sat down and wrote us the following :

"HERALD OFFICE, *New York, Dec.* 5, 1855.

"My DEAR SIR:

If circumstances permit, I would like to have you leave this afternoon for Kansas Territory, to act as the correspondent of the *New*

York Herald. In addition to the important political events that may take place, and of which you will furnish us with the particulars, I would suggest that you send us full information of the agricultural and industrial progress of the new territory and people. I shall hope to hear from you in a week or ten days.

Very truly yours,
F—— H——
for JAMES G. BENNETT.

G. Douglas Brewerton, Esq."

In addition to this "letter of instructions," we were kindly provided by a very popular Ex-Senator, with a brace of introductory epistles to the "distinguished consideration" of Governor Shannon and Senator Atchinson. By this time the advent of one o'clock reminded us that Time and steamboats wait for no man, and that if we meant to leave that evening we had better be going. So we made our adieu to the ministering angels (?) of the Herald, with many a hearty prayer (not to mention some expressions of incredulity), as touching our safe return; and then went forth to make the necessary preparations for a trip to the seat of war in Kansas.

And now as we can't plead the old-fashioned apology "excuse haste and a bad pen"—we will simply beg your mercy, if want of space should jolt our style into the Doe-sticks or railroad order. *En avant!* then, let us progress—even though it be at high-pressure speed—so follow us, good people, if you can.

We plunged into Broadway—met a shop with flaring glass windows—be-lettered from top to toe in many hued-capitals, setting forth the names of cities and places to an extent which might have induced the bewildered spectator to hazard a supposition that the "man inside" must have begun his travels at an early age, and kept on until he had mastered the geography, got over the maps, and bothered the terrestrial globes. We "limbered up" accordingly, and straightway concluded that if the proprietor of this establishment didn't sell tickets to St. Louis, which (as everybody ought to know) is the first *long* step to Kansas, nobody else did ; so we dived in—violated the sanctity of the railed pen-marked " no admittance behind the counter"—met a hatchet-faced man, with keen eyes, a faint moustache and consumptive-looking whiskers to match—told hatchet-faced man that we wanted to go to St. Louis, and required information—found hatchet-faced man polite, with a very glib tongue, or, as Samuel Weller, senior, of the " Belle Sauvage," would have expressed it—with " the gift of the gab werry galloping." Indeed, we had barely intimated that we wanted to go West, when he opened his mouth, and out came such a Niagara of words, that we were fairly swept away by the torrent, and listened patiently *per force;* for, in less time than it takes to write it, Hatchet Face had put us in possession of all the " favorable facts " connected with five separate lines, or thereabouts, for which he was the sole agent ; and, strange to relate, (if Hatchet Face spoke the truth ; and being a railroad agent, he could by no means have done otherwise), these five different and differing lines had each and all one most uncommon similarity, inasmuch as there was no one of them that didn't save the traveller who had the good fortune to pursue that particular route, a " mint of money,"—" without possibility of collision," or " missing of connections," and put him through in " five hours less time than by any other track," with fewer changes of cars, and (as a Scottish landlord says when the bill of fare is exhausted), just anything else you please. In fine, we never knew before, or *since,* how delightfully easy it had become to travel westward ; we even found ourself embarrassed by the multiplicity of advantages, until in our perplexity we had almost determined upon putting all the lines—no—their " prospectuses " we mean—into our hat, and taking the first drawn out at a venture. So, trusting to luck, we said "The Suspension Bridge and Canada, via Detroit, and the Illinois Central"—paid our money. receiving, as a "certificate of deposit," a little package of tickets curiously stamped, countersigned and hung together, and withal so wondrously enveloped that the whole affair resembled a diminutive *billet-doux.* Being thus accredited to the road, we shot out of the office, bade Hatchet Face a hasty adieu, and wended our way to Bolen's, where we purchased pow‑ der, caps, and balls ; then stationery—quite a wholesale lot— was to be procured ; and finally we discussed the relative merits of divers and sundry carpet-bags with a shrewd old Yankee, who took our measure at a glance, and suited us with an article which we will make bold to say has held more manuscript than any other single specimen of all its leathern kith and kin.

Ding, dong, ding—three o'clock again—we "broke like a quarter-horse" for our residence in Brooklyn, where we spent the hours until five P. M. in packing up, bidding good-bye, and writing "last lines" generally. Six P. M. found us on board one of those "floating palaces" (when they are clean), a North River steamboat, and fairly under weigh.

Nine hours through the dark water, cleaving our way beneath the giant shadows of the dusky hills that walled in our steamer's trackless path, brought us to that most unromantic of all com‑ monplace localities, the Albany dock; then came a hotel, sought out amid the darkness of a gloomy winter's morning ; and then a breakfast, served up with all that overplus of hospitality which is only to be had at so much per day—a meal, to be eaten in haste, with your loins girded, which in our case meant an overcoat and a many-hued worsted comforter. And then we sallied forth to view the railroad train for Buffalo, and pick out the passenger-car next to the last, in which (as we had been caught in a railroad smash up before), we selected a seat which seemed safer than the rest ; that is to say, it was "convenient" to the door, with a window opposite, which might be kicked out at short notice upon an emergency.

And permit us to inform you, friend reader, as we go, that there is—accidents excepted—a deal of fun in railroading it. For, if we remember aright, it was Mr. Pope, or some other behind-the-age worthy, who declared that,

"The proper study of mankind is man."

Now had Mr. Pope known human nature better, he would have recommended woman. But if man—or for that matter, woman either—be the prescribed course, and mankind the pupil, we can suggest no better school than a first-class passenger-car ; for there is to us something really refreshing in the frankness with which the *genus homo* throws off even the affectation of unselfishness when he leaves his own peculiar orbit to traverse the public highway.

It is so easy, too, to classify the bipeds around you. There is the *nervous* man, who shivers at every blast of the steam-whistle, and hears an "awful catastrophe" in the rush of an approaching train, which never fails to conjure up a vision of broken legs and arms, and, it may be, a coroner's inquest in the prospective. To this class we belong—for, in this respect, we are a person of terrible experiences.

Then comes the *obdurate* man—he of the mulish temperament, who has "paid for his rights, and means to get 'em"; who would see a woman "in that extremity" first, and her baby to boot, before he would budge either his precious body or his almost equally valuable valise.

And then, there's the *jolly* man—your thorough-bred, gay, devil-may-care sort of fellow—funny by profession, and happy by habit—one of those deuced clever chaps, who would crack his joke at your nearest relative's funeral, just by way of "keeping up your spirits," or recommend "lemon-*aid*" to the young lady who sits beside him at table, as a recompense in full for having spoiled her new pattern dress—the only one of its kind —by upsetting his soup into her lap.

And then there's—but we must stop moralizing, or we shall never get to Kansas. So let us shift the scene to the Niagara Suspension Bridge—Canada side—where we arrived about nine o'clock on the evening of the 6th. Here we were detained, while waiting for the departure of the Detroit train, which did not go out until some two hours later. But on reviewing our note-book, we flatter ourself that we must have improved our time ; for our adventures—or rather those of our neighbors— while sojourning at Suspension Bridge, were " considerable if not more so." But they shall speak for themselves.

Upon leaving the cars we wended our way into the dingy (at least by night-light) depôt, and finally penetrated to the yet more comfortless eating-room, where a dirty-looking supper stood waiting for customers at fifty cents per head. Here we sought, but searched in vain, for an unappropriated seat ; for though vacant chairs were plentiful, and likely to continue so, they were ranged for possible occupation about the supper aforesaid. But had we entertained any doubt upon this head, it would have been dispelled by the information which was tendered us " free gratis " by an officious waiter (in dirty slippers, and a dilapidated apron), to the effect that " if we didn't want to eat we mustn't move the chairs." So we were fain to wander forth from this inhospitable apartment into a crowded antechamber, warmed by an enormous stove (our particular abomination), and fairly reeking with filthy odors—those of frying tobacco-juice and half-smoked cigars predominating.

As we edged our way through the throng, to get a little fresh air, our attention was attracted by a half-intoxicated enthusi-ast (a very " Hinglish " individual, by-the-way, in a rough top-coat, with an upper finish of Canadian fur-cap), who was amus-

ing his auditors by an ultra free-soil harangue, which he delivered in a somewhat boisterous, not to say incendiary, style.
The following specimen will serve as an exponent of this ora-
tion :

"Gentlemen, we may be thankful, hold Hingland may be
proud hof 'er provinces. Yes, we hopens hour harms to the
hoppressed (hic). The miserable Hafrican (hic) flies from the
American lash (hic) and finds a refuge in this hour (hic) land
hof real hand huniversal liberty (hic)."

Here the speaker paused, and throwing himself into an attitude, gazed round him with a drunken gravity, which seemed to
say, "I wait for a reply ;" and verily the answer was at hand,
for it came instanter, butt-end foremost, in the shape of an excited Southerner, who had likewise been indulging too freely in
the "extract of the corn."

"Stranger !" said the new-comer—a very raw-boned gentleman, in unmistakably home-made clothes—"Stranger ! yeou're
a *dog-gaun* fool."

We will draw a veil over the wordy war which succeeded this
most unceremonious interruption. Suffice it to say, that it was
ridiculous in the extreme. But as the disputants waxed wroth,
and their conversation grew more decidedly personal, we wearied
of their wrangling, and escaped to the comparative quiet of the
cars "going West," which were still stationary, but now rapidly
filling up. Here, at least, thought we, we shall hear nothing
more sonorous than the long-drawn snore of some indigestion-
haunted sleeper. But we "counted without our host," for we
had not yet "got shet" (as the Missourians say) of the "nigger question." In fact, we had barely composed ourself for a
traveller's nap, when an impertinent darkey came sauntering
through the car, where he ordered about the passengers, and
attempted to arrange their seats with such scanty ceremony,
that the exhibition of his "little brief authority"—if authority

it was—called forth some very energetic remonstrances from those whom he attempted to address.

Among others, a choleric old Yankee, with a perfect signboard of a nose, broke out thus :

"What under the canopy do yeu mean ? By thunder, I guess yeu own this train ; jest tell us, will yeu, if yeou're a regular nigger, or have there been so many accidents on this road that the company thought best to put the conductors in mourning, and ordered you painted black accordingly ?"

To this "call for information," the irate darkey returned no particular reply, beyond a general statement to the effect, that in Canada "all men were born free and equal," or, in other words, that a white man might be as good as a nigger, if he chose to exert himself. Now all this might have passed off unnoticed, if our darkey, in the bitterness of his heart, had not finished his remarks by requesting his interrogator to proceed to the "unmentionable to ears polite," with all convenient speed. This was *too* much—the Yankee's blood was up—he grasped the poker—and we really believe that if the affrighted African had not vanished from the cars, without even a hesitation by the way, that poker would have "played Hail Columbia" (as our Yankee expressed it), upon his thick-skulled pate ; but he departed ere his fate could

"Point a moral or adorn a tale."

and then as the train rolled out, the pugnacious Yankee thrus his huge paw into a great-coat pocket, and produced a worsted night-cap, whose hue rivalled the scarlet of its owner's "signboard of a nose," with which he forthwith proceeded to envelop his head ; but in so comical a manner, that the tassel vibrated like a pendulum above the wearer's left eye, while the sympathetic optic kept winking and blinking as it moved. To complete his preparations, our Yankee then turned over the seat back in front of him, so as to secure a very unfair share of body room ; and then, with his short legs elevated upon a cushion, and his night-capped head propped snugly against the window-blind, he settled himself to a slumber which we envied, but tried in vain to imitate.

CHAPTER II.

INCIDENTS BY THE WAY.

OH, what a dreary thing is night travel upon a railroad—whiz—bang—jounce—a yell that might wake the dead—fifteen miles an hour—shake—shake—shake—balance all—thirty miles an hour—everything dancing—nervous old maid opposite in fits—stout gentleman vibrates up and down, as if his understanding was worked by springs—carpet-bags come jostling from their racks. "Got a cinder in your eye, sir?" "Yes, dern the cinder." "Blow your nose, then, and pull down the eyelid." "How the deuce am I to blow my nose, sir, when it's almost knocked off by that last jump of this infernal car?"

Bang—crack—yell—forty miles an hour.

Shu—shu—shu—shuing growing fainter—you are getting drowsy—shuing ceases—you have just dropped off—sudden shock—somebody shakes your elbow—you start from your recumbent posture, and rub your bewildered optics—an uncompromising looking personage stands before you—you regard his coat, and the idea of a police-officer suggests itself—you contemplate his legs, and believe him to be an out-door clerk—your eye wanders upward to his cap, and you discover your mistake—for the man is labelled like a medicine, which might be taken by mistake—yes, the magic word "Conductor" is fairly writ in characters of gold upon his hat-band, so that he who runs may read, even at the rate of forty miles per hour. He is a man of few words withal, who knows you not as Governor A, or General B, the gentleman who has written a book and figured in the newspapers, but simply as the man in the brown coat, who is going so many miles, and must, therefore, pay the sum indicated by the Company's fare-table. Like poor Poe's raven, he has but one reiterated cry—'t is " ticket, sir," and

" Nothing more."

You draw down your beaver to shield your visual organs from the glare of the lantern, with which this implacable official is throwing some light upon your tickets (as he nips another hole, the sixth since you started, in them, with the little patent shoemaker's pincers which he carries in his right hand), or, it may be, is aiding the suspicious inspection of the circulating medium, which, in the innocence of your heart, you took confidingly from his brother employee, upon the " down train." You pay your money, and receive an oblong piece of paste-board, marked " Good to Blank, for this trip only," on one side, and labelled with the names of places which you never heard of, and distances that you don't believe in, upon the other. You conclude your business with the conductor, and sink back into your place, where you strive in vain to compose yourself, but it won't do, for you are now thoroughly " waked up," and must wrestle fruitlessly with the drowsy god, who will not stay to bless you, until a brace of squeals from the locomotive, followed by a sudden application of the brakes, brings the train gradually to a halt, when the coldest door is thrown open, and a " gruff voice " looks in, with the cry of " Squashtown—train stops twenty minutes for refreshments." You are hungry and athirst ; you are young and inexperienced ; you anticipate great things from Squashtown ; you follow the crowd of half-famished bipeds, who rush out into the bleak night air ; you step upon the icy platform ;

your heels go up and your head down ; you have a free ticket to
the fireworks, you recover yourself, and begin to realize that
you are a "stranger in a strange country," to which you may
shortly add, "and they took me in." You look about you, are
blinded by the glare of unexpected lights in extraordinary places,
and almost deafened by the tintinnabulations of vociferous din-
ner-bells, which are being frantically rung by anxious-looking
landlords, who stand shivering before the entrances of various
rival man-traps, marked "Refreshment Saloons." You still follow the crowd, you approach one of these competing establish-
ments, you believe in the sign-board, you allow yourself to be
humbugged, you enter with the throng, you sit down, or more
frequently stand up, to a long table, or greasy counter, well
covered with *crockery*, consisting of plates, containing a diminutive triangle of waxy, cold apple-pie each, pitchers of milk, and
sugar-bowls, which suggest strange doubts as to the possibility
of obtaining water in the Squashtown vicinity. There are
cups too, that can be filled with a compound, styled coffee, at a
York shilling per cup. You don't like cold apple-pie at midnight, but you will take coffee ; a distracted waiter hears, and
at length pays attention to your demand ; the coffee is produced ;
did you observe that he served you with the dirty cup, which
has just been emptied by your neighbor on the left ? You
didn't ? Well, never mind ; but we will make our affidavit that
you got something more than "sugar and cream" for *one*.
Here comes your coffee, *scalding* hot ; don't like it, hey ? burnt
your mouth, may-be ? "Why, waiter, I say, this isn't coffee,
it's more like burnt peas ; give us a cup of tea." "Tea, sir ?
yes, sir ! one shilling, sir ! thank you, sir !" But the advent of
the tea is marked by a yell of warning from the locomotive, a
cry of "all aboard," and an *exeunt omnes* from your fellow-passengers. You "follow suit," perforce, and resume your seat, a
"sadder, if not a wiser man," for you are minus a quarter for

"refreshments," and plus—the vexation of being imposed upon.

And so you go rushing along, with a shriek and a roar, across the night-shrouded landscape, waking the echoes of the frowning hills, and startling the slumberers in way-side bed-chambers, as the iron horse, with his great red eyes and iron sinews, drags on his quivering load—"faster—faster—faster."

The morning of the 7th found us in safety at Detroit, from whence we journeyed onward through chilly Michigan, until a "cut off" by rail brought us to the Illinois Central Railroad; here we changed cars, and traversed the last-mentioned State, under the heavy disadvantages (so far as scenery was concerned), of a wet, dismal, sloppy day, with a stormy sky above, and a boggy, rain-drenched prairie below. What wonder then that we "blessed our stars" when it "cleared up cold," just as we were approaching the town of Alton, where the passenger for St. Louis shifts himself from the rattling train, to embark upon a wheezy, snorting, broken-winded steamboat, which labors on, in a succession of convulsive jerks, until you "tie up" beside the levee at St. Louis.

As speed was everything, for, we wanted, if possible, to overtake the Kansas War, we did not intend to tarry in St. Louis, but "man proposes," and the facilities for travelling in Missouri "disposes," as the French proverb, does *not* say. So, after chartering a boy, and lugging ourself through the mud to the Pacific Railroad depòt, we found that it did not connect, and until the morrow nothing else did. Now this was bad enough, but it couldn't be helped, and we were therefore fain to put up at the "Planters," a good house *once*, that is to say eight years ago, since when it has bravely gotten over it.

Here our first care was to descend to an office on the ground floor, situated in one corner of the building, where you can buy tickets to go almost anywhere beneath "the glimpses of the

moon," a second edition, in short, of our hatched-faced friends' in
Broadway. But our business was no longer with railroad men ;
we had got, alas ! to the "end of our tether," in that respect.
We must now travel by stage, or not at all. It was therefore to
find out a representative of the firm of Smashup, Breakdown
& Co., stage-agents and proprietors, that we entered the
"Planters" subterranean, and would that we had never found
them, or, having found them, had never trusted ourself to
their tender mercies. Hear us then, good travellers—hearken,
we pray, and beware how you enter their office, (under the
"Planters" in St. Louis), unless, indeed, you should be tired of
this life, or, being obese, desire to be reduced in flesh. But
listen to the facts, for we were most egregiously "*done*," and if
Smashup, Breakdown & Company are not entitled to a "first-
rate notice," we don't know who are—so here goes.

It was on the evening of Saturday, Dec. 8th, that we entered
their taking-in-trap for unsuspecting travellers—we saw Smashup
—we intimated that we were a newspaper correspondent, who
wanted, not a "free ticket," but reliable information as to the
best and quickest route to the Kansas frontier. We were
informed that the road to a certain place, which shall be nameless, was not more beguiling, nor more easily to be traversed
than theirs from St. Louis to Fort Leavenworth—always supposing the pilgrim to have a through ticket from Smashup—we
believed Smashup—we trusted him—Smashup was a man with
iron-grey hair—or an approximation to it—he looked amiable—
had a Christian expression of countenance—we would have lent
Smashup five dollars (if we had it), on his face alone. In
short, we let Smashup take us in. We asked the price of a
ticket to Fort Leavenworth ? the answer (given in a most
insinuating tone of voice), was *only* twenty-eight dollars—the
distance is about three hundred and twenty miles, and the sum
mentioned is exactly what our through ticket cost us from New

York to St. Louis, Mo. "But," said the amiable Smashup, "as you are a representative of the press, we *must do something*, so we will only charge you twenty-five dollars—in fact, sir," added the agent, with generous warmth—" we will make an exception, and deduct *three dollars*." Feeling that twenty-five dollars was quite enough, we made no objection, the more so as the Company charges only fifteen dollars for the return trip, over the same road. We accordingly disbursed the pecuniary consideration, and received in return a homœopathic card, whose inscription ran thus :

"Stage ticket—*good for this trip only*, from St. Charles, (distant eighteen miles by railroad from St. Louis), to Fort Leavenworth. December 10th, 1855. S. S. Blank, agent."

"But what kind of stages are we to have, Mr. Smashup?"

"Good stages, sir, and careful drivers."

"And the time?"

"We run night and day, and will put you through in four days from the date of your ticket. The omnibus will call for you on Monday morning. That will be your first chance to go."

As we have said before, we believed in Smashup, so we pocketed our ticket and bade that amiable gentleman farewell, without even a foreboding that like that oft-quoted and juvenile bear—" all our sorrows were to come."

Upon our return to the upper chamber of the "Planters," we learned that General Clarke of the United States Army was sojourning in the house, so, presuming upon an old introduction, and the fact that we were in pursuit of information—as regarded matters and things in general, and Kansas in particular—we took the liberty of sending up our "pasteboard"—and was soon after shown to his room. And a fine specimen is General Clarke of the hale, hearty old gentleman; he is moreover, in some respects, a soldier of the rough and ready—or may we not as well say at once of the American—school ? for few possess more of that wonderful desideratum (in this age of practical humbug), good, strong, hard, common sense. The general confirmed the statements which we had previously heard made, by those well qualified to judge, as to there being a sufficiency of United States troops then stationed in Kansas within striking distance of the scene of difficulty to put down -ny violations of law and order in the Territory. General Clarke, however, expressed the hope that so sad an ultimatum might never become necessary—as it should be the very last argument resorted to—to which we, as in duty bound, said a fervent amen.

The following, from our journal of the 9th, is of that days' experience, all which seems worthy of being chronicled here.

It blew here last night as if Old Boreas had left all his store-house doors open. Some of the boats on the river broke loose from their moorings. We hear, however, of no very serious damage being done. At Jefferson Barracks the brick and plaster work suffered considerably, and an officer who left there this morning, tells us that the parade-ground is littered with fragments of roofs, walls, porches, etc. When the gale was at its height a fire-alarm was sounded—we turned out immediately, in a light undress, consisting of a shirt and drawers, without stockings, for, like the Hibernian at the Astor, we didn't even know that the hotel was insured, and we were quite positive that we were not. The fire, however, proved to be upon Fourth street, it having broken out in the interior of two small brick stores, where it was very wisely permitted to burn itself out. Apropos to fires, we will back the St. Louis Fire Department, even against the B'hoys who " run wid der mashine" in the Empire City, for making a " confusion worse confounded" upon these occasions, for, despite the howling of the storm we never heard such a " human rumpus" at a fire before. But perhaps it is as innocent a way of evaporating one's animal spirits as any other which could be devised—and far be it from us to inter'ere with the pleas ures of the people.

We have met to day, for the first time in three years, with our valued friend—Assistant Surgeon Joseph B. Brown of the Army—one of the best officers of his grade on the Medical Staff. We had been comrades upon

the frontiers of Mexico, had ridden side by side, through many a weary
mile of Texan chaparral, and broken commissary biscuit at the same table,
amid the swamps on the head waters of the Los Moras. But our time for
"comparing notes" was of the shortest, for we found that the Doctor was
leaving that morning, with his "wife and bairns," for Old Point Comfort
Va.: from whence he was ordered to embark for service with the Ninth Infantry in Oregon. May the Indians spare him.

And so ends Sunday, December the 9th.

We began our Monday by breakfasting at early dawn, and
then getting into a chilly omnibus and driving in company with
five miserable-looking beings (the whole party, ourself included,
presenting the general appearance, as seen by the uncertain light
of a bitter winter morning, of having been up all night), to the
starting point of the North Missouri railroad—from whence an
eighteen, or as some call it thirteen miles' ride, brought us to the
Missouri river shore, just opposite the town of St. Charles,
which we reached in due course of time, by a steam ferry-boat,
whose exterior at least would have astonished a New Yorker to
a very considerable degree.

St. Charles, Mo., is, to our fancy, about the *meanest* town
which it has yet been our misfortune to set foot in—being half
French, three-quarters Dutch, and, as an Irishman would say,
the other half "nigga."

On our arrival here, we went to a "groggery" looking sort
of tavern—where a couple of "foreigners" drinking Schnapps, a
low ceiled room, and a high bar with quaint old drinking glasses,
made up a very Flemish interior. In this Gerald Douw-ish seeming place we were detained half an hour, when a cry of "here
comes de stage," brought us to the door, to catch a glimpse of
the vehicle in which we felt so deeply interested, and, oh horror!
how shall we describe the "thing" which met our affrighted
gaze—for really "Miss O'Dowd's convaniency" was a "fool to
it."

But let us attempt a description. It was what the Missourians call a "mud cart"—a cross . in fact between a second-hand bakers' wagon—and a hospital ambulance which had seen hard service ; this blessed institution was calculated to hold six by the builder, and, as we afterwards discovered, nine by the stage company. In short, it was to us a terrible surprise—a kind of waking nightmare that we couldn't get over. But as Smashup, Breakdown & Company were just eighteen miles in our rear, and the "Wakarusa war," supposed to be raging ahead of us, we strove to make the best of a bad business by hoisting ourself into the "mud-cart," which didn't improve upon a closer inspection, where we shoved our carpet-bag under our feet, and proceeded to insert ourself into the still unoccupied half of the front seat, for the place by our side had already been taken by a very clever seeming Virginian, with whom we had just scraped an acquaintance upon the cars, which bade fair to increase and prosper. The back seat was also full—a hale old gentleman and his daughter, a rather pretty Missourian girl, who looked anything but charmed with our conveyance, being its occupants—yet the middle bench was still empty. Well thought we, this is not so *very* bad after all, if the "mud-cart" is a humbug, it is at all events not crowded, and that in staging is no small advantage ; but even this hope was destined to be dispelled, for our landlord cried, "Driver, don't forget those passengers, they're all ready to start."

"What passengers?" shouted we, as our Jehu began handling his lines ; "how many ?"

We caught the landlord's reply, which overtook us on the road, as we rattled down the mud-hole of a main-street. It was a staggerer, for it said, "*only* ten." Ten ! we turned pale at the very thought ; ten and four made fourteen—and fourteen in a stage mud-cart ! It seemed an impossibility. "Smack went the whip, on rolled the wheels"—"was ever man so sad ?"

till we halted at the door of a—a far Western Hotel, Class No. 2, and depreciating at that. And there, dreadful to relate, stood the ten, the expectant ten, all waiting to be jammed, with such a wagon-load of luggage, and so many little things which must be carried inside, that we felt assured that our hypothesis of an impossibility would be correct, and thereby save us perforce, at least in part.

But who were the ten? They consisted, so far as a bird's-eye view could inform us, of three very " Deown East " looking Yankees, with two "ladies," old and young—neither being pretty—and a little girl to fill up their half dozen, for these six went in a lot, all, Yankee-like, anxious to get ahead, while the remaining four, two of whom were Hibernians, stood looking on, as if it were a matter of perfect indifference to them whether they spent the day where they were or not.

In the meanwhile the St. Charles agent of the stage-line—a little Dutchman with a mulish face—had made *his* appearance, way-bill in hand, on the pavement before the inn, where he stood looking distractedly from the document in his fist to the eager group of Yankees, who had evidently made up their minds to get in " whether or no." Time was passing, and the driver becoming impatient ; but the Dutchman could get no light upon his dilemma. He couldn't jam even six more inside ; he might squeeze in nine in all ; but he wouldn't hire an extra coach. He scratched his head ; he pondered ; he couldn't cypher it out. At length a brilliant thought seemed to have struck him ; he had determined to do it by subtraction.

" Sir," said he, to our half-frozen self, " your name ish last upon de bill. You ish expected to ride on de driver mit de outshide."

To this modest proposition a voice (it was ours, speaking from the inner fold of a mammoth woollen comforter), mildly objected, and the following dialogue ensued :

He.—"But you mush git out ; dese peoples mush go on. Mein Gott, but you mush."

We.—" But I have paid my money, sir. Here is my ticket, duly made out, good for this day, and this day only."

He.—" But I cannot help him, sir ; you mush git out, or ride mit de outshide on de driver."

We.—" But I won't. I've got a bad cold."

He.—" You musht. You may go back and sue mit de company, if dere ish anyting dat ish wrong." ·

We.—" But I won't. I haven't time to go back and sue the company. My business is to go ahead, and I'm going."

He.—" You mush get out, or I shall make you."

At this stage of the conversation we opened our great coat, and displayed' the mild-looking butt of a persuasive revolver (for we had taken the precaution to bring with us at least *five* good reasons for being politely treated). Having turned the handle of this weapon somewhat ostentatiously into a more come-at-able position, we assumed, so far as our very amiable countenance would permit, the manner and style of the " Blood-drinking Border-Ruffian," as we had seen those worthies set forth in Crockett's Yarns, and Far-Western Almanacs, and delivered ourself as follows :

" Stranger, we war raised in South-Western Texas, we war. We can't be crowded—not much. We air considered hard to run against—we air a reg'lar pine-knot. Ef we air moved from this hyar cart, we must be lifted. But ef yeou feel like it, stranger, don't restrain yeourself—pitch in. We're considered as numerous as most folks, we are."

In fact, we defined our position, and " rared back " upon our " reserved rights " generally, at the same time intimating to our krout-eating friend, that if he wanted his " har raised off his head, like a wild Ingin's, he had better take a hand."

The agent grows civil and disappears. We supposed the

fight was over, and was just congratulating ourself upon having gained a very easy victory, in which (as the bulletins *have* said) we " had to regret the loss of *none* killed and *none* wounded." But we were never more disappointed in our life.

Interval of twenty minutes, during which we sat munching an underdone ginger-cake. Time up. The agent returns, accom panied by a short individual in a long nose, red hair, and a light, saffron complexion, to accord. Small individual looked fierce, and remarked that his name was Johns ; we suggested that we were glad to hear it, and thought the appellation rather pretty than otherwise.

" But I want you to know, sir, that I 'm the city marshal."

We intimated that it was a gratification to us to receive that interesting piece of intelligence.

" But, sir, you must get out of that stage."

We stated that we were sorry to refuse so pleasant-spoken a gentleman, but that, under the circumstances, it would be utterly out of our power to gratify him.

" But you must."

" But I shan't."

" But it's a law, sir, in the State of Missouri, that the tenth passenger rides outside."

We intimate a doubt, and express a desire to see chapter and verse ; the marshal steps forward threateningly ; we produce our five-shooter, and begin dandling it upon our knee.

An awful pause.

We admit our willingness to acknowledge the majesty of Missouri law, by submitting to any legal process, reserving to ourself, however, the right to demand the writ, and surrender our body under protest, with a promise to prosecute the red-haired individual for an assault with a battery to boot, should he overstep the powers of his office. We wind up our business with the saffron-colored functionary in these words :

"It strikes me, Mr. Marshal, that you're making a fool of yourself. If you have got a warrant for me, show it; if you have not, mind your own business, and save trouble; for, without intending to threaten, I want to assure you that I intend to protect myself."

The marshal hesitates—he will not take the responsibility—five minutes more—our logic has triumphed—the marshal has succumbed. The red-haired man takes his long nose and saffron-colored complexion out of our visual horizon—the stage-agent is discomfited, and goes with his head cowed down, like the tail of a cur in difficulty, to procure an extra hack, into which steps the hale old gentleman with his pretty daughter, leaving our back seat to be refilled (oh, most unhappy change), by the old and young Yankee ladies with the little girl aforesaid—two Yankees, male specimens, then pile into the middle seat, while the third perches himself upon the box, beside the driver; and so, being "all *wrong*," we "roll out" for Kansas.

The agent, mounted upon a rat of a mule, whose expressive countenance seemed modelled after its rider's, trotted by our side until we were clear of "the town," where he took his departure, and as he did so, we thrust our body half out of the place where the mud-wagon's curtain ought to have been, to wave an ironical adieu, and desire our "most particular regards to his red-haired friend, the city marshal."

CHAPTER III.

A HARD ONE FOR THE AUTHOR.

FROM this time forth, until the day of our return to St. Louis, we may truly say that we suffered "some." For if the happiness of life be composed of trifles, it is equally indisputable, that little discomforts make up its miseries. And oh, that dreary day ! the first of a long procession of dreary days, each gloomier than the last ; which, even now (as we scribble up our experiences amid the superfluities of a city residence), give us a shiver, as we recall them to mind ; for they have left upon the tablet of our memory a most un-Gignoux-ish winter scene, with no sunshine in its leaden sky, full of huge trees, dismantled by the December blast, with great arms rocking to and fro, and unthrifty-looking farms, where the half-frozen cattle sought shelter in vain, or crowded against each other to keep out the piercing cold ; and then the searching, bitter wind, the vain attempts to guard yourself from the weather ; the getting chilled and restless, and sleepy ; the conversation growing shorter and more snappish as the day wore on ; the quarrels for room ; the difficulties between your legs and the lower limbs of your fellow-passengers, which could not be compromised ; the ruts ; the mud-holes, masked with ice that wouldn't bear ; with a finale at night-fall, in the shape of a halt at a log-cabin hotel, where the "stage got supper," and the landlord, a very old settler, brought out a bottle of corn-whisky, and a bowl of brown sugar, and asked us to "step up and take a little something before tea."　After which, supper was announced, and we walked into the kitchen (an establishment, by the way, that reminded us strongly of the houses which we used to build out of corn-cobs, when a boy), to eat it ; and now, with your permission, we will chronicle that supper, as a fit exponent of our wayside meals, with two blessed exceptions, from the Alpha to the Omega of our recent far Western travel.

Imprimis.—It was in " killing time," and hog-meat was everywhere ; so we had sausages at both ends and ribs in the middle, flanked by other and less recognizable preparations of the unclean beast.　Then there were dried apples, underdone hot biscuits, with what Willis would call two stomach-aches in each, and coffee, considered such by courtesy—a beverage not to be indulged in with impunity—all of which was provided at the very moderate rate of four bits (a bit being the universal appellation for a York shilling in Missouri) per-head. -

N. B.—We forgot to add three dirty " niggers" who served the repast, and a white woman who took the head of the table, where she seemed ill at ease, and appeared to us like the personification of chills and fever, and an overworked one at that.

And then the driver, who had supped with " the stage"—for the Far West levels all social distinctions—thrust in his head with

" Stage's ready—all aboard, gentlemen !"

We gathered our coat about us—wrapped our comforter more closely about our ears—seized our carpet-bag—cast " one last, long, lingering look behind " at the huge log-fire and the ruddy light within, and then anathematized the stage company, and resumed our seat.　If the dreary day had been full of sorrows, what was that night ?

<blockquote>

"No stars—no moon—
All dark—all gloom—
We rumbled on—still on."

</blockquote>

Till with a whoa ! and a sudden pull up, the driver poked in his head at the termination of the first two miles' jolting, and requested all hands to get out, as "he allowed he'd broke a king-bolt."

There was no use in grumbling—we descended—we stepped into a mud-hole—we wet our feet—we swore, I am afraid we did—we got a rail—we made a mechanical power of ourself— we helped to hoist the mud-cart upon its wheels ; and then being all wrong, got in again ; but we might have spared ourself the trouble, for it was first a hill and then a descent—a "corduroy" road, or it may be an insinuating suggestion from the driver, such as :

" Here's a *dog-gaun* bad place, gentlemen ; ef yeou don't want yeour necks broke, yeou'd better git out ; but it don't make no difference to *me*—I don't kear—you may stay in ef yeou'd drather."

It is needless to say that we didn't " drather." And thus the night wore on, between shaking inside, and " footing it " out, until two o'clock in the morning, when one of our " ower careful " drivers got out to " pick a place " at which to cross " a slew," or what Western men call a " branch," which intersected the road immediately in front of us. Having found what he was pleased to designate as " a heap the best crossing," he remounted his perch, seized the reins, urged on his cattle, and dashed in ; the leaders scrambled out of the half-frozen ditch, for such it was ; the wheelers followed, but not so the coach— there was a sudden stop—a crash—a heavy fall—and then a sort of smothered howl from the driver, with a noise like a locomotive running away, induced us to poke our head out into the night for information—and a pretty prospect it was which met our eye. The stage, with its cargo of passengers and luggage, was embedded in the slew, while the luckless driver sat upon the ground some ten feet in advance of his box, from whence he had been dragged by the lines ; and where he was just then engaged in feeling of his bones, as if to assure himself that they were unbroken, with interludes, as the small bills say, of tender manipulations in certain back settlements, which wouldn't, at that particular moment, bear any great amount of friction. The team in the meanwhile was out of sight, but we couldn't complain, as they had certainly been pleased to make a very equal distribution of the spoils, by taking with them *their* share of the concern, the fore-wheels and their appurtenances, and leaving to us the body of the mud wagon, with its hind wheels and boot-load of luggage attached. As we afterwards discovered, they ran about half a mile, strewing sundry fragments here and there as they went, as if to mark their road ; nor is it probable that they would have halted short of the next station, full two miles further on, if they had not grown weary of dragging one of their companions, the rear wheeler, who had the ill luck to fall, and whom (as they were too much hurried to give the beast time to pick himself up), they consequently pulled after them by the harness-leather across the frozen prairie ruts, until the unfortunate animal was literally flayed alive from the tip of his nose to the very end of his scraggy-looking tail, when they magnanimously condescended to stop and permit themselves to be caught.

Having accomplished this much, we all, driver included, left the vehicle, with our " plunder," and that famous traveller, Uncle Sam's Mail, to take its chance upon the broad prairie, while we "put out" in search of fire and a shelter ; these were finally obtained, after some hunting about in the gloom of that dreary hour which immediately precedes the breaking of day, in a little hill-side log-cabin, where, thanks to a good-natured Missourian, who got up and opened the pin-fastened door to receive us, our benumbed passengers found a Western welcome to such comforts as its very limited accommodations could afford. So we made the best of a bad matter, and forthwith crouched down upon a low stool before the heaped-up wood-fire—burning one side, and shivering upon the other, as we turned ourself, like a perambulating meat-jack, to its blaze, until the first faint glimmer of the morning light crept in through the unchinked logs to herald the coming of the dawn, when we once more took the road, and in company with our Virginian friend, pushed on to "the station," where, in the proper course of events, the mud-cart should have changed horses some hours before, at which we arrived, per Shanks mare, without further casualty. Here we breakfasted at "the hotel"—a log-cabin, of course—on the stereotyped bill of fare—attended to our ablutions, and repaired damages generally—and then passed two very unentertaining hours in company with a brace of Missouri hog-drivers, whose conversation, save when it turned upon the mysteries of their trade, contained, as our city journalists say, when referring to the arrival of the "Southern mail"—"nothing new." At ten o'clock, A. M., our driver, a very independent sort of person, after refreshing himself with hog meat, coffee, "a sleep and a smoke," thought proper to go down and look after the mud-cart, which was still reposing most ingloriously in the ditch. It was nearly noon, therefore before we finally got under way again, and went jolting over a road which grew worse at every mile. The close of another miserable day found us at a blacksmith's shop and groggery, of a town whose very name we have forgotten, and another, and yet more comfortless night—with some little assistance from an intoxicated driver, brings us to an upset, which *we* consider noticeable, the more so, as it came within an ace of making a very striking impression upon our brain, in a double sense.

It was a December night—a credit to the family of such nights, dark, frosty, and depressing. We had two drivers upon the box—one a "native," very drunk, and the other a Dutchman, who was only partially so, "by chance." The Dutchman had the lines—we were half a-sleep—having got as near a state of " blessed unconsciousness," as we ever do in a night-coach, when a quick tipping of the " stage," followed by a general smash up, apprised us (even without the exclamations of " Oh, Lord ! we're over." " Oh, murder !" " Oh, somebody ! take me out," which came dolefully from the Yankee ladies in the back-seat), that the mud-cart was done for. Fortunately for us, however, the vehicle was so accommodating as not to turn over upon our side—a matter, by the way, of small congratulation to the poor Virginian, upon whom we fell heavily. Upon reaching the ground we found ourself at the top—(thank fortune for *that*)—of a confused mass of arms, legs, bodies, and travelling-bags—and as it is very difficult to prevent mistakes in the dark—and we didn't like to tarry longer in a place which might prove unhealthy, if the horses started—we forthwith proceeded to extricate ourselves, with more speed than ceremony. What wonder then, that, in helping ourself out, we should have committed the trifling *impoliteness* of setting one foot in the old Yankee's mouth, as he afterwards declared, to the great detriment of his front teeth—while we kicked his better-half in the stomach with the other, until a change of position allowed us to make a step-ladder of our Virginian's back-bone, as he lay snugly coiled up below—from whence another stride brought us out of the place where the upper window-glass ought to have been. Being once more head uppermost, and safely landed upon *terra firma*, we flew to the assistance of the fairer portion of our companions, one of whom at least, if she were susceptible of cholic, must have been suffering severely from the external application of our buffalo soles. Nor was it a difficult matter to decide upon the precise whereabouts of these females in distress, for the locality into which they had been tumbled by the catastrophe was made evident by a series of squalls in the duet style, the old lady doing the first, and the younger the second treble, with very opera-like effect. To out knife and cut away the leather curtains which fastened them in, was the work of a moment ; to put in our hand and get hold of *something*—we believe it was the old lady's —— limb, was the work of another, and then with a yo-he-oh ! we tugged away, until we had succeeded in hauling the venerable matron into the outer air, where she arrived in a very flustered condition—quite wrong side up with care. Having thus happily accomplished the deliverance of the senior, we turned our attention toward ameliorating the condition of the younger lady, whose outcries still continued to

" Vex the drowsy ear of night,"

in which laudable effort we were assisted by our Virginian, who had by this time picked himself out, with, as he expressed it :

" Thank God no broken bones—but a very sore back, for *somebody*—one of those vile Yankees he believed—had kicked him there, right on his spine, in their efforts to save themselves, and he'd be derned if he didn't just wish that he knew which one of them it was."

We thought that we might have given him some insight into the matter, but judiciously refrained—so after much poking, and some awkward mistakes, in the course of which our Virginian came very near getting even with the male Yankees still struggling inside, we got hold of the young lady, and placed her beside the elder. And as we watched the damsel who stood shaking out her petticoats, it occurred to us that, in one respect at least, she had got *ahead* of her venerable companion, insomuch as she had been delivered by a head instead of a feet presentation, having been literally lugged out by the hair.

Our next procedure, after having counted noses, and assured ourselves that there were no bones broken, was to pass a general vote of censure, or, in other words, we uttered curses both loud and deep against the firm of Smashup Breakdown &

Co., general stage-agents of St. Louis, Mo., and their devices :
with a particular application of our remarks to the offending
stage-drivers then and there present, for their excessive stupidity and unpardonable drunkenness, to all of which " the Native," a surly sort of fellow, hiccoughed out something about his
" havin' known of a feller that once got his neck bruk " on an
" Ingianny" stage, who had bin paid as much as five thousand
dollars for doin' it, by the stage folks ; and he jest allowed that
ef any on us war killed, the company would hev to pay *us* for
the privilig;" an assurance which, though it might have been a
comfort to an Irishman, had no more soothing effect upon us than
to draw forth the remark, that we didn't want to put Smashup
to any such expense, at least upon our own personal account.

" But, stranger (continued the Native), I (hic) jest *know* that
I'd her (hic) my neck broke (hic) for that ; couldn't a feller buy
a few acres and a nigger (hic) or two niggers, may-be—*well* he
could (hic) yes—(here a pause for reflection)—yes, I'm *dog-
gauned*, stranger, ef they mayent (hic) break my neck and smash
my (hic) legs to eternal smash for five thousand dollars, (hic)
well they may."

As for the Dutchman, he (being the soberer of the two, or,
perhaps we should rather say, the more *sympathetically* drunk)
took a penitent view of the matter ; and, like a tender-hearted
railroad employee whose negligence has just assisted at the
smash-up of a few car-loads, seemed inclined to condole with
our misfortunes to an extreme limit, for he assured us :

" Dat he would drather give five dollar of his money dat he
make stage-drivin' dan have dish ting happen ; dat he never
upset nobodies not more dan nine, may-be fifteen times, and he
drive six month ; but dat he didn't know dis part of de road,
and only drives for his friend dat is shic mit de whisky, but
dat he never drunksh nothin, himself, but takish some schnapps
mit his friend when tish cold."

CHAPTER IV.

" OLD MAN RHYMER " AND A BOONSVILLE " HOTEL."

WE reached the town of Rocheport, Mo., late on the evening
of the 12th, when we were forthwith rattled up to what the
stage-driver—a new specimen of the genus, who for a wonder
kept sober, called " old man Rhymer's tavern," of whose extraordinary conveniences he had spoken in such favorable,
not to say enthusiastic terms, that we felt really curious to see
that *rara avis*, at least in the interior of Missouri, " a first-rate
hotel ;" but we found to our cost that in this, as well as in our
other Far Western travelling experiences, the

"Distance lent enchantment to the view ;"

for even " old man Rhymer's " tavern proved upon a closer
acquaintance to be no better than it ought, if half so good ;
in fine, it was as dirty, ill-kept, and unprepossessing a village inn
as we had yet encountered upon the road ; and we very much
fear that our loquacious stage-driver, in expatiating upon the
accommodations of this establishment, had a personal and, it
may be, pecuniary interest in drumming customers into the
clutches of mine host. Mynheer Rhymer, his very poetical name to the contrary notwithstanding, appeared at the door
of his " hostelrie " as we drove up, in the shape of an obese,

bull-headed, uncleanly-looking old Dutchman, with an oily voice and a fat smile. His first salutation ran thus:

" Mill you hash supper, gentelmen ; dere is no stage here, so you mill hash to stay all night." .

Here was another damper ; but after three days and nights of travel over the very roughest of all rough roads this side of Jordan Turnpike, a night in bed was something "not to be sneezed at." So we gave into this *nolens volens* detention with the best grace possible, and supped on the unclean beast as usual. Then came bed-time, and our couch a feather-bed of course, for how could a Dutchman sleep soundly upon straw. And if a poor road-worn mortal ever felt the full force of Tom Hood's

> "O, bed ! bed ! bed ! delicious bed :
> That heaven on earth to a weary head,
> Whether lofty or low its condition,"

we were that mortal that night, for as we lay submerged in a feathery sea, we rolled, and tumbled, and dreamed of dire upsets and desperate runnings-away, and then woke up to bless our stars, and enjoy the luxury, as we turned to sleep again, of stretching out our cramped-up legs without running the risk of breaking a neighbor's shins.

December 13th.—Morning, and a late breakfast, not yet ready. *Scene.*—The " bar-room," the principal actors being the fat landlord and ourself, with the loquacious stage-driver in the background. This wrangling dialogue ensues :

We.—Mr. Rhymer, would you have the goodness to let your servants give me a bit of chicken for breakfast. I have been ill, and Missouri hog's meat seems to owe me a grudge, for we can't agree.

He.—Shicken—shicken—mein Gott—de shicken ish too big to kill. Dish ish not de time for de shicken ; dish ish de shea-son for de hog.

Here the loquacious. stage-driver, whose feelings appeared to have been deeply outraged by our request, broke in with the following most unauthorized observations. We shall take the liberty to reduce the oaths to blanks, and thus diminish his comments by fifty per cent. at the least.

"By the great-jumping-flat-footed ———, where the —— did yeou come from? Yeou can't eat hog-meat, hey? Yeou're delicately raised—you air, by ——. I'll be —— ef we hadn't better send out and kill a few patridges for yeou—*well* we had, by the eternal ——. Send I may be ——. Chickens, hey? chickens!"

Here the enthusiastic driver halted for want of breath, and we embraced the opportunity to assure him that if he would do us the favor to step out and kill those "patridges" we would eat them with the greatest pleasure, whereupon the driver stared, and seemed really impressed with an idea that we took things—for an Eastern man—mighty coolly. As for our fat host, he waddled out, and ordered a piece of turkey's breast, fried brown in *pork*, for our own private use and benefit, on which we breakfasted gloriously, very much to the amazement of our Virginian, who was in the habit of amusing himself with our very Jewish dislike to the "entire animal."

Upon finishing our repast, we, in company with our fellow-passengers, resolved ourselves into a "committee of the whole," to contrive "ways and means" for getting on; for it was but too evident that our fat landlord was correct in his assertion, that, so far as "stages" were concerned, Smashup, Breakdown & Co.'s line had at length "given out for good."

It was finally determined by our passengers, in council assembled, that "old man Rhymer" should take the responsibility of furnishing a suitable vehicle, and as he was the duly accredited stage-agent of Smashup, Breakdown & Co., at Rocheport, look to those worthy gentlemen for his pecuniary reward—an arrangement, by-the-way, which seemed to afford but slender gratification to mine host, whose tavern gained nothing by our exit. But, overcome by our importunities, he finally saw fit to grunt out an assent, and accordingly went rolling out to order up the necessary transportation.

In half an hour's time, "the stages" were reported ready, and we once more sallied forth to embark in whatever new instrument of torture it might please Providence and "old man Rhymer" to bestow us in. And there they were, sure enough ; for one of the stages alluded to was a dilapidated hack, which held one male Yankee, and three ladies inside, while our Virginian, who had perched himself upon the driver's seat, after a round or two of argument as to the right of position, more than completed its complement. As for the other vehicle, in which we felt more particularly interested, it was nothing more than an ordinary lumber-wagon, which we should say—judging from its odor, and inside cleanliness—had been very recently engaged in the transportation of manure ; or it may be that its body had been on detached service as a hen-roost. When we came to take our place, we found the wagon already filled up with the Yankees' luggage, on which the balance of our party had already seated themselves, in compliance with a request to "pile in, cf they wanted to make Boonsville that day." So we were fain to follow their example, and scrambled up upon the heap of trunks, boxes, and bundles, which made up the plunder of our fellow-travellers, where we selected an eligible seat, which means—took up our position upon a leathern trunk, studded with large brass knobs, and lettered at either end with nails of a similar material. And in this "blessed institution" we rode some eighteen miles or more, in a light, drizzling rain, and a very wet overcoat. So don't wonder if our style of description should grow curter as we revive the recollections of that day—for our troubles were beginning to tell upon us, even to the suspension of our good-nature. We had not gone a league, when the driver—a near relation, we should say, of our friend of the " chickens," and a surly brute into the bargain—asked us very coolly to get out and walk, to save old man Rhymer's horses, up a very steep hill, and through such deep mud as the world never produced out of the State of Missouri. We were irritated— we regarded ourself as being humbugged, swindled, done for, and imposed upon, and, in the excitement of the moment, consigned "old man Rhymer," his tavern, horses, kith and kin, to the " unmentionable to ears polite," with a codicil in favor of stage-drivers. We intimated, however, to the driver, that if *he* felt like saving old man Rhymer's horses, we should be most happy to handle the ribbons, and let *him* walk up the hill, or for that matter, all the way to the Missouri river. His answer was an emphatic one, and quite a " laconic " in its way.

"Stranger, do yeu think I'm a *dog-gauned* fule ?"

In answer to which, we very frankly admitted that upon *that* point we had not yet made up our mind, but when we did, we would let him know, and immediately relapsed into a misanthropic reverie, which lasted until we reached the banks of that mighty tributary to the Great Father of Waters, which is here to-day—gone to-morrow—and as generally uncertain in its ups and downs, as that nigger, who is sure to *run* away—" In point of fact," as Wilkins Micawber says, we allude to the Missouri. As Boonsville is situated upon the opposite bank, it became necessary to embark upon a ferry-boat, which plies from the point at which we struck the river, to the " City levee." This boat was a six-horse power affair, and we feel confident that our calculation is correct, for in this instance, the sole motive agent was a circular tread-mill, worked by half-a-dozen (we don't mean as the bakers count), old blind mares, with their bones so wonderfully developed, and their bellies so singularly small, that you

would have sworn that life itself was a burden to these unfortunate beasts, who panted and heaved while they walked

"Their weary round,"

as if it were part of their business to imitate the puffing of a
high-pressure engine, and thus delude the beholder into a belief
that the whole concern went by steam, and really nothing else.
But the old proverb cautions us to "speak well of the bridge,
which carries us safely over." So we are bound to make honorable mention of the mares, for although it was—pull mares—pull
Missouri, and a very close thing at times, between our "six-
horse power," and the current, they *finally*, that is to say, in
something less than an hour's time, brought us triumphantly to
the Boonsville landing, where we remounted our trunk, and was
conveyed to the City Hotel, one of the two " blessed exceptions,"
to which we referred when denouncing Missouri inns.

There was one thing about this hotel, with which we were
more particularly pleased, and this was the air of home comfort
in its sleeping apartments. What *decent* traveller is there,
who will not sympathize with us when we say, that it is so gratifying to escape from the bar, or general sitting-room, for, in a
Far Western tavern, these luxuries, (?) are but too frequently
united, with its foul odors and unprofitable discourse, to such a
sanctum as was our chamber at the City. Let us describe it for
you, for it has "a place in our memory" still. Imagine, then, a
large, airy room to begin with, which has two heavily-curtained
windows, and a broad, open fire-place, whose well-swept hearth,
and high brass fenders, bore tokens of recent attention from
careful hands. But the fire ! ah ! that was. the great success ;
you should have seen it when we came in ; it wasn't one of
your poverty-stricken, just large-enough efforts ; none of your
single back-log, with one-or-two-sticks-on-top-of-it affairs, which

might burn out, like a three-inch tavern candle, before you went to bed ; but a free-handed, generous, rollicking blaze— a *roarer* of a fire, in fact, who was now fairly started, and off upon a spree, and being so, meant to go it with a rush, and crack every log that came in its way, without reference to expense. It was one of those fires, too, that open a man's heart ; for it seemed to warm you right through, morally and physically. You felt its genial influence, the moment you entered the chamber ;—why, to us, it almost appeared to talk, as we came in, for it leaped up, and danced, and uttered a roar of welcome, as if it wished to say, " How are you, old fellow ?—glad to see you—sit down, draw up your chair—extend your legs, and make yourself at home." Our benison on that fire, say we, and on the man—or woman, perchance, who built it ; for, we repeat it, it *was* a brilliant success—an undoubted one—and the whole world couldn't argue us into any other belief.

And then there was the bed—the beds, we should have said, for there were two of them—why, they're a paragraph in themselves ; such beds ! such

> " First class carriages of ease
> To the land of Nod, or where you please."

as Hood has it, were surely never seen before ; they made us think of Dickens's old John Willet, and the May-pole Inn ; why, the state couch of that snug hostelry is no where by comparison. You could hardly call either of them beds for two, they seemed rather to have been built for three—or perhaps, we might say, with a view to the accommodation of small families— and, for the matter of that, we verily believe that, if Smashup, Breakdown & Co., general stage-agents, who understand packing, had owned an interest in the " City," Smashup would have got half-a-dozen into each. They were, moreover, curtained with some warm-tinted fabric, which accorded well with the cheerful hues of the carpet and window drapery ; and as for sheets and pillowcases, why, we must refer the reader, for their counterpart, to the linen-presses of Dandie Dinmont's "gude wife," at the Liddesdale sheep-farm, for a description of which see Guy Mannering, fair ladies, and "when found," follow up the suggestion of Captain Cuttle, and "make a note of it."

There was a sofa, too—a wonderful sofa—so soft, so practical, and, best of all, so *old-fashioned;* and then there were chairs that seemed natural, and, what is more to the purpose, *agreeing* relatives of the sofa ; which stood round the room upon their sturdy legs, as if they felt themselves to be a credit to the establishment, and—so they were.

But stay, we mustn't forget the wash-stand.   Not much in a wash-stand, hey ?   Why, you were never more mistaken in your life, my good reader !   Nothing ? pooh, nonsense ! why, there's everything in a wash-stand !   Think of the dimpled hands, that lave their tiny fingers over them sometimes, and the bright morning faces, that catch their first glimpse of sunshine from the reflection of their own optics in the basin, and then, we won't say a word, you know, about toilette mysteries.   But believe in the wash-stand, or not, as you choose, *that* doesn't alter the fact that *our* wash-stand was just the thing ; a big, overgrown, apoplectic one, of real Spanish mahogany, turned black with age ; and now throw in a couple of huge, wide-mouthed, and scrupulously clean, white pitchers, filled with unexceptionable water, with quaint-looking accompaniments to match, and a long mahogany rack, hung with towels, white as the driven snow, and we will let our sketch of a comfortable interior go from us without further touching, save this—if you are hard to move, and don't believe in its truthfulness, just try it for yourself, after four days and nights of winter staging in the Far West, and we will "eat our head," *à la* Grimwig, upon the result of your decision.

The morning of the 14th, found us, so far as a conveyance

was concerned, worse off, if anything, than we had been at
Rocheport : for the stage line had again "given out," and the
agent would not even procure a wagon to take its place ; we
tried entreaty, flattery, and even threats, but it was all in vain,
we might as well have talked to the Missouri ; the stages were
all up the country, or all down ; he had none to give us ; he
might have a stage next day, or he might not for a week ; in
fact, our getting on was, so far as his assistance went, quite a
matter of ¿ *Quien sabe* ?

What was to be done ? The Kansas War would be getting
cold—the Herald wouldn't have the news ! It was clearly our
duty to push on ; we accordingly consulted with our Virginian,
who had a wife and youngsters near Lexington (our next principal stopping place, *en route*), from whom he had been for some
time separated. We were, therefore, but from widely differing
causes, most anxious to proceed. "I have it," cried he, after
considerable reflection, "I have just learned that there are some
empty hacks going back to Lexington, so we will leave the
stage-agents to their devices, by cutting them dead, and hiring
our own conveyance.

And to this proposition we acceded, for although, we did not
consider it pecuniarily to our advantage to employ a private
conveyance, to transport us over a road which we had already
paid ten cents per mile, for the privilege of traversing, we felt
compelled to adopt the expedient, as the only one which seemed
calculated to extricate us from the annoyances of a vexatious
delay. So we sallied forth with the Virginian, and sought out
the senior hack-driver, a negro, black as the ace of spades (his
junior being a white man), with whom we entered into a verbal
contract forthwith, wherein it was stipulated, that for a certain
consideration, to be by us "the party of the first part," duly
paid, he, Nigger Jim, as "the party of the second part," should
undertake to bring us, bag and baggage, in safety, to Lexington.

the next "principal city" upon our route, by nightfall of the
ensuing day.

But ere we leave Boonsville, upon paper, let us, to do all things
properly and in order, make a few extracts (in another chapter), from a "letter home," which we dated from our cosy
chamber at the "City Hotel."

CHAPTER V

FROM OUR CORRESPONDENT EN ROUTE.

Boonsville, Mo., *Thursday, December 13th, 1855.*—We remember once, ere we "put our sword upon the peace establishment," and our tongue, or—what comes to the same thing, with an author—our pen, "upon the civil list"—or in plainer language, when we used to *do* tactics in the army of our ungrateful Uncle Sam—to have heard one of our men—a *very old* soldier—from the Emerald Isle, of course (for who doesn't know that the "regulars" of Native American Uncle Sam are for the most part "demmed furriners)," close some unbelievable yarn which he had been spinning for the edification of a newly-joined batch of recruits, with this pithy sentence :

"Yis, gintlemen, av the littel advintures that have happened to me, in my lifetime, an' more perticularly since I've bin a solger-in', was to be put inter a book, it's jist my imprision that they'd fill about five hundred family Bibles in the smallist kind of prent."

And so, in good truth, may we speak of *our sufferings*, since your correspondent and his carpet-bag, got into the hands of that most atrocious of humbugs—the Smashup Stage Company.

(For the subject-matter of a hiatus which occurs here, we must refer the reader to our inklings of miseries by the way, already recorded.)

  *   *   *   *   *   *   *   *   *

And now, having told you of our troubles, we think that you

must allow, that in our pursuit of knowledge under difficulties, in your behalf, we are furnishing you with *proofs* which ought to *set us up* for ever in your estimation, for though we do everything upon the *square*, and strive to work by the golden *rule*, we may even yet be *leaded* by some Border Ruffian, or enthusiastic Free Soiler, in which case please head our obituary with—

𝔇𝔦𝔢𝔡,
OF KANSAS AND A MISSOURI STAGE ROUTE.

There, don't be angry with us for trying to be funny. It's no small effort, under existing circumstances, we can assure you, for really, our *understanding*—our physical one we mean—has been damaged to so great an extent, within the last four and twenty hours, that we shouldn't even like to sit upon a jury.

(We would here refer the reader to our lumber-wagon experiences from Rocheport, to fill another break.)

*   *   *   *   *   *   *   *   *

But enough of egotism, and now for Kansas, whose "Free State War" seems to resemble the yellow fever in New Orleans, in this—that, as you approach more closely to the scene of its active operations, the agent which does the mischief is less talked about. Such, at least, has been our experience in Kansas news-hunting, so far, for in answer to our numerous queries, the Missourians give one stereotyped reply, running thus :

"We don't kear much about it, stranger, but ef our boys go up to Lawrence, I hope they'll kill out those *dog-gauned* Abolitionists. And I jest expect they will."

Indeed we had almost begun to despair of gaining any intelligence at all, until actually upon the spot, in *propria persona*, when in comes the stage from Westport, with a whole grist "of live Yankees," every "mother's son of them" being Free State men—if nothing stronger—and all fresh from the seat of war. What they were doing there is probably nobody's business but their own. Well, we have seen these worthies—talked with them—"*pumped*" them, if a Yankee *can* be "pumped"—tried to separate a mountain of lies from its mole-hill foundation of truth, and have gained the following :—

As this intelligence has been superseded by more reliable testimony, which we afterwards collected upon the spot, we will spare the reader a reiteration of our news items, which, indeed, were, at that early date, summed up in the information that, so far as Lawrence was concerned, the " pomp, and pride, and circumstance of glorious war," had taken up its *nunc dimittis*, or, in a military phrase, its " line of march " for other regions, leaving both sides victorious, and nobody satisfied with that somewhat extraordinary result.

*　　*　　*　　*　　*　　*　　*　　*　　*　　*

We have the following statements from an Abolitionist, who, as we have every reason to believe, took an active, if not violent part in the troubles at Lawrence ; we suppressed his name at the time, because of our promise to do so, for our informant seemed in mortal fear of tar and feathers. So agitated was he in fact, that we verily believe the nightmare herself could have visited him only in the shape of a pro-slavery jack-ass, with bowie-knife legs, and a revolving tail. But to return—he watched us as we were " takin' notes," and hearing that we really meant to " prent em," he beckoned us aside, and very cautiously proceeded to open up his version of the " affairs in Kansas," to which we were all attention ; but it is no more than right to say that our gentleman mistook us for a correspondent of the Blank, a paper, whose proclivities are avowedly Free Soil, or it is just possible that he might have been a little *less* communicative ; at all events, he certainly regarded us as " a friend and *brother*," for he gave our hand a peculiar grasp, which, as we don't belong to any secret societies, save the Good Fellows, and others of that *genus*, we are free to confess we didn't understand ; but remembering that all stratagems are fair in love and war, we could not see why it should not be the same as regards the acquisition of newspaper intelligence, so we squeezed back as vaguely as we conveniently could, which called forth another telegraphic pressure from our friend, who looked mysterious, made signs of caution, drew us outside the door, said something about pro-slavery men being pugnacious, and having sharp ears, and finally, muttered something between his teeth about its being "all right." We had our private suspicions that our friend might find it all *wrong*, but didn't see fit to express them.

(Our new acquaintance then proceeded to enlighten us upon various points, which, for reasons already given, would be uninteresting, if recapitulated here ; there was, however, *one* statement made, which we wilh chronicle as worth reading.)

Our informant tells us, that the so-called settlement of the difficulties at Lawrence, between the Free State and Pro-slavery leaders, was, on the part of the Free State people, nothing more than a "cute Yankee trick," amounting simply to this—that the citizens of Lawrence, after making a show of resistance, until they found that they might be overpowered by a superior force, avoided a fight, by intimating to Governor Shannon that they were willing to submit themselves to the laws, and permit the sheriff of Donglas County to arrest the persons against whom he held writs, and whom they had hitherto been harboring—a settlement was accordingly made, but not until the fugitives in question had been warned by the Free State party, and allowed time to make good their escape, which they were not slow to do.

"But," queried we, "are the Lawrence people going to back down, and give it up so—won't they try it again ?"

"They're bound to," was the reply, and so our conference ended. Upon parting with us, our mysterious little friend desired, as a particular favor to himself, that we should state, in case any inquiries were made, concerning him, that we had known him in Louisville, Ky., from whence, as we afterwards discovered, upon reference to the record of the hotel, he had seen fit to register himself. " My real name," said he, " is S. N. W***, and I am a prominent Free State man in Lawrence ; but, for Heaven's sake, don't breathe my name here, it's as much as my life's worth." As we didn't want to place Mr. W*** life in danger (in case the Missourians might take it into their heads that he was *worth* killing), we have kept these matters to ourself, even till now. Oh, we had almost forgotten to say, that little W***—for he *was* a little man, and not over handsome at that—seemed very anxious that we should make the acquaintance of some of the prominent Free Soilers in Lawrence, or, as the Yankees pronounce it— *Lar*-ence—to which we assented, as we were sincerely desirous of information, and didn't care from what source it came, black, white, or grey, for be it remembered, that we were after facts— facts of the stern hard-shell kind, for the Kansas news are as grist to our pen and ink mill, and we would even have coveted " a free fight," if we could have been " counted out," for the sake of adding to our items.

And now, ere we close this long-winded epistle—for the candle is flickering in its socket, and our watch indicates that witching hour, when

" Churchyards yawn," and drowsy watchmen sleep—

let us send you a veritable narrative, which we have learned from the lips of a New Yorker (hailing from Delaware County), who got it upon the spot. And we will here take the liberty of dedicating this yarn to the ultra-Emancipationists in general, with a reservation in favor of Mistress Blank (no relation to our Blanks up to date, by the way), if that distinguished authoress should feel inclined to add an extra Key to the Uncle Tommia. It may be called—A BLACK DIAMOND— THE GEM OF THE KANSAS SEASON.

"It would appear, that among the Pro-Slavery warriors, who besieged the far-famed fortifications of Lawrence, there was a certain good man, and true—one Mister Magee, from Clay County, Mo., or thereabouts (everybody comes from counties at the West). Now Mister Magee owned a "nigger," who had worked in the yoke of slavery, until it ought to have scarified his shoulders, but had not. Of the precise baptismal designation of Mister Magee's nigger we are unaware, but, for convenience sake, we will presume his cognomen to have been Cæsar—Julius Cæsar, if you please—or, if you prefer it—Augustus. And our Cæsar was evidently no coward, but rather a valiant man-of-war, who, like Mr. Norval,

"Had heard of battles;"

in short, he was "a fighting darkey," and accordingly accompanied his master to prove, by doughty deeds, that a "colored passon" has his rights and won't be freed without his consent being previously obtained, "anyhow you can fix it." Now, it so happened that Cæsar, while serving in the Wakarusa camp, was charged with the performance of some scouting duty, in the execution of which he discovered an Abolitionist lurking about his post. Cæsar hailed him, and inquired into his business there. The Abolitionist gave replies which Cæsar regarded as being highly unsatisfactory. The Pro-Slavery darkey forthwith advanced upon this philanthropic upholder of human rights with an energy which, while it spoke volumes for his party zeal, said but very little for his pacific intentions. The pale-face turned and fled—it is not even on record that he lingered to say—"*Et tu Brute*"—or, as it is matrimonially translated—"and you too, you brute." Cæsar was swift of foot, as well as valorous of heart; he darted forward in pursuit. The white man quickened his pace, but Cæsar put his long heels down as if he were after a runaway locomotive, and ere long overhauled the panting fugitive, who "surrendered at discretion," at the same time begging for his life, and delivering up, as an evidence of his submission (in compliance with Cæsar's particular request), a Sharp's rifle, a brace of Colt's revolvers, and an improved bowie-knife, with which he had *encumbered* himself. Our narrator goes on to state that Cæsar "toted" the fellow into the Wakarusa camp, and then and there delivered up his prisoner and the spoils, to the manifest amusement of the Pro-Slavery men, and the no slight increase of the military reputation of Fighting Cæsar. It is now generally supposed in Clay County (adds our informant), that a "white man may be as good as a nigger," under favorable circumstances.

And now, farewell ; we have two or three nights more of staging before us, from which may the Fates send us a safe deliverance, for it is "raining like blazes ;" the country is all afloat, the rivers up, and the bridges down, and your "war correspondent" given out to such a degree, that, like a certain distinguished personage, he may be said to sit uneasily in his seat.

We shall write you soon, from *somewhere ;* but we are going to have a row with the stage-agent to-morrow, and there's no telling what may come of it ; he may be too much for us ; we anathematized a driver yesterday—result—stage upset, *accidentally*, of course, just half-an-hour afterwards.

Truly yours, &c.,
HIAWATHA.

CHAPTER VI.

OUR VIRGINIAN FRIEND ON SLAVERY.

But let us get back to Boonsville; to our private hack, and the morning of December 14th. We were all ready to start— bill paid; porter satisfied; landlord smiling benignantly; Nigger Jim handled the reins; and Virginia (as I shall henceforth call him), and "our correspondent," made ourselves comfortable upon the back seat, the front, for we were the only passengers, being already occupied by our carpet-bags.

As we drove on, until nightfall, over a most abominable road, we whiled away the hours by chatting with "Virginia," whom we had already discovered to be a sensible, well-informed, and high-bred gentleman, of the old-fashioned Southern school Among other matters, we discussed that much-vexed theme, the slavery question, but more particularly as to the effect of this institution upon the welfare of the slave; and upon this point, we found our friend to be excellently posted, for he was, himself, a considerable slave-holder, owning a large farm, and some eighty negroes, in the vicinity of Lexington, Mo., of whom, not more than thirty, as he assured us, really paid for their keeping.

We are indebted to "Virginia" for much valuable information in regard to the mode of life, habits, morals and general management of slaves, as at present existing in Missouri; and we very much regret that our business engagements prevented us from accepting an invitation, which was most kindly ten-

dered, to visit his plantation and take up our abode at his residence, where we could investigate the subject at our ease, enjoy
some good shooting, and see negro slavery, not as Northern fanatics would paint the picture, but as it really is to be found ir
many a Southern home, where the relation between the master
and his slave is, in nine instances out of ten, a more kindly
one than that which exists between the Eastern manufacturer
and his sickly, pale-faced operative.

And now we must ask the reader's indulgent criticism ; for
it is no easy task, after an interval of weeks, to select from
a mass of facts, stated in a rambling and oftentimes interrupted
conversation, just such material as would be most interesting
to the inquirer. We must, therefore, make the circumstances
under which these things were told to us our best apology for
the disjointed style in which we are compelled to present them
But let them tell their own story.

Slave women differ very much in their affection for their
children ; some exhibit great solicitude for the welfare of their
offspring, while others seem perfectly reckless as to their fate.
The old women are, for the most part, employed in looking after
the children and cabins during the absence of the negroes in the
field ; this is the more necessary, as the young darkeys are wonderfully mischievous, as much so as juvenile monkeys ; indeed,
were they left to themselves they would be quite as likely to
amuse an idle hour by burning down the "old folks' cabin," as
in any less incendiary way. When the youngsters get large
enough, they are frequently taken into the planter's house, where
they do light work, stuff themselves with eatables, and, in many
instances, get petted until they become completely spoiled.

Singular as it may appear, we find it very difficult to obtain
good house-servants ; for the negro seems better fitted for out-
door employment. This is even the case with those who are
brought up in our houses, for as they approach the age of

fifteen or sixteen years, they grow restless and discontented, and begin to envy what they consider the greater amount of freedom which falls to the share of the field-hands, who have their stated and regular hours for work, and are, therefore, at liberty, when their labor is done, to enjoy themselves, or, as a negro says, "joy themselves" in any way they please.

We give our hands, both male and female, two full suits of clothes per annum, with under-clothing in proportion; these suits are made of a coarse, but very warm and durable fabric, which costs between one and two dollars per yard. When one of our slaves desires to marry, he goes to his master, confesses the "soft impeachment," and asks his consent. If the object of his adoration belongs to another plantation, the master of the girl is waited upon for the same purpose. These requests are scarcely ever refused. As the negro has a great idea of doing things like "quality folks," their weddings are state occasions, where Cato and Pomp are expected to support their dignity by behaving with the utmost decorum; while high-bred colored ladies show their "manners" to the fullest extent; and though there be no presentation of plate at the nuptial feast, the bridal gifts are, nevertheless, of a very substantial kind; for, beside the remembrances of their companions, it is usual for the planter to present the newly-married pair with a four-poster and mattress, or it may be a new brass kettle with which to set up house-keeping. The slave has also his little garden, which he may till with self-interest; as an incentive, the proceeds are his own, to be disposed of as he thinks proper. He is also permitted to keep a hog, and, if he desires to do so, chickens. There is, probably, no slave who might not purchase his freedom, if he were so inclined and would exert himself sufficiently to obtain the requisite means (for we are told that when such an intimation is made to the master, he is generally willing to value his servant at a much lower rate than he would hold him at in negotiating with another party).

"The negroes are usually particular in the moral training of their children. A sort of school was established upon my place, and kept up for some little time by an old negro of mine, quite an 'Uncle Tom' in his way, who seemed to take great pleasure in attempting to teach the slave children, and for that matter, their parents, to read and write ; but it was labor thrown away, for though his pupils were zealous enough in undertaking their education, their literary courage soon oozed out, for your true African is anything but a book-worm. As regards temperament and disposition, my negroes were formerly very gay; they were at it from morning till night ; the fiddle and the banjo made constant music in the quarters, dancing was the rage, and a 'hoe-down' just the thing. But.

' A change came o'er the spirit of their dream,'

they took a religious turn, and my Uncle Tom got up 'a revival,' which was what the preachers call 'most abundantly blessed.' The sable converts were numerous, and, as they would do nothing by halves, while on the road to salvation, the fiddle was tabooed—the banjo put away—dancing interdicted, and even the innocent 'hoe-down' voted a child of 'de debble,' and a 'mighty sure' trap, to 'catch de sinful nigger's soul.' Since then the excitement has cooled down, and, as in similar cases among more refined people, many of the 'renewed,' have 'slipped back.' But the influence of the event, combined with the continual admonitions of my Uncle Tom, is still sufficient to restrain them from any extraordinary exhibition of their animal spirits. So we continue to miss their dancing, and instead of a harvest-song, get Old Hundred most dolefully lined out.

"The negroes, for the most part, adopt the family name of their respective masters, but the given name, or, more frequently, an abbreviation of it, is their only practical designation. In spite of all that has been said and written to the contrary, the negro women are generally chaste, and faithful to their lords. I have but one family upon my plantation whose women bear a doubtful character in this respect, and they are looked down upon and despised by their fellows. If one of my negroes falls sick, he sends word to the house, when my wife usually goes down to visit the patient, and if it be a simple matter, within the reach of our family medicine-chest, she prescribes, and treats the case herself. But if the symptoms are violent, or, the disease assume a graver character, we send immediately for a physician, the best that can be obtained. A negro's hopefulness is small. When ill, they lose much of their elasticity of mind, are low-spirited, highly superstitious, and quite ready to imagine that they are certainly 'going to die.' Our white children are very fond of playing with the negro boys, more so, I think, than with those of their own color. I have a couple of youngsters, who sometimes get into trouble with their colored playmates ; on these occasions it very frequently happens that my boys are thrown down, and sometimes get a sound thrashing from their sable companions, the children of my slaves, but, unless they have been manifestly imposed upon, I never interfere, but let them fight out their own battles.

" As regards our method of slave discipline the *whip* is but seldom resorted to, and then only in extreme cases. An increase of labor, or a deprivation of some customary privilege, will usually suffice to bring the offender to his senses. A negro rarely suffers for an offence which he has not committed, for though the circumstantial evidence against him be ever so strong, when it comes to the moment of punishment, one of your old darkeys, of known character and discretion, will generally step out with some such expostulation as this :

"'Massa John, what you gwyne whip dat nigga for? he no do it. More like to be dat lying nigga, Pete, Massa,' &c.

"Christmas and 'Christmas week,' are the negro's great holidays. They have other 'gala days,' but the anniversary of our Saviour's nativity, is the 'festival' *par excellence*, of the slave.

"I have quite a good-looking young negro girl, some sixteen years of age, who has been brought up as a house-servant in my family, and it is a matter of no little amusement to my wife and self, to watch this sable damsel getting through the difficulties of her first flirtation ; for she has a lover, a young fellow from a neighboring plantation, as black as black can be, who drops into our kitchen on Sunday evenings to 'hab de felicity to pay his respects to Miss Dinah,' but Miss Dinah is very modest, and prefers sending for some young colored girl about her own age, who 'plays propriety,' and assists her in entertaining 'Mister Tom.'"

And now, we have given the subject matter, if not something more, of our talk with the Virginian.

Supper time brought us to Marshall, where we halted for the night, after accomplishing about half the journey to Lexington. The following is an extract from our "journal letter," of that day :

MARSHALL, *Saline Co., Mo., Dec.* 14.

We have progressed, since writing you from Boonsville, some forty miles upon our way, over such roads as no Christian ever dreamed of out of the Far-Western country, where every little "branch" is a creek, and every creek a swollen river. Vehicles are detained, horses killed, and passengers indulge in the use of strong expressions, until the *voyageur* begins to suspect, that if Job himself, of much enduring memory, had been sent (instead of being afflicted with boils, and a wife), to traverse, with his better half for a blister, the stage routes of the 'Missouri bottom," he would have knocked under before the first change of horses.

And *apropos*-to the roads, we give our forethought credit, for, had we trusted to that "through ticket," of Smashup's, we would have been in Boonsville at this present writing, but being enterprising, we are here ; yet the exertion has cost us something withal, for a long day's travel in an open hack, with December's icy wind whistling in one's teeth, is a sorry joke, as our half-frozen limbs can testify.

And now, could you look in upon us, you would echo the old saw, which tells us, that "one half the world don't know how the other half live." To locate ourself, then, let us give you an unvarnished description of the very primitive apartment in which we are now writing. It is the best, and almost the only room of a two-story "hotel," log-cabin ; a huge fire of Missouri coal blazes upon the hearth (the only cheerful-looking thing in the establishment); the furniture consists of a large double-bed, of the old-fashioned, short-legged, four-poster breed, which fills up one corner of the room, and at present accommodates an *almost* sober stage-driver (who has turned in with his boots and overcoat on), and occasionally interrupts his nap by rolling over, with his face toward the company, so as to join in our conversation ; a very rickety wash-stand is placed opposite the bed, garnished with a tin hand-basin, not over clean, and a brace of empty whisky-bottles, one of which does duty as a candlestick ; over these hang a crooked looking-glass, which will caricature your face into a monkey's, if you are bold enough to consult its dusty surface ; or if you would regenerate your hair, look to the right of the mirror, where you will find a half-worn brush and very greasy comb, which are attached to long pieces of red tape, and hang pendant from the wall, *pro bono publico;* add to these, a rough board table, whose uncertain legs interfere sadly with our penmanship ; and a tallow dip in a sea-green brass candlestick, which reminds one strongly of a badly-managed revolving light, and you have an inventory of the *regular* accessories to this very primitive apartment. As for the *irregulars*, they are all around us ; for the dingy walls are literally papered with "circus bills," unreadable business cards, notices of sheriffs' sales, stray cattle, and patent medicines, "good for the chills ;" nor are these all ; cloaks, hats, and riding-whips are suspended from every available peg, and a rifle, flanked by its bullet-pouch and horn, rests above the door, while the tobacco-stained floor under our feet is littered with a mingling of buffalo over-shoes, robes, Mackinaws, and such like travelling gear.

And oh ! if it were only in our line, how we should like to sketch in the group around the fire—but "we kānt, we rēally kānt," it isn't in ouēr way. If we were Doesticks, or Dickens, or Widow Bedott, or somebody else, whose name doesn't occur to us just now, we *might* do them justice, but as we are ourself, and nothing more, we must confine our pen and ink delineations to an outline ; so here goes for a slap-dash description.

"Misery makes strange companionships—so do's travelling ; what incongruities—were ever such opposites united before ?"

So ran our mental criticism, good reader, as our wind-damaged eyes wandered from one to another of our associates for the time being, and it was a mixture of which we shall give you a taste of the ingredients.

In the very warmest corner—a seat most judiciously chosen— sat an old Yankee, with a long, sharp nose, and keen grey eyes, over which a pair of heavy eyebrows arched themselves. ever and anon, as if they said, "Wael, I never—du tell !" These with a strip of yellow forehead, a bilious complexion, and a most unyielding head of hair, complete a face, which would have been a letter of credit for its owner's "all-fired smartness," from Persia to the Poles ; as for dress, Jonathan was rigged out in a coat, that was built among the granite hills of cold New Hampshire, or nowhere—a swallow-tailed thing, with huge pockets, and bright brass buttons ; to this add a generous allowance of shirt-collar, a free-and-easy neck'erchief, a pair of striped breeches, whose legs were a world too short for his long shanks, and an unpolished sample of eastern-made boots, and we flatter ourself that you have a tolerably correct likeness of as unmitigated a Yankee as ever whittled a stick, or talked about "hum," as connected with the land of wooden nutmegs.

Next to the Yankee, sat our friend the Virginian, the living antipodes of the character which we have just been attempting to portray. In face and form he was just what "sweet sixteen," with her pretty head filled with

" Tales of old romance,"

would have fallen in love with at first sight. Yes, there's no denying it, for though "verging upon the forties," "Virginia" was as gallant a looking fellow as you would meet with in a long day's march. And for his age, why, as the fire-light brings out his features into bolder relief, we are disposed to think, that the hand of Time has dealt wisely with him, in strengthening the lines of the mouth and brow, and thereby adding a maturer dignity, ere in his ceaseless flight he brings the strong man to the full perfection of meridian life. Virginia is over six feet in height, well proportioned, and very Spanish in his style, for his hair and flowing beard are dark "as the raven's wing," with eyes to match. Take him all in all, he is a true son of the Old Dominion, an F. F. V. "*sans peur et sans reproche*," whose dress, and air, and manner, somewhat imperious though it be, bespeak the gentleman born and bred, of the real Virginian school, where men *are* men, not black-coated fops.

And now we crave room, plenty of room, or he may " clar the ground " himself, for another character, and a peculiar one withal. He is a type of the *genus* " Border Ruffian," a frontier

Missourian, just fresh from the Kansas Wars, where he has been figuring as an incendiary Pro-Slavery volunteer, and "don't kear a dog-gaun who knows it." He is a tall, gaunt man, all bone and muscle, with ape-like limbs, cast in no classic mould, but nevertheless sufficiently strong to "wrap 'em a'way round a b'ar," and make Bruin grunt with anguish at every hug. In short, you may regard him as a fair exponent of that eccentric class of Western men, who, being persons of terrible experiences, claim to "scream louder, jump higher, shoot closer, get more drunk at night, and wake up more sober in the morning" than "any other human" this side of the Rocky Mountains, and "ef you don't believe it" it's "I'm easy to whip, stranger, I *am*, just pitch in, will yeou, and don't stand on ceremony," with, mayhap, a flourish from a horn-handled bowie-knife to second the invitation.

Our Border Ruffian is just now regarding the Yankee as if he would give the best horse he ever rode for a reasonable excuse to "jump him up," but the returned volunteer "will hardly get a chance ; for though Jonathan evidently dislikes his neighbor, he has no notion of engaging in a row, where he "don't feel himself to hum."

The Borderer is careless, even to a fault, in his costume ; he sports a sky-blue blanket overcoat (a favorite color in Missouri), from the side-pocket of which the butt "of a six-shooter peeps threateningly out, and if you will take a look into his right boot-leg, we should say that a serviceable bowie-knife *might* be found inserted between the leather and his tucked-in Kentucky jean pantaloons. He has hard, weather-beaten features, long brown hair, and a restless eye ; his teeth are good, and his mouth, though somewhat large, might have been called handsome ; but an inveterate habit of tobacco-chewing has drawn down the left corner, from whence a leak lets the juice of the weed dribble gently down.

How do you like our last effort, Miss Precise ?—think it

colored hey? Not at all; it's done in simple white and black, nothing more we assure you, but you think he's a "horrid beast." Oh, you do; well, we congratulate ourself twice; first, that we are not your big brother; and secondly, that the subject of our sketch is unacquainted with your very flattering opinion of him. But seriously, Miss Precise, did you never hear of an unpolished gem? Never mind our Borderer's *rough-setting*. He is a diamond of the purest water for all that. An honest single-hearted sort of creature, rather Indian in his nature, who loves and hates with equal zeal. He'd cut your throat if you insulted him, and his idea of an insult includes any disparagement of the South or her peculiar institutions; but on the other hand, he would share his last dollar with you if you needed it, and if a woman or a child be in the case, he is one of the tenderest hearted fellows in the world. Of such are Kit Carson, born in Boonslick County, Missouri, and the whole-souled pioneer men of the Far West.

But our outline has already tempted us too far from our marked-out track. We have yet to reach Kansas and the War, and these digressions delay one sadly; so complete our fire-side group with a stage-driver (not the gentleman on the bed), a "Hoosier," a trio of hog-drivers, a Missouri landlord, and a "special correspondent," and then fill in the picture to suit yourself.

One paragraph more, and we will complete our journalizing in Marshall. We are writing in a mild Bedlam. The Demon of politics has stirred up our companions. The Free State war is before the house. The Yankee is defining his position. The Missourians, with equal earnestness, are defending theirs. The arguments on both sides grow "fast and furious," and already threaten personalities; and, to crown all, the sound of "de fiddle and de bow" is to be heard from an adjoining cabin, where a long-legged Kentucky amateur plays a tuneful violin, and a nigger, stripped to his breeches and shirt, is "breaking down" to that good old tune "The Arkansas Traveller," as if his life depended upon the elasticity of his legs.

Dec. 15.—Breakfast over—sun just getting out of a snow-bank—hack at the door—Virginia and ourself inside—carpet-bags ditto ; we drive off. Stop, hold on : we have forgotten something—our note-book was missing. We go back to look up the lost sheep, and reënter the "hotel" just in time to hear a Missourian say :

" That man—why, he's a correspondent of that vile Abolition paper, the New York *Herald.*"

We concluded that the " schoolmaster " might be " abroad" in Marshall, but didn't think it probable. We recovered our property, and then made good our retreat without beat of drum. "That vile Abolition paper, the Herald "—O, Tempora ! O, Moses ! as Mrs. Partington feelingly remarked, when Ike tumbled into the barrel of soft soap : " Isn't it a blessed thing to editorialize for an appreciative public ?"

Another miserable day, and more of it. Virginia too cold to talk, and " your correspondent " too sleepy. Nigger Jim, who has a bottle of Red-eye whisky, " warranted to kill forty rods round the corner," in his pocket, thaws out under its influence and become gradually enthusiastic, whereupon we ask Nigga Jim what he thinks about the "Kansas War," who makes answer as follows :

" Can't say, massa ; never form no 'pinion ; dis nigger ain't a gwyne to 'stress himself bout politics ; don't reckon much on dese Abolitionists, no how ; but jest know dis, massa, dat dis nigga's jest as happy and 'joys himself as much as if he owned de whole town of Lexington ; bein' slave is may-be mighty hard on white folks, but it's dreadful good for nigga."

We fell asleep well satisfied, for we had gained a new idea, or, to speak more correctly, had an old one verified, by evidence from a "most undoubted authority," whose opportunities for acquiring practical information rendered him well qualified to judge.

Night-fall again—sun down in another snow-bank—a streak or two of yellowish white light in the West—dark grey clouds overhead, while

> " Out of those frozen clouds the snow
> In wavering flakes begins to flow."

We enter Lexington " City," and draw up at the door of Walton's Hotel. The hack is halted—the door opens—we descend, and our carpet-bag follows. The fare, as stipulated in Boonsville by " the party of the first part," is duly paid, and Nigga Jim and " Our Correspondent " are parted for ever.

An hour later—inside the hotel—we have had supper, and a difficulty with the landlord, by way of dessert ; it has, however, just been arranged in a highly satisfactory manner to both parties, by a visit to "the bar," by which the reader may understand, not the bar of justice, but the "saloon" next door ; and we consider it about as *cheap* a row, by the way, as we ever got into in our life ; for a "drink" of old Rye (which is at times regarded in Missouri as the pledge of peace, though it is oftener the cause of feud), costs just one dime per glass ; so that our late difficulty with "mine host" stood us in twenty cents precisely, a clear saving of lawyers' fees and costs of court, not to mention vexation and the possible necessity of " a surgeon and a friend " in the morning—think of this, ye pugnacious people, but two dimes to settle a fight ; *mirabile dictu!* was there ever so cheap a luxury ?

Eight o'clock, P. M ; we are *solus*, with a bed-chamber, two tallow candles, a shaky table, and pen, ink and paper for company ; with which, half-past eight found us writing away at our Journal, for the subject matter of which see the next chapter.

CHAPTER VII.

LEXINGTON.

As our location indicates, we are still *en route* for Kansas; but, *n'importe*, we are in advance of the mail, and *did* mean to have continued so, but at this place, we have come to a dead lock; for, until the stage arrives, there will be nothing going on, we fear (alas!) in any respect. We might "foot it," it is true, and *would*; but there's our carpet-bag—ah! that's a drawback; and then, what with broken bridges (we crossed one chained to a tree to-day, to keep it from sloping down stream), swollen streams, swampy bottom-lands, and rut-ploughed prairie roads, the De'il himself couldn't make much headway on his own private hoofs, even with the assistance of his tail for a cane, over a Missouri highway in winter. So "Shank's mare" is not to be thought of; but there's some hope left still, though it be founded upon possibilities, for this untoward weather cannot last for ever; and then the stage *may* come up; and we *may* get a seat, and thus reach Westport, if we have *very* great good luck, within four and twenty hours from this present writing, when, "please the grunters," we will enter Kansas—yea, even though it should be through an army of Border Ruffians and upon the rump of a Mexican jackass.

O Kansas! Kansas! Thou longed for "haven where we would be," but not "at rest," when shall we tread thy snow·

clad prairies, and gaze upon thy Lawrence—the hope and pride of thy Free State men's eyes—a locality which must, from this day forward, be more than classic ground to every "Woolly Head," of the veteran white-coated brigade? Oh! would that we had been there when the bloody ensign hung out upon the outer wall of that beleaguered city. Would we not have "pitched in?" Ah! no, but we'd have sat, like Marius among the ruins of Carthage, or anybody else you please, with a grey-goose quill in our fur-mittened right hand, and taken notes in most unreadable abbreviations. Aye, that we would, even among "flames and blazes," the

"Wreck of matter and the crush of worlds."

So much for fun—we'll grow more serious anon.

Sunday, *Dec. 16th.*—We held converse to-day with a number of Missourians, who have just returned from " the seat of War, in Kansas," where they have been serving in the ranks of the Pro-Slavery, or, as some call it, Governor Shannon's army. They are full of talk about " the War ;" indeed, to do the good people in this vicinity justice, Kansas, and " the vile Abolitionists," are in everybody's mouth. They are shouted in the bar-rooms, they are sounded in the streets, until the very parlors catch the oft-repeated echoes, and packages of Missourian beauty, done up with care, in the last new fashion from New York (and a very liberal one it is, so far as hoops and flounces are concerned), talk resistance and disunion as they discuss " Kansas and the Wakarusa War." We have even heard of an enthusiastic fair one, residing in the territory, who declined giving her hand to a gentleman Free-Soiler in the dance, alleging as a reason, that *she* was a Border Ruffian, and under such circumstances, wouldn't get up " an affinity " with any " Cromwell of them all."

The Kansas excitement is certainly at a white heat in this region. Old men shake their heads and express decided opinions while young Missouri, yet more determined, looks revolvers, and talks bowie-knives, as he openly declares that "the boys ought never to have left an infernal Abolitionist alive in Lawrence."

Among those with whom we have talked the matter over to-day, was an aide-de-camp of General Strickler's, who has just returned from his arduous campaign, with what, to our thinking, may not improperly be called the Field and Staff Brigade, for, may we be placed in that extremity, if we have as yet seen a man, of all those "fire-eating" sons of Missouri, who volunteered "for the war," who was not a subaltern at the very least. The Colonel (we think that was his title, and desire to apologize if we underrate his rank), informed us that he had written a short history of the "Wakarusa War." We were most anxious to see it, and therefore intimated to the aide-de-camp that his manuscript, or even an abridgment of its contents, would be a very acceptable addition to our gleanings of intelligence by the way. But the gallant Colonel's modesty got the better of his desire to oblige us, so we shall therefore be compelled, though most reluctantly, to disappoint public curiosity, so far as the publication of our Pro-Slavery military friend's reminiscences are concerned, though we offered "a first-rate notice" as an inducement, and the New-York Herald for a publisher.

While engaged in conversation with this gentleman, Col. Walton (mine host of the city, and formerly an officer of Doniphan's command), called our attention to a burly, black-smithy looking dark-complexioned individual, in the general sitting-room, which adjoined that in which which we were standing. The person pointed out seemed, for some reason, but for what we could not understand, to be the cynosure of every eye ; nor were the glances directed toward him of either a flattering or an amicable description ; on the contrary, men scrutinized him as they might have examined a newly-imported wild animal at a show, and then nodded their heads, and jogged the elbows of

their neighbors, who looked up and stared as if Barnum's mer-
maid had just walked out of the glass case, with her tail under
her arm.

"It's him."

"It isn't."

"It's that rascally Abolitionist, I tell you. I'd know him
among a thousand," were the muttered comments of those about us.

"Who is it?" we asked.

"Why it's P———," answered mine host.

"But who is P———?"

"Why P——— is the prisoner that our people took, as he
was travelling from Lawrence to Lecompton. He is one of the
Free State men, an agent, the financial one, I believe, of the
Kansas Emigrant Aid Society, and a prominent man among the
Abolitionists beside. He is now travelling under the name of
Clarke, and claims to be a Baptist preacher, but he might save him-
self the trouble, for there are fifty men here who recognize him."

Whew! thought we—"the murder's out." Here, then, is one
of the famous Lawrence men, a *bona fide* sample of those doughty
warriors, who are setting the American world by the ears. One
of the Free State Sharpe's rifle and Colt's revolver breed—a
veritable specimen, all alive and kicking. We got excited, we
already scented a column of private information, "exclusive to the
Herald," from the Yankee side of the question. So we determined to make P———'s acquaintance, even at the risk of being
taken for "a bird of that feather," in which case our chance of
being lynched for a Down Eastern Agitator, who might or might
not "steal niggers," as opportunity offered, would have been
exceedingly good.

"Introduce us," cried we to Col. Walton.

We were led up accordingly. Pro-Slavery men, with whom
we had previously been conversing in a very amiable way,
looked ferocious, but we didn't quail.

"General P———, let me make you acquainted with Mr.
———. The Special Correspondent for Kansas, of the New York
Herald." We exchange the usual compliments, and the fol-
lowing dialogue ensues :

Correspondent.—So, General P———, you are just from
Lawrence ?

Free State General.—Yes sir, I was a prisoner in General
Strickler's camp for four or five days. They took me as I was
travelling.

Correspondent.—Is it possible ? We hope they used you well.
Did they threaten you ? We presume, however, that they did.

Free State General.—Yes, the rabble, that is, the common
men, threatened me, but their officers restrained them.

Correspondent.—Oh ! the officers took care of you, did they ?
Well I suppose they gave you plenty of corn dodgers, good coffee,
and all that sort of thing ?

Free State General.—Yes, I lived as well as the officers.
I was liberated about the time that the troubles were settled,
but they took me out of their camp (the one on the Wakarusa
creek), very quietly at midnight, when they let me go, for it was
supposed by the Pro-Slavery leaders that their soldiers might
do me a mischief if I fell into their hands. So General Strickler, with General Richardson, and Senator Atchinson, released
me secretly for fear of the mob.

Correspondent.—Now, General P———, could you not give
us some notion of the state of affairs at Lawrence ? How about
those "breast-works," cannon, Sharpe's rifles, &c.? We learn that
your people had a white flag flying over Doctor Robinson's
house (the Commander in Chief of the Free State Army). Is
that so, and what terms did you make finally ? Come, post us
up, let us have the items. The readers of the New York
Herald will be glad to hear your story. Nothing like both
sides of the question being fairly stated, you know.

4*

Free State General.—Well, I guess the New York papers know all about it now. The Tribune's had a man out there these six weeks, a person named Winchell, or something like that. Then, there's Phillips, he writes letters for the New York Times, and Tom Shankland too, he sends news to the Tribune sometimes ; I reckon they have heard all about it by telegraph, anyhow.

(We intimated that the telegraph wires were down, and communication by mail at that season of the year, very uncertain.) General P——— continues :—

" Well, as to the breast-works, we had them, I can tell you, with trenches, and rifle-pits too ; I guess they cost as much as five thousand dollars. We didn't have as many men as was reported, but we had a cannon and plenty of Sharp's rifles. There was a white flag a-flying over Doctor Robinson's house. Doctor Robinson was down in the town, and his women folks hoisted it. As to the terms of the capitulation, there's all sorts of stories about it, but I guess there was no particular agreement, anyhow. That's what it will turn out to be in the end, we didn't give up our arms nor agree to do so, either."

(Note: We fancy there was some mistake, or it may be a desire on the part of Gen. P——— to mislead us, as to his know'edge of this treaty ; for Gen. Robinson afterwards gave us to understand that P——— was acquainted with the terms of the treaty at the time when this conversation took place. Indeed Gen. Robinson supposed that it was from *him* that we obtained copies of the " stipulations " agreed upon between Governor Shannon and the Free State leaders, with its *accompanying* document. In this, however, he is mistaken, for though we certainly *did* make accurate transcripts of these papers previous to our entering Kansas, and at a time when it was presumed that there were but three copies in existence, we received them from another quarter, a gentleman deep in the councils of the Free State party, but whose name we are in honor bound not to divulge.)

Correspondent.—With such excellent opportunities as you must have possessed for forming a correct judgment, General P———, your opinion as to the cause and growth of these disturbances at Lawrence, would be valuable ; could you favor us with it ?

Free State General.—Well, I guess it was just a misunderstanding all around and nothing more. Some folks in Lawrence are mightily hot-headed one way, and some the other. There are people among the Free Soilers who made a great deal of talk and stirred things up considerable, but I guess they would have been *wanting* if it had come to a fight ; and then there's others who kept still, and didn't say much, that would have fought till they died.

Correspondent.—Who are the real leaders of this Free State movement at Lawrence ?

Free State General.—Well, General Lane I guess, and Doctor Robinson too, are leading men.

Here the " down stage " in which General P——— *alias* Mr. Sam Clarke (for our Free State "*militaire*" had, as Col. Walton informed us, found it more convenient, and it may be *safer*, to register himself in that name, of which more anon), had taken his seat, was reported ready. Whereupon the General turned to us and said :—

" Mr. ———, as you are collecting information in regard to Kansas matters, for the Herald, I will give you a letter to some of the Lawrence people ; it will help you along."

As we were very willing to be " helped along " so far as our fact-gathering was concerned, we expressed our willingness to receive any documents which might tend to the elucidation of that very knotty problem, the state of affairs in Kansas. Whereupon, the General very politely stepped up to the landlord's desk and in a few moments furnished us with a specimen of his chirography in the shape of a brief letter of introduction to Doctor Robinson, the chief *par excellence* of the Free State movement in Kansas for which the giver will be pleased to accept our thanks, but may the Peace Society deliver us, if these bloodthirsty and fire-eating Missourians should catch us with such a document upon our person ; for it would most assuredly be our credential to anything but a polite reception ; indeed, we should expect a coat of tar and feathers at the very least ; or, as a terrible alternative, be obliged to prove the soundness of our political principles ; and, as the Border Ruffians express it, show ourself to be "all right upon the goose," by accepting a plantation with half a hundred "niggars," and adding a guarantee to shake out the remainder of our days upon the rich timber-land of the " Missouri bottom."

And now to write more seriously : during our passage through Missouri, we have been studying the "genius of the people" pretty constantly, and we think that we may now safely say, that the good citizens of this State, though, as a general thing, endowed with a fair proportion of hard common sense, are still somewhat fallible, not to say stupid, in their very summary way of judging Eastern, or Free-State-born men ; for they would appear to be firm believers in the adage, that " none can touch pitch and not be defiled." To have been " raised " on Deown East Johnny-cakes, or even Ohio corn, is a certificate in full for Abolitionism and fanatical proclivities, or Free Soilism at the best. Indeed, the " black North " is but little understood ; for, as we stated in our journalizing from Marshall, we heard ourself spoken of as " an agent for that vile *Abolition* paper, the Herald ;" the *Herald*, a good joke is it not ? yes, it may be to *you*, but *we've* made a mental note of it, nevertheless, and don't intend to come West again, as a newspaper correspondent, at any price, unless " our paper " furnishes us with the political character of the sheet, so "fairly writ" as to please everybody, with, if you please, a certificate appended, to the effect that the New York Herald don't and never did belong to the "Woolly Head" faction, or its representatives. But we must cry a truce to this, for we find that we have been imitating the example of the Camden and Amboy railroad, insomuch as we are running *off* the track of our subject, in trying to *get on;* so, lest we should carry out the simile, and conclude with a "smash up," we will even "get back to our mutton," which, by this time, must be moderately cold.

Let us see—we were in the bar-room of the Lexington City Hotel, hearing everybody talk Kansas. Well, our friend, General P———, got off with a whole skin, somewhat, as we fancied, to his surprise, for he made a most obsequious bow to the little crowd of Lexingtonians, who gathered round him as he mounted the steps of the stage, from whence his " I wish you a very good morning, gentlemen," was evidently spoken in deprecation of any contemplated violence to his person, for though it was a sort of farewell benediction, and nothing more, it seemed to say, "don't hurt me, if you please, I'm only one, and so little ; now be merciful, and don't."

Upon returning to the store, to rejoin what Dickens, in his American " Diary " (where he " handles us without gloves ") would have called the circle of tobacco-spitters, we found the generality of the crowd all busily engaged in warming themselves physically, by the fire, while they heated their indignation by a discourse, in which that accursed thing, " Abolitionism," figured as the text, and General P——— as a "horrible example." To have listened to the running fire of injurious observations, which was kept up on every side, one might have supposed that a contribution-box, labelled " Proofs of depravity, as exhibited in the political character of Mr. Abolitionist P——— ; the smallest favors thankfully received," was being passed round, so anxious seemed every one to pitch in his mite. From the sum total of these collections, after duly counting the receipts, and throwing out a quantity of *base* metal, we have gathered the following :

That Mr. Abolitionist, or Free Soil P———— was travelling under the name, as before stated, of Sam Clarke (this we verified by the hotel register), who, *as* Sam Clarke, claimed to be a Baptist preacher, whether "Hard Shell," or "Close Communion," this deponent is not prepared to say, but that the *soi disant* Sam was really named P————, who had been a Free State warrior

"Of Indifferent fame,"

but who was better known as a financial agent of the "Eastern Aid Societies." Indeed, as we afterwards ascertained from Governor Shannon, P———— had, upwards of fifteen thousand dollars in money and drafts upon his person, when arrested by the Pro-Slavery scouts. P————'s reason for travelling as Mr. Sam Clarke (as we understand it to have been stated by himself to others), is as follows :

" I had a clerk in Kansas named Sam Clarke, and wanted to send him to St. Louis on business. I accordingly took a place for him in the stage ; but when the time came for him to go, he "took to chilling " (that is to say, had fever and ague), and was, therefore, unable to start, so I took his place and used his name."

All right, general ; but, as Colonel Walton of the city very pertinently remarked, "Was it necessary that you should eat and sleep as Sam Clarke, as well as ride for him ?"

CHAPTER VIII.

TREATS OF THINGS RELIGIOUS AND SECULAR.

Apropos to would-be preachers—but not always to such like—
Governor Shannon afterwards related to us a good story, which,
though it be a digression, may as well find its way into these
pages before we enter upon the grand " theatre of events."

There is now living at what is called the Quaker Indian Mission,
which is located on the Indian Reserve and within three miles of
the Shawnee manual labor school, where the Governor has established his temporary residence, an old Quaker who is, for aught we
know to the contrary, everything which a disciple of William Penn
—even of the "straightest sect"—ought to be.   But we all have
our little failings—as somebody once said of Mr. Seven Stars'
fondness for the ladies ; and in our Broad Brim's case, politics
were an "amiable weakness."   He went in for Reeder, to speak
figuratively, body and boots ; and not only to the extent of his
own body and boots, but even to those of his neighbors, as what
we are about to state, on Shannon's authority, will abundantly
prove.   The election for delegate to Congress—we think it
was—came on ; and the backers of Reeder were not backward
in casting in their paper mites at the ballot-box ; among others
friend Broad Brim, as we shall call him, came also, even as did
Satan of old.   He voted once ; he voted twice ; he voted
thrice ; yea, a fourth time ; and, verily, a fifth : and every time
for Reeder, and " nary lick " for anybody else.   Now, how did

he, a pious and a God-fearing man, manage it ? or, how could he " do this thing " and still compound with his conscience, and, what is almost as much to the purpose, clear his skirts before his brother Broad Brims of " the meeting ?" Reader, he did it thus : he voted *once* for himself, and on *four* other occasions, at the same ballot-box and for the same candidate, as a *proxy* for his particular friends, Messrs. A., B., C., and D., all of whom, as he affirmed, *would* have voted for Reeder, but unfortunately *wa'nt there to do so.*

We understand that this mode of voting by *proxy* was extensively permitted, and we fancy upon both sides, in Kansas. They have singular notions in the West.

But this is not the only peculiarity about friend Broad Brim; he is, at least so says Dame Rumor, a red-hot Emancipationist; and once, when Henry Clay, the " Harry of the West " was addressing a large political meeting at Indianapolis, Ia., of which assemblage friend Broad Brim formed a unit, this identical old Quaker stepped forward, and insulted the great statesman and orator, whose memory is enshrined in so many thousands of American hearts, by rudely breaking in upon his remarks, and crying out, " Why don't you liberate your niggers ? Go home and do it before you talk to us." Or, as the military courts say, " words to that effect."

It is reported that Clay paused, looked at him for a moment, and then said : " Go home, sir, yourself, and attend to your own business, for my slaves are better fed, better clothed, and, judging from your very abrupt interruption of my remarks, better *mannered* than yourself."

Rumor adds, that upon receiving this very pointed rebuke, friend Broad Brim settled down an inch or two in his boots, and then slunk away, so marvellously discomfited that he is even reported (in his extreme agitation) to have uncovered and made a hasty exit from the room, minus his *sombrero.*

But to return to our " tobacco-spitters;" their indictment further set forth that Mr. Free Soil P——— (for if he travel with one *alias*, why should we not provide him with another ?) was riding near the picket-guards of the Pro-Slavery, or "law-executing army," then encamped upon the Wakarusa creek, in the vicinity of Lawrence ; that Mr. Free Soil P——— was requested, somewhat abruptly, to halt, by the Pro-Slavery picket aforesaid, which he, P———, seemed unwilling to do, until a Pro-Slavery man had argued him into it by drawing a bead upon him with his long Missouri rifle, one of "Jake Hawkins' best," and bound to "shoot centre" anywhere within two hundred yards. The charge goes on to state that our Free Soiler, having halted, did, thereupon, like Major Andre of Revolutionary memory, offer then and there ten dollars in current "shin-plasters" to bribe his captors into liberating him, at the same time stating that he was travelling upon urgent business, and would willingly sacrifice *even* that amount for the privilege of "getting on." But our Missourian was a second Van Woert— a wag, and moreover a patriot of that stern and inflexible school who never make good aldermen. It is, therefore, upon record, that he *accepted* the pecuniary consideration without demur, and did immediately convey the same into the recesses of his breeches pocket, whereupon Mr. Free Soil, thinking it was "all arranged," made another effort to progress, when he was once more detained by the facetious Missourian, who, without reflecting that he was "adding insult to injury," was so impolite as to apply the end of his thumb to the tip of his nose, at the same time extending the remaining digits and gently agitating them in the air. But while we thus digress, Mr. Free Soiler is still ten dollars out of pocket, and only half captured to boot. Not content with this indignity, the Pro-Slavery man next proceeded to "bag," *à la* South Africa Cummings, the person of Mr. Free Soil, and carry him, will-I nill-I, into General Strickler's camp, where their despondent prisoner arrived in a most miserable state of bodily fear, not to mention mental trepidation. Here the advocate of darkey rights was placed under guard, if we heard aright, in General Strickler's own marquee. He had not been there long, before one of his captors, the ten dollar man, approached Gen. Strickler, who was standing beside his quarters, when the following decidedly unmilitary dialogue ensued between the Brigadier and his "high private:"

High Private.—General, I want the prisoner to come out hyar, I've got some of the old cock's money and want to give it to him.

General.—It can't be done, sir, I can't permit him to come out, but I can pass you in.

"But I tell you, General Strickler," urged this unabashed representative of the citizen soldiery, "I *must* see him."

How the General settled this delicate point of military etiquette we are unable to say, but certain it is, that when captor met captive, the former handed out the X, with a " Here, old cock, is your money, I dont kear about it."

It is reported, that before P ———'s liberation from his confinement as a "prisoner of war," in the Wakarusa camp, he was overheard talking to a fellow-captive who had been brought in that day (and who being in great fear of his life, which he already considered sacrificed to the bloodthirstiness of the Border Ruffians, whom the Free State people hold to be little better than devils without horns, was shedding tears copiously), in the following strain:

"Don't be alarmed, my dear sir, don't be alarmed. You may consider yourself as being now in the very *safest* place which this section of the country can afford."

And now a word for Lexington. It is really "considerable of a place ;" a sort of nine pound baby city, healthy and likely to grow, with perhaps this very Western drawback that " the

town is so large you scarce can see the houses."   To-day, Sunday,
dawned upon it gloriously, until even the leafless trees of the
broad "Missouri bottom," brightened up under its influence,
and as the pretty (?) girls came tripping by in answer to " the
church-going bell," we fairly caught the infection, donned our
" Sunday-go-to-meeting " gear, got a nigger to re-touch our
boots, slicked our whiskers up, and our hair down, and then,
took the field, armed with a pocket edition of the " Psalms and
.Hymns," to find some " sect " with whom to fraternize in their
worship, and we were not, all things considered, very long in
accomplishing it—a result which was effected by mingling
with a "living stream," albeit, somewhat thin, who were then
on their way to be "refreshed with the Word," as it is
preached by the Groaners, a branch of the "Hard Shells."   And
verily, "in all our rough experience of harm," as the Yankee
Skipper has it, I never before had met so strange a " meeting-
house "   But never mind an *exterior* description ; we won't
comment upon the outside, but reserve ourself for the interior.   So,
as far as the building goes, you may imagine almost any sort of
oddity that you please.   The ancient and modern styles of
architecture, for instance, trying to cross the breed, and " eventu-
ating " a monstrosity, may, perhaps, be not very far out of the
way.   This "particular kind of Religionists," as the sermom on
" a Harp of a thousand strings " has it, is, we understand,
quite fashionable in Missouri, and if the specimen of the persuasion which we beheld in Lexington, be a fair criterion, there
must be a deal of fun in them.   If you don't believe it, my
vinegar-faced friend, just read the following, and judge for yourself :

We reached the church (we beg the church's pardon, meeting-house, we should have said), entered, and got an unnoticeable
seat.   The service was already under way when we arrived, for
we had been vain enough to hold on, in some hope of creating
a sensation among the rural damsels by the display of what a

Missourian would call " store clothes," " which, alas ! have since
then found a most unnatural end in Kansas ;" but we are anticipating.

Their minister was certainly a study, he had just such a
face and air as a clever artist might have chosen to characterize the bell-wether of some hill-hiding Covenanter flock
In short, it was stern, hard, and uncompromising. Nor was
his garb less singular, for he sported (may we be forgiven
for the phrase), a snuffy-brown coat, of strange and antiquated cut, which bore but too evident tokens of long and not
over careful usage. The continuations were of yellowish-grey
cloth, with stove-pipe legs, built like an Irishman's hurricane,
" straight up and down," and encased below the knees in
serviceable-looking buckskin riding-leathers, well stained with
Missouri mud ; add to these a pair of buffalo overshoes, a sur-
prising shirt collar, and a wonderfully starched linen cravat,
whose complicated folds and puritanical stiffness would have
broken a " New York washerwoman's heart at first sight," and
you will have a very accurate delineation of this reverend gentleman's outer man. We must not forget, however, a pair of
wide-bowed horn spectacles which divided their time between
the top of his venerable head, and the bridge of an independently cocked-up nose, thereby adding not a little to the gro-
tesqueness of this somewhat unclerical *tout ensemble*.

The text we have forgotten, for we always forget texts, nor
can we at this present call to mind the precise locality in which
it "am to be found," but to make another extract from that
much-quoted discourse, by " the capting of a Mississippi flat-
boat," " It air to be discovered in the leds of the Scripters, and
somewhar between the book of Generations and the book of
Revolutions."

As for the " sermonizing," it was literally and distinctly *some*,
being quite *à la* Elder Knapp, or in other words, a sort of uni-

versal raking over the coals, with a promise of a bigger fire to come, for not going to prayer-meetings, winding up with a special allusion to one unlucky night, upon which the parson and a certain deacon Ephraim Graves had been the only persons "on hand," a shortcoming which proved fatal to that evening's exercises, for how could they do the psalmody in an orthodox way, when, as Parson Jones expressed it, "Deacon Graves couldn't sing nary lick, and he himself was hoarser nor an owl."

A lack of attention to the Ten Commandments in general, and to the minister in particular, was also a theme upon which our preacher waxed not only eloquent but personal. But to give you a "taste of his quality," we will select a few "elegant extracts," which, as they caught our drowsy ear, between a succession of what Eastern matrons call "cat naps," yet linger in our memory, and we are the more inclined to quote them, as they are not only *very* peculiar in their style, but withal, a fair exponent of a certain class of "hard shell" discourses, which have long been popular, and it may be serviceable among the "rough and tumble religionists" of the primitive Far West Our first selection runs thus :—

"Yes, my sin-stricken bretherin and sisters, thar Lord only knows how I'm to bring this hyar congregation out of the gall of bitterness and the bonds of iniquity ; whar's the sense of my wrästlin's in prayär ? whar's the good of my groanin's in sperit ? whär's the use in my ridin' down hyar every Lord's day mornin', an' thar corderoy mighty bad at that, to try an' save these hyar sinners from the brimstone and fire as is to come ? whär's the sense, I say, my bretherin ? for I tell yeou all, an' I jest allow that thar Lord knows it too, that thar's some of yeou a settin' hyar, that dance out at thar toes in a week, all thär religion that thar minister kin hammer inter thar heads, let alone thar hearts, with prär-meetin's, and preachin', and singin' of psalms, through a 'hull year round. Yes, my brethrein and sisters, it's thar wick·

edness of Christmas week, thar dancin', and thar foolin', and thar drinkin' and thar gamblin', that does thar devil's work hyar ; an' whar will yeou be, my bretherin ? yes, whar will you be, I say, when Satan comes a huntin' his own, or as is remarked in thar Scripters, like a roarin' lion a goin' round to see what he kin devour ? take kear, my bretherin, take kear."

And again—in allusion to the prayer-meeting business :—

" Whar's the good in invitin' yeou inter prayār-meetin's, when yeou air always excusin' yeourselves and never thar ? Ef it war a corn-huskin', wouldn't yeou be thar ? Ef it war a keard-playin' party, wouldn't yeou be thar ? Well, yeou would ; and I jest *know* ef it war a hoss-race, yeou'de be sure to be thar. But how is it, when we want yeou to serve thar Lord, and call on yeou to " come up an' help us," are yeou thar *then ?* *Well*, yeou ain't, bretherin, an' why ain't yeou ? Why, because thar ain't no keards, nor quarter horses, nor fiddles, nor danciu', nor foolin' with the gals, *thar's* the why. An' how was it tother night, my bretherin, when deacon Graves and yeour preacher war all that war thar ? Well, it rained, s'pose it did ; air yeou sugar or air yeou salt ? and wouldn't yeou hev gone, ef yeou had bin sugar or salt, ef it war to a frolic ? *Well*, yeou would. Yeou're a travellin' thar broad road, the 'hull ou you ; it's dreadful nice now ; it ain't steep aud hain't got no ruts inter it, but yeou'de better be a goin' the narrer one ; yes, ef it war all corderoy and hog-wallow, yeou'de do well to be a goin' of it ; for when thar folks as travel it air a shoutin' glory, an' halleluya, whar will yeou be ? A wailin' and a 'nashin' of yeour teeth, *thar's* whar."

And again :—

" When I go inter thar house of a professor of religion, an' see thar, thar begammon board, and thar dice-box, or may-be, a pack of keards a lyin' on thar table, I allow that thar, in that house, thar's somethin' wrong. Do yeou see them air things in my cabin, my bretherin, or in Deacon Graves's cabin ? *Well*,

yeou don't. But thar's a Bible thar, an' a hymn-book thar, an'
a sound of prayār, an' a shout of thanksgivin' thar. *Well*, thar
is."

Now it just struck us, after listening to this very *un-common*
sense harangue, that there is such a thing as checking up a
horse, whether quadruped or biped, a little *too tight*, and furthermore, one might imagine that in a new country, not to particu-
larize the State of Missouri, a parson might be pretty well satisfied if his flock fenced in their consciences, without expecting
them to "improve" every acre of the land. We wonder what
the reverend man would have said to our New York hoops and
habits.

And so endeth our Sunday in Lexington, Mo.

CHAPTER IX.

OUR AUTHOR ENTERS KANSAS.

BY the way, it might be amusing enough to an *uninterested* spectator to see the crowded stages as they come in from the South to store their bedevilled cargoes in the " City Hotel," until such time as their good fortune—the elements and the " agent"—may permit them to proceed. In the meanwhile, was there ever such a " merry Bedlam kicked up" by any one set of worried mortals before? Such complaints ; such threats of actions and damages ; such yarns of mud knee-deep, which almost realize the waggish idea of that " hat," with its submerged wearer, and the " good horse under him ;" and then such stories of travelling vexations, which our last week's travelling expe- rience assures us are but too true ; such grumbling ; such growling ; such cursing and swearing. Did one ever hear the like ? But there's some *fun* in it after all ; indeed there's fun in everything, if one has only a disposition to grasp life by its smoothest handle—from that introductory joke the cradle to that gravest of all grave subjects, the grave; for instance, while we sat watching the " current of events" in the smoky sitting-room of the " City" to-day, we saw a broad-shouldered, powerfully-built Missourian, who must have stood about six feet two in his stockings (if he wore any), come striding into the hotel ; and our eye singled him out at once as one who had evidently seen harder times than the rest of his travel-worn fellow-passengers ;

for his face was battered and bruised, his sinister optic considerably "the worse for wear," and his nose particularly "mapped out." We watched him closely, as he stepped up to the bar and ordered a "whisky straight," with all the air of a man who has reached comfort at last, and means to enjoy himself, and heard him say, in reply to some bystander's inquiry as to "how he had got along :"

"Got along, thunder ! Wāall, stranger, I kin jest tell yeou that I've hed an awful time—what yeou mout call all sorts of a time—fur I've bin a travellin' thar road whar those *dog-gauned* Dutchmen live, an' thar bound to crowd yeou ef they git a chance ; but jest jump a few on em, an' thar mighty apt to let yeou alone ; they didn't trouble *me* much, I allow— *well,* they didn't ; an' that air ain't all 'nother, stranger ; I've whopped a few stage-drivers as I come along—jest a *few*— somewhar about five, I reckon. You see it happened this way. I jest made up my mind to lick every one on em that upsot thar coach ; fur it's jest liquor and *dog-gauned* carelessness makes em do it anyhow—thar's *one* on em, I allow, will remember *me* ; he upsot us in a mud-hole on the road back a piece betwixt hyar an' Boonsville. I got out when the old mud-cart war a rolling over, and I felt bad, I tell yeou *some*, fur my cousin, a young gal that I war a takin kear of, got hurt considerable; so as I reckoned we war imposed upon, I jest stepped up to thar driver : 'Look a hyar, stranger,' says I, ' I'm a thinking of droppin' yeou.' 'Yeou'd better not on yeour own account,' says he ; ' it's agin' the law to whip a stage-driver in thar State of Missouri. ' *Dog-gaun* thar laws of Missouri an' thar stage-drivers, too,' says I ; and about that time," added the man who had seen "all sorts of a time," parenthetically (for his drink had been compounded and was now in the act of proving itself to be a " whisky *straight*" by taking the shortest road down its new proprietor's throat), "and about that time, stranger, I histed him, as I should reckon, nigh on to four feet, *well* I did."

And here our journalizing at Lexington, for Dec. 16th, must give place to extracts from our log, written up at Westport, Mo. —which is, however, but half a mile distant from the frontier-line of Kansas Territory—on the night of the 17th.

We had retired to rest at a late hour, on the night previous to our departure from Lexington, in the blissful expectation of a whole night's sleep in bed, for we had been informed by the stage-agent that the "stage" (for we were promised a *real* stage this time), in which we were going, was not to start until after breakfast upon the ensuing day ; imagine then, our astonishment, to say nothing of our consternation, at having our first half-hour's sleep—for we had sat up writing until after midnight—broken in upon by a gruff voice and a tallow candle, which admitted themselves by the door of our apartment at the somewhat unusual hour of one o'clock, A.M. We were so *very* sleepy when they arrived, that we shouldn't have been surprised if they had gained an entrance by the window. The gruff voice said : "The nigger tried to wake you, sir, but you slept so soundly that he couldn't ; you must be quick if you are going ; the stage is all ready, and it's snowing hard ;" and having delivered itself of this interesting communication, the gruff voice took itself out again, leaving the tallow candle, by way of substitute, to throw some light upon our getting up ; and such a getting up. Did you ever, most amiable reader, turn out of a warm bed—in which you had just succeeded in generating a sufficient amount of animal heat to keep yourself comfortable—at a moment's notice, with a disagreeable journey before you and *worse* coming ; with the mercury, like your spirits, down ; a driving snow-storm without ; no fire within, and your miserable self in a night-shirt and— nothing else in particular ? If you have, sympathize with us. We did it, though—after an almost superhuman effort ; turned out, dressed, woke obliging landlord, paid unobliging Bill, in two senses of the word—that being the name of the porter ; and then sallied forth, carpet-bag in hand, into the dark night and wintry gale, to seek the spot where a glare of lanterns and the presence of sundry somnambulic black helpers, who looked like spirits of darkness amid the swiftly-falling snow, marked out the position of the stage. And the stage, oh ! would you believe it ? the stage ! that solemnly promised *real* stage, turned out to be but another, and, if possible, a still more dilapidated " mud-cart," which looked for all the world like the identical vehicle in which we had rolled out from St. Charles, that is to say, if that " blessed institution " can be supposed to have been engaged during the period which had elapsed since our last meeting, in a succession of disasters from which it didn't appear likely to recover. But in good earnest, and all joking aside, this *new* imposition was what you might call a *solemn fact*, for it had been rent, and torn, and battered, to such a degree, and was, moreover, troubled with so many complaints, such as a leaning to one side, and a weakness in its wheels, not to dwell upon a tongue, which, though *longer*, was not half as serviceable as an old maid's, that it became a matter of pleasing uncertainty whether the mud-cart would, or would not, condescend to hang together, until it brought us to Independence. But as the stage was " going, going " and almost " gone," by the time we reached it, there was no opportunity for expostulation, so we tumbled in and kept our sorrows to ourself.

And oh ! what a night—the very recollection of it prompts us to breathe a prayer that we " never shall look upon its like again," for the snow fell, and the wind blew, and howled amid the road-side forests, until the increasing storm seemed multiplied into the Retreat from Moscow, or Kane's journey to the Pole, as the icy particles came pelting in through every nook and cranny—and their name was legion—of our shackly old conveyance. It would not have been easy to frighten us into better behavior by any Miltonian description of Pandemonium at that time. Oh ! no—we should have said, " How are you ?" to brimstone, and " Glad to see you," to fire. We are not even prepared to say, that we should not have taken the Old Harry's *warmest* claw, had he proffered it in good faith, or it may be, have gone the " entire animal," and, like Doctor Faustus, sold out altogether, for a consideration, and it would have been in *our* case, neither silver nor gold, but what, if rumor speaks true, might be a much easier bargain for Satan, for the thing *we* wanted most, was to see a right jolly blaze. Nay, we would even have accomplished that which our greatest general found difficult to perform, by *facing* "a fire in our *rear*," and charging the enemy right gallantly to boot, for through the dreary hours of that apparently interminable December night, we suffered, in company with our balance of six inside, and one out, quite as much as any one, if we except, perhaps, an Esquimaux, ought to endure. And, oh ! how we longed for daylight, and wondered, as we skirmished for room with our neighbor's half-frozen legs, whether the dawn would *ever* come, until at length, in our despair, we lost confidence in the truthfulness of highly respectable watches, cursed the maker of the Almanac, and even swore, in the bitterness of our heart, that the State of Missouri was as far behind the *time* in her sun-rising as in everything else.

But after all, we " hadn't ought to " grumble, for the long-wished for dawn came stealing in at last, and 9 o'clock, A. M. found us thawing out, under the moderating influences of a good fire, and what we have elsewhere termed a " bad hog breakfast," *alias* " four bits " worth of " choice selections." And here we may remark *en passant* (though we have already " cut and come again " upon this subject), that Missouri seems hog-crazy. The roads are blocked up with swine upon their travels, while little pigs squeal, and venerable porkers grunt, from corn-field and farm-yard, until the very air grows vocal with their music. It is, moreover, as we have already stated, "killing time," and as all swinedom is but pork, the flesh of these hapless beasts is served up to the yet more unfortunate traveller, until his soul sickens over his meat, and he is almost ready to declare himself a Jew, if he could thereby obtain a reasonable excuse for rejecting those too —*too* unctuous fragments, which are the never-failing accompaniment of every road-side meal. But adieu—a long adieu, we trust, to the hogs, for we have matters of greater moment to chronicle.

WESTPORT, MONDAY, *December 17th.*—We have passed Independence, which we had not seen, since we rode up to its brick tavern at two o'clock of an August morning, some eight years ago; but are now, as the date indicates, at Westport, a flourishing town, supported for the most part by the Indian and Santa Fe trade, and situated—oh ! happy thought to us—upon the very verge of the Kansas frontier. We are at last within striking distance of our ultimate object ; for the residence of His Excellency, Governor Shannon, is, or has been, at the Shawnee Indian Mission, or Manual Labor School, distant some two and a-half miles from this place, where we had hoped to have talked over the "Kansas War" with the Governor, ere this, had not His Excellency been temporarily absent at Lecompton, a new-born Kansas city, which looks uncommonly well upon *paper*, and which we hope to observe for ourself ere we be a fortnight older. The Governor, as we understand, is now building at Lecompton, with the view of preparing a residence for his family, who are at present residing in the more tranquil State of Ohio.

The latest bit of hear-say intelligence, in regard to the Kansas difficulties, comes to us to-day, in the shape of a statement, made by the youthful editor of a Pro-Slavery journal (that is just about to be). He says, that all parties are dissatisfied with Shannon, for the Governor would neither let the Missourians "wipe out" the Abolitionists on the one hand, nor would he

permit the citizens of Lawrence to resist Sheriff Jones, and set
the Territorial laws at defiance upon the other, or, as we translate
it, he committed the unpardonable error of endeavoring to preserve peace on both sides—about as difficult a task to accomplish,
we fancy, in the bear-garden state of things then existing at
Lawrence, as to attempt an interference between man and wife,
from which folly from which may our good angel deliver us.

December 18th.—Though we still date from Westport, we may
be congratulated, for we have not only seen, but *entered* the
"promised land." Yes, it is even so, for our host, "old man
Harris," as he is familiarly styled, evidently imagines, thanks
to an old Army Commission of ours, and to something which
he seems to have picked up in relation to our having come out *special*,
that we are at the very least, a bearer of dispatches, or, perchance, a Minister Plenipotentiary to the Court of Shannon, with
documents from Washington to the Governor, containing full
powers to hang, draw, and quarter, every Abolitionist in the Territory; so he opened his heart toward us, and although, apparently
not given to generous deeds, has offered us the loan of his private
and particular mule, a clumsy, ill-made beast, with no amiability
of character, to convey us to Shawnee Mission (Governor
Shannon's residence), where, though his Excellency was absent,
as we have already stated, at Lecompton, we could obtain ample
information in regard to the probable duration of his stay, from the
employees of the Manual Labor School. We, moreover, desired
to carry our "news hunt," into the Indian range, and post ourself up in relation to the management, working, and apparent
results of the Indian educational system, as pursued in these
Missions, or labor schools, of which this Shawnee establishment
is most probably a favorable exponent.

With those objects in view, we thought proper to accept the
offer of our good-natured landlord, who forthwith ordered one
of "his niggers" to parade the animal, who proved, as we have

already hinted, upon a more familiar acquaintance, to be an ob-
stinate, not to say sulky beast, with prodigious ears, and a
short scraggy tail. We mounted gallantly, however, with a big
stick by way of "persuader," for it's no use trying "moral suasion" with a mule, "Martin, on Animals," to the contrary, notwithstanding.

Upon reaching the "State line," we felt, as somebody says,
"the influence of the scene." So we reined in our long-eared
steed, and considered the fearful responsibility which we were
about to incur. We might be treated to a coat of tar and
feathers ; we might be planted in the miry soil, a rich vegetable
mould, of the Kansas Bear Garden, in which case, we should
undoubtedly, have been carried "through a course of very re-
markable sprouts." But we "didn't keār ;" we summoned up our
resolution, knit our brow, hit the mule a thundering lick upon
the ribs, murmured "let her rip," and then, like Mr. Cæsar of
old, plunged in, accoutered as we were, to Kansas and a mud-
hole. The mule shy'd ; we regret it, for it upset our dignity
considerably ; we have since, upon mature deliberation, been induced to suppose, that the beast being raised in Missouri, was a
Pro-Slavery mule, which would very naturally account for her
unwillingness to enter Kansas.

There was, we are compelled to admit, no particular sensation
as "Our War Correspondent" crossed the line. No convulsions,
no earthquake ; the trees stood firm, ditto the log-cabins ; the
mud was as deep, the winter wind just as piercing ; in fact, the
only things which appeared to be interested in our entrance were
a two-year-old hog (that omnipresent representative of the
largest commercial interests of Missouri), who poked his inquisitive snout through a clump of wayside bushes, as if to say,
"What new fool comes now ?" and a venerable old rooster, who
welcomed us with a crow, which we were fain to interpret into
an omen of good luck to come. May the divinites that "shape

our ends" grant it, for this going to Kansas in troublous times, to get the war news, is "skeary business." In sober earnest we begin to feel as the old Connecticut deacon did when his horse ran away down hill ; " he trusted in Providence *until* the breeching broke, and after that didn't place any particular dependence on anything." May not "the breeching" be almost broken with us ? Who knows ? 'Tis a fearful thing to contemplate ! Was ever newspaper correspondent in such a fix ? Stop, let's reconnoitre our position. If we "crack up" the Pro-Slavery men, the Free Soilers will make " no bones " of us in Lawrence. If we abuse the Border Ruffians, we shall (even without the staging), never escape alive from the State of Missouri, and if we stride the fence, and don't do either, we shall be most particularly blessed by both parties, and for aught we know to the contrary, by the New York Herald into the bargain. Well, be it so ; if we must succumb, we must, but as we live by hog-meat and bad coffee, we will kick vigorously to the last.

CHAPTER X

THE SHAWNEE MANUAL-LABOR SCHOOL.

AND now, to return, or rather to go ahead, we pressed on, and after some two miles and a half of hard trotting travel, with something to boot from taking the wrong road, "hove in sight," as the sailors say, of the Shawnee Methodist Mission, consisting of three long two-story brick buildings, with sundry cabins and out-houses, which, while they had rather a dilapidated appearance, looked as if they might be *Western* comfortable inside.

Upon reaching the board fence which enclosed a sort of flower-garden, just in front of the Superintendent's dwelling, we rode up to a tying-post, and having reined in our mule, who was, because he liked it, very willing to stop, we dismounted, hitched Long-ears so securely that he couldn't very conveniently run away, and then proceeded to arouse the inmates of the "most responsible looking" house, but as our knocking called forth no reply, save the growling of several ill-looking curs of low degree, who kept up a dismal racket in our rear, we made bold to walk in, the more so as the front door stood invitingly open ; but we traversed several rooms, got out of the back door, and finally wandered into the kitchen ere we lighted upon anything human, which, however, turned up at last, in the shape of a voluble old darky, with a bullet head, and elongated heels, who informed us that "Massa Johnson" (the Superintendent of the Mission), was not at home, and would not be back until night.

5*

"But who is?"

"Well, dars de man dat takes care ob de place when Massa Johnson's gwyne away."

"Can't you find him, and let him know that a gentleman would like to speak with him?"

"Well, dis hyar niggar's mighty busy just now, massa, s'pose I mout find him, though—'spect I might try, but I'm dubersome about it."

As this uncertainty was removed by a quarter, "the man who took kear ob de place" was found, and speedily made his appearance. Upon transferring our inquiries to him, we learned that Governor Shannon was, as we had previously understood, at Lecompton, some fifty miles distant from Westport, whither he had gone to buy up some claims ; our informant added that the governor's son who is also his private secretary, and the Secretary of State, Mr. Woodson, were with him, but that the whole party were expected back in the course of a few days. After communicating these facts, our new acquaintance, who seemed a plain well-meaning sort of person, and a strong Pro-Slavery man into the bargain, invited us into a sort of sitting-room, where we will venture to say that we asked him as many questions in five minutes' time, as if he had been undergoing a cross-examination by a Philadelphia lawyer (though for that matter, we are free to confess that we don't exactly see why a legal man, because he comes from the Quaker City, should be any keener than his brethren of the long robe, elsewhere), but be this as it may, here follows an abridgment of the information elicited by our inquiries.

The Shawnee Manual Labor School has been established for nearly twenty years ; at first, under the fostering care of the Board of Missions for the Southern Methodist Episcopal Church, in connection with the patronage of the general government. Latterly, however, as the institution grew better able to support itself, or it may be, as Uncle Sam became more liberal, that amiable old gentleman has stood sole paymaster ; at present, under the treaty stipulations with the Shawnee Indians, the school receives the interest of one hundred thousand dollars, at five per cent. per annum, amounting, of course, to five thousand dollars ; that being the sum appropriated for educational purposes in the Shawnee Nation. To this income, may be added the earnings of the very large farm attached to the mission, which, at this time, consists of fifteen hundred acres of fenced land, of which, from six to seven hundred acres are under cultivation. The soil being a rich loam, from twelve to fifteen inches in depth. During the past year they have raised upon this farm, one hundred and forty acres of corn, sixty acres of which grew eighty bushels of grain to the acre (not bad that, even in Kansas), and one hundred acres of oats, which yielded from thirty to forty bushels per acre. There is, also, a large vegetable garden, and they have two hundred and fifty head of cattle, who, so far as the *females* are concerned, are very like the Dutchman's cow of notable memory, which " gave very goot milk."

The Institution is under the direction of a general superintendent, a school superintendent, and his assistant (to whom we are indebted for interesting information), and a farmer who oversees and directs its agricultural operations. There is, also, a superintendent of the boarding-house, who was our informant in regard to many matters connected with his own department, as well as in relation to the history (for he is an old settler) of the mission.

The buildings, as we have before stated, consist of thin, long, two-story brick houses, not very substantially built, and from present appearances, considerably in need of repair. As a summer residence they might be moderately comfortable, but as a winter one, and particularly in severe weather, they are, owing, I should say, to the shiftless way in which things appear to be managed, a most undesirable home. The arrangement too, for persons lodging there, are bad, as the boarding-house proper is some fifty yards distant from the dining-room or rather kitchen, in which the inmates take their meals. The children's school-house and dormitories are open to the same criticism, being about twice that distance from the main building.

This mission is located upon the "Shawnee Reserve," a tract of land some twenty-four miles in width, by thirty long, which is secured to the nation by their final treaty with the United States government. This treaty gives two hundred acres, as soon as its survey is fully completed, which is expected to be the case by the 1st of July next, to each Shawnee Indian, whether man, woman, or child. These tracts are to be selected by the parties concerned, as nearly as possible to the vicinity of the individual's present residence in the Shawnee Indian Territory. The choice to be made and declared within sixty days, or, as other authorities say, ninety, from the conclusion of the government surveys. Thirty thousand acres are to be reserved for non-resident Shawnees, who may come in to claim their share. The remnant of this (once powerful) tribe, now resident upon the Reserve, amounts, all told, to about seven hundred and fifty souls. The remainder of the "Shawnee Reserve" will then, if we understand the matter rightly, be thrown into the market to become subject to locations at the *usual* government price ($1,25 per acre). In view of these facts, we have been informed that a secret society has been organized in Missouri, or rather in certain border counties of that State, for the purpose of settling the whole of this tract, as soon as it is made liable to entry, with *bona fide* Pro-Slavery settlers. This society, we learn, numbers nearly eight hundred men, who are pledged to each other to do all in their power to make Kansas a slave State, and to support the peculiar institutions of the South. We hear that they have already made very favorable arrangements with the Shawnees, as to the entry of these lands. This club may be regarded as an humble imitation, which will, however, in all probability, accomplish quite as much as its progenitor, the Massachusetts Aid Society.

The number of children at present under instruction in the Manual Labor School is about forty of both sexes ; among these are some half-a-dozen Wyandots and one Arapahoe. Some of these children are orphans, placed here by their guardians, others have parents residing upon the Reserve. But few of these Indians are full-blooded, yet the physical peculiarities of their race seem strongly marked in each ; the dark, restless eye, the prominent cheek-bone, the straight, coarse black hair, and pigeon-toed gait being visible in all.

These children pay seventy-five dollars per annum each, to the superintendent, as a receipt in full for board, washing, and tuition. Their instructor assures us that they will compare favorably, in mental capacity, with the same number of ordinary, every-day, non-precocious children at the North. They speak, as a general thing, no language but their own upon entering the school ; the first care of their instructor is, therefore, to teach them English ; this they soon learn to speak well, though a slight, yet not unpleasant accent seems in almost every case to betray their *foreign* birth. As *children*, they are playful out of doors, romping with each other in very un-Indian-like style, while in school they appear to be quite as mischievous as the offspring of the pale face. If they misbehave, the system of discipline is nearly the same as that *formerly* in vogue in New England. They do not, however, care much for any species of punishment, save that of the rod, a peculiarity which is appreciated by their teacher, who is a firm believer in that portion of the wisdom of Solomon, which says, "spare the rod and spoil the child." The branches taught are those necessary to a good English common-school education.

Their daily routine of life is as follows—at five, A M., they are awakened by the ringing of a bell, when, if it be summer, they do light work about the farm until seven o'clock, when they breakfast, a horn being blown by way of signal before each meal, which gives them ample time for preparation (if in the winter-time, their morning work, before eating, is confined to the preparation of fuel, milking the cows, some thirty or forty in all, and feeding the stock). At nine, the school-bell summons them to their studies, which are kept up, with a short interval for recess, until twelve, M. They dine between twelve and one o'clock, and then resume their mental pursuits until four. Their tea-hour is six, P.M., and their evenings are spent in the preparation of lessons for the ensuing day until eight o'clock; they are then allowed to indulge themselves in in-door recreation, until half-past eight sends them to their dormitories for the night. The only religious services which are held during the week are the reading of a chapter in the Bible, followed by prayer, just previous to the morning and evening meals. Saturday "forenoon" is devoted to work, the afternoon is. a holiday, and the evening is spent in the bath-room in "cleaning up for Sunday." The Sabbath is devoted to devotional services.

As regards general character and temperament, the Indian pupils are accounted as generally docile, teachable, and good-natured. When sick, they are stupid and silent, have much fear, are easily depressed, and sink more rapidly, when prostrated by disease, than the white. They quarrel but little among themselves; in their juvenile attachments they appear to have a greater "affinity" for members of their own tribe, and would, we are told, resent an insult more quickly if coming from a child belonging to another. Indolence is their greatest and most besetting sin.

In the little Arapahoe we felt particularly interested, as he is a full-blooded Indian, who came to the Institution as wild as a hawk, when he could speak but a very few words of English, and even these had been learned upon his way thither from a white man, who had accompanied him from the hunting-grounds of his tribe. The date of this juvenile's reception into the school, was the 27th of October, 1855, and in three days after his admission, he knew his letters perfectly—his teacher tells us that he now spells readily in words of one syllable.

As regards their table—for we had not time to inspect the dormitories, we should say that, so far as *quantity* is concerned, the children fared remarkably well ; though the cookery, to our taste, was little better than an illustration of that oft-quoted proverb, which talks of Heaven's sending the raw material, and Satan's providing those who dress it. Of this we were well able to judge, as we had dined at the board of these "children of the Red-men," or, to speak more correctly, at one just like it, which is common to the superintendent and his family, as also to visitors, and the other officers and *employees* of the Institution. All things considered, however, these little aborigines may regard themselves as being extremely fortunate ; for we could not but contrast their living favorably with our own early recollections of the "fashionable boarding school starvation system," which is but too frequently tolerated at the East.

The superintendent of the boarding-house informs us that workshops were formerly attached to the Mission, where the pupils, in addition to their daily routine of studies, learned various trades. These, however, have of late years been discontinued, as it was thought better for the intellectual advancement of the children, that their minds should not be too much diverted from their books. They are not, for a similar reason, allowed to labor in the field or do any other than light work upon the farm. (It occurs to us that there might be another object in this prohibition, which is, to prevent a dishonest or interested superintendent from following the example of that amiable pedagogue, Wackford Squeers, who pursued the very practical system at his delightful academy for young gentlemen at Dotheboy's

Hall, where youth "were" boarded, washed, furnished with pocket-money, &c. of teaching a boy a thing, and then fixing it upon his memory by letting him *go out and do it*.)

These very general facts, in relation to Shawnee Mission and its Manual Labor School, are gathered in part from our own observation, for with true Yankee curiosity we visited, in our pursuit of facts, the school-room, where we saw the Indian children at their desks, and heard them recite, and we can assure the reader, that (physical peculiarities excepted), they seem, to our eyes, to differ but little from any " district school " interior, which educates the juveniles of some New England village, amid the green valleys of Connecticut, or the rocky hills of the old " Bay State." For we saw one youngster munching an apple, with an occasional side-look at the master and his rod, another doing anything but a sum, unless the sum had a nose and a mouth, with a crest of eagle's feathers upon its head, while a third tried hard to post up her neighbor, a very stupid-looking Shawnee, as to the correct reading of some forgotten arithmetical rule, while the urchin in question stood scratching his head, and looking woefully perplexed, as he tried in vain to catch the muttered information in time to answer promptly.

Finally, then, as touching the interior economy of the Shawnee Mission, this school is said to have done a vast amount of good among the Indians, for whose benefit it has been instituted. We are informed by those interested in the establishment, that a number of the female pupils who have grown up and received their entire education at the Mission (for there are several of them), have, on graduating, married well. Some of them to white men, and in their after lives done credit to its training ; *apropos* to this, we understand that a relative of the present superintendent (Mr. Johnson), was united in matrimonial bonds with one of these fair descendants of the very oldest inhabitants, not many months ago.

And here we may remark, that so far as our own taste in such matters goes, although some of the Shawnee girls, now members of the school, are called pretty, we have as yet been unable to discover this alleged beauty in these copper-colored damsels. Their manner of walking, for instance ; is ridiculous, indeed it was with the greatest difficulty that we refrained from laughing outright, as we saw them file out (on a signal rap from their teacher's fork), at the dining-room door, for the only thing which we can think of as approximating to their peculiar gait, might, perhaps, be a lame, and very short-legged duck, if you can suppose so common sense a bird to be attempting an imitation of the last fashionable "teter" for young ladies. Add to this, that they stoop, have round shoulders, no figure at all, and "too much color" in their faces, and then if you be a *connoisseur*, sing their praises, if you please—*à la* Longfellow's "Hiawatha."

CHAPTER XI.

RED-SKINS AND INDIAN YARNS.

THE people of the Shawnee Nation, particularly those who have been educated at the Mission, are *said to be* industrious, hard-working farmers ; and as a general thing, peaceable, law-abiding citizens. As a practical commentary upon which, it is pretty generally admitted, that some nine or ten of their " warriors " tendered their valuable services as " fighting men" to the good people of Lawrence, during the late difficulties ; and *on dit* that a portion of the Delawares, with a number of the Sacs and Foxes, followed this very " law-abiding " example. As to the "Delaware offering," they are said to have been such enthusiastic Free State sympathizers, that a few of them insisted upon going to Lawrence, where they remained about town " talking big, and drinking whisky," so as to be on hand if Pro-Slavery and Free Soil should come to loggerheads. It is, however, but justice to the people of Lawrence to add, that they (in common with the Pro-Slavery party, to whom other Indians offered their coöperation), declined to accept the assistance of these volunteer aids.

In other matters, as regards their character and moral proclivities, we can but judge from a very superficial observation of such " *specimens* " as chance threw in our way, and these usually turned up in the shape of *something-drunk-in-a-blanket*, with a very loud voice, and a very guttural notion of using it. The missionaries speak favorably of them, and we are not disposed to gainsay either the honesty of these gentlemen, or their superior opportunities for becoming acquainted with the fact ; but we do declare that if an inquirer should say to us, " Mr. Correspondent, what do you think of the proclivities of the Shawnee Nation ?" we should answer candidly : " Very bad." For if medical men speak the truth, a great proportion of the Indian women in Kansas, not only want chastity, but are afflicted with diseases, so loathsome, that modern prudery forbids that we should even give them a name. One physician, indeed, remarked to us, that he regarded a visit which a party of the Caws had recently paid his town, a very small one, by the way, as being quite a handsome sum in his pocket ; " For," said he, " they camped near us, stayed two months, and increased my practice by nearly four hundred dollars." And if merchants are to be credited, a respectable pickpocket, with a good city reputation, should bear a very fair character among an assemblage of these copper-colored braves. It is reported, for instance, that a Caw will steal the blanket off your back, while you are saying how-do-ye-do, to him ; and unless Dame Rumor do some of the Sacs and Foxes foul injustice, your eye-teeth would not be safe in your head, should any of these amiable gentlemen take a fancy to them. Apropos to these little thievish traits of Indian character, a gentleman from Lecompton tells us that it is no uncommon thing among " the traders," for a red-skinned customer to enter a store with plenty of money in his pocket, make his purchases, and then turn coolly round and inform the individual from whom he has bought, that

" Me no money now—bimeby kill deer—squaw dress skin—sell 'em—then Ingin plenty money—then come pay."

" Well, but what does the trader do then—will he wait ?" queried we.

" Do !" said my informant, " why, he upsets him, pulls off his blanket, takes away his money, helps himself to his due, and then lets Mr. Indian walk with the balance, if there be any in his favor."

Since we are upon this very *original* subject, we may as well relieve ourself of a frontier yarn or two which we have picked up among the Indian agents. The first of these was related to us by a friend whom we shall call Major Ramrod, for want of a less military *sobriquet*, who used to tell the story as a veritable extract from his own personal experiences, while acting as the Government Indian Agent for a certain tribe who (as we wish to preserve his *incognito*), shall be nameless. It runs thus :

"Some two years ago, in the course of an official tour, I had occasion to visit, for the first time, a remote portion of the tribe, over whose interests I held jurisdiction. I had ridden hard, but the way was long, and it was not until the close of a warm, sultry, August day that I approached the creek, or, as they call it in the Territory, river, on which the Indians with whom I desired to confer were encamped. Upon trotting up, however, to their lodges, or temporary shelters, which had been erected upon the edge of the prairie, and outside the timber of the ' river bottom,' I found no one to answer my call ; for though the fires were lighted, and a piece or two of deer-meat basting over the coals, their camp seemed deserted, save by two or three mangy, ill-favored curs, who yelped spitefully, but at a most respectful distance, as I rode in. Judging, however, from these signs of recent occupation, that those whom I sought must be somewhere in the immediate vicinity, I dismounted, and having hobbled my mule, turned her loose to graze, while I sat down to await the return of the Indians. Of this, however, I soon wearied, for as you know, solitude doesn't agree with me, nor is Robinson Crusoe-ism my *forte*, so it was not long ere I turned my back upon the lodges, and strolled leisurely towards the heavy timber which marked the location of the stream, through which, after some

clambering over fallen logs, and an occasional botheration from
a slew, I finally made my way, and was already in sight of its
wood-embowered waters, when, mingled with the rippling of the
swiftly-flowing tide, I fancied that I heard a distant shout, and
as I paused to listen, it was repeated with an unction which made
the presence of some near neighbors no longer a matter for question ; so following the direction of the sound, as I was guided
by its reiteration, I passed on, until a sudden bend in the river
brought me full in view of about as primitive a bathing-party as
had ever been gotten up since

> "The good old days of Adam and of Eve,"

Yes, there they were, papoose, and squaw, and warrior bold, all
busily engaged, though up to their necks in the stream, in kicking
up a pow-wow, that reminded me strongly of some fashionable
beach-scenes, which I have witnessed, during ' the season,' at
Newport and Cape May. .

" But to my tale—it required but a glance at these copper-colored bathers, to assure me that the whole party was in that very unusual condition which is most decently expressed by intimating
that they were in a ' state of nature,' and furthermore, that
the softer sex was largely represented, and being—don't laugh—
quite a modest man, at least in those days, I was for retreating
with all convenient speed, until these fair belles of the wilderness could find time to make a more elaborate toilet ; but as I
turned, like Joseph of old, to shame Satan and fly, my ears were
saluted with a sound of hi ! hi ! coupled with some unpronoun
cable gutturals, which signified, as I afterwards learned, " Brother,
who are you ?" This degree of relationship, however, was instantly changed, upon their discovering who I was, into a cry
of " How do you do, father ?" that being the title (our friend
was about two and thirty years of age), by which the Indian is
accustomed to address the agent of his tribe. But the courte-

sics, alas ! were not destined to terminate here ; no, they soon let me understand that they would give me a still warmer welcome, and verily, if a popular agent was ever received with *all* the honors by his charge, I certainly was that day. For, imagine my feelings, my outraged diffidence, perhaps (quit your laughing now) I should rather say, when I tell you that the redskins, one and all, matrons, wives, and maidens included—the latter, between you and me, being foremost in the race—scrambled out of the creek, and then, all unaccoutered as they were, with their huge mouths full of guttural welcomes, and not a rag upon their sun-tanned backs, they rushed into my arms and almost smothered me with a succession of embraces which left me dripping like a newly-washed Newfoundland dog, and as for the Eve-like squaws—but I draw a veil over my sensations— come, let's step into the grocery and take something to drink."

Having imbibed, the Major next proceeded to enlighten us as to his "adventures" upon returning to the Indian camp, with a distinct understanding, however, that the female barbarians had gotten their rigging on in the meanwhile, or we should have most respectfully declined to jot down another of our friend Ramrod's "little incidents."

"I presume that you know something of Indian cleanliness ; if you don't, and should ever think of returning to the Rocky Mountains, I should advise you to keep clear of their cookery, at least until it is upon the board, and even then, if you *will* take 'pot luck' with them, don't scrutinize the platters, and above all, use your own table tools, come what may."

We intimated to the Major that we had once dined with a Eutaw chief, off a "hotch potch" of stewed grass-hoppers and lizard's tails ; and Ramrod went on,

'"Well, I reckon then, as you have travelled *some*, that I may run the risk of spoiling your supper by relating the first of a number of annoyances which bedevilled me during my stay in what I shall name, for convenience sake, the Bathing Indians' camp ; for you must know that, upon my return to their lodges, I found myself somewhat fatigued from the excess of hospitality which I had so recently undergone, and being thirsty withal, I begged one of the squaws to give me a drink of water—"

(Here we looked up, and having closed our right eye, threw our head a little to that side, gave a long whistle, and at the same time pointed significantly with our thumb over the left shoulder.)

"Well, can't you wait until I have finished the sentence ?" cried Ramrod, half peevishly, in answer to this pantomimic interruption ; "come, don't be poking fun at a man until he gets through ; I didn't say that I intended to take it *raw ;* but you've put me out ; let me see, where was I ? Oh, now I recollect, I had just asked the squaw, a good-looking half-breed by the way, to get me some cold water. So, being an obliging girl, she half filled a small tin pail with the element and placed it beside the buffalo-robe on which I was placidly reclining. I had taken up this water-holder and was just in the act of qualifying it with a modicum of prime old rye whisky from my 'private tickler,' when it struck me that the tin pail might be a great deal cleaner ; so I made bold to suggest an amendment in this respect, to the copper-colored damsel, who forthwith emptied the pail and was wiping it out with a wisp of freshly-gathered prairie-grass, which she had pulled for the purpose, when an old chief, who had hitherto sat quietly by my side, where he had been, to all appearances, completely absorbed in the enjoyment of the pipe-full of tobacco with which I had supplied him, sprang suddenly to his feet, and interrupted the operation by snatching the utensil out of her hand, at the same time telling the woman, in their language, that she must be a fool, that white folks were particular and liked everything very clean, but that if she watched him, she would know how to clean a drinking.vessel another time, in

a manner which would satisfy even the most fastidious pale face.
So suiting the action to the word, while the squaw looked on in
mute admiration, and I, if the truth be told, in considerable
mental distress, he seized the tin pail with one hand, while with
the other he cast loose his breech-clout, and then, oh, horror of
horrors ! proceeded to polish most faithfully, the *inside* of the
vessel with this somewhat exceptionable garment. Is it necessary for me to add that I went supperless to bed that night ?
And now, stranger, *won't* you take *another* drink ?"

We will add a paragraph here, which might very properly be
headed, "A real blessing to mothers and nurses," or an infallible
receipt to stop babies from crying whether or no, and then we
shall say farewell to Mr. Ingin, at least for the present.

We had noticed that Indian babies didn't cry ; we had seen
these cunning-looking, hairless, black-eyed, dear darling little
angels (we quote from enthusiastic young *unmarried* ladies now),
as they hung in a most neck-breaking fashion from their mothers'
backs, with their heads poked out of the Mackinaw blanket-folds
(in which the little innocents were enveloped to an extent which
threatened their speedy suffocation), so as to admit of their peep-
ing over the maternal left shoulder ; but still no cry, no whim-
per—no, not even with a cholic to provoke it—gave notice that
little How-wow-bob-er-ry was in pain. "But why," methinks
we hear the inquisitive reader exclaim, "was this ? Was the
long-named cherub dumb ? Had the pretty copper-colored pet
been tongue-tied from the hour of its birth ?" Oh, no, nothing
of the sort ; it had been better trained than the child of the
pale face, that's all ; for the wigwam is a stern school, and the
Indian a most impartial teacher ; and little How-wow-what-do-
you-call-him, though not yet twelve moons old, knows better
than to squall, for his infant memory still retains the recollection
of a time when his first unlucky squall was greeted by a duck-
ing in the nearest creek, administered by his papa, that cele-

brated warrior, Wont-stand-any-such-humbug ; and his second by ditto repeated, until he had learnt to reason from his former aquatic experiences that the same thing might happen again. So the "recollections of the past," all sombre though they be, warn him to "keep a stiff upper lip," even though he don't "feel jolly." From "all of which and singular" you may perceive that as "a burnt child" is said to "dread the fire" upon this side of the Mississippi, so a ducked one may fear the water upon the other. And, finally, under this head, we would, with all due deference, beg leave to recommend this system of immersion to indulgent mammas in general ; for they may rest assured that there is nothing like *Hydropathy* for converting a "squalling brat" into "a treasure of a baby."

And upon re-reading what we have just written, we are convinced that the Temperance people, at least, should think well of us ; for, have we not given the reader three most undoubted *cold water* yarns, all duly strung together like a flock of wild geese (let us hope that the simile ends there), and what is more to the purpose, a moral to each—if one could only hunt it out ?

So much for our first visit to the Shawnee Manual Labor School and its inhabitants.

CHAPTER XII.

NEWS-HUNTING IN WESTPORT.

WE got back to our Westport "inn" rather *inexpressibly* mule sore, an hour by sun, and straightway "dropped round town" into various shops (or, as we Americans call them, "stores"), and so forth, with our ears wide open and our note-book at hand ; nor was our news-hunt in Westport less successful than that in which we had been engaged at the Mission ; for we "bagged" the following from an old frontiersman, who had seen our friend Kit Carson—*the* Kit—in October last ; and it may interest those who have read of his wild adventures "by flood and field," to know that Kit Carson of the Rocky Mountains—the hero of many a border-fight and romantic expedition—has at length "settled down for good." Yes it is even so ; for our Nimrod of the West has laid aside the rifle and bowie-knife to take up the yard-stick and scales ; and now, instead of sending hostile Indians to their long account, he is sending *long accounts* to them.   'Tis true he *charges* still, and we doubt not as freely as before ; but these attacks are only on his customers ; and if he "*posts* a man," he does it in the ledger. But a truce to punning—for we hate a pun—the more so as it is rumored that those who perpetrate such things "would even steal a sheep ;" and as we have little desire to be charged with mutton-thieving, we will tell you in so many words, that Kit Carson keeps a store, or, as they say out West, "is engaged in selling goods" in the city of San Fernando del Taos, New Mexico, where, as our informant states, Carson has entered into partnership with a Mr. Maxwell, a gentleman who, if we remember rightly, was himself an " old Mountain man." The style of the firm is Carson & Maxwell. We were, moreover, pleased to learn that Kit has been restored to his office of Indian agent, from which he was for a time suspended by order of the Governor of New Mexico. From all that we could gather in relation to the difficulty which led to his suspension, we understood that Carson had directed some sheep belonging to the Mexicans to be killed for the use of the Indians—under what circumstances we were unable to discover. This drew forth a complaint from the Mexicans to the governor, who called Carson to account ; and finally got into a difficulty with the old mountaineer, in which the latter played a very independent part. The whole affair was then referred to the proper authorities at Washington, and there settled (as we should judge from the result), in the pioneer's favor. Kit talked of coming to " the States " this fall, but has deferred it until another year.

From Carson the conversation very naturally turned to poor Aubrey, who, as the reader doubtless knows, was recently killed in New Mexico, where he fell, after braving death in every form, by the hand of an American, and in a private quarrel.

It is not generally known that Aubrey rode, in the fall of 1848, from Santa Fe, N. M., to Independence, Mo., a distance of 775 miles in five consecutive days, and sixteen hours. But in his anxiety to perform a feat which no man has yet equalled, and in all human probability never will, he nearly sacrificed his life to his ambition, for on arriving at his journey's end, he was literally lifted from his blood-stained saddle. We remember meeting Aubrey at the crossing of the Arkansas in the summer of that year ; he was then just returning from a similar ride, which he had made in something less than eight days. In person, Aubrey was a small but very active man, all bone and muscle, just the figure for such an expedition—for who doesn't know that there's no telling what a *little man* cannot do when he tries ?

We met a prominent Free State man, a correspondent of the New York Times, here to-day, who is on his way *out* of the country. This gentleman gives us the following in regard to the Secret Military Organization of the Free State party. He says : that it extends through the States of Illinois, Indiana, Iowa, and Northern Michigan, from which some fifteen hundred fighting-men were already on their way to assist the citizens of Lawrence, when a settlement of the difficulties there, rendered the presence of a reinforcement unnecessary, and induced them to turn back. From which it would appear, that " the hour and the man " of Free State-ism, or Pro-Slavery-ism, for we can scarce say which, is yet to come.

We hear too, from the same source, of a serious misunderstanding between Generals Robinson and Lane, the Free State leaders. Its origin was thus : It seems, that after the settlement of difficulties in Lawrence, it was thought proper to give a supper and ball, at the Free State Hotel, or Eldridge House which is to be, to celebrate the happy termination of the Wakarusa War, and hail the advent of

> " Those piping times of peace,'

as Shakespeare has it. Now this ball was free to all comers. Indeed it was not only a jollification, got up without distinction of party, but a sort of soothing plaster to cement the blessed re-union which has just been consummated between Free-Soilism and Pro-Slavery, and heal the wounds of all parties concerned. Among other distinguished personages, General Robinson tendered a special invitation to the Pro-Slavery sheriff, of Douglas County (Jones), a person at that time highly obnoxious to the Free-Soilers, who regarded him as being little better than a fit emissary of what they looked upon " with as favorable eyes as Gabriel on the Devil in Paradise "—the so styled " Bogus Legislature." After tendering this invitation, and receiving Jones's acceptance of the same, General Robinson went back to the supper-room, and then asked (which we fancied might better have been done at first), if it were agreeable to the company present that Sheriff Jones should attend ? to this an almost unanimous cry of " Yes, let him come," was the response. When General Lane got upon his legs, and made what we have heard styled a very inflammatory speech, in which he stated that he had talked with a committee from three of the Lawrence companies of Free State Kansas Volunteers, who had declared that the men of those companies would not be present, if Jones was permitted to become a guest. This called forth a shout of " Keep him out then." In answer to this, Robinson immediately rose, and expostulated with those present, at the same time pointing out to the malcontents, that he *had* invited Jones, who must therefore be considered their guest, and as such entitled, by every law of hospitality, to courteous treatment at their hands. To this Lane replied, by stating that he " had rather a million of Joneses should stay away, than that one of his men should be prevented from coming." He then went on to speak of the killing of the Free State man Barber, making use of this unhappy circumstance as a theme well calculated to excite the indignation of his hearers. General Robinson then declared that Jones should come, or he himself would stay away, whereupon, our informant adds, high words passed between General Lane and himself, which ended in Robinson's going up to the room in which Jones was stopping, and reiterating his invitation. Jones, having, in the meantime, heard of the opposition to his being present, declined the supper, but upon being urged by the Free State General, accompanied him to the ball, where he was introduced to several of the Lawrence belles, who, by the way, are strong politicians, and even more belligerent in their Wakarusa War notions, than their Free State "lords and masters." And thus it was that the very pugnacious Jones became the lion of the evening, and the cynosure of every eye. It is even hinted that one of the fair ladies present intimated a desire to see him *safe* home, that is to say to Franklin, a distance of four miles, which, with the mercury at zero, and at two o'clock in the morning, strikes us as being a very masculine undertaking. The Missourians are reported to have fought shy of this festivity, as a general thing. And it is even hinted that one of the Free State Volunteers, who must have been little better than a beast, avowed his determination to murder Sheriff Jones in cold blood, as he entered the ball-room. It is on record, however, that he *didn't* shoot, and we sincerely trust that if he had, there would have been manliness enough in the soldiers of the Free State Volunteers to have taken the fiend out of doors and hung him upon the neare   tree, and we believe, moreover, that it *would* have been don.

CHAPTER XIII.

WE JOURNEY TO LECOMPTON.

AND now we will resume our quotations from our letter en route :

HOUSE ON THE PRAIRIE, NEAR LECOMPTON, K. T., *Dec. 20th,* 1855.

We left Westport, Mo., at 9 A. M., yesterday, in an open wagon loaded with doors, carpenter's tools, bedding, etc. (this being the first conveyance to Lecompton), with the understanding, duly entered into between ourself and the driver, that we should walk up the bad hills and down the steep ones, which, as it was no more than we have been doing for the benefit of Smashup, Breakdown & Co.'s humbug of a stage-line, ever since we left St. Louis (not to mention packing a rail), seemed no very great hardship. We had for company on the road, beside the driver, who had been " raised in Illinois" (where he had followed the example of that eccentric Westerner who swore, that if a man hadn't a right to get the chills in a new country, he hadn't a right to do anything ; and very nearly shaken himself to death in carrying out the principle), an Empire State man, a very seedy specimen, going to seek his fortune at Lecompton (which, as your readers ought to know, has been selected as the capital of Kansas), and a certain Mr. Stewart, the recently appointed superintendent of Public Buildings at that place. These, with your very humble servant, " Our Correspondent," made up the complement of bipeds. As for the animal motive power, we had a couple of rat-like " Ingianny " horses, of which our driver seemed particularly proud, though for what particular good quality it was impossible to say, and a short-tailed mule of Stewart's which did duty both as a riding-animal, and as a leader to our team, when a steep hill required an extra effort.

At 2 o'clock, P. M., we halted at Donaldson's, a Kentuckian who married the daughter of a Shawnee chief (Captain Parks), and is therefore entitled to reside upon the " Indian Reserve;" his dwelling, a new stone house, just erected at a cost of $2,800, is, for " these diggin's," quite an aristocratic affair, being two stories in height, with doors, windows, and such like luxuries, and wonderful to relate, lathed and plastered inside. Here we dined, at " two bits" (York shillings) per head, on hog-meat and wild honey, and then progressed, feeling, so far as our individual self was concerned, considerably better, on our way to Bean's Hotel (?) on Wakarusa Creek, where we proposed halting for the night.

As we journeyed slowly on, our friend Stewart pointed out to us a rude wooden enclosure, standing solitary and alone, upon a ridge of the prairie ; " There," said he, " I witnessed a strange ceremony last spring. The friends of an Indian brave, whose spirit had sought the hunting-grounds of his fathers, were burying their dead out of their sight beneath yon snow-covered mound. As I rode up, the interment had been completed, and the mould filled in. The horse of the dead chieftain was then led forth and shot beside the grave, with a favorite hound of the deceased ; for it is the custom of their people, when the red man goes forth upon that unknown trail, to send his fleetest steed and faithful dog to bear him company."

During this day's travel our way lay, for the most part, over long rolls of up-swelling prairie, with here and there a long line of timber, marking the location of some creek, or bottom land ;

but as a general thing, the earth boasted neither bush nor shrub.

Poets who eulogize what Bryant styles

> " —The gardens of the desert,
> For which the speech of England has no name,

should ride over them—as we have done to-day—in the teeth (and they ought to be aching ones) of this December blast, on the top of a loaded wagon, with their eyes a fountain of waters, and their noses an indigo blue, and we will venture to say that they would quote from Shakspeare as we once heard an Irishman do, and declare with practical Pat, that " a prairie is divil a bit better than jist flat, stale, and unprofitable."

We know that " Our Correspondent " found it so, for as the sun went down, and the biting gale came sweeping over the long, unprotected " rolls," we would have given all the romance of strange travel in a yet stranger country, for the every-day creature comforts of a warm room and a hot supper. Yes, we will be candid ; be it confessed, then, that we shivered, and shook, and played the old Harry's tatoo with our chattering masticators, until, between " the influence of the hour," and the indigestion naturally arising from a hog and honey dinner, we got the blues—grew desperate—wished Kansas, " the war," and the New York Herald in that extremity, and your humble servant, the writer, safely back again in the " Empire State." But " Bean's Hotel," brought us up handsomely at eight, P.M., and we assure you that we had not taken our half-frozen body out of the wagon over half-an-hour before we thawed out, and, *unlike* Mark Tapley—who was always doing well under " depressing circumstances "—" turned up jolly " under the genial influences of a big log-fire, and a hot cup of coffee. But we should do the reader, ourself, and mine host, Mr. Bean, an injustice, if we neglected to describe his " hotel,' inside and out.   It is a log-cabin, or rather two log-cabins, with a connecting link between, in the shape of a porch, which is obtained by continuing the flooring and room, but omitting the sides ; to either end of this Siamese twin house is attached a huge chimney, of such tremendous dimensions, that it quite carried out an idea which we heard hazarded once by a certain Miss Biddy O'Rourke, of " a house built to a chimney ;" but fuel is cheap in a new country, and there are worse things after a long day's ride than a heaping wood-fire, with its sparkles and flashes of light, and its great red coals, which peep out like fiery eyes ; not to mention the glowing pictures which the day-dreamer fancies, as he watches, with thoughtful brow, the upward course of the glowing sparks ; and then for furniture (for we always love to locate ourself to the reader, even at the risk of being taken for an upholsterer on a tour), we have a pile of books, a chest of drawers, *antique*—a table, *very shaky*—a big bed, quite primitive in its way—a little ditto, which, with a small armory of rifles and other murderous utensils, complete the inventory. And then there's the group around the fire ; but it would require too great an effort to do them justice, and moreover, if we remember aright, we have already given the reader " a taste of our quality," in the way of fireside descriptions ; so we won't repeat the dose, at least at present, the more so as we are in honor bound to write Kansas, and really " nothing shorter." A truce then, to any description of character, be the originality ever so striking, or the temptation ever so great ; suffice it to say that we slept that night the sleep of a weary man, on a feather bed, with a buffalo attachment (where we dreamed of Rocky Mountain snow-drifts), in a thorough draft, with a door half a foot too short on one side, and an insecure window, whose glasses were absent without leave, upon the other ; and so ended our first day and night in Kansas.

In the morning, we breakfasted and started betimes, so that

in spite of our snail pace motion, we reached the town of Franklin about noon, where, as our orders include, "the industrial and agricultural prospects of the new Territory and its people," we obtained the following "facts," which we give you as they were told us, having first, to guard against misrepresentations, deducted twenty per cent. for any personal interest which our informant might have had in settling that particular vicinity.

Franklin, Kansas Territory, is what the geographer would call pleasantly situated on a somewhat prominent hill or prairie ridge. It was first settled by one Wallace of Iowa, in October, 1853, but permanent buildings were not commenced until June of the present year. As regards the value of land, town lots, sixty by one hundred and twenty feet, bring, according to location, from $25 to $100, although, for that matter, we should much prefer to buy at a less rate, and at a greater distance from the main body of the place, for we understand that the whisky-drinking and gambling propensities of the good citizens of Franklin are pretty generally known. Timber, principally oak (various kinds), and black walnut, is to be had in *present* abundance, at the distance of a little over a mile from the town. Excellent water may be obtained by digging to a depth of from twenty-five to thirty-six feet; but these wells sometimes go dry. For building purposes, pine lumber may be obtained at Kansas city—the nearest point—at a cost, including transportation to Franklin, of $80 per thousand feet. Agriculturists say that the yield of corn in that vicinity—first crop—taking a range of two miles from Franklin, has been sixty bushels to the acre, in lands on the Wakarusa bottom, and twenty-five bushels in sod on the prairie. A two-story frame building, forty-two by thirty-two feet, comfortably furnished inside, has just been put up at a cost of $1,400. We were afterwards invited to attend a house-warming upon the completion of this dwelling by its owner, who very kindly offered to send a conveyance to Lawrence, where we were then stopping, to bring us down, and we regret that our engagements and the severity of the weather should have prevented us from seeing a social fandango in Franklin, where, to do the people justice, they are said to get up those sort of things in very good (frontier) style.

But to return. There are some twelve houses and cabins built or in progress of erection.

The population of this place is from seventy-five to one hundred souls. It is a strong Pro-Slavery town, and furnished a large quota—nearly sixty men—to the Governor's forces for "the War." It has a steam saw-mill of eighteen horse power. The citizens claim to have had no cases of that great Western bug-bear, the all shaking fever and ague, as yet ; but we should say that the location, with the large swampy bottom in its vicinity, was favorable to the production of swamp miasmas.

Franklin is distant by some thirty-eight miles from Westport, Mo., fifty-five from Independence, three from Lawrence, and fifteen from Lecompton, the capital of Kansas Territory.

We are indebted to Mr. Stewart, our fellow traveller, for much useful data *in re* Kansas and her prospects.

The following "facts and figures," which have been derived in part from the gentleman just alluded to, and others well qualified to give accurate information, may, we think, be regarded as reliable, and, we trust, prove useful to those who contemplate "moving into the Territory." These calculations, it should be remarked, will apply equally well to a large portion of Eastern Kansas.

Day laborers command $1 35 per day and find themselves ; mechanics from $1 75 to $2 00 per day, without board ; washing—as there is a lack of females as yet—is high, say $1 25 per dozen; single-team wagons—calculating the average day's travel at twenty-five miles—may be had at from $4 50 to $5 00 per day. You may reckon thirty bushels to the wagon. Fencing

may be estimated, where you hire the laboi, at $4 00 per hun-
dred rails ; this includes everything, splitting, hauling, and setting. Though authorities differ upon this point, we should say
that it would be a saving to the emigrant if he were to purchase
his building materials, fully manufactured, in St. Louis, and
transport them to the site selected. When we say building
materials we mean doors, sashes, frame-work, flooring, &c. It is
not only a saving in the transportation of bulk, which of course
is greater in the undressed material, but the difference in the
prices of labor, lumber, &c., will, in the present state of the
market, make a saving upon the articles purchased in St. Louis
of nearly 20 per cent. Frame houses, which are built entire in St.
Louis, or, to speak more properly, their components, have already
been transported to Kansas for erection, at a considerable saving
to their owners. For instance, the Auditor of the State, Mr.
Donaldson, has such a house at Lecompton—it is two stories
high, has two rooms in the lower, being lined with dressed pine
boards inside, and there are two rooms above, say sixteen by
eighteen feet each—which cost its proprietor when finished
including transportation by steamer to Kansas City, and from
thence by wagon to Lecompton, $800. We are told that in
many parts of the Territory concrete is the cheapest building
material ; it can be put up at an expense of fourteen cents per
cubic foot. This speaks well for the building stone and quarries
of Kansas.

It costs about $8 00 per acre, lowest estimate, to " improve a
claim." Of the claim system, so universal in our Territories, we
shall speak more fully elsewhere. Under the same head fall
" squatter laws " and " preëmption rights."

And now, having given the reader this much of sober dollar
and cent facts, we will go on with our pencillings by the
way.

At one, P. M., as we rolled up "a rise," our delighted though somewhat mud-blinded optics beheld for the first time the far-famed city of Lawrence. How shall our feeble pen express our sensations ? We gazed upon the scene as did the patriarch of old when he beheld the promised land. But in good earnest we felt a deep interest in Lawrence ; and as we watched her snowy banner floating in the breeze, we snuffed up the pure, albeit some what freezing gales of the prairie with a keener relish, and murmured " This air Lawrence." We didn't apostrophize her, because we didn't feel equal to the task. We didn't curse her, because the inhabitants of that city are stern republicans—" black" though they be—and we have the fortune—good or bad as it may be —to hail from the Knickerbocker State. We didn't drink her health, because Stewart was out of whisky ; but, though we didn't say much, we followed ·the example of the sagacious bird, the owl, in keeping up *a think ;* and what we thought, shall be chronicled as soon as, in Missouri phrase, we "get shut of Kansas." To be serious, however, Lawrence —even without taking into consideration her high military reputation—is " considerable of a town," above which that " large stone building," the Kansas Emigrant Aid Society's Free State Hotel—that is to be—loomed up pre-eminent. We would fain have approached to do it reverence ; but as we were pushing on to Lecompton, to confer with his Excellency Governor Shannon, and as the wagon wouldn't stop, we were compelled to postpone our pilgrimage to this political shrine until a more convenient season.

So, like the Priest and Levite, we passed by upon the other side, and mounted the steep bluff, which reaches down to within five hundred yards of the main body of the town, and which, in a military point of view, commands the place. But we won't be so *uncivil* as to handle Lawrence in a military manner here ; no, let her glory in her boasted strength, until we get an opportunity to fire our paper-bullets at her earthen " breast-works," when we *expect* to prove (we don't mean *hope*) that Lawrence can be taken, and badly taken to boot, her Sharpe's rifles and Kansas Brigades to the contrary notwithstanding, in something less than two hours, by the watch.

At three P. M. we entered the woods, where the capitol of Kansas Territory, partly is, and principally is to be, and drove up to a shanty that covers a sort of "general store," which will doubtless expand itself with the progress of the place. Upon the stoppage of our conveyance, we picked a "soft place,"—no difficult matter, for the noon-day sun had began to thaw the frozen ground—and jumped off, to the no slight detriment of our "boots." Upon alighting, and entering the store, which seemed to contain a little of everything, but more particularly cheese and corn whisky, we were introduced by our friend Stewart to a "small crowd" of very frontier-looking gentlemen, a little rough on the outside, but evidently very good fellows for all that. Upon making inquiries for "the Governor," we were informed that he was making his residence, during his stay, at a "House on the Prairie"—the residence of Major Clarke, Indian agent for the Pottawatomies—distant some three miles from Lecompton. We were accordingly just "putting out" upon friend Stewart's mule—which he had very kindly placed at our disposal—when a letter-posted informant suggested, that the Governor and Secretary of State, Mr. Woodson, were in another part of "the town," which he designated. Upon the receipt of this intelligence, we mounted, and rode through a piece of woods, found the "other part of the town," consisting of two houses, and the Governor, who made his first appearance to our eyes in the form of a stoutly-built, elderly gentleman, clad in a rusty suit of black, with iron-grey hair (and if the *governing* of Kansas is not enough to turn any man's hair grey, we don't know what trouble would), under a most "dilapidated tile." He was sitting upon a white horse, *à la* General Taylor—or as the

"great unwashed" delight to call him, "Old Rough and Ready"—
and looked dignified, as a Governor should, but good-natured
withal. So we felt emboldened, reined in our mule, made our
politest bow, and presented our credentials in the shape of the
letter of introduction from the distinguished ex-Senator already
alluded to. The Governor dropped his bridle, put on his
spectacles, read the document in question, and then shook us
warmly by the hand and welcomed us to Kansas. Then turning to the Secretary of State (Woodson), who was riding at
his side, he gave us the initiative to an acquaintance, which we
afterwards took great pleasure in cultivating. We then rode
down together, to the residence of Dr. Rodrigue, a prominent citizen of Kansas, who has informed himself thoroughly in
relation to the natural resources of the Territory ; with Doctor
Rodrigue, we found Sheriff Jones. We found him rather a
fine-looking young man, of some eight and twenty years of
age, or thereabouts, who, unfortunately for our young lady
friends, is married to a very nice wife. Well, we shook hands
with these new friends, and then pursued our way, in company
with Woodson and the Governor, by a short cut, to " House
on the Prairie," where we arrived in safety, as the sun was
going down, and met a hearty reception from its inmates.

After supper we entered into conversation with Governor
Shannon and his private secretary—a son of the Governor's,
whom we were introduced to at Major Clarke's—upon the
multiplicity of matters which our duties, as a newspaper correspondent, make it our province to investigate, and the Governor
very kindly promised to give us a history of " the war."

CHAPTER XIV.

HOUSE ON THE PRAIRIE.

AND now it seems proper to say something of Major Clarke, from whose hospitable mansion we are writing, as well as to put the reader in possession of some of the dangers to which "Our special Correspondent" may be exposed, while pursuing his vocation even in the pacific and law-abiding Territory of Kansas.

To go back "to the beginning," Major Clarke (who is from Arkansas, where he formerly edited a paper, and was a member of the State Legislature), has taken, or has had the credit of having taken—which, with an enemy, always comes to the same thing—a very decided Pro-Slavery stand during the recent dificultes in Kansas. He was, moreover, one of the two men—his companion being Colonel Burns of Weston, Mo. who fired upon Barber and his party. These acts have made him particularly obnoxious to the Free State men of Lawrence, and as his residence is within eight miles of that town, he has been repeatedly threatened with violence, in proof of which the following may be stated.

Even before Barber was killed, a party of some ten or twelve Free State men, armed to the teeth, surrounded Mr. Doak (a brother-in-law of the Major's, who resides with him), as he was returning home from Lecompton, and told him that, " Now was the time that they were going to have the difficulty with Major Clarke settled ; that he, the Major, could not live ;" with many similar expressions.

Since the death of Barber, a party of some twenty men stopped at the dwelling of Judge Wakefield (a prominent Free-Soil politician, who has since figured upon both their regular and irregular tickets), on the California trail, some three miles distant from Major Clarke's, and there swore, in the presence of a certain "Squire Crane—'a very reliable man'",—that "Clarke should not live; that he must die," alleging at the same time as a reason, that Clark was with the party who killed Barber. Barber's two brothers were said to have been with these men.

In addition to these matters, of which Major Clarke has at various times been notified, it may be mentioned as an additional proof of the hostile intentions of his enemies, that a Doctor Johnson, a son of the present governor of Virginia, who has been residing at " House on the Prairie," for the last two weeks, —his own dwelling being in the immediate neighborhood—to assist in defending Clarke's house from any attack that might be made upon it, has been fired upon no less than three times, the ball—upon the last occasion—passing through his coat. The circumstances under which these attacks were made are as follows : In the first instance, which occurred just after Dr. Johnson arrived at " House on the Prairie," three suspicious-looking men rode up in front of Clarke's house ; this was after nightfall. To ascertain their intentions and business there, Doctor Johnson stepped out into the yard and hailed them ; to this they returned no satisfactory reply ; the Doctor then fired upon them with his pistol, upon which two of the strangers wheeled about and returned the fire, after which they immediately rode off. No person was hit, so far as could be ascertained, upon either side.

Upon the second occasion—which dates back to the Monday preceding our visit—Doctor Johnson was walking up from Benicia, some two miles from Major Clarke's, and when about midway between the two places, a man mounted upon a grey horse, rode out from the bushes, and called out : "Is your name Dr. Johnson ?" to which the Doctor answered, "Yes." The man replied, "Then you are the rascal I have been waiting for ;" and immediately fired upon him with a pistol—for this would-be assassin had no gun—the ball, as before stated, passing through the skirt of the Doctor's coat. Before the Doctor could draw his pistol to return the shot, the man had ridden off and disappeared in the brush. Dr. Johnson begins to grow superstitious about these repeated attempts to take his life ; he says that they come nearer and nearer every time, and he fears that the next attempt will be successful.

Major Clarke's residence has now been regularly guarded, for upwards of two weeks ; loaded rifles rest against the walls, and "six-shooters" lie "handy" upon the tables. Some of Clarke's Pro-Slavery friends are constantly there, and if an attack be made, the assailants may count upon a most desperate resistance. There is hardly any room to doubt that if an overt act be committed in this quarter, a war of extermination would be the result. For, were Major Clarke's residence to be molested in his absence, the Missourians would be almost certain to cross the frontier, and level Lawrence with the ground : at least, such is the impression of those best qualified to judge.

To give some idea of the state of excitement and apprehension which exists among the members of the Major's family, we may mention, that Major Clarke has already fired upon, and wounded one of a party of his friends who were approaching his house, late in the evening, under the impression that they were enemies. Indeed, a knock at the front door this very evening caused a muster of the "tools," and it was not until the name and business of the stranger were fully understood, and deemed pacific, that the door was (even then), cautiously opened for his admission.

For ourself, we are free to confess, and we don't care who

knows it, that we shall, during our stay in Kansas, deny ourself the luxury of moonlight rambles, or the pleasure of paying visits after sundown.

The annexed letter will come in very properly here. It is a communication from Major Clarke to Governor Shannon, dated from House on the Prairie, which he sometimes calls Camp Clarke, and addressed to His Excellency, at Shawnee Mission. The following is a literal copy :—

CAMP CLARKE, Dec. 3, 1855.

DEAR SIR:—I hasten to write you by an express that is now on its way (12 o'clock at night). My house is a fortification. I am compelled to keep a guard with sentinels all night. Unless the violators of the law are disarmed, the country is ruined. If the troops should withdraw without this being done, a partisan war will continue. Murders, house burnings, and all the outrages incident to civil war will follow; or we (the law-abiding men) will have to withdraw from the Territory, to our great pecuniary distress.

The outlaws have marked our men. They keep their movements secret, and we know not who is first to be attacked, or when it will be made. We have learned, upon ample authority, that more than one hundred Sharpe's rifles are distributed in the immediate neighborhood. My next door neighbors have them in possession, and only two days ago ten armed men surrounded a member of my family with threatening language, and ended the interview with a threat to dispose of myself.

We, the law abiding men, appeal to you, and insist that nothing less than the surrender of the arms now held by the traitors can satisfy the community. They are in open rebellion—they have their arms for the special purpose of resisting the laws and avenging supposed injuries—with these arms they have already forcibly rescued prisoners from the hands of the officers—they threaten to rescue others; they are protecting men who have broken custody, and in every sense they are traitors, and giving aid and comfort to traitors.

In haste, your friend and obedient servant,

GEORGE W. CLARKE.

To Governor WILSON SHANNON, Shawnee Mission.

Major Clarke, it should be remembered, has been for the last three years (as Indian agent of the Pottawatomies) an officer of the general government, stationed in the Territory. He is represented as being an impetuous, and highly excitable, but withal, kind-hearted person ; a democrat and ultra-Pro-Slavery man in his politics ; in fact, what is usually called a thorough-going Southerner.

It is admitted that the Major was one of the Pro-Slavery men who took part in that unfortunate rencounter, which resulted in the killing of the Free State man, Barber.

The following may be regarded as a correct statement of the circumstances attending this deplorable transaction, as we have learned them from the most reliable Pro-Slavery authorities. For the Free State versions of. the affair, we must refer the reader to the narratives of Barber and Pierson, the brother and brother-in-law of the deceased, which will be found under their proper head. We should also remark, that we finally obtained an account of the matter from Major Clarke himself, but as this paper has been unfortunately lost, we are compelled to give his side of the story as it has come to us, through a person to whom he related the alleged facts ; it is, however, substantially the same, if we mistake not, as that which we received from Major Clarke.

On the 7th of December, at noon, Major Clarke left the Pro-Slavery camp at Lecompton in company with a party of its leading men, among whom were Major General Richardson, commanding the Militia of Kansas, Judge Cato of the Supreme Court, and Judge Woods of the Police Court of Douglas county. These gentlemen were going, in compliance with the request of Governor Shannon, to confer with his Excellency at the Wakarusa camp.

While on their way, they perceived a party of three mounted men coming from the direction of Lawrence ; and as verbal

orders had been issued to arrest all suspicious persons, it was
proposed that an equal number should be detached from their
party to intercept and question these people ; and if their
answers should prove unsatisfactory, arrest them. This suggestion was about to be adopted, when Colonel Burns of Weston,
Mo., one of the persons selected, said : "Why do we want so
many ?—two of us are enough to take these vile Abolitionists,
anyhow." Burns and Major Clarke were accordingly detailed,
and rode out to overtake the Free State men. This they did ;
and, after halting them, a conversation ensued, in which the
Free State men not only declared that there was no law nor
order in the Territory, but declined to surrender themselves, in
compliance with the demand of Clarke and his companions.
Upon this, both parties commenced drawing their arms—that is
to say, with the exception of one of the Free State men (who
was most probably the man killed) ; this person sat upon his
horse a little apart from his companions ; he had a switch in his
hand, but drew no arms, nor did he appear to have any. Both
parties " squared to each other," and fired—pistols being the only
weapons used. On the part of the Pro-Slavery men, Clarke
was armed with a small five-inch Colt's revolver, while Burns
had a Navy revolver, which is heavier and carries a much larger
ball. After exchanging shots, the Free State men galloped
off. Burns proposed to send a "long shot" after them
from his rifle, but Clarke objected, saying, "Let them go."
Burns is said to have admitted, that he thought he hit the man
whom he fired at, as he saw him press his hand to his side, or,
as others state it, " Saw the fur fly from his old great coat."
When the Lawrence men rode off, they showed no appearance
of being hurt. Clarke declares that he had not the slightest suspicion that they had wounded one of their antagonists, until
news was brought at a late hour that night to the Wakarusa camp that a Lawrence man had been killed in this ren-

counter. It was rumored, that upon the receipt of this intelligence, Colonel Burns left the camp and returned to Missouri ;
this, however, is incorrect, as both Burns and Clarke remained
with the Pro-Slavery faction until the termination of the Lawrence difficulties.

Neither Clarke nor his companion knew any of the men
with whom they had this fight. There was, therefore, no personal malice nor previous quarrel between them. It seems
proper to add, that Major Clarke not only does not wish to
shun a thorough judicial inquiry into his own conduct in this
affair, but actually desires such an investigation. He is, moreover, willing to abide by the result. It is understood that the
Major is at present at St. Louis, upon business connected with
his Indian agency, but will shortly return to his residence near
Lecompton.

And now, as our letter is already of the largest we will forbear further writing until General Whitfield's mules shall have
hauled us to Shawnee Mission, for we have accepted an invitation
to accompany the Governor to that place, from whence we hope
to date our next epistle.

CHAPTER XV.

THE EXECUTIVE OFFICE AT SHAWNEE MISSION.

I AM writing in the Executive office, and for that matter, the private bed-room, public parlor, library and general sanctum of his Excellency Wilson Shaunon, Governor of Kansas Territory. Now, as some of your readers may suppose that to be Governor of Kansas is a very high, very mighty and very easy office—a sort of sinecure, in fact, where the favored incumbent wears "purple and fine linen," and "fares sumptuously every day"—I will take the liberty to dispel the illusion, and convince the boldest visionary that the Governorship of Kansas is a reality of the sternest kind, by a pen and ink sketch of our present surroundings ; and remember, too, that this is the most responsible looking building which we have as yet seen in the Territory, built of brick and of considerable dimensions.

Well, to locate the Gubernatorial apartment—it is some twenty feet square, has a door opening out upon (that Americanism) a "piazza ;" also a window, with a *vis-à-vis* of two windows, which look out upon a picket-fenced back yard, a hill-side and some trees. The windows are shaded by faded chintz curtains, which. even in their original freshness, never cost a fortune ; a double curled-maple four poster, which assists the sleeping of the Governor and his private secretary, occupies one corner of the room ; a wash-stand that even a "fashionable Biddy" would look askance at, stands opposite ; between the two, a little table, a crooked looking-glass, and a huge pile of law books, fill up " the aching void ;" while a rusty stove, with its rustier pipe, warms one-half of the apartment, which is, however, kept even more than comfortably cool by the ill-hung door, that lets in more air than a regiment of patent ventilators ; in *medias res* stands a larger table, littered with piles of public documents, newspapers, and writing materials, with a blue Mackinaw blanket by way of covering, on which " Our Special Correspondent " is at this moment driving a pen ; the corners and sides of the room are piled up with books—law predominating. Everything, in fact, bespeaks the residence of one, who cultivates the brain rather than the body. The Territorial seal, which, with a-half gallon of Marquand's ink, and an old pair of breeches, occupies a box at the foot of the bed, is all that tells of the power vested in its occupant. Add to this, that the floor is uncarpeted, and the walls more than slightly dilapidated, and I think that the reader will concur with me in pronouncing Wilson Shannon the most literally democratic Governor in these United States. For ourself, we are willing to go even a step farther, and declare that if the " sovereign people," after such convincing proofs of his stern republicanism, don't make him next President, they will do themselves and everybody concerned rank injustice.

I bade farewell to our hospitable friends at House on the Prairie, near Lecompton, from whence our last letter was forwarded early yesterday morning, and we regret to add that we departed with a sad foreboding that ere we met again their pleasant home (which, as we stated in our last, had been threatened with violence) ; might be made the scene of strife and bloodshed, for suspicious persons were heard moving about the place during the night, and we, ourself, at about two o'clock in the morning, heard distinctly the trampling of a horse, and the jingling accoutrements of its rider, as he twice rode round the house. The day, even for December, was intensely cold (the mercury standing at zero) ; the landscape looked cheerless in the extreme, and the sky grey and wintry. But our team, with a long ambulance attached (the whole belonging to General Whitfield, now in Washington), proved a good one ; and the vehicle, which, like most ambulances, or "prairie wagons," as they call them here, proved rather airy, was made comfortable by wrapping ourselves in buffalo robes and moccasins. So with the Governor's private secretary (Mr. Shannon), for a driver, we rolled out upon the road, with the Governor occupying a seat beside his son, while the Secretary of State, his little boy, a bright-looking youngster of nine, and " Our Correspondent," crowded the inside of the conveyance.

If we except a halt at Bean's, where we ate a primitive dinner of waxy-cold biscuits, and that external " hog meat," which, if possible, was colder than the bread, and some few gettings out to walk at bad places—for the natural roads of Kansas Territory proper, are equal, if not superior, to any in the world—there was little to interrupt the shivering, wearisome monotony of our ride ; for though men may be companionable in staging it at the start, their conversational intercourse generally terminates, unless you do some " leg stretching," with the first twenty miles, when the travellers, in most cases, subside into a gloomy, misanthropic, half dreamy state, which lasts until a halting-place thaws them out. But as our friend Woodson, the Secretary of State, did talk to us during a portion of the trip, and as Woodson began life by sticking type in " old Virginny," and ended his adventures in that section of country by becoming the editor and proprietor of a journal in Lynchburg ; and as Woodson is a clever fellow, who knows how to tell a good story well, we know that you will be pleased to get the derivation of those much quoted " Westernisms "—Lynch law and bowie-knife— as we heard them from his lips.

Lynch law owes its title to a certain Squire Lynch—a stern

and uncompromising old patriot, who lived during " the times
that tried men's souls," on his plantation, distant some three
miles from the present site of Lynchburg, Va. It was the custom in those stirring days of the Revolution, for his neighbors,
when they caught a tory, to bring the unlucky culprit before
Squire Lynch, who at once organized a court of his own selection, in which he himself was judge, jury, and counsel for the
prisoner. If the crime were proved, he would proceed to pass
sentence, by awarding from fifty to one hundred stripes, to be
well laid on ; or, it may be, even a graver penalty, in proportion
to the magnitude of the offence. And it is note-worthy, that as
this was a court from whence there was no appeal, few thought of
preaching " higher law," or taking exception to his Honor's
findings.

Our informant adds, that the old man's memory is still greatly
revered in that section of the " Old Dominion," while his descendants are justly reckoned among those highly respectable people,
" the first families of Virginia." A grandson of the Judge,
Charles H. Lynch, Esq., still resides upon the paternal estate ;
and a venerable oak, one of the real old settlers, is even now
pointed out to the curious, as the canopy under which Judge
Lynch held his rough and ready court ; those who have seen it,
say that the notches are still visible upon its moss-grown trunk,
which, in " old lang syne," kept the cords from slipping, while
the tory got his dose. The town of Lynchburg takes its name
from the Judge, and it is rumored that the grandson would
sooner lose an arm than part with the old homestead and its tory-
haunted tree.

The bowie knife yarn is simply this :—Mr. Sam Bowie, who
patronized Arkansas in those good old times when Arkansas
was what it used to be, being " curious " in his style of fighting,
wanted tools to suit himself. He therefore invented a singular
knife, which he wore inside his coat back, and as this peculiar

instrument gained a wider and bloodier popularity, it took the name of its originator, until the bowie knife has outlived the recollection of a man who knew how to use his favorite weapon as well as any citizen of the once far-famed Territory of Arkansas.

Our next paragraph should be headed "How a Governor and his Suite Look while Travelling in Kansas." And how they do look ! You should have seen His Excellency Governor Shannon yesterday, as we footed it up a steep hill at Wakarusa Creek. The Governor was ahead ; he sported, what a New York " b'hoy " would have termed a " most shocking bad hat," while his great coat and continuations looked almost as rusty as the country-built boots, which had evidently known no blacking for a week. Add to these habiliments a red worsted comforter, with the ends tucked in at the breast, and a pair of buckskin riding-gloves, and you will have a very precise inventory of the Governor's outer man upon that memorable occasion. As for the Secretary of State, he was " deil a bit better off for clothes" than his chief ; in fact, he himself affirmed that he looked more like a " Border Ruffian " than any of us. The private secretary was an improvement on either, and we flatter ourself that your humble servant, the writer, was the most fashionably (to quote from Toots) " got up " individual in " the crowd," and even he didn't cut a very insinuating figure with a smashed-up cap and a pair of gray breeches turned up over his boots—to say nothing of the butt end of a six shooter and the nozzle of a whisky flask which peered out suspiciously from either side-pocket. To complete the picture, add, forms doubled up with the cold, watering eyes, blue noses, frost-pinched cheeks, and such like " compliments of the season," and we will add no more on this head.

CHAPTER XVI.

THE PRO-SLAVERY SIDE OF THE KANSAS WAR.

AND now it is high time to be serious. We must really "quit poking fun" at Kansas, at least for this letter. Governor Shannon has been kind enough to state the facts as they have come to his knowledge, in relation to the rise, progress, and temporary termination (for we are but too fearful that the present calm is but a lull in the wild conflict of contending factions) of the unhappy difficulties in this Territory. We believe that we are in possession of the main chain of evidence ; for the details, we must refer the reader to the accompanying affidavits, letters, and official despatches, which, with statements taken down by "Our Correspondent," would seem to place the "Pro-Slavery party" in a generally favorable position. The genuineness of the documents presented may be implicitly relied upon, as they have been carefully copied by ourself from the files at the Territorial Executive office. In giving the Governor's narrative of events, which we have taken down from his own lips, we disclaim any responsibility for the subject matter, beyond the mere style of its composition. We therefore ask an impartial hearing for Governor Shannon's statement of facts in relation to the late troubles in Kansas Territory, as he has derived them from his own personal observation, or the depositions, correspondence, and verbal statements of reliable men of both parties in and about the Territory.

He says :—" On or about the 24th of November, 1855, a difficulty occurred between a Pro-Slavery man of the name of Coleman, and a Free State man named Dow, in relation to " a claim ;" this resulted in a rencounter, in which Coleman killed Dow. This gave rise to considerable excitement among the Free State people in that neighborhood, which is known as the Hickory Point settlement. In this place there are about one hundred Free State, and fifteen or sixteen Pro-Slavery, families. The excitement ran high, and the Free State men threatened to take Coleman, try, and hang him, without any legal judicial investigation, by a court and jury of their own.

" There were also among the settlers at Hickory Point two men, named Buckley and Hargis. They were Pro-Slavery men, friends of Coleman, and witnesses to the difficulty between himself and Dow. Some two days after the killing of Dow, a party of seventy-five men—a majority of whom resided in and about Lawrence—went to Hickory Point, to the residence of Hargis, and demanded of these friends of Coleman what their testimony in the matter would be. They repeated the circumstances as they intended to relate them. To this these Free State men, who were all armed with Sharpe's rifles, replied (at the same time cocking their guns and pointing them at the breasts of Buckley and Hargis), " What you say is false ; the circumstances are not so. We give you until Monday to make a correct statement of the facts. If you refuse we will kill you." This was on Saturday. Before the time given had expired, the Free State men burned down the houses of Buckley, Hargis and Coleman. In so doing they turned the family of Buckley out of doors. This family saved nothing of their wardrobe or furniture but the clothes in which they fled."

The following affidavits of Buckley and Hargis will come in very properly here—

AFFIDAVIT OF HARRISON W. BUCKLEY, IN RELATION TO THE RESCUE OF BRANSON, AND THE DIFFICULTIES, HOUSE-BURNINGS, ETC., AT HICKORY POINT.

United States of America, Territory of Kansas, ss.

Be it remembered, that on this 6th day of December, in the year A. D. 1855, personally appeared before me, J. M. Burrell, one of the Associate Justices of the Supreme Court of said Territory of Kansas, Harrison Buckley, of lawful age, who, being by me duly sworn, saith that he is a citizen of the County of Douglas, and has resided therein since 30th day of March last, and has resided during all that time at Hickory Grove; that he was informed on good authority, and which he believed to be true, that Jacob Branson had threatened his life, both before and after the difficulty between Coleman and Dow, which led to the death of the latter. He understands that Branson swore that deponent should not breathe the pure air three minutes after he returned, this deponent at this time having gone down to Westport, in Missouri.   That it was these threats, made in various shapes, that made this deponent really fear for his life, and which induced him to make affidavit against the said Branson, and procure a peace warrant to issue and be placed in the hands of the Sheriff of Douglas County. That this deponent was with the said Sheriff (S. J. Jones) at the time the said Branson was arrested, which took place about two or three o'clock in the morning.   That Branson was in bed when he was arrested by said Sheriff; that no pistol or other weapon was presented at the said Branson by any one.   That after the arrest, and after the company with the Sheriff had proceeded about five miles in the direction of Lecompton, the county seat of Douglas County, the said sheriff and his posse were set upon by between thirty and forty men, who came out from behind a house, all armed with Sharpe's rifles, presented their guns cocked, and called out asking who they were, when said Branson replied that they had got him a prisoner, and these armed men called on him to come away.   Branson then went over on their side, and Sheriff Jones said they were doing something they would regret hereafter, in resisting the laws; that he was Sheriff of Douglas County, and as such had arrested Branson.   These armed men replied that they had no laws, no Sheriff, and no Governor, and that they knew no laws but their guns.   The Sheriff, being overpowered, said to these armed men that if they took him by force of arms he had no more to say, or something to that effect, and then we rode off. This deponent further states that there have been three houses burnt in the Hickory Grove settlement; one was this deponent's house, another belonged to Josiah Hargis, and the third to said Coleman. All I had in the world was burnt up, leaving my wife and children without clothing. This deponent's wife and four children fled to Missouri, where they still remain with their relatives. The house of deponent was burnt down, as it is said, shortly before daylight in the morning. The wives and children of both Coleman and Hargis also fled to Missouri, where they still remain. There were about fifteen or sixteen law-abiding families in the settlement called the Hickory Grove settlement about the time these differences sprung up; they have all been forced, by terror and threats of these armed men, to flee with their wives and children to the State of Missouri for protection, and still remain there. These armed men have repeatedly, in my presence, said that they would resist the law by force, and that there was no law in this Territory. These threats have been repeatedly made by these men for the last three months: And further this deponent saith not.

H. W. BUCKLEY.

Sworn and subscribed, the day and year above stated, before me, J. M. Burrell, Associate Justice Supreme Court, Kansas Territory.

Here follows the Affidavit of Josiah Hargis, a Pro-Slavery man, and a member of the Sheriff's *posse* at the time of Branson's rescue from Sheriff Jones.

AFFIDAVIT OF JOSIAH HARGIS IN RELATION TO THE RESCUE OF BRANSON, AND THE DIFFICULTIES, HOUSE-BURNINGS, ETC., AT HICKORY POINT.

United States of America, Territory of Kansas, ss :

Be it remembered, that on this 7th day of December, A. D. 1855, personally came before me, S. G. Cato, one of the Associate Justices of the Supreme Court of the Territory of Kansas, Josiah Hargis, of lawful age, who, being duly sworn, deposeth and saith that, on or about the 26th day of November, 1855, in Douglas County, Sheriff Jones called upon him, with nine others, to act as a posse to arrest one Jacob Branson under a peace warrant issued by Hugh Cameron, Justice of the Peace; that he proceeded with said sheriff to Hickory Point, in said county, and there arrested said Branson, with whom they proceeded in the direction of Lawrence; when near a house on the Wakarusa an armed mob, amounting to between thirty and forty men, rushed from behind said house, and by force did rescue said Branson out of the hands of said sheriff and posse, and, in defiance of said sheriff's command, did take said Branson, and refuse to deliver him to said sheriff; that the said sheriff told the said mob that he held said Branson under a peace warrant, properly issued by a legally authorized officer, and that he was sheriff of said county of Douglas, and charged with the execution of said writ. The leader of said mob replied to said officer that they knew him as Mr. Jones, but not as sheriff of Douglas County. He then told them that he would call out the militia to enforce the law. Their reply was that he could not get men to enforce said laws. He told them then, that he would call on the Governor for assistance, to which the said mob replied that they had no laws and no officers, and to pitch in. Said mob stood with their guns cocked and presented at the time of said rescue.

This deponent further saith, that one H. W. Buckley, of said County of Douglas, was with said sheriff at the time of said rescue, as one of said sheriff's posse; that, during the same night on which said rescue was made, said affiant saw a light in the direction of said Buckley's house, and that he fully believes said house was at that time being burned; that he believes, from circumstances within his knowledge, that said house, together with his own, was burned by persons concerned with said mob; and that he has reason to believe that some of said houses were fired by said Branson aforesaid, assisted by a German commonly called Dutch Charley, and that they were counseled and advised thereto by one Farley. This affiant further says that, at the time of the rescue of said prisoner, he was at a house near Hickory Point, and that he there saw three women who told him that there had been an armed force there that day, who had notified them to leave, and all other Pro-Slavery families in the neighborhood, since when said families have left said neighborhood and fled to the State of Missouri. Said affiant further says that he believes there were at that time in said neighborhood about fifteen Pro-Slavery families, nearly all of whom have fled as aforesaid to the State of Missouri for protection. Said armed force was represented to consist of from one hundred to one hundred and fifty armed men. And further this deponent saith not.

JOSIAH HARGIS.

Sworn and subscribed before me, S. G. Cato, associate Justice, Supreme Court, Kansas Territory.

[NOTE.—The number of these men was probably exaggerated. There is also a discrepancy in the two affidavits as to the direction in which the

7*

[Sheriff's party was going at the time when this rescue is alleged to have been effected. One deponent says towards Lecompton, and the other seems equally positive that it was Lawrence.]

" Terrified by these lawless proceedings, the sixteen Pro-Slavery families residing at Hickory Point fled with their women and children into Missouri, where their accounts of the treatment to which their friends had been subjected, excited the most intense indignation among the Slaveholders of that State. From these stories, exaggerated as they spread, and it may be too highly colored by their original narrators, the impression became current throughout Missouri that the Free State party of Kansas, armed with Sharpe's rifles and revolvers, intended to expel the Pro-Slavery men from that Territory. It is alleged that such threats were made by individuals of the Free State party ; but as they do not appear to have come from responsible persons, it would be unfair to infer that this is the avowed purpose of their party. In the meantime, Buckley, Hargis, and Coleman —who had fled so soon as they could escape from the band who were threatening their execution—made their way to the Executive office at Shawnee Mission, K. T., to have an interview with myself. I was absent at the time. When I returned, Coleman had surrendered himself to the Sheriff of Douglas County (Jones), who happened to be at the mission. Buckley and Hargis stated their grievances to me, and informed me that a man named Branson, of the Free State party, and one of the residents at Hickory Point, with whom Dow (the person killed) had resided, was the leader of the band who had threatened and endeavored to extort false evidence from them. Upon these representations, I advised Buckley to go before a magistrate, or any judicial officer of the Territory, make affidavit to the facts as regarded the threats of Branson, obtain a peace-warrant against him, and thus have him bound over to keep the peace. As Sheriff Jones was about starting with Coleman in custody, and Buckley and Har-

g.... company, on their way to obtain a peace-warrant against
Branson, an express arrived from Hickory Point, which had
ridden all night, advising Coleman and his two friends not to
return to that settlement, as they would certainly be killed by
the Free State party. Sheriff Jones, with much difficulty, and
by guaranteeing their safety, at length succeeded in persuading
them to accompany him to Lecompton, the county seat of
Douglas County, in which all these difficulties had occurred, and
from whence it was of course necessary that the peace-warrant
should be issued. On his arrival there, Buckley, in pursuance with my advice, went before a justice of the peace—
Mr. Cameron—made affidavit against Branson, and obtained
a peace-warrant, which the justice placed in the hands of
Sheriff Jones for execution, who immediately summoned a
posse of ten men (citizens of Douglas County) to serve the
writ."

The affidavit of Samuel J. Jones, sheriff of Douglas County,
which we introduce here, will put the reader in possession of the
facts connected with the rescue of the prisoner Branson from
his *posse*, as alleged by the Pro-Slavery party.

It will be perceived that the sheriff's deposition is corroborated
for the most part, by those of Buckley and Hargis.

AFFIDAVIT OF SAMUEL J. JONES, SHERIFF OF DOUGLAS COUNTY, K. T., IN
RELATION TO THE RESCUE OF HIS PRISONER BRANSON, AND THE CONDUCT
OF THE FREE STATE PARTY IN LAWRENCE.

United States of America, Territory of Kansas :

Be it remembered, that, on the 7th day of December, A. D. 1855, per-
sonally came before me, S. G. Cato, one of the Associate Justices of the
Supreme Court of the Territory of Kansas, Samuel J. Jones, Sheriff of the
County of Douglas, and Territory aforesaid, of lawful age, who being by
me duly sworn, deposeth and saith, that on the 26th day of November,
A. D. 1855, he received from the hands of Hugh Cameron, a legally

appointed justice of the peace for said County of Douglas, a peace-warrant issued by said justice of the peace, and to him directed as sheriff, obtained upon the oath of one II. W. Buckley, against one Jacob Branson, and immediately after receiving said warrant he summoned a posse of ten men and proceeded to the house of said Branson, and made the arrest, and on his return he and his posse were met by a mob of some forty men, armed with Sharpe's rifles, who forcibly rescued the prisoner out of his hands, and defied his recapture, swearing at the same time that they recognized no law in the Territory, or no officers, from the Governor to the lowest officer, and relied only upon their rifles as the law of the land, and would at all times defend themselves from being arrested by any process issued by any officer of the said Territory; that he immediately made requisition on Governor Wilson Shannon for a sufficient force to arrest the said Jacob Branson, and execute other process in his hands as sheriff of said county; that the said Jacob Branson was taken into the town of Lawrence, in said county, and there, as he verily believes, as he was informed by good authority, tried and acquitted by the citizens of the said town, without any legal investigation; that a mob of some fifteen or twenty threatened to tar and feather and inflict other punishment upon the justice of the peace who issued the warrant; that he, as sheriff, has been repeatedly insulted by the citizens of the said town of Lawrence, and threatened with violence if he attempted to execute any process in his hands against any citizen of that place, and he verily believes that he would be resisted, and violence committed upon his person, in attempting to execute a legal process in said town; that the citizens of that place and vicinity are all armed with Sharpe's rifles for the avowed purpose of resisting the execution of the laws of this Territory; that they are daily being drilled for that purpose alone; that the mob who rescued the said Jacob Branson out of his hands, he verily believes, were induced to do so by the citizens of Lawrence, and that the public newspapers of that place openly recommend and call upon the citizens to resist the laws of the Territory, and that the prisoner, Jacob Branson, and a portion of the mob who rescued him from his custody, he verily believes to be at this time in the town of Lawrence, or secreted by the citizens of that place, and that warlike preparations are being made by the citizens of Lawrence for the purpose of resisting the execution of the process in his hands, and that it would not be prudent to attempt to execute said process without a very strong force to assist him, and further this deponent saith not.

S. J. JONES,

Sheriff, Douglas County, Kansas Territory.

Sworn and subscribed before me, S. G. Cato, Associate Justice of the Supreme Court of Kansas Territory.

The Governor continued—" This rescue took place on Tuesday morning, the 27th of November, at about two, A.M. The rescuing party then returned to Lawrence, where they held a meeting, at eight o'clock, A.M., on the same day. Branson, the prisoner, presided, dressed, as it is said, in a military uniform, while S N. Wood, the leader and spokesman of the rescuing party, made speeches of an incendiary character, glorying in the triumph of the Free State men over the laws of the Territory.

The following document comes in here, as being pertinent to matters alluded to by Governor Shannon in the foregoing paragraph.

STATEMENT OF JOHN P. WOOD, IN RELATION TO CIRCUMSTANCES WHICH OCCURRED IN THE TOWN OF LAWRENCE, SHORTLY AFTER THE RESCUE OF THE PRISONER BRANSON, FROM SHERIFF JONES; TAKEN DECEMBER 7, 1855.

Mr. Wood states that he was in Lawrence on or about the 27th and 28th of November, 1855, and was going up street when he met a Mr. C. W. Babcock, who informed him that on the night before, Branson had been rescued from Sheriff Jones, by a number of armed men. As Babcock and Wood continued up the street, a man named S. N. Wood approached them, dressed in a military uniform, with sword on, etc. Some one proposed three cheers for S. N. Wood, the rescuer of Branson. I heard Wood admit that he was with the mob who rescued Branson; he moreover gave the names of seven or eight others, among whom were those of Abbot, Smith, and Curless. I saw Curless afterwards, and asked him why he was engaged in such an outrage. He or some one else told me that the leaders informed him that Sheriff Jones had no writ for Branson, but had only arrested him to prevent his giving evidence against Coleman.

NOTE.—Governor Shannon's secretary informs us that the

gentleman who makes this statement (Mr. John P. Wood) is an
Illinoisian, a citizen of Lawrence, and Probate Judge of Douglas County ; he is also, a Pro-Slavery man in his politics, and a
large property holder in Lawrence, from whence he is at present
an absentee, for fear of personal violence, with which he has
been threatened by the Free State party in that town.   He has
made himself obnoxious to the Free Soilers, by holding office
under what they call "The Missouri Bogus Legislature"

CHAPTER XVII.

GOVERNOR SHANNON'S HISTORY OF THE WAKARUSA WAR.

" FROM this day forth the Free State party in Lawrence openly
commenced their military organization, by drilling, sending out
their runners—as is proven by the fact that they collected men
from points even as far distant as eighty miles—and otherwise
putting their town in a position to resist, by force of arms, the
legally constituted authorities of Kansas Territory."

"Upon the same night, about eight o'clock, I received a dispatch, by express, from the Sheriff of Douglas County (Jones),
informing me that his prisoner, Branson, had been rescued by an
armed mob. This dispatch was brought by Mr. Hargis, who
stated verbally, at the same time, that the Free State party had
that day threatened to take Coleman (then in the custody of
Sheriff Jones) from the sheriff, hang him, and also kill
Jones. The sheriff's letter asked for three thousand troops, to
protect him in the execution of the law. It was evidently written under a state of considerable excitement and apprehension."

The annexed is a copy of the letter from Sheriff Jones, asking
for *three thousand* troops—a good round number by the way—to
subdue but *forty* Free State disorganizers.

SHERIFF JONES TO GOVERNOR SHANNON:

DOUGLAS COUNTY, K. T., *Nov.* 27, 1855.

SIR.

Last night I, with a *posse* of ten men, arrested one Jacob Branson
by virtue of a peace-warrant regularly issued, who, on our return was res-

cued by a party of forty armed men, who rushed upon us suddenly from behind a house upon the road-side, all armed to the teeth with Sharpe's rifles.

You may consider an open rebellion as having already commenced, and I call upon you for *three thousand men* to carry out the laws.　Mr. Hargis (the bearer of the letter), will give you more particularly the circumstances.

Most Respectfully,
Samuel J. Jones,
Sheriff of Douglas County.

To His Excellency,
　　Wilson Shannon,
　　　　Governor of Kansas Territory.

" As these facts had reached me in an official manner, from a source of undoubted reliability, and were, moreover, corroborated by much verbal testimony as well as written evidence ; and as these latter acts of outrage (upon the part of the Free State party of Lawrence) seemed but the carrying out of their previously declared intentions, as expressed in the incendiary resolutions passed at their public meetings, which have from time to time been held in different parts of this Territory, and of which the following may be quoted as a specimen :

*　　　*　　　*　　　*　　　*　　　*　　　*　　　*

" *Resolved,* That we owe no allegiance or obedience to the tyrannical enactments of this spurious legislature ; that their laws have no validity or binding force upon the people of Kansas, and that every freeman amongst us is at full liberty, consistently with all his obligations as a citizen and a man, to defy and resist them, if he chooses so to do.

*　　　*　　　*　　　*　　　*　　　*　　　*　　　*

"*Resolved,* That we will endure and submit to these laws no longer than the best interests of the Territory require, as the least of two evils, and will resist them to a bloody issue so soon as we ascertain that peaceable remedies shall fail and forcible resistance shall furnish any reasonable prospect of success ; and that, in the meantime, we recommend to our friends throughout the Territory the organization and disciplining of volunteer companies, and the procurement and preparation of arms.

*　　　*　　　*　　　*　　　*　　　*　　　*　　　*

[These resolutions are literal copies of the originals, as they appeared in the *Herald of Freedom* for September 15, 1855. This paper is published in Lawrence, K. T., and is one of the avowed organs of the Free State party in Kansas. The resolutions quoted were passed at the Free State Delegate Convention, holden at Big Springs, K. T., on the 5th September, 1855, which convention also nominated Governor Reeder as a candidate for Congress, and fixed upon a different day for the election from that prescribed by law. This nomination Governor Reeder accepted.]

" I therefore deemed it incumbent upon me, as the chief executive of Kansas Territory, to enforce the laws and protect the sheriff, and his prisoner Coleman, from the violence and rescue which had been threatened and in part carried out by this mob, for I firmly believed (being in possession of the facts), that the overt acts just committed by the Free State party were but the commencement of a settled plan and determination to resist and bid defiance to the Territorial laws, in accordance with the resolutions already quoted.

" Under all these circumstances, I felt that I must either furnish Sheriff Jones with a sufficient posse to carry out his instructions or be forced into the disgraceful alternative of surrendering the Territorial government into the hands of an armed and lawless mob.

" And it may here be stated that the militia of Kansas were at this time (and are still) totally unorganized. The legislature had, it is true, elected two major generals in the Southern and one in the Northern division, as well as some brigadiers ; but so far as the rank and file are concerned, the organization was not even commenced.

" With the view of furnishing the sheriff with a sufficient force to serve his writs, as well as to protect himself and his prisoner Coleman against the threatened violence of the Free State mob in Lawrence, I issued orders to Major General William P. Richardson (then residing in Doniphan County), K. T., to collect as large a force as he could in his division, and repair with his men, with all practical speed, to Lecompton, where he was desired to place his command under the orders of Sheriff Jones.

"This order resulted in the collection of from one to two hundred men. Within six days from the date of my order, these men were at Lecompton, where General Richardson placed himself and his command under the orders of the sheriff. To the best of my belief these men were all citizens of Kansas. The Southern division of the militia being wholly unorganized, I simply requested Brigadier General Strickler, then residing at Tecumseh, distant only twelve miles from Lecompton, to gather as many men as possible, and report himself and command in the same manner as General Richardson.

"These instructions bore the same date as General Richardson's order, and resulted in the collection of from fifty to one hundred men."

The following are copies of the official orders issued in this emergency to Generals Richardson and Strickler :

COPY OF GOVERNOR SHANNON'S INSTRUCTIONS TO MAJOR-GENERAL WILLIAM P. RICHARDSON, COMMANDING THE MILITIA OF KANSAS TERRITORY—CALLING OUT THE MILITIA AND DIRECTING THE MANNER IN WHICH THEY SHALL BE EMPLOYED.

HEAD QUARTERS, SHAWNEE MISSION, K. T., *Nov.* 27, 1855.

MAJOR-GENERAL WILLIAM P. RICHARDSON:

SIR:

Reliable information has reached me that an armed military force is now in Lawrence, or in that vicinity, in open rebellion against the laws of this Territory; and that they have determined that no process in the hands of the sheriff of that county shall be executed. I have received a letter from S. J. Jones, the sheriff of Douglas County, informing me that he had arrested a man under a warrant placed in his hands;

and while conveying him to Lecompton, he was met by an armed force of some forty men, who rescued the prisoner from his custody, and bid open defiance to the law. I am also duly informed that a band of armed men have burned a number of houses, destroyed personal property, and turned whole families out of doors. This has occurred in Douglas County; warrants will be issued against these men and placed in the hands of Mr. Jones, the sheriff of that county, for execution; who has written to me, demanding three thousand men to aid him in preserving the peace and carrying out the process of the law.

You are hereby ordered to collect together as large a force as you can in your division, and repair without delay to Lecompton, and report yourself to S. J. Jones, Sheriff of Douglas County. You will inform him of the number of men under your control, and render him all the assistance in your power, should he require your aid in the execution of any legal process in his hands.

The forces under your command are to be used for the sole purpose of aiding the sheriff in executing the law, and for none other.

I have the honor to be,

Your obt. servt.,

WILSON SHANNON.

[NOTE.—This order reached Gen. Richardson, by special messenger, at his residence, in Doniphan County, K. T.]

Here follow the orders to General Strickler :

COPY OF GOV. SHANNON'S ORDER TO GEN. STRICKLER, CALLING UPON THAT OFFICER TO COLLECT MEN, AND GO TO THE ASSISTANCE OF THE SHERIFF OF DOUGLAS COUNTY.

HEAD QUARTERS, SHAWNEE MISSION, K. T., Nov. 27th, 1855.

GEN. H. J. STRICKLER:

SIR:

I am this moment advised by letter from S. J. Jones, sheriff of Douglas County, that while conveying a prisoner to Lecompton, whom he had arrested by virtue of a peace-warrant, he was met by a band of armed men, who took said prisoner forcibly out of his possession, and bid open defiance to the execution of law in this Territory. He has demanded of me three thousand men to aid him in carrying out the legal process in his hands. As the Southern Division of the Militia of this Territory is not yet organized, I can only *request* you to collect together as large a force as you can, and at as early a day as practicable, and report yourself, with the men you may raise, to S. J. Jones, Sheriff of Douglas County, to whom you will give every assistance in your power towards the execution of the legal process in his hands. Whatever forces you may bring to his aid are to be used *for the sole purpose of aiding the said sheriff in the execution of the law, and none other.*

It is expected that every good citizen will aid and assist the lawful authorities in.the execution of the laws of the Territory and the preservation of good order.

Your obt. servt.,
WILSON SHANNON.

To GEN. STRICKLER,
    Tecumseh, Shawnee Co.

"I presumed as a matter of course, and intended, that all these men should be drawn entirely from the citizens subject to militia duty in Kansas Territory. At that time—as the seat of difficulties (Lawrence), is distant some forty miles from the State line of Missouri—it never for a moment occurred to me that the citizens of that State would cross into Kansas or volunteer their aid to carry out her laws. I at first presumed that the forces collected under the orders issued to Generals Richardson and Strickler would have been sufficient to have protected the sheriff in the performance of the duties entrusted to him. But upon the concentration of the forces under these officers at Lecompton, which gave us a total of but two hundred and fifty men, the Free State faction collected their people in the town of Lawrence, until their reported strength reached an aggregate of six hundred men, armed, as was undoubtedly ascertained, with Sharpe's rifles and revolvers.

"This would have given the Free State faction a superiority over the militia of three hundred and fifty men, without reckoning that which they would derive from the immense superiority of the repeating arms with which they were amply furnished ; while General Richardson's command were principally supplied with fowling pieces, some having pistols and bowie knives."

CHAPTER XVIII.

CONTAINS A DIGRESSION.

"I can thus account for the intense excitement which was generated among the Pro-Slavery men of the Missouri frontier by these events, and which finally resulted in their flocking to the aid of the upholders of Territorial law in Kansas.

"Missouri has fifty thousand slaves in that portion of her territory which borders upon the frontiers of Kansas. By estimating the average value of each of those slaves at $600 (a low rate), we have a total of $30,000,000. Now, should Kansas become a Free State it would be ruinous to the slaveholding interests of Missouri. Her negroes have in several instances, already been tampered with and run off by Abolitionists ; and such acts, with the stern retaliation they are calculated to call forth, must sooner or later result in a deadly feud between the Free State and Pro-Slavery factions, which, if Kansas becomes a non-slaveholding State, would finally be handed down from father to son, and thus engender feelings of bitter and uncompromising hate on both sides.

"These facts are well known to every planter in Missouri. Nor is this all. The mere pecuniary consideration was the least exciting motive to move in this matter—their feelings had been worked upon ; they had listened to the stories of men, women and children, who had fled from homes in Kansas, made desolate by the threatened and actual violence of the Free State party

Even granting that these stories were exaggerated by the fancy
or indignation of their narrators, there was still enough of truth
in their representations to excite a smouldering fire of wrath,
which only required some new act of outrage to fan it into an
unextinguishable flame ; and this came at length in the reports
from the town of Lawrence. The men of Missouri heard that
the Territorial laws were set at defiance ; that the sheriff of
the county—a Virginian, well known and highly esteemed, and,
moreover, a strong Pro-Slavery man—was actually threatened
with death by an armed Abolition mob ; they heard, too (for
when did rumor ever lose strength as it flies ?) that these outlaws were fortifying themselves, drilling day by day, were sending to distant States for men, were amply supplied with the
most deadly weapons which modern skill has devised, and even
provided with artillery. They knew, too, that this was no disturbance born of a transient excitement, and nurtured by the
passions of an hour. On the contrary, it was understood to be
a cold-blooded, long-foreseen, and carefully prepared-for thing.
And what was the most natural result ? The gathering in the
camp at Wakarusa may best answer the question. Missouri
sent, not only her young men, but her grey-headed citizens
were there ; the man of seventy winters stood shoulder to shoulder with the youth of sixteen. There were volunteers in that
camp who brought with them not only their sons, but their
grandsons, to join, if need be, in the expected fray. Every hour
added to the excitement, and brought new fuel to the flame.
What wonder, then, that my position was an embarrassing one !
Those men came to the Wakarusa camp to fight ; they did not
ask peace : it was war—war to the knife. They would come ;
it was impossible to prevent them. What, then, was my policy ?
Certainly this : to mitigate an evil which it was impossible to
suppress, by bringing under military control these irregular and
excited forces. This was only to be accomplished by permitting

the continuance of the course which had already been adopted, without my knowledge, by Generals Richardson and Strickler—that is, to have the volunteers incorporated as they came in into the already organized command. A portion of these men, who were mostly from Jackson County, Mo., reported themselves to Sheriff Jones—by giving in a list of their names—as willing to serve in his *posse*, and he, after taking legal advice upon the question, decided to receive them. They were accordingly so enrolled. It was decided that he had a right to employ them, from the fact that as they were present in the county, the sheriff had a right to call upon them to aid in the preservation of law and order within said county, even though they might be citizens of another State, in which case, if they chose to act, their services would be legal."

ANOTHER DIGRESSION.

Although this may seem a most unwarrantable digression from what should properly be the " Governor's talk " and not ours, we will take the liberty of mentioning a fact or two which have come to our knowledge from "undoubted authority," in relation to the very fierce party zeal that was exhibited by the Pro-Slavery " Border Ruffians " who joined the forces in the Wakarusa camp. The reader will find that they endorse Governor Shannon's statement as regards an extraordinary excitement to the fullest extent.

Among those who answered to the war-signal of Strickler, or it may be to the cry of " Come up and help us," which persecuted Pro-Slavery—sent forth from Hickory Point settlement—was a very old man, a resident of one of the frontier counties of Missouri—who, so far as temperament went, was as Irish a gentleman in his " suddenness in quarrel " as ever came from that sweet spot for broken necks and duelling—County Galway. In fact there was no cooling him. Time had tried it but given

up the job in despair, for though the snows of seventy odd winters had whitened upon his head, the warm blood of five-and-
twenty yet lingered around his heart.   He was Pro-Slavery—
withal—to the back bone.   With him to hate the Abolitionists
was to "do God service."   So the old-man was not only among
the first to take the field himself, but literally carried out the
assertion of the Governor by bringing with him not only his
son but his *grandson* to join, if need be, in the expected fray.   And
it is related of this veteran, that while enduring the hardships,
which, owing to the severity of the season, were peculiarly
severe, of a soldier's life in the Wakarusa camp, he one day
exhibited his musket, an antiquated flint-lock of the condemned
old fogy pattern— which he paraded with no little pride, at the
same time giving vent to these very decided words :—

"Gentelmen," said this warrior of seventy—"Gentelmen,
this hyar old firelock war carried by my father through thar
dark days of thar Revolution—the days that tried men's souls
—as I heerd a chap say when he war a makin' a stump speech
down in Arkansaw ; but I'll be (here the old man ripped out a
very English oath, and brought down the butt of the piece
with a·crash to the ground); yes, I'll be derned, gentelmen, *ef
she war ever carried in a better cause than this.*"

Another "returned volunteer" yarn·goes on to state that
some of these "fire-eating" Missouri Pro-Slavery boys were
even heard to *affirm*, in their very un-*friend*-ly way, that they
"*didn't kear whether thar whisky gin out or not*"—that they
"had come thar for a fight, and jest allowed to stop whar they
were, ef it should be fur a month of Sundays, but what they'd
git one."

Touching which, if you don't know far-western men, my
amiable reader, we can assure you that there is a terrible signi-
ficance in their being,willing to stay where they were, " whether
thar whisky gin out or not ;" for when a frontiersman says

that, he means something, for under such circumstances, the main spring of action, whatever it may be, must " have the strength of forty jackasses," as, without " the corn," a Borderer—to use his own expression—is " no whar ;" indeed it has even been hinted by very old settlers that the " Old Scratch " himself couldn't keep a Missourian quiet, even for four-and-twenty hours, in that place which shall be nameless to Methodistical ears—unless he had a gourd full of highly rectified along with him, and mayhap a fiddle beside.

What wonder then, that our new-made Governor should have found himself very much in the position of the unlucky Scotch man in the story, who stood on a cliff, " with the Deil on on side and the deep sea upon the other." What a dilemma indeed was his, for a newly-fledged Territorial Executive. With him it was indeed both " save me from my friends," and " preserve me from my enemies." Let us explain our parallel between Governor Shannon's position, and that of the bedevilled Sawney, just alluded to. The gubernatorial throne of Kansas may well represent the cliff, with this exception, perhaps, that it is hardly lofty enough to break even a democratic politician's neck were he to tumble from

" His high estate."

Then for the De'il : what apter illustration could you find than those Satanic Border Ruffians, whom all Lawrence count as children of wrath, and servants of the arch-fiend himself. And for a similitude to the deep sea, we point most triumphantly to the Free State party, who are, or say they are—which in American politics comes, now-a-days, to very nearly the same thing, as mighty as the sea, and for all we know to the contrary, as *deep*. Were a Pro-Slavery man to carry out the idea, he would probably say, that as regards the loaves and fishes of office, they would carry out our Oceanic thought to a charm, by swallowing them up, as did the rock which closed on Korah, Dathan and

8

Abiram. But stay, there's something else. We must suppose the "Deil," in this instance, to be upsetting the gubernatorial throne with a pitchfork, which, on a close inspection, will be found to be labelled, Black Republicanism and the opinions of the press. What wonder, then, we repeat, that our friend Shannon should find himself in a situation, which can only be expressed by the somewhat vulgar comparison of " a divil of a mess."

How easy it is for us, good quiet people that we are, to chat over " the troubles in Kansas," in our well-furnished drawing-rooms after dinner, where we say, Shannon should have done that, and the Governor ought not to have done this ; *apropos* to which, my very self-sufficient friend, did you never observe, that when the journals of the day are filled with the particulars of some terrible disaster upon the storm-swept ocean, there are hundreds of warmly-housed citizens

" Whose souls would sicken on the heaving wave,"

who sit down in their snug chambers, and speak, as they toast their slippered toes at an anthracite heaped grate, of the sea-faring man—who hoped, and struggled, and battled manfully to the last, until he had vainly exhausted every resource which experience or skill could devise, to save the gallant bark committed to his care—as an ignoramus, a coward, and an ass—a stupid fellow who ought never to have had a command, coupled, perchance, with what *they* would have done, or what they *think* they would have done under like circumstances. And now, who shall say that these remarks are not quite as applicable to the unwarrantable criticisms which are so frequently passed upon those whose curse it is to sail that most unmanageable of all storm-driven craft, " the Ship of State ?" Yet does not every day prove, how nicely—*upon paper*, our good people at the North, many of whom never saw a log-cabin, and do but dream of " outside barbarians," *could* " take in the rags" for a Kansas

Governor, where the wind "blows great guns" from the South, or put his bark under "close reefed taup-sails," when a Free State tempest is at hand?   But we, for one, should be mighty pleased, as we have but a "Union interest" in this "Ship of State," to see some of these bold pretenders try a "trick at the wheel," which, and we mistake not, would most probably "eventuate" in their being rolled into the lee scuppers with her first lurch to port.

But let us get back, with an apology for interrupting him, to the Governor's history of the "Wakarusa War."

"The Pro-Slavery forces thus collected, including the militia, amounted on the 1st or 2nd of December, 1855 (as it was then stated to me at the Shawnee Mission), to about 1,500 men, and it was also reported that about an equal number of Free State men had concentrated at Lawrence. I became satisfied that in all probability a deadly collision must take place, and that the only way to avoid that collision was to request the aid of the general government.   I was, moreover, in the receipt of a communication from Brigadier-General Eastin, of the Northern Brigade, K. M., putting me in possession of information from Lawrence, and recommending the employment of the United States forces at Fort Leavenworth."

The following is the communication referred to from General Eastin.

LEAVENWORTH, K. T., Nov. 30th, 1855.

GOVERNOR SHANNON:

Information has been received here direct from Lawrence, which I consider reliable, that the outlaws of Douglas County are well fortified at Lawrence with cannon and Sharpe's rifles, and number *at least* one thousand men. It will, therefore, be difficult to dispossess them.

The militia in this portion of the State are entirely unorganized, and mostly without arms.

I suggest the propriety of calling upon the military at Fort Leaven worth. If you have the power to call out the Government troops, I think it would be best to do so at once. It might overawe these outlaws and prevent bloodshed.

(Signed)   L. J. EASTIN,
Brig. General, Northern Brigade, K. M.

"To obtain the coöperation of the general government, I telegraphed on the 1st of December from Kansas City, Missouri, to President Pierce, that I requested authority to call upon Colonel Sumner, commanding at Fort Leavenworth, for such military aid as should enable me to protect the sheriff of Douglas County in executing the laws, and preserving peace and good order in the Territory."

[NOTE.—As this dispatch, with the President's reply, as also the Proclamation of Governor Shannon, dated on the 29th of November, from the executive office at Shawnee Mission, have already been published, until they have become as threadbare as Paddy O'Flaherty's Sunday coat, it is hardly worth while to recapitulate them here, the more so, as there is "sorrow a taste of divarsion" in either of them.]

"I also dispatched a messenger to Col. Sumner, 1st Cavalry, U. S. A., at Fort Leavenworth, notifying him of what I had done, and requesting him to hold himself and command in readiness, in case the orders should be received ; to which he promptly replied that he would be ready to move with his men at a moment's warning, as soon as the requisite instructions should come."

Here follows a copy of Col. Sumner's letter to Governor Shannon in reply to the dispatch just referred to. Of the Governor's letter, which was dated from Shawnee Mission on the same day, no copy was retained, but its contents are embodied in "the statement." Col. Sumner's letter runs thus :

HEAD QUARTERS, 1ST CAVALRY, FORT LEAVENWORTH, *December* 1st, 1855.
GOVERNOR:

I have just received your letter of this day. I do not feel that it would be right in me to act in this important matter until orders are received from the government. I shall be ready to move instantly whenever I receive them. I would respectfully suggest that you make your application for aid to the government extensively known at once, and I would countermand any orders that may have been given for the movement of the militia until you receive the answer. I write this in ——.

With much respect, your obdt. servt.,
(Signed) E. V. SUMNER,
Col. First Cavalry.

His Excellency,
    GOVERNOR SHANNON.

NOTE.—This letter was received by Governor Shannon on the 2d of December, at Shawnee Mission. The Governor immediately adopted the suggestions contained therein, and accordingly addressed letters to General Richardson and Sheriff Jones, which are annexed as follows, together with Sheriff Jones's reply, and a communication from General Richardson to the Governor, asking permission to demand a surrender of the arms then in possession of the Free State party in Lawrence.

Copy of instructions from Governor Shannon to General Richardson commanding the Territorial militia to carry out the suggestions contained in Colonel Sumner's letter of the 1st:

GOVERNOR SHANNON TO GENERAL RICHARDSON.

EXECUTIVE OFFICE, SHAWNEE MISSION, K. T., *December 2d*, 1855.
MY DEAR SIR:

I have written a letter to Sheriff Jones, informing him of what I have done, and putting him in possession of the fact that I am in constant expectation of receiving authority from Washington to call out the regular troops at Fort Leavenworth. I have notified Colonel Sumner of this, and am in receipt of his reply, assuring me that he will be ready at any moment to move with the whole force at his command, so soon as the orders are received from the General Government. These orders are confidently expected in a day or two. I am desirous to employ the United States forces, as it would have a most salutary effect upon these lawless men hereafter; for when they find that the regular troops can be used to preserve the peace and execute the law in this Territory, they will not be so ready to place themselves in a hostile attitude. In the meanwhile you will remain with Sheriff Jones, and retain a sufficient force with you to protect that officer, and secure the safety of his prisoner; the remainder of your men will be kept at a distance, but be held in readiness to give their services whenever they may be required to act. You will be careful in preserving order, and in restraining your people from any illegal act. *Let everything that is done, be for the preservation of law and order.* Your duties are to protect the Sheriff, and enable him to serve the legal process in his hands; when these objects are accomplished, your command will retire.

I shall accompany Colonel Sumner with the United States forces, when they move.

Yours, with great respect,

WILSON SHANNON.

MAJOR GENERAL RICHARDSON,
Camp at Lecompton.

[NOTE.—This letter was forwarded by express, together with the communication to Sheriff Jones.]

Copy of instructions from Governor Shannon to the Sheriff of Douglas County—Samuel J. Jones—to carry out the suggestions contained in Colonel Sumner's letter of the 1st:

GOVERNOR SHANNON TO SHERIFF JONES.

EXECUTIVE OFFICE, SHAWNEE MISSION, K T., *December 2d*, 1855.

SIR:

I am in receipt of Colonel Sumner's reply to my dispatch, in which he informs me that he will be ready at a moment's warning to move with his whole force, if desired, on the arrival of his orders from Washington. My telegraphic dispatch to the President must have reached its destination by this time, and an answer should soon come to hand. I have no doubt but that the authority which I have requested—to call upon the United States troops—will be granted. Under these circumstances, you will wait until I can obtain the desired orders before attempting to execute your writs. This will save any effusion of blood, and may have a moral influence hereafter, which would prevent any farther resistance to the law; for when these lawless men find that the forces of the United States can be used to preserve order, they will not be so ready to adopt an opposing course. And if necessary, steps will be taken to station an adequate force in the disturbed district to protect the people against mob violence, and to secure the fulfillment of the laws.

You will retain a sufficient force to protect yourself and guard your prisoner; anything beyond this had better remain at a distance, until it can be ascertained whether their aid will or will not be needed. The known deficiency in arms, and all the accoutrements of war which must necessarily characterize the law-abiding citizens, who have rushed to your assistance in the maintenance of order, will invite resistance from your opponents, who are well supplied with arms; it would be wrong, therefore, to place your men in a position where their lives would be endangered, when we shall in all probability have an ample force from Fort Leavenworth in a few days.

Show this letter to Major-General Richardson, and also to General Eastin, who, as I am advised, have gone to your aid. Their destination is Lecompton, but they will join you wherever you are. Their forces are but small, and may be required for your protection until advices are received from Washington.

I send you, with this, a communication to General Richardson, which you will please deliver to him at as early a day as practicable. As I refer him to this my letter to you, for my views, you will permit him to read it. Let me know what number of warrants you have, and the names of the defendants. I shall probably accompany Col. Sumner's command,

Yours, with great respect,
WILSON SHANNON.

SHERIFF JONES, *Lecompton.*

SHERIFF JONES'S REPLY.

CAMP, AT WAKARUSA, *Dec. 4th,* 1855.

HIS EXCELLENCY, GOVERNOR WILSON SHANNON:

SIR:

In reply to your communication of yesterday I have to inform you that the volunteer forces, now at this place and at Lecompton, are getting weary of inaction. They will not I presume, remain but a very short time longer, unless a demand for the prisoner is made. I think I shall have a sufficient force to.protect me by to-morrow morning. The force at Lawrence is not half so strong as reported; I have this from a reliable source. If I am to wait for the Government troops, more than two-thirds of the men now here will go away, very'much dissatisfied. They are leaving hourly as it is. I do not, by any means, wish to violate your orders, but I really believe that if I have a sufficient force, it would oe better to make the demand.

It is reported that the people of Lawrence have run off those offenders from that town, and, indeed, it is said that they are now all out of tne way. I have writs for sixteen persons, who were with the party that rescued my prisoner. S. N. Wood, P. R. Brooks, and Saml. Tappan are of Lawrence, the balance from the country round. Warrants will be placed in my hands to-day for the arrest of G. W. Brown, and probably others in Lecompton. They say that they are willing to obey the laws, but no confidence can be placed in any statements they may make.

No evidence sufficient to cause a warrant to issue has as yet been brought against those lawless men who fired the houses.

I would give you the names of the defendants, but the writs are in my office at Lecompton. Most respectfully yours,

SAML. J. JONES,
Sheriff of Douglas Co

The following is a copy of a letter from Major-General Richardson to Governor Shannon, in which the General requests permission to demand the surrender of the Free State people's arms.

GENERAL RICHARDSON TO GOVERNOR SHANNON.

LECOMPTON, K. T., *Dec. 3d*, 1855, 12 *o'clock*, P. M.

HIS EXCELLENCY, GOVERNOR WILSON SHANNON:

DEAR SIR:

I believe it to be essential to the peace and tranquillity of the Territory that the outlaws at Lawrence and elsewhere should be required to surrender their Sharpe's rifles. There can be no security for the future safety of the lives and property of law-abiding citizens unless these unprincipled men are (at least) deprived of the arms, which, as we all know, have been furnished them for the purpose of resisting the law—in fact, peaceable citizens will be obliged to leave the Territory, unless those who are now threatening them are compelled to surrender their rifles, and artillery, if they have any.

I do not, however, feel authorized from the instructions which you have given me, to make this demand. Should you concur with me in my opinion, please let me know by express at once.

A fresh rider had better be sent up in lieu of the bearer of this, as he will be fatigued. I am diligently using every possible precaution to prevent the effusion of blood and preserve the peace of the Territory. As the Sharpe's rifles may be regarded as private property by some, I can give a receipt for them, stating that they will be returned to their owners at the discretion of the Governor.

Very respectfully your obdt. servt.,

WILLIAM P. RICHARDSON,
Major-General, commanding Kansas Territorial Militia.

"On the 4th of December, the telegraph lines being down between Lexington and Jefferson City, Missouri (my dispatch being therefore sent by special messenger during the interval), I received a reply, dated December 3d, from the President, stating that the Executive would use all the power at his command to preserve order in the Territory, and to enforce the execution of the laws, and as soon as the proper orders could be made out at the War Department, they would be transmitted. I immediately forwarded a copy of the President's telegraphic dispatch to Col. Sumner, requesting him to march (on the strength of that dispatch), with his men to the Delaware crossing of the Kansas—twelve miles above its mouth, at which post I would meet and accompany his command to the scene of difficulty.

"Col. Sumner replied that he would do so, as it was a case of extreme emergency. (I had written him that time was everything, as things were rapidly coming to a crisis.)"

Here follows a copy of Col. Sumner's reply :

8*

COL. SUMNER TO GOVERNOR SHANNON.

HEAD QUARTERS FIRST CAVALRY, *Dec. 5th*, 1855, 1 *o'clock*, A. M.
GOVERNOR:

I have just received your letter of yesterday, with the telegraphic despatch from the President. I will march with my regiment in a few hours, and will meet you at the Delaware crossing of the Kansas *this evening.*   With high respect, your obedient servant,
(Signed)   E. V. SUMNER,
Col. First Cavalry.

His Excellency,
WILSON SHANNON.

[NOTE.—This letter was received by the Governor, at Shawnee Mission, early on the morning of the 6th.]

"About this time a committee waited upon me from Lawrence, of Free State men—claiming to represent the citizens of that town (Messrs. Lowry and Babcock). They stated that the people of Lawrence were surrounded by a body of armed men, who were threatening to demolish their town, and requested me to exercise my authority to preserve peace and save their city. They produced a letter signed by the leading men of Lawrence."

The following, although the date of its receipt is not given, must have reached Governor Shannon about this time :

CAMP ON WAKARUSA, *Dec. 4. 1855.*
SIR:

Inclosed is a dispatch from Gen. Richardson. I have the honor to inform you that I was in Lawrence yesterday, and found two hundred and fifty men under arms, and about six hundred men in the town willing to bear arms against the officers. In camp Wakarusa there are now about two hundred and fifty men under my command.
Yours respectfully,
H. J. STRICKLER,
Com. S. Division.

GOV. SHANNON.

Finding that affairs in Lawrence and its vicinity were fast tending to a crisis, I determined to repair there immediately, in person.

"I accordingly addressed a communication to Colonel Sumner, apologizing to him for not meeting him at the Delaware crossing, as I had promised, and adding that as I was going to push on, ahead, I hoped he would follow with his command, as rapidly as possible. It was my desire to have had the Colonel's men stationed in Lawrence, for I knew, if it could be effected, it would prevent an attack. On the night previous to my leaving for Lawrence, I sent a special messenger, with three separate dispatches, to Generals Richardson and Strickler, and to Sheriff Jones, to prevent an attack or disorder of any kind"

CHAPTER XIX.

THE GOVERNOR CONTINUES HIS NARRATIVE.

"At half past three o'clock, P. M., on the 5th of December, I left Shawnee Mission, went to Westport, Mo. (distant some two and a half miles from the Mission), and requested Col. Boone—a grandson of Col. Boone of frontier memory, and the Postmaster at Westport—to accompany me to Lawrence, and, as his acquaintance with the leading Pro-Slavery men who were then in the camp near Lawrence was extensive, give me the benefit of his influence in keeping down an excitement and preventing any rash act upon the part of the troops then threatening that town. This he instantly agreed to do, and I owe much to his valuable assistance in restraining the volunteers. We journeyed in company to the scene of action. Shortly after leaving Westport we met a dispatch from Colonel Sumner, First Cavalry, stating that upon reflection he had concluded not to march with his command until his orders from the War Department had been received.

Here follows a copy of Col. Sumner's dispatch, written upon "maturer reflection :"

COLONEL SUMNER TO GOVERNOR SHANNON.

HEAD QUARTERS FIRST CAVALRY, FORT LEAVENSWORTH,
Dec. 5th, 1855.

GOVERNOR:

On more mature reflection I think it will not be proper for me to move before I receive the orders of the Government. I shall be all ready whenever I get them. This decision will not delay our reaching the scene of the difficulties, for I can move from this place to Lawrence as quickly (or nearly so) as I could from the Delaware crossing, and we could not, of course, go beyond that place without definite orders.

With high respect, your obedient servant,

E. V. SUMNER,
Colonel First Cavalry.

His Excellency,
WILSON SHANNON.

"We then proceeded as rapidly as possible to the Wakarusa camp (within six miles of Lawrence), which was occupied by that portion of the Pro-Slavery forces under the command of General Strickler, and reached it about three o'clock A. M. on the 6th.

Early on the morning of the 6th, I sent a request to Major General Richardson to meet me at the Wakarusa camp, and bring with him the leading men of the Lecompton camp. One of the objects in dividing the Pro-Slavery forces into the two camps of Lecompton and Wakarusa, distant from each other by eighteen miles, was to prevent those men in Lawrence against whom the sheriff had writs, from escaping, another was to take advantage of the very favorable camping ground afforded by the Wakarusa bottom, as its facilities for obtaining fuel, water, and sheltering timber, rendered it a desirable location for the troops.

About 3 P. M., General Richardson, with a number of the most prominent men from the Lecompton camp, arrived at my quarters (which I had established at an Indian house on the east side of the Wakarusa, and about a quarter of a mile from the Wakarusa camp). I had been engaged during the day up to the very moment of Gen. Richardson's arrival, in conference with the leading men of the Wakarusa camp, with the view of ascertaining their feelings and intentions, and if possible prevailing upon them to co-operate with me in carrying out my views. For myself, I had two leading objects, which I had determined to use every exertion to accomplish :—One, to prevent the effusion of blood ; the other, to vindicate the supremacy of the laws. I found in the Wakarusa camp a strong disposition which appeared to be almost universal, to attack Lawrence.

For the purpose of furthering the objects I had in view, I invited between thirty and forty of their leading men from the two camps to meet me on the night of the 6th, at my quarters, with the intention of explaining to them my desires and purposes and inviting a similar confidence on their part in return.

They convened at my quarters, accordingly, at eight o'clock P. M., when I addressed them at length, defining the position which I intended to occupy and the ends which I hoped to gain, and finally begged them to explain freely, their wishes and expectations as to the settlement of the existing difficulties. I soon discovered that there was but one person present who fully approved of the course which I desired to pursue. The others wished to go further ; some would hear of nothing less than the destruction of Lawrence and its fortifications, the demolition of its printing presses, and the unconditional surrender of the arms of the citizens ; others, more moderate, expressed a willingness to be satisfied, if the Free State party would give up their Sharpe's rifles and revolvers. Under these unfavorable circumstances the conference broke up at midnight, having accomplished nothing beyond the interchange of opinions on either side. Before its adjournment, however, I informed them that I would enter Lawrence upon the ensuing day (the 7th), and ascertain what arrangements the Free Sate party were willing to make, and what terms they would accede to. On the part of the Pro-Slavery men there seemed to be so fixed a purpose to assault the town that I almost despaired of preventing it, unless I could obtain the services of the United States troops at Fort Leavenworth. With the intention of communicating my wishes to Col. Sumner, the commandant of that post, I made arrangements with Gen. Strickler, commanding in the Wakarusa camp, to furnish me with an express rider at daybreak, to start immediately for Fort Leavenworth. I at once wrote a pressing letter to Col. Sumner of which the following is a copy :

GOVERNOR SHANNON TO COLONEL SUMNER.

WAKARUSA, December, 6th, 1855.

COL. SUMNER, 1st Cavalry, U. S. A.:

   SIR :

I send you this special dispatch to ask you to come to Lawrence as soon as you possibly can. My object is to secure the citizens of that place, as well as all others, from a warfare which, if once commenced, there is no telling where it will end. I doubt not that you have received orders from Washington, but if you have not, the absolute pressure of this crisis is such as to justify you with the President, and the world, in moving with your force to the scene of difficulties.

It is hard to restrain the men here (*they are beyond my power, or at least soon will be*), from making an attack upon Lawrence, which, if once made, there is no telling where it may terminate. The presence of a portion of the United States troops at Lawrence would prevent an attack—save bloodshed—and enable us to get matters arranged in a satisfactory way, and at the same time secure the execution of the laws. *It is peace, not war, that we want*, and you have the power to secure peace. Time is precious—fear not but that you will be sustained.

With great repect,
WILSON SHANNON.

N. B.—Be pleased to send me a dispatch.

COL. SUMNER'S REPLY.

HEAD-QUARTERS FIRST CAVALRY, FORT LEAVENWORTH, Dec. 7, 1855.

GOVERNOR :

   I have received your two letters of the 5th and 6th inst. I regret extremely to disappoint you, but the more I reflect on it the more I am convinced that I ought not to interpose my command between the two hostile parties in this territory until I receive orders from the Government. We know that the whole matter is now in the hands of the Executive, and it is an affair of too much importance for any one to anticipate the action of the Government. I am momentarily expecting to receive orders, and whenever they come I shall move instantly, by.night or by day. If you find those people bent on attacking the town, I would respectfully suggest that they might be induced to pause for a time on being told that the orders of the General Government were expected every moment, and that there was no doubt but that these orders, framed from an enlarged view of the whole difficulty, would give general satisfaction, and settle the matter honorably for both parties.

I am, Governor, with much respect, your obedient servant,

E. V. SUMNER,
Colonel 1st Cavalry, Commanding.

His Excellency WILSON SHANNON,
    Governor of Kansas.

"At 2, P. M., 7th December, Gen. Stricklercame to my quarters, and informed me that he had been advised that a plan had been laid in the Wakarusa camp to intercept my dispatches to Col. Sumner at Caw River crossing. To avoid this, I requested the General to start the messenger immediately. He did so ; and the express rider finally left at 2 o'clock, A. M., and was directed to a ford upon Caw River (not the usual crossing), by an Indian guide from the Caw bottom, who had been procured for the purpose by Col. Boone. To his letter I received no reply until after my return to the executive office at Shawnee Mission, when an answer reached me on the 11th of December.

"The object of the Pro-Slavery men in attempting to intercept the dispatches, was to prevent, if possible, the arrival of the United States troops, who, they feared, would restrain them from attacking Lawrence. By gaining time, they expected to make the assault before any force could be brought to mediate between the conflicting parties."

NOTE : The following letter from Mr. J. C. Anderson, may very properly be introduced here, as an evidence of the highly excited state of feeling then existing in the Pro-Slavery camp,

to which Governor Shannon refers, when—in his communication
to Col. Sumner—he speaks of these people as being beyond his
control.   Mr. Anderson's letter is addressed to Major General
Richardson, the commander of the Pro-Slavery forces.   The
writer is a member of the Kansas Legislature, and resides at
Fort Scott—is strongly Pro-Slavery in his politics, and though
quite young, took a leading part in the so-called " Bogus Legislature ;" he is said, moreover, to be a person of considerable
ability.

J. C. ANDERSON TO GENERAL RICHARDSON.

[No date. Governor Shannon's secretary suggests that they were so
busily engaged in the Wakarusa camp, at the period when this epistle was
penned, in trying to get a chance at *Eternity*, that they lost all track of
time.]

MAJOR GENERAL WILLIAM P. RICHARDSON:

  SIR:

      I have reason to believe from rumors in camp that before to-
morrow morning the *black flag** will be hoisted, when nine out of ten will
rally round it, and march without orders upon Lawrence. The forces at
the Lecompton camp fully understand the plot, and will fight under the
same banner.

If Governor Shannon will pledge himself not to allow any United States
officer to interfere with the arms belonging to the United States now
in their possession,† and, in case there is no battle, order the United States
forces off at once, and retain the militia, provided any force is retained—
all will be well, and all will obey to the end, and commit no depredation
upon private property in Lawrence.

I fear a collision between the United States soldiers, and the volunteers,
which would be dreadful.

Speedy measures should be taken. Let the men *know at once—to-night*

---

* The " black flag" was to be the signal for action, in case the more incendiary portion
of the Pro-Slavery forces should determine to take the punishment of the Free State party
into their own hands.

† Most probably referring to certain United States arms (it is said muskets), which some
of the Clay County (Mo.) Volunteers are reported to have taken from the arsenal in that
vicinity.

—and I fear that it will even then be *too late to stay the rashness of our people.*

Respectfully your obedt. servt.,

J. C. ANDERSON.

"On the morning of the 7th I repaired to the town of Lawrence, having on the evening of the 6th been invited, by a committee representing the citizens of that town, to visit their place, for the purpose of arranging, if possible, the difficulties which then threatened them. On my road to Franklin, which lies midway upon the route, I was met by a committee of ten citizens of Lawrence, who escorted me into their town, where I was courteously received. I was conducted to an upper chamber in the Emigrant Aid Society's Hotel, and had a long interview with Generals Charles Robinson and James H. Lane, the commanders of the Free-State forces, who were appointed on the part of the Lawrence people to confer with me in relation to the then existing difficulties. They seemed to feel no hesitation in assuring me that the territorial laws should be executed, and that there should be no obstacle presented to the serving of any legal process ; they, however, as representatives of the citizens of Lawrence, reserved to themselves the right of testing the validity of these laws in the Supreme Court of the United States. They both claimed that the majority of the citizens of Lawrence and its vicinity had never taken any other ground. I did not—although well aware of the incendiary nature of the resolutions which had been repeatedly passed at the various meetings of their party—consider it necessary at the time to enter into any controversy with them in relation to their previous position as regarded the execution of the territorial laws —though they had repeatedly declared those laws null and of no effect, and avowed their determination to "resist them to a bloody issue.' I felt it to be my duty to accept their present declaration as an apology for the past, and an assurance (hollow though it

might be) of improvement for the future. While I was determined, by every means in my power, and even if necessary by
an appeal to arms, to exact obedience to the law, I felt urged
by every dictate of humanity to prevent a collision which would
inevitably have resulted in the utter destruction of Lawrence
and its inhabitants. This was, indeed, no time to revive past
offences, for I felt fully convinced that so far as Lawrence and
its inhabitants were concerned, ' *moments were hours.*'

"I satisfied myself, however, that there was then no person in
the town against whom writs had been caused to issue, as the
parties had left the place several days before. I then, moved by
the consideration of the fearful danger in which their people stood,
stated to them that so far as I was concerned, as the chief executive of the Territory, the arrangements which they appeared
willing to enter into in good faith would be satisfactory to me ;
that my sole purpose was to secure a faithful execution of the
laws ; that I asked nothing more, and that object obtained, I
should at once disband the *posse.* At the same time I explained
to them the difficulty of prevailing upon the highly-incensed
forces then surrounding Lawrence to retire without attacking
the place or demanding the surrender of the Sharpe's rifles and
revolvers, with which they were well known to be armed. I
added, moreover, that the idea was universally prevalent, both
in the Lecompton and Wakarusa camps, that these weapons had
been furnished from the East for the purpose of resisting the
execution of the Territorial laws of Kansas, and making her a
free State. The committee declared that these weapons had
neither been procured nor distributed for any such end, but
simply to defend the ballot-box from invasion. Yet it cannot be
denied that they admitted to me that these arms were forwarded
in boxes from the East, having been written for by General
Robinson for the purpose aforesaid. It was also claimed by
General Robinson that these arms were now the property of

individuals, as they had been distributed to, and a certain amount of moneys paid for them by the persons in whose hands they then were; that is to say, each man who received a Sharpe's rifle paid *something* as an equivalent; but, from what has transpired, it is my belief that the amount so paid bore no proportion to the real cost or value of the arms; in fact, it is currently reported that the sum paid for these Sharpe's rifles by their receivers did not average over three dollars per man. It is computed that there are now in this Territory 1,200 Sharpe's rifles, which have been brought into it for the purpose of arming the Free State faction. The cost of these arms, calculating them at $30 each, would give a total of $36,000. Now, supposing that this rumor be true, that each of these deadly weapons bring but $3 in Kansas, or a total for the 1,200 of but $3,600—who, let me ask, loses the difference of $32,400? And it will be perceived that this calculation makes no allowance for the expenses of transportation from the East.

"As I found that to insist upon the Free State troops in Lawrence giving up their arms, or to make it a *sine qua non* in our arrangement, would inevitably lead to a conflict, which as I have before stated, I most earnestly desired to avoid, I therefore merely *suggested* to the committee that they should surrender their arms to Major General Richardson, and I would direct that officer to receipt for the weapons so received; it being understood that in the event of their so doing, the arms thus receipted for, should be restored, when, in the opinion of the chief executive, it could be done with propriety; or, if they preferred it, they might, in the same manner, surrender them to me. I had hoped that this arrangement could have been effected, as it would have enabled me to induce the forces then threatening Lawrence to withdraw without committing any acts of violence. This proposition was positively declined. The committee qualified their refusal, however, by stating, on the part of the citizens of Lawrence, that if at any time I would make a requisition in writing, stating that those arms were required for the purpose of preserving peace and good order, they would use their influence to comply with that requisition. I then closed the interview, being satisfied that they would not deliver up their arms without a fight. I returned to the Wakarusa camp, which I reached about half-past 10 o'clock, P. M. I immediately sought an interview with the most influential men of that camp, stated to them the result of my visit to Lawrence, and reported what the citizens of that town would, and would *not*, do in the matters under consideration. To a large majority of the Wakarusa camp the concessions made by the Lawrence people were wholly unsatisfactory, but a number of the leading men, although dissatisfied with the terms offered, agreed to use their influence with their companions to induce their immediate and peaceable withdrawal.

"At 1 A. M., Dec. 7, I learned fram a reliable source that a plan was on foot to raise the "black flag," with the view of throwing off the authority of the Territorial executive and its officers and attacking Lawrence upon their own responsibility. I renewed my endeavors for peace, and with the leading men did all in my power to dissuade these hot-headed people from so unauthorized a movement."

NOTE.—The following orders were issued by Governor Shannon upon the 8th of December, to Generals Richardson and Strickler, to prevent any unauthorized attack from being made by the Pro-Slavery volunteers upon Lawrence, during the negotiations which were then pending between the leaders of the opposing parties :

GOVERNOR SHANNON TO GENERAL RICHARDSON.

WAKARUSA, *December 8th*, 1855.

MAJOR GENERAL RICHARDSON:

SIR:

You will repress all movements of a disorderly character, and take no steps except by order from me. If any unauthorized demonstration should be made upon Lawrence, you will immediately use your whole force to check it, as in the present state of negotiations an attack upon Lawrence would be wholly unjustifiable.

Your obdt. servant,
WILSON SHANNON.

GOVERNOR SHANNON TO GENERAL STRICKLER.

WAKARUSA, *December 8th*, 1855.

GENERAL STRICKLER:

SIR:

You will repress any movements of a disorderly character. No attack must be permitted upon the town of Lawrence in the present state of things, as with the concessions they have made, and are willing to make to the supremacy of the law, such an attack would be wholly unjustifiable.

Your obdt. servant,
WILSON SHANNON.

CHAPTER XX.

GOVERNOR'S NARRATIVE CONTINUED—THE TREATY.

"On the morning of the 8th of December things looked still worse. I was advised by a prominent man that unless the citizens of Lawrence gave up their arms, the place would be attacked, and I had better consult my own safety and keep out of danger. My reply was, that I should consider any such attack, after the declarations which had been made by the people of Lawrence, as wholly unjustifiable, and that I should use every means in my power to prevent it. This I at once made preparations to do. Early in the morning I left my quarters and repaired to the Wakarusa camp, and again sought out some prominent individuals and secured their assistance. Upon consultation with these gentlemen, one of the most distinguished, proposed to select a committee of thirteen captains, to meet at Franklin a committee from the Lawrence camp, with the view of frankly interchanging opinions, and if possible, coming to some amicable settlement of our difficulties, which were now becoming hourly more complicated. I immediately approved the suggestion, and prepared myself without delay to visit Lawrence, where I hoped to procure the appointment of a similar committee on their part, and bring them out to Franklin, which had been selected as a proper place for the negotiation. While on my way to Lawrence I halted at Franklin for a short time, and while there the committee of thirteen captains arrived, and at my request promised to remain there until I could return with the representation from Lawrence. When I entered that town I found that the people had held a meeting the night before, and had reduced to writing the terms on which they proposed to treat.

"These written stipulations were, so far as their promise to execute the laws was concerned, identical with those verbally agreed upon the day before. But there were other matters which entered into this document, distasteful both in their subject-matter and phraseology. These I caused to be struck out. The remodelling and correction of this paper delayed us until four, P.M., when Generals Robinson and Lane repaired with me, as a committee authorized to act for the Lawrence people, to Franklin, where we procured a room and organized the committees for business. I then addressed the committees, stating to them the two great objects which I so earnestly desired to accomplish, informing them of what had been done, and urging upon them, in the strongest terms, the importance of acquiescing in the arrangement which I had made, by inducing their men to retire quietly. After closing my remarks, General Lane addressed the committees. He was followed by Colonel Woodson, of Independence, and by General Robinson.

"After a conference of three hours, during which opinions were freely interchanged on both sides, the committees concluded to withdraw and report to the men of both parties that they were satisfied, and would settle matters as I wished. We then returned to the Wakarusa camp, which we reached at ten, P. M., where I still continued to press upon the leading men the importance of withdrawing with their men, and acceding to the terms offered."

THE TREATY.

The following is an accurate copy of the treaty stipulations, entered into between His Excellency, Wilson Shannon, Governor of Kansas Territory, and Generals Robinson and Lane, the Commanders-in-chief of the " enrolled forces," in the city of Lawrence.

WHEREAS, there is a misunderstanding between the people of Kansas, or a portion of them, and the Governor thereof, arising out of the rescue at Hickory Point of a citizen under arrest, and other matters. And *whereas,* a strong apprehension exists that said misunderstanding may lead to civil strife and bloodshed; and *whereas,* as it is desired by both Governor Shannon and the citizens of Lawrence and its vicinity, to avoid a calamity so disastrous to the interests of the Territory and the Union; and to place all parties in a correct position before the world. Now, therefore it is agreed by the said Governor Shannon and the undersigned citizens of the said Territory, in Lawrence now assembled, that the matter is settled as follows, *to wit:*

We, the said citizens of said Territory, protest that the said rescue was made without our knowledge or consent, but that if any of our citizens in said Territory were engaged in said rescue, we pledge ourselves to aid in the execution of any *legal* process against them; *that we have no knowledge of the previous, present, or prospective existence of any organization in the said Territory, for the resistance of the laws;* and we have not designed and do not design to resist the execution of any legal service of any criminal process therein, but pledge ourselves to aid in the execution of the laws, when called upon by *the proper authority,* in the town and vicinity of Lawrence, and that we will use our influence in preserving order therein, and declare that we are now, as we have ever been, ready to aid the Governor in securing a *posse* for the execution of such process; *provided,* that any person thus arrested in Lawrence or its vicinity, while a foreign foe shall remain in the Territory, shall be only examined before a United States District Judge of said Territory, in said town, and admitted to bail, and *provided further,* that all citizens arrested without legal process, shall be set at liberty; and *provided further,* that Governor Shannon agrees to use his influence to secure to the citizens of Kansas Territory remuneration for any damage suffered in any unlawful depredations, if any such have been committed by the Sheriff's *posse* in Douglas County. And further Governor Shannon states, that he has not called upon persons, residents of any other States to aid in the execution of the laws; that such as are here are here of their own choice, and that he does not consider that he has any authority to do so, and that he will not call upon any citizens of any other State who may be here.

We wish it understood, that we do not herein express any opinion as to the validity of the enactments of the Territorial Legislature.

WILSON SHANNON,

(Signed,)   CHARLES ROBINSON,

J. H. LANE.

Done in Lawrence, K. T. December 8th, 1855.

"It was not, however, until daybreak on the 9th, that I felt safe in issuing my orders as Chief Executive of Kansas Territory, to Sheriff Jones, and Generals Richardson and Strickler, to disband their forces. I did so ; my instructions were complied with, and the forces assembled in camps Lecompton and Wakarusa retired without committing any depredation or act of violence, so far as I have heard."

And here it will become our duty to finish our summing up, or, to speak more correctly, Governor Shannon's summing up, of the Pro-Slavery argument *in re* Kansas and her war, by adding the last link to

"This strange eventful history,"

in the shape of a copy of His Excellency's official orders to Major General Richardson, and others, disbanding the militia and sheriff's *posse*, or, in other words, giving the Border Ruffians, then and there assembled, a full and free permission to take up their *nunc dimittis*, with, we fancy, more than one inward prayer on the part of the care-worn Executive, that they might keep in mind as they went, the farewell caution of Bombastes Furioso, who dismissed his followers with

"Begone, brave army—don't kick up a row."

But in all sober earnest here follow the orders :—

CAMP WAKARUSA, *Dec. 8th*, 1855.

SIR:

Being fully satisfied that there will be no further resistance to the execution of the laws of this Territory, or to the service of any legal process in the county of Douglas, you are hereby ordered to cross the Kansas River to the north side as near Lecompton as you may find it practicabl. with your command, and disband the same at such time and place, and ii such numbers as you may deem most convenient.

Yours, with great respect,
WILSON SHANNON.

MAJOR GEN. RICHARDSON.

KANSAS TERRITORY, CAMP WAKARUSA, *Dec. 8th*, 1855.

SIR:

Being fully satisfied that there will be no further resistance to the execution of the laws of this Territory, or to the service of any legal process in the county of Douglas, you are hereby ordered to disband your command at such time and place as you may deem most convenient.

Yours, with great respect.
WILSON SHANNON.

GENERAL STRICKLER.

KANSAS TERRITORY, CAMP WAKARUSA, *Dec. 8th*, 1855.

Having made satisfactory arrangements by which all legal process in your hands, either now or hereafter, may be served without the aid of your present *posse*, you are hereby required to disband the same.

Yours, with great respect,
WILSON SHANNON.

S. J. JONES, *Sheriff of Douglas County.*

We doubt whether His Excellency, the Governor of all Kansas, ever signed documents with a greater degree of satisfaction, than he must have experienced in putting his autograph to these.

Here endeth the "Governor's History" of the so-called "Wakarusa War"—a "most parlous" campaign—which will doubtless render the shallow creek from whence it takes its name (and that name by the way, like many another sweet Indian appellation, won't bear translation, at least to "ears polite," in this most modest nineteenth century), as well as the Yankee-built city of Lawrence, famous throughout all coming time—"So mote it be."

Governor Shannon tells us that it seemed to him as if the very elements fought for him; for it turned cold, and blew as it never blew before in Kansas—until Bean's "Wakarusa Hotel" was so full—as its good landlady expressed it—that "you couldn't have crowded another man in edgewise."

Had it been in the pleasant summer time, or had the weather been less *seasonable* than it was, the "Border Ruffians" might be scouting about the Wakarusa Creek at this present writing; but December's winter blasts threw cold water upon their quarrel, until, as the knowing ones say, it is hard to determine whether the gale of Saturday night or the pacific counsel of the Governor did most towards bringing about that very desirable event—an almost bloodless termination to "the Wakarusa War." And now for another matter.

A copy of a certain document, addressed to Generals Robinson and Lane, the Commanders of the Free State party in Lawrence, and signed by Governor Shannon, had come into our possession before we entered Kansas. And we had promised that, so far as we were concerned, that document should not be given to the world. But as it was rumored that a disposition existed, on the part of certain members of the Free State party, to make capital out of the existence of this paper, we mentioned the fact—in the course of conversation—to Governor Shannon, that we were aware of his having attached his signature to such a document, at the same time exhibiting to him its duplicate in our note-book. The Governor seemed very much surprised at our having obtained it, but admitted its authenticity, and remarked, that he had not even taken a copy for himself. The document alluded to is a communication (which we publish below at the request of Governor Shannon), authorizing the Free State Generals to use the force under their command for certain purposes therein named. But let it speak for itself—it runs thus :—

TO C. ROBINSON AND J. H. LANE, COMMANDERS OF THE ENROLLED CITIZENS OF LAWRENCE:

You are hereby authorized and directed to take such measures and use the enrolled forces under your command in such manner, for the preservation of the peace and the protection of the persons and property of the people in Lawrence and its vicinity, as in your judgment shall best secure that end.

WILSON SHANNON.

Lawrence, Dec. 9th, 1855.

With the view of reconciling this apparent inconsistency in the official conduct of Governor Shannon—in first calling out the Territorial militia to suppress an armed mob, assembled in direct violation of the law, and then legalizing the existence of that mob by an official letter, authorizing the same persons to act as a military body, at their own discretion, and for an unlimited length of time—we took the liberty of addressing a communication to Gov. Shannon, in which we requested His Excellency to furnish us with any explanation which he might feel disposed to give. The following is his reply :—

GOVERNOR SHANNON'S REPLY.

EXECUTIVE OFFICE, SHAWNEE MISSION, K. T., *December 25th, 1855.*

DEAR SIR:

Your favor of this day's date is before me. In reply I have to state that the arrangement of the difficulties with the citizens assembled in the town of Lawrence during the recent disturbances, was reduced to writing by myself, and intended to be on liberal terms, and honorable alike to all parties. In my arrangement with them my great object was to secure the supremacy of the law, and bring about, if possible, a more

friendly feeling between the two conflicting parties, and thus secure a lasting
peace and amicable relations. I knew the object would be defeated by insist-
ing on any terms that would be humiliating to the parties concerned, and
I was determined to extend to the citizens assembled in Lawrence every
opportunity for placing themselves in what I deemed a correct position in
reference to the execution of the laws. The paper which was shown you
was probably a correct copy of the arrangement entered into on the 8th
instant.

As to the paper dated on the 9th instant, and purporting to be addressed
to C. Robinson and J. H. Lane, I desire to make an explanation, so as to
present the truth in relation to the manner in which it was obtained, as
well as my object in signing it. In order to understand this matter, it is
necessary that I should make some preliminary statements.

On the morning of the 9th, about sunrise, I issued my orders for disbanding the forces assembled around Lawrence. I remained at the Wakarusa camp until the forces at that place had retired. This they did in
good order. About 10 o'clock A. M. of that day (being Sunday), I went in
company with Brigadier General Strickler to Lawrence, where, with Sheriff
Jones and others of the Pro-Slavery party, I spent a considerable portion
of the day. In the evening I was invited to attend a social gathering of
ladies and gentlemen of the town of Lawrence, at the Emigrant Aid Society
Hotel, which I accepted. There were but two rooms finished in the hotel;
they were small, and in the third story, and were, therefore, very much
crowded by the company assembled. The time was spent in the most
friendly and social manner, and it seemed to be a matter of congratulation
on every side that the difficulties so lately threatening had at length been
brought to a happy termination. In the midst of this convivial party, and
about ten o'clock at night, Dr. C. Robinson came to me, in a state of
apparent excitement, and declared that their picket guard had just come in
and reported that there was a large irregular force near the town of Lawrence who were threatening an attack; adding that the citizens of Lawrence
claimed the protection of the Executive, and to this end desired me to give
himself and Genl. Lane written permission to repel the threatened assault.
I replied to Dr. Robinson that they did not require any authority from me,
as they would be entirely justified in repelling by force any attack upon
their town; that the law of self-preservation was sufficient, and that any
authority which I might give would add nothing to its strength. The
Doctor replied that they had been represented as having arrayed themselves against the laws and public officers of the Territory, and that he

therefore wished me to give him written authority to repel the threatened assault, so that it might appear hereafter, if a rencounter did take place, that they were not acting *against*, but *with* the approbation of the Territorial executive. With this view, amid an excited throng, in a small and crowded apartment, and without any critical examination of the paper which Dr. Robinson had just written, I signed it; but it was distinctly understood that it had no application to anything but the threatened attack on Lawrence that night.

I had, during my negotiations with Dr. Robinson, as one of the committee on behalf of the citizens assembled in Lawrence, repeatedly assured him that if the people of that place would acknowledge the validity of the Territorial laws until otherwise determined by legitimate authority, and would place themselves under their protection, I would exert all the power vested in me to protect the citizens of that town, both in their persons and property, and in securing them from an attack. And I will here state that after an arrangement had been made with those assembled in Lawrence, and after my assurances of protection, so far as in my power lay, I should have looked upon any assault upon the town of Lawrence on the night of December the 9th as an outrage, and wholly unjustifiable, and I should have felt myself bound, both in duty and honor, to have exerted myself to the utmost to have prevented so unwarrantable an act of violence.

It was under these circumstances, and with the view of carrying out in good faith my assurances to the citizens of that place (pending negotiations) and to avoid all cause of complaint on the part of the people of Lawrence, on any pretext, for breaking from the stipulations concluded but the day before, that I signed a paper authorizing C. Robinson and J. H. Lane to repel the threatened attack on the town of Lawrence. It was done on my part with the kindest and best of motives, from an earnest desire to restore harmony and confidence. It did not for a moment occur to me that this pretended attack upon the town was but a device to obtain from me a paper which might be used to my prejudice. I supposed at the time that I was surrounded by gentlemen and by grateful hearts, and not by tricksters, who, with fraudulent representations, were seeking to obtain an advantage over me. I was the last man on the globe who deserved such treatment from the citizens of Lawrence. For four days and nights, and at the cost of many valuable friends, whose good will I have forfeited by favoring too pacific a course, I had labored most incessantly to save their town from destruction and their citizens from a bloody fight.

On the next morning after this transaction took place, upon the most diligent inquiry, I could not learn that any force whatever had ever made its appearance before Lawrence upon the previous night; and on a full inquiry into the matter since, I am now satisfied that there was no hostile party at any place near Lawrence on the night of the 9th.

This paper, obtained as I have stated, has, I presume, been shown by Doctor Robinson, and copies permitted to have been taken and used, for the purpose of giving an air of legality to the acts of the citizens assembled in Lawrence previous to its date. No such purpose was contemplated by me, and I repeat, that the paper I signed was only intended to apply to the alleged threatening of the town of Lawrence by an armed force, on the night of December 9th, and if it was obtained, or has been used for any other purpose, it is an exhibition of base ingratitude and low trickery, which should render infamous the name of every one connected with it.

Yours, with great respect,

WILSON SHANNON.

If the reader should be so curious as to ask the motives which actuated us in addressing this "call for information" to General Shannon, in regard to the nature and intention of the document just alluded to, we should answer that, we had two reasons for so doing. The first, being a desire to sift thoroughly, and weigh well the statements which had been made to us, for the journalist must ever be a convert to the rule of believing but half that he *sees* and almost nothing that he *hears.* And where, let me ask, can you find an apter illustration of the necessity of this "ower carefulness," if such it be, than in the present instance? We might even, had we been so minded, have preached from this unlucky paper as from a text, and proved thereby that the Governor of Kansas was little better than a walking contradiction; at least, we should have made this clear to all who looked no further than the document in question. Yet, who does not know that "it is the *letter* that kills" while "the spirit giveth life." To sum up the whole matter, this legalizing of the "armed outlaws" in Lawrence, is either a mountain or a mole-hill; take it as it appears, and it is a Mount Pelion; explain it, and lo ! the mountain has been in labor, and brought forth—a *mouse*. So much for our first motive.

As regards the second, we are free to confess that we have taken a fancy to the Governor—he did all he could to lighten our news-hunting labors—he gave us a hearty welcome, and seemed to regret our departure; and that, too, in a country where we were literally " a stranger among strangers." This is a cold world, and kindness should be reciprocal. Governor Shannon is, moreover (or at least we think so), in his anxieties for the best good of Kansas, a very single-hearted man ; he has also occupied a somewhat prominent position in the world of American politics, in which he has filled various offices—such as Minister to Mexico, Governor of Ohio, and others of lesser note, with credit to himself, and satisfaction to those whom he has represented. And finally upon this subject, if a third reason should be required, we will add it in the form of an article of our creed, which enjoins upon us the belief that every individual and every party is, at all times and in all places, entitled to the benefit of what they call, in Western Texas, "a white man's chance." And in saying this, we are compelled to admit that we have followed the very ladylike practice of keeping our strongest reason for the *last*.

By the way, there *is* one little incident connected with the reception of the Governor's letter of elucidation, which will bear repeating. Governor Shannon asked us, as we glanced over his epistle, if we thought he had made it *strong* enough. We were reading the concluding sentence at the time, and we made bold to assure him that it would be " painting the lily," in *that* respect, to alter a single line ; for if this explanation be not *strong* enough, we only wonder how His Excellency contrives to get his powerful ones through the mail-bags, for we should fancy that they might almost rival the " Artful Dodger's celebrated tea," which had arrived at that degree of strength 'that it required a safety-valve to the tea-pot to prevent an explosion.

The following epistle has just been handed us. We copy from the original document, a much mutilated and not over cleanly bit of paper, six inches by four, badly spelt, and evidently written with a view to disguise the hand. It was folded in a self-sealing note-envelope, with an ornamental seal pressed into the paper of so peculiar a stamp that an expert policeman could hardly fail, in a small town like Lawrence, to discover its author. It is directed to "Sheriff Jones, Lawrence, K. T.," by whom it was recently received, through the Lawrence post-office : it reads thus, "short and sweet " :—

[No date.]

Sheriff Jones—You are notified that if you make one more arrest by the order of any magistrate appointed by the Kansas Bogus Legislature, that in so doing you will sign your own Death Warrant. Per order.

Secret Twelve.

This dispatch is as " ultra " in its tone as the most enthusiastic agitator could wish.

We have just learned by a gentleman this day from Lecompton, that he was in Lawrence on the Tuesday following the disbanding of the militia, and then and there saw some fifteen or twenty men engaged in digging entrenchments. To use his own expression, " they are adding some circular earth forts " Our informant also states that they have a flag still flying over the town—a tri-color—red, white, and blue—the stripes running in the same manner as those of the American ensign, but no stars. What does this strengthening of breastworks mean ? Is not peace made, ratified, and concluded ?

CHAPTER XXI.

CHRISTMAS IN KANSAS.

CHRISTMAS-DAY—cold, bitter, freezing, seasonable as it ought
to be ; a little too " seasonable," perhaps, for the like of this, in
the way of biting winter weather, has never been known in
Kansas, even in the memory of that highly respectable individual—the oldest inhabitant.   The ground is covered with snow.
At Council Bluffs it is said to be six feet in depth ; and for the
past three days the mercury here has indicated from ten to
twenty-two degrees below zero; other authorities say *thirty-three*,
but we have no desire to make it any *worse*—it's bad enough as
it is—in fact we have been so much annoyed of late by weather-
wise observers, who will insist upon quoting their different and
differing thermometers for our especial benefit, that we begin
to entertain almost as decided an " enemosity " to that sensitive
instrument as did the old lady down East, who, on being informed
upon a certain scorching day in August, that " the thermometer
made it five degrees hotter," begged her son John to " take the
darned thing out of doors afore it sot the house on fire." We
forget whether this thrice-told tale has been credited to Mrs.
Partington or not.

But to return—we even hear of people being frost-bitten on
lonely prairie roads,

" Smoothed up with snow,"

where, if the traveller should wander from the unbeaten track, his chance—unless he be a better path-finder than new-comers generally are—is small indeed.   Old Kansas settlers say that last year some people froze to death ; and we can readily imagine it, for Siberia itself could hardly look more frigidly repulsive than these frozen, snow-drifted wastes of Eastern Kansas.

And this is Christmas !—Dear, old-fashioned, merry-hearted Christmas !—which we have longed for, and welcomed, and honored truly from a boy.   But there's some mistake this year ; for though to-day is, beyond a doubt, December the 25th; on which, as everybody knows, Christmas ought and *used* to come, we haven't seen it yet—*our* Christmas we mean.   Alas ! what evil fortune—*our* festival, with its friendly gifts and right good wishes ; its turkey dinner, pleased little ones, toasts, mince pie, evergreen decorated church, sermon, and all that sort of thing, is on the t'other side of those far-off Alleghany mountains.   So we must even make the Christmas of 1855 a working-day, if only in self-defence to occupy the mind and drive away those confounded visitors—the Blue Devils, which will intrude themselves, though all unbidden, when the "*voyageur*" treats himself to that most dangerous luxury, a fit of musing, which bears him back, "on Fancy's restless wing," to distant friends and home.

And thus it happened that "Our Correspondent's" Christmas-day dwindled down into plain December the twenty-fifth, which we passed in writing—bating a meridian egg-nog—until the gloomy winter evening was deepening the shadows in the Governor's as yet unlighted chamber, when we received a special envoy in the person of Mr. Johnson, the superintendent of the Mission, who intimated to us that his good lady would be happy to see Governor Shannon and his suite—of which we, by courtesy, formed one, for the time being—in their private "sitting room," where she would have the pleasure of introducing

to our notice an "apple toddy," with accompanying refreshments, concocted by her own fair hands ; an invitation which
we were not slow to accept. Reader ! did you ever taste
apple toddy ? If you haven't, try it ; when it is just possible
that you may discover why we don't like it, too. "Take an
old man's advice, and never mix your liquor, Charley," was
the recommendation of that veteran stager, Major Monsoon, to
his young friend O'Malley ; and we firmly believe that if old
Monsoon had been requested to imbibe apple toddy, he would
have pronounced it a terrible compound, involving an awful
waste of "the groceries." But if the mixture was questionable, its accessories were not ; and better still, we found, upon
descending to Mistress Johnson's sanctum, a huge open wood
fire (our old favorite), and plenty of children (another pet of
ours), all busily engaged, like Mrs. Bradford's " Benny," in

> "Digging deep among the goodies
> In their crimson stockings hid ;"

and raising the very Ancient Edward himself in their boisterous
glee. It was a pleasant thing to mark their gambols, and to listen to those little ones, too ; for their merry shouts filled that
"fire-lighted chamber" with joyous echoes. But as we watched
their sport there came up to our mind

> "A fearful vision fraught with all that lay between,"

of that uncertain future whose sorrows would, in coming years,
wrinkle those fair young brows and dim those gaily laughing
eyes—and then, as we turned from the far-off Future to walk
sorrowfully with the recent Past, what bitter recollections
came crowding in of Death's stern doings within the year which
was now growing grey and old—and oh ! how chillingly they
fell upon our heart, as our spirit drifted out—-borne up by the

Ghost of Christmas Past, into the chill December air—to sweep over many a snow-clad mount and ice-bound river, and traverse plain, and lake, and leafless forest, until it reached the spot, made sunshine but a twelve-month ago by the presence of one too pure for earth, whose infant form now sleeps that long last rest which knows no waking, beneath the frozen clods of a sea-side city of the dead. What wonder, then, that we are sad to-night!

It may interest the New York juveniles to know that in the Far Western country, a child's first Christmas salutation to every one it meets, is "Christmas gift—Christmas gift." They catch you always, if they can. We tried to get ahead of a blue-eyed, curly-headed little lady this morning—a daughter of Mr. Woodson, the Secretary of State—but Miss Betty was too smart for us, and cried "Christmas gift," before we could open our mouth.

So much for *our* Christmas day in Kansas.

Shawnee Mission, Dec. 26.

We must talk politics to-day or nothing, so we will even extract the very lightest paragraph from our latest journalizing, and introduce it here.

Judge S——, the Free State candidate for ——, had a long conversation with Governor Shannon in the executive office yesterday. The Judge is, as we are informed, a New Yorker; that is to say, from the interior of that State. He is reported to have left there in disgust, because, to quote from his Honor's own words, as expressed to a distinguished individual in the Territory, "He would not live in a State where his next door neighbor—a better man than himself—who had, however, the misfortune to be naturally dark-colored, with a slight kink in his hair—could not cast his vote, because he was not a free-holder." As may be presumed from this, the Judge is an Abo-

litionist, "dyed in the wool." But be this as it may, the Judge
is spoken of as a man of his word, and a person whose statements
may be relied upon. We therefore attach more importance to
the following dialogue :—

Judge.—Do you really believe, Governor, that there will be
any appeal to arms made by the contending parties in this Territory ?

Governor.—Everything tends that way at the present time,
sir. I think that this must be the final result, for I have not a
particle of confidence in the present state of quiet.

Judge.—As I am now going East, I will, in such an event,
send out men and arms to the Free State party in Kansas. The
Missourians talk of 'wiping us out,' but they can't do it, sir—
they can never do it—for the Free States can raise twenty
dollars to one, and four men to one over the slaveholding States.

Secretary of State.—I reckon you are going East for that
purpose, anyhow, Judge.

To this insinuation the Judge returned no definite reply, but
smiled significantly.

Governor.—Do you not think, Judge, if your folks get to
fighting in Kansas, that the war will extend to other parts of
our country, and finally terminate in the dissolution of the Union ?

Judge.—Certainly it will. I think the Union won't last six
months, or a year at the most.

And here we came away—or our informant did, who formed
one of the party.

The following may be relied on as a part of the *present* intentions and prospects of the Free State party in Kansas. It
comes from one of their most prominent men, whose name has
been placed upon their ticket for State officers.

They intend putting their Free State government into operation at any cost. They have no hopes that Congress will admit
Kansas as a State, during its present session, but declare that

they have positive assurances that, to favor their views, no appropriation for the support of the Territorial government in Kansas will be made, even if it should be necessary to defeat the General Appropriation Bill in so doing, in which event, they hope the Territorial government will "die out," and permit their State administration to step into its shoes. This is to be done in the House of Representatives. They do not claim strength in the Senate. But whether this takes place or not, they have decided that their Free State government is to go into operation on the 4th of March next, at which time they will inaugurate their State officers.

To-day is December 27. And now, if there be any fun in the Kansas question, we will extract it, if we can ; but don't be critical, kind reader, for it's about as hopeless a task to get blood from a stone, as a *good* joke out of political wire-pulling ; but if the subject have a "sunny side," we'll find it, for the present, upon its Southern exposure, so we shall, therefore, indulge ourself in a few Pro-Slavery yarns, which, as they are veritable facts, and withal, "nuts to crack" for somebody, may as well come in here.

Yarn the First.—We are assured that the standard of the Pro-Slavery company, which marched to the seat of war from Jackson County, Mo. was carried by a slave—a slave born, and bred, and dyed in the wool ; in short, what a certain person we wot of would elegantly designate, as "a long-heeled, thick-lipped, flat-nosed, and kinky-headed specimen of the benighted and down-trodden Sons of Africa," who nevertheless marched gallantly in the van, bearing aloft the banner of Pro-Slavery, and withal, "armed and equipped as Border law directs," to encounter those who "had been *talking*" of shedding their life's blood for his benefit. And this is what these ferocious "Border Ruffians call "*putting the seeds of dissension in the lead.*"

Yarn the Second.—Some months ago a slaveholder in Lafayette County, Mo., passed through the town of Westport, in that State, on his way to select a farming location in Kansas Territory. He was accompanied by half a dozen likely negroes from his own plantation, all well mounted and completely armed, each fellow having a Colt's navy revolver tucked into his right boot.

"Where the deuce are you going to with those niggers?" shouted an inquisitive friend to the planter; as the cavalcade trotted into Westport.

"Going?" was the reply, "why, where should I be going? I'm bound for Kansas to hunt a claim, and as I knew I'd have to go by Lawrence, and down among those vile abolitionists, I thought I'd better have a body-guard, and brought some of my niggers along accordingly."

YARN THE THIRD.—An old negro man, a slave, belonging to a gentleman in the vicinity of Westport, was asked whether he did not "want to go and live among the Free State men in Lawrence?" when he instantly replied :

"No! s'pect not, massa, dis nigger been raised 'mong quality —couldn't think of gwine thar, sir ; drather stay at home 'mong white folks."

It is currently reported in these parts, that when a planter wishes to scare a refractory darkey into good behavior, he has only to threaten selling him to a Lawrence man, which operates as effectually as a hint to a nigger in the Old Dominion, that he's off for New Orleans, if he dont amend.

If strong Pro-Slavery sympathizers are to be believed, the South must be "up and rising" upon the Kansas question. She will, they say, pour a tremendous emigration into the Territory in the early spring. The following items may, we think, among a mass of rumors which want foundation, be relied upon, as we have derived them from the highest and most respectable sources .

From one county in Georgia, one hundred *bona fide* emigrants have already made their preparations to start. More will leave from other counties in that State.

From Mississippi no less a personage than Gen. Quitman himself, with some hundreds of the boys of the Cotton State, are confidently looked for. Gen. Quitman has (it is said), given \$2,500 to promote the objects of the Southern Kansas Aid Emigration Society. This may not be the proper title of the association, but it has the peopling of Kansas by Pro-Slavery men for its aim.

Colonel Buford, of Alabama (writes our informant), has con tributed from his own purse \$25,000 for a similar purpose. He himself is coming out to the Territory in March with 300 Alabamians, who will settle in Kansas, cast their votes to make her a slave State, and, if necessary, handle their rifles in the same cause, a procedure, by the way, which we deprecate exceedingly.

Apropos to *possible* Kansas Aid Emigration Societies in the South, we have made the following extract from Col. Buford's address to " Kansas emigrants, and the friends of the South generally," as we find it published in the Alabama " *Spirit of the South.*" In selecting these extracts, we have carefully endeavored to strike out all that was *partisan,* our object being simply to present the reader with a fair specimen of the practical organization and proposed arrangements of one or two of the numerous Pro-Slavery Kansas Emigrant Aid Societies, which are now forming, or said to be forming, in almost every city of the sunny South :

From the Alabama Spirit of the South.

TO KANSAS EMIGRANTS AND TO ALL FRIENDS OF THE SOUTH.

I had proposed to start with my company of Kansas emigrants on the 11th of February next, but many of them being unable to get ready by that time, and others being unwilling to go before spring, and especially as I am advised by my correspondents that the Missouri and Kansas rivers are already impeded by ice, I have determined to postpone starting till the winter breaks.

The emigrants may rendezvous at Eufaula, on the 31st March next, at Columbus, Ga., on the 3d of April, and at Montgomery, Ala., on the 5th of April next—so that I can start from Eufaula, via Columbus and Montgomery, collecting on the way those I find at the different places of rendezvous. The company will travel from Montgomery by steamers, via Mobile and New Orleans, or else by railroad via Atlanta to Nashville, and thence by steamer to Kansas. I engage to transport no baggage except six blankets, one gun, one knapsack, and one frying-pan to each emigrant. For baggage over and above this, the emigrant himself must engage transportation; many will have no more, and I must treat all alike. While I thought my company would be small, I expected to be able to take women, children, and slaves; but I find I must leave them to give place to men, who are now greatly needed in Kansas to preserve the public peace and enforce the laws. I now expect over four hundred men, and I will take no females, nor slaves, nor minors under eighteen years of age. Women and children should not be exposed there in tents in the spring, but the husbands should go first and prepare houses.

The regiment will be divided into companies of forty or fifty men, under the usual military officers, elected by the men. Officers have no emoluments, and the organization is on the principle of volunteer militia to sustain the laws; a majority of each company may expel any member. Rations, transportation, and fare, that of soldiers in service. By way of remunerating me for the privilege of joining my party, for subsistence and transportation to Kansas, and for furnishing means to enter his preemption, each emigrant agrees to acquire a pre-emption, and to pay me, when his titles are perfected, a sum equal to the value of one-half of his pre-emption, which obligation he may discharge in money or property at a fair valuation, at his own option. I had heretofore, from misinformation, supposed pre-emptions assignable before patent, but on examining the act I find they are not. Neither does the donation act apply to Kansas, but each male of full age, widow or head of family who has not had a pre-emption under the act of 1841 and does not own 320 acres of land, and who has improved and settled on it—not to sell on speculation, but for his own use and cultivation—is entitled to enter 160 acres, at $1 25 per acre, payable any time before the land sales.

I have simplified my proposals to a single proposition, as above, in order to be more easily understood and to obviate the many questions that overwhelm me.

Besides taking only free males over eighteen, the great number of applications compels this further modification, i. e. :—I will receive only those emigrants who rendezvous at the places above designated—at either of which places, i. e., Eufaula, Columbus, or Montgomery, I will receive all males over eighteen from any Southern State, who join me at the time above designated; their rations to begin from the time above-named for rendezvous. Emigrants must pay their own expenses to the place and day of rendezvous. Those gentlemen in California and other States, forming companies to join me, can very easily obtain free transportation for their companies by proper application to the directors of the railroads over which they must pass.

*　　*　　*　　*　　*　　*　　*

I have before told you what Judge Cato (Judge of the Territory) says of that fertile region. In his letter of November last, he writes:—

"Corn is plenty at twenty-five cents per bushel. This is as fine a country as any on earth; the profits on its productions far exceed that in the cotton regions. All grain, grass, clover, and hemp give large returns —at least from thirty to forty dollars per acre annually. I have seen no poor lands; it all seems richer than the best Chattahoochee bottom, and the most of it is just like adjoining Missouri lands that now sell at twenty to fifty dollars per acre. The estimated average of the corn is one hun-dred bushels per acre, and six tons hemp per hand, worth $140 per ton. I can give no idea of the beauty and fertility of the soil of the country. Good wells can be obtained anywhere, and running streams are frequent."

Dr. Walker, a long resident of its borders, and of high character and intelligence, says:

"As far as health, climate, and profits of labor are concerned, Kansas is better than any part of the Union. There is no country where a man can be more independent, and make his bread and meat with less capital, than here; ten or twelve furrows will make ten barrels of corn to the acre. One thousand pounds hemp per acre is a common crop. There are swarms of cattle and good markets for everything."

Another distinguished resident of Western Missouri, in his letter of the 30th December to me, says:

"Planters are making twice the money per hand that they are in any other part of the Union. One hand will raise five tons of hemp, and this don't interfere with the corn, wheat, and oat crop; planters have no supplies to purchase, but everything to sell. A near neighbor last year, with fourteen hands, men, women, and boys, averaged eight hundred and thirty-six dollars per hand—negro fellows, field hands, hire for $300 per annum—mechanics $600; white men $25 per month; any number of young men in the spring can find ready employment at that price, and then they have other advantages."

Kansas is the starting point for California, Oregon, Utah, and New Mexico—thousands of wagons leave every spring; they carry three millions of goods per annum to New Mexico, besides immense government supplies to pay Indians and sustain our military posts, &c.

Let every one wishing to go urge his neighbors to hold meetings who will appoint agents to solicit every man's contribution, either in money or note, payable after the emigrants are taken out. Contributions must not be to individual members, but for the common benefit. I could by the last of March raise five thousand men, if the contributions reached, say $10 per head—for that would enable me to furnish all with their military and agricultural outfit.

I am asked, "What military and other service do I require?" *None*, except that when he gets to Kansas, the emigrant shall begin some honest employment for a living—if it be working on his claim—that will give him credit to buy bread on. On his way there he is expected to be orderly and temperate, to attend the reading of the Scripture and prayer, night and morning, learn to fear God, to be charitable to our enemies, gentle with females and those in our power, merciful to slaves and beasts, and just to all men.

All who intend to go, will please write me immediately.

W. P. Belcher, Esq., Abbeville C. H., S. C., and Capt. E. B. Bell, Graniteville, Edgefield, S. C., I understand, are raising companies to join me. They, doubtless, can get free transportation for them to Columbus, Ga., and Carolina emigrants might do well to come with one of them.

All editors friendly to the enterprise, it is hoped, will copy this address in full.

J. BUFORD.

EUFAULA, ALA., *Jan.* 19, 1856.

The following comes from E. B. Bell, Esq., of South Carolina; we have taken the liberty of treating Mr. Bell's letter in the same manner as that of his predecessor, by extracting its political *pepper*—for, with all due deference to these gentlemen, we do not intend in this, *our* Kansas war, to permit any one to meddle with the *spice* box but ourself. And if we cannot succeed in basting both sides to their entire satisfaction ere we cry, "Hold, enough," we will invite all parties concerned to proceed forthwith to the plains of Kansas, a most unbounded battle field, and there fight out the quarrel with Sharpe's rifles ard Bowie knifes if they please, while we stand by, to *see* the fight.

From the Edgefield (S. C.) Advertiser.

HO! FOR KANSAS.

At the solicitation of many friends, I will commence the organization of a company of one hundred men to proceed to Kansas about the last of March.

This pioneer band needs the aid of our moneyed citizens. They go to a far-off country for the purpose of securing homes, and at the same time to defend Southern institutions. They appeal to their native State for aid, with the hope that their appeal will not be in vain.

It is impossible that the people of South Carolina can hear without emotion the news which daily comes to us from Kansas.

* * * * * * *

We trust that these questions may be answered in a worthy and liberal manner. Let patriotism, State pride, and Southern spirit be expressed in some suitable, practical form of aid for Kansas.

E. B. Bell

Were further testimony necessary of there being some reality in this action on the part of the South, it might be added from Georgia, Mississippi, and other slaveholding States—for from the dark forests of Kentucky, as well as from the rice-fields of the sunny South, comes up the cry, "Hurrah for Kansas!

To change the subject—Hunters just in from the plains report buffalo in great abundance. They came in this fall to within fifteen miles of Council Grove ; this is nearer than they have come for years. A party of men arrived here, or in Independence, some ten days ago, with four wagons loaded down with their meat. Would it not be a good speculation for some enterprising fellow—a Yankee, of course—to come to the Territory and go into the buffalo butchering business ?

And yet another change : Editors make mistakes sometimes both in and out of Kansas—here is a specimen ; we clip our text from the "Herald of Freedom," Dec. 15 :

Major Clarke, Pottawatomic Agent, reinforced the mob at Lecompton yesterday, with a party of Indians. As this party passed through Topeka they boasted that they would not return without a scalp—one on each shoulder.

Clarke attempted last evening to shoot a Free State man, but the ball passed through the leg of one of his own friends, shattering it very much, rendering it quite probable that it will have to be amputated.

The real facts of this affair—which was, after all, what an Irishman would call, "just a thrifling mistake, and divil a bit more"—were, as we have received them from Major Clarke, the gentleman alluded to in the foregoing paragraph, substantially as follows,—

Major George W. Clarke, United States Indian Agent for the Pottawatomics, being in the Indian Reservation, and learning that the country through which he was about to travel, with a large amount of public funds, was filled with armed and incendiary parties, adopted the precaution of bringing with him an escort composed of employcés of his agency, among whom were five Pottawatomics, whom he sent back the next day, and who did not participate in any manner in the territorial difficulties. Upon returning to his residence, near Lecompton—having in the meantime left his escort at that place, distant by some two and a-half miles—he found his family in great alarm from a threatened attack to be made upon his house that night. In the course of the evening, and at an early hour, he was aroused by the screams of his family, who were alarmed by one of its members, who came running in, and stated that the house was attacked by an armed party, and that the assailants were already in the yard. Major Clarke seized a loaded fowling-piece which happened to be standing in the hall, ran out of the back door, turned a corner of the house—it being very dark at the time. Upon doing so he perceived a number of men just entering the front door. Fully believing that a set of desperadoes were about carrying out their blood-thirsty intentions—in accordance with the repeated threats which had even upon that very day been made by certain individuals· of the Free State party, to the effect that they would shoot Major Clarke, he did not hail, but hastily fired; the piece was loaded with small bird shot (not "ball," as the "Herald of Freedom" states.) The load most unfortunately entered the leg·of one of the men, who proved to be one of a party of Major Clarke's neighbors, who had come at Mrs. Clarke's request to assist in protecting her house against the violence with which it had been threatened by a Free State mob. After some moments of confusion an explanation was made, and the injured man was carried into the house, where his wounds were as well cared for as circumstances would permit. At his request, Major Clarke then carried the victim of this sad accident home in his (Major Clarke's) carriage. The gentleman injured (Mr. Bolder) is now rapidly recovering, and is at present able to walk about, and, as Major Clarke is most happy to declare, stands in no danger of being called upon to submit to an amputation.

Nothing like having both sides of a story, is there?

CHAPTER XXII.

LIFE AT THE MISSION.

December 29th—morning. At Shawnee Mission still. The weather (and why shouldn't we quote the weather as well as Professor E. Meriam or any other warmly-housed philosopher), has got into a "cold circle" in these regions just now, and if you should ask us when it's going to get out, we could but reply in the words of an eccentric lieutenant of artillery—a musical man, and odd fish generally—who once informed his tailor, who seemed over anxious about "that little bill of his," that "he couldn't pay it then, and the Lord in his infinite mercy only knew when he could," and it's just so with this Kansas cold weather. But we would have you to understand that we shall, while it lasts, warm our indignation at its continuance, and thus verify the old adage about its being "a very *cold* breeze which blows nobody any good." But it *is* biting, though, in sober earnest, cold enough, in fact, to freeze the Free State question and thereby make Kansas respectable in spite of herself.

Reports from Lawrence say that "the enemy" are still entrenching themselves—a waste of labor—if it be true; do they fancy that the "Border Ruffians" are going to enter upon a campaign, even with their "*summum bonum*"—a fight with the Abolitionists as an incentive in such a temperature as this? Why, the Missouri army of invasion would be out of necessaries ere it had marched twenty miles; for all the whisky in

"Pukedom" would not last the Pro-Slavery forces—with the mercury below zero—for even a single day. No, Free Soilism may bless its favoring stars, for it may now exclaim with Nicholas (late of all the Russias), "Have we not Generals January and February to fight our battles?" and Brigadier Jack Frost too, with his rimy beard and icy armor of proof? Pooh! niggers and Pro-Slavery men can't stand such a climate as this.

But we are weary of this hum-drum monotony—our mission life don't suit us—as a specimen which we will give you presently shall most abundantly prove. So, blow high—blow low—come ice, or hail, or snow—we take the Lawrence road to-morrow, where we shall both see and hear for ourself. We are therefore determined and shall start for the late "seat of war," from whence, if we escape the Abolitionists, and be not congealed upon the road, the world in general may expect to hear from us within eight-and-forty hours from this present writing.

But we promised the reader a sample of the half-dozen dreary days which we spent at Shawnee Mission. So let us shorten our style and write it up in brief.

Morning at the Mission.—Six o'clock, and the mercury two dozen degrees below zero. Scene.—A large double-bedded room, with ill-made windows, a badly-hung door, and not even a spark in the fire-place, its sole tenant being "Our Correspondent," just then in bed, the tip of his intellectual nose, of whose existence he has had serious doubts for the last half-hour, being the only feature visible. First, breakfast-bell rings violently—no, it don't—but Nigger Bill blows the preliminary horn, which in this instance comes to the same thing. "Our Correspondent" is reminded of Tennyson's "Bugle Song," which he proceeds to quote, with a difference, as follows:—

> "Blow, bugle, blow—the kitchen-maid's replying,
> And answer echoes, answer—frying—frying—frying.

"Our Correspondent" meditates. Breakfast is a necessity not to be had at Shawnee Mission after eight o'clock, A. M., but the road to that necessity lies through getting up, and getting up with the mercury *down*, is a fact of the stubbornest kind, a very jackass of a fact. "Our Correspondent" continues to reflect, and finally extends one leg outside of the covering to act as a feeling thermometer, but brings it back again hastily, for the leg doesn't like it ; it might have suffered more, had not "Our Correspondent," like a prudent man, emulated the example of

"Diddle, diddle, dumpling, my son John,"

by literally "going to bed with his breeches on ;" for if "misery makes strange bed-fellows," there is no reason why it should not suggest strange bed-clothes—particularly where Mackinaws are scarce—which we regret to say is the case at Shawnee Mission. But, to return, we—for "Our Correspondent" takes up too much space—had gotten our pedal extremity into bed again, and were once more resolving ourself into a committee of ways and means when, like a knell, we heard the

"Tintinnabulations that so shiveringly swelled
Of the bell, the breakfast bell,
Ringing out above our head."

The foregoing is from Poe's "Song of the Bells," we believe, but we're not certain as to the accuracy of the quotation. And the signal had its effect, for it was the second and "last time of asking." We "made an effort"—even Mrs. Dombey would have "made an effort," under like circumstances—so we determined to get up, and accordingly protruded our legs from their, comparatively speaking, comfortable interior of covering ; but don't be alarmed, fair reader, for remember they had breeches on them ; our body followed—we made a desperate jump—and then landed in the middle of one of the very "coldest circles" off of Brooklyn Heights.

As we were already dressed, with the exception of a coat and a pair of half frozen boots, it required only a shake or two—*à la* Newfoundland dog—to make our toilet, but our ablutions were of the scantiest; for the bathing conveniences—a tin wash-basin and pitcher—proved themselves to be a practical commentary upon Sam Weller's suggestion of

"Werry delightful climate for them as is well wropped up, as the polar bear remarked, when he vent a skatin' vith his intimate friend—for water in the hand-basin is a mask o' ice, sir."

We were, therefore, compelled to sacrifice that virtue, which ranks "next to godliness," at least, for the present; and then, with a heavy worsted comforter bound round our neck, ran at top speed through the snow-drifted hall, and from thence into the long dining-room, where we took our place upon a wooden bench, with a huge tin coffee-pot, one of a long and illustrious line of tin coffee-pots; ranged at regular intervals upon the board, for a *vis à vis*, and forty young Indians, besides a sufficiency of "white folks," by way of company. Then came a Western breakfast, and then we made a bolt for the Executive office, situated in another building, which we reached by a half beaten path through the piled up snow, where we passed our time between writing and getting "exclusive information" from Governor Shannon, with an occasional visit to the stove to thaw out the benumbed fingers, which could scarcely hold the pen, until the somewhat primitive hour of noon brought us to our dinner, and another journey through the snow; then came the afternoon with its continuation of our literary labors, varied, perhaps, by the arrival of some chance visitor with news, or it may be, by Woodson's bringing in the Eastern mail from the Westport post-office, when Kansas items were extracted and read over, and Free State editors with Abolitionist proclivities "handled without gloves," by the Governor and his suite, until the supper-bell put an end to the discussion. As for the evening, it was but a repetition of the afternoon, prolonged by our scribbling into two or three o'clock in the morning, when we once more ploughed through the snow, on our way to the main building, in which we would seek out our icy, comfortless chamber, and then (all accoutered as we were) scramble into bed, where it was often daybreak before we had grown sufficiently warm to slumber, and even then, our over-tasked brain would be ridden, as by a nightmare, with Kansas politics, and Kansas news, and Kansas questions in general, till, in our spectre-haunted dreams, Free Stateism took the form of a long-limbed, red-headed negro, in a shocking beaver, shambling legs, and dirty white coat ; while Pro-Slavery shook his fist at the apparition from the other side of our couch, in the shape of a ferocious Border-Ruffian, with a slave whip in one hand, and a revolver in the other, until, as somebody says, we would awake, and swear a prayer or two, and then fall to our sleep again.

"All of which," to quote from the secretaries, "is respectfully submitted" as a faint outline of our daily routine of life—if such an existence can be called living—at the Methodist Shawnee Mission.

December 29, *Evening.*—At "old man Harris's" most uncomfortable "hotel," in Westport. We are once more settled in our old chamber, which has, at present, an additional tenant, in the person of Major Clarke, the Pottawatomie Indian Agent, elsewhere alluded to. Now, Major Clarke, differing opinions to the contrary notwithstanding, is, to our thinking, a fat, warmhearted, jovial little man ; and so we like Clarke, and "don't kear" who knows it ; and our reason for fancying him is just this (and a very Irish one at that) there's a deal of *fun* in him. He has shot one or two men it is true ; has fought a brace of duels, and it may be more ; but we can't help liking him, for, as we have already said, he has

"A marvellous humor of his own."

So we shall journey on to Kansas to-morrow in company, and while together, be comrades in all good fellowship.

Evening.—Major Clarke and myself have just made ourselves as comfortable as circumstances will permit, by visiting the rooms of our fellow-lodgers, where we have quietly emptied every wood box, and removed their contents to our own apartment, thereby providing ourselves with a stock of fuel for this night's consumption.   A somewhat selfish but very prudent move, suggested by the fact that, in "old man Harris's" establishment, a nigger is not to be had, even when stimulated by a dime, unless, indeed, you break the darkey's head daily ; and when you do get a servant, it's ten to one that he cuts the fire-wood six inches too short for your stove, and then you may freeze in bed, or out, as you prefer ; or, if you don't know the ways of the house, spend your time and breath in shouting for some sable functionary, who grows stone deaf, on principle, after nine o'clock, P.M.

CHAPTER XXIII.

COLEMAN'S NARRATIVE.

WE have a visitor in our chamber as we write—Mister—everybody is Mister in the democratic Far West—Franklin M. Coleman, who has gained a Kansas, and perhaps even outside notoriety from having been "the murderer—so say the Free State prints—of Dow.

And we are about to present the reader with a narrative of the circumstances attending his unfortunate rencounter with the deceased, together with the difficulties which led to it, as we have taken the story down from Coleman's own lips.

We do this for two reasons ; in the first place, the killing of Dow (a Free State man) seems to be generally referred to and decided upon as one of the initial—if not *the* initial point of the recent Kansas difficulties. And in the second place, this matter has been so garbled, both in the communications of interested letter-writers, and in the paragraphs of a one-sided local press, that we feel it is but just to give to the world, for the first time, the statement of the principal actor in this most deplorable tragedy. It runs thus :

FRANKLIN M. COLEMAN'S NARRATIVE.

"I am a native of Brook County in Virginia. I left that State in 1849, and removed to Louisa County Iowa, from whence I emigrated to Kansas City, Mo., in April, 1854. Here

I kept the Union Hotel until September of last year. From this place I moved with my family, consisting of a wife and child (a boy of six years old), to Hickory Point, on the Santa Fé trail, distant some ten miles from Lawrence, K. T.

" At this time, the greater part of the land near Hickory Point was held by three Indianians, who occupied, partly by their own claims, but mostly as the representatives of certain friends of theirs in Indiana, who, though non-residents, claimed title by them as their proxies. Time passed on, and the absentee claimants neglected to comply with the requisitions of the ' Squatter Laws,' thereby forfeiting their claims. Three of their claims were accordingly taken by Missourians, who learned that they were lying vacant, in November of 1854. Some few days after these claims had been entered upon, the absentee Indianian claimants arrived. This led to one of the ' jumped claims ' being referred to arbitration—the arbitrators being twelve in number, a majority of whom belonged to the Free State party. It was settled by these in favor of the Missourians. On the strength of this decision, in partnership with John M. Banks, a Free State man, I ' jumped a claim ' held by a man named Frasier, a non-resident of Kansas. We notified this person that we had ' jumped his claim,' and as we did not wish to take any undue advantage of him, would give it up if he could show any legal right to the land in question. We afterwards discovered that Frasier had sold this claim to one Jacob Branson, then residing in Missouri but formerly from Indiana. This we learned from Branson himself, who came out forthwith to Hickory Point (I had known Branson while in Kansas City), I remarked to Branson that I had taken the Frasier claim ; he replied : ' I have bought that claim from Frasier, and paid him fifty dollars for it, and I intend to have it.' I then said to Branson, that the claim in question was forfeited by Frasier's non-compliance with ' the Squatter Laws,' and that I was willing to submit it to arbitration. This he refused, stating that if the laws took a man's claim away he would defend himself and have his claim, or ' die right where he was.' I then closed our interview by telling him that it was not worth our while to talk about it. On the morning following this conversation, Branson came (during my absence), to my house, with a wagon-load of household stuff, accompanied by Louis Farley, a Free State man from Indiana—Mr. Banks and a young man named Graves—a Free-soiler—were the only men at my house on the occasion of Branson's visit. Branson and his companion tried to force his property into my dwelling. Banks requested them to let their goods stand until they could send for me ; he did so, and I came immediately. Upon entering my house, Branson and Farley being within, I reminded Branson that he had said that ' he would have my claim or die upon it.' I then drew a single-barrelled pistol from under the head of the bed and told him that I should defend myself, and if he was determined to settle the matter in that way, I was prepared to do so. Farley then attempted to mediate between us. During this conversation, Branson kept his hand upon an ' Allen's revolver ' which he had with him in his pocket, but made no motion to draw the weapon, nor did I threaten him with my pistol, further than to exhibit it as a proof of my intention to protect myself. I cannot remember the precise date of this difficulty; I think it occurred in November, 1854. Branson and myself then agreed to compromise the matter by submitting our difficulties to an arbitration. This was accordingly done, and the arbitrators, twelve in number, and mostly Pro-Slavery men, decided against my partner and myself, insomuch, that instead of allowing our claim to the whole Frasier tract, amounting to two hundred and forty acres, they awarded one hundred and sixty acres to Branson as his proportion. Branson then promised, in the presence of the arbitrators, to measure off his share. But this he subsequently refused to do. Banks and

10*

myself then reminded him of his agreement to submit to the decision of the arbitrators, adding that we desired peace. He said that he did not crave our friendship, and that we should never have a single foot of the lumber which grew upon the greater part of the claim. He then stated that he had measured the entire ' Frasier claim,' with one of his neighbors, and found it to contain but one hundred and twenty acres—called us a set of base thieves, who had swindled him out of his rights, and with whom he wished to have no intercourse, etc. We then parted for our several homes.

"Banks, Graves, and myself then measured off the claim, allotting to Branson his full proportion (all timber land) of 160 acres, and marking the boundary line which divided our claim. This division was never accepted by Branson. He still claimed the whole tract. Branson then turned his attention to strengthening the Free State party—to which he himself belonged—in the vicinity of Hickory Point. This he did by encouraging Free State men to settle about him, giving them timber from his land, and informing them of vacant claims. In pursuance of this object, he and his friends invited a man named Dow, an Ohioan and Abolitionist, to occupy a claim adjoining my own. This claim rightly belonged to one William White, of Westport, Mo., a Pro-Slavery man, who had made some improvements on it, and therefore held it under the 'Squatter Laws.' The ' improvement ' was a log-cabin, which was burnt down by the Free State party, on or about the day of Dow's arrival at Hickory Point. Dow then entered upon White's claim and commenced building. Upon this, twelve men of the Pro-Slavery party at Hickory Point, I being one of their number, waited upon Dow, to inquire into the 'jumping' of White's claim, and the burning of his house. We accused Dow of being accessory to the act. He asserted his innocence as regarded the destruction of White's cabin. Upon being asked if he was not aware of the intention of the Free State people to destroy it, he answered that that was his business, and none of ours. I then observed to him, that as my claim adjoined his, I would be his nearest neighbor, and should be very sorry to suspect that the man who lived next to me could be guilty of such an act, but as he had affirmed his innocence, as regarded the burning of White's house, I would (if it proved to be true), be a kind neighbor to him, and added that he was welcome to visit at my house if he wished to come. He thanked me, and we parted. These occurrences took place during the winter of 1854 and '55, and from this date up to the very day on which I killed Dow, I met him on several occasions, and always in a friendly manner, although I had at various times heard of his threatening me.

"In July or August of 1855, a branch of the Kansas Free State secret military organization was established among the Free State settlers around Hickory Point. Branson being their commander. Not long after this, I learned that he had not only threatened to use this force to put down and set at defiance the Territorial laws, but had stated, on several occasions, that he had an old grudge to settle with me—that he would like to meet me—that I should not live in the Territory, but that he would have his revenge before I quitted it, &c. It was also reported to me, some four days previous to my rencounter with Dow, that he (Dow), had declared, that 'he would beat my d—d brains out, if I went into the grove '—on my own claim—' to cut timber.' I was also warned by a Free State man, a friend of mine named Spar, 'that my life was in danger from the ill will harbored against me by Branson and Dow.'

"On, or about the 27th of November, 1855, between 11 and 12 o'clock A. M., I was at work making a lime-kiln, on my claim, in company with a young man named Harvey Moody.—Moody is a Free State man—I had been busy there since early in the morning, as I had been for several days previous. Dow came to the place where we were working ; he was alone, and apparently unarmed. He quarrelled with me about my claim—said he intended to stop our working there, and after making several threats left. I continued on with my work. In a short time after this visit from Dow, Moody called out to me, 'Here comes Branson and Dow.' On looking up I saw them approaching, armed with Sharpe's rifles. Both Moody and myself were entirely unarmed. I immediately left my claim without waiting for them to come up, for it was my belief that they intended to kill me, and were then coming upon me with arms in their hands for that purpose. Moody, being a Free State man, remained at his work. Moody has since informed me that on coming up they ordered him from the claim, stating that they would not hurt him ' this time,' but if they caught him there again, they would do him an injury ; they furthermore said, that they 'just wanted to see me, and asked Moody where I was? to which he replied, that 'I had gone home.' Upon hearing this, Dow took his gun and followed me. Moody states it as his belief, that they would have killed me if I had stayed for their coming. From my claim, I went immediately to the house of Mr. Hargis, a Pro-Slavery man, whose claim bordered upon my own, informed him of my being ordered off, and begged him, as I did not wish to trespass upon my neighbors, to come to my house that afternoon and assist me in establishing the dividing lines between his (Hargis) and my claim ; this he promised to do. I then armed myself with a double-barrelled fowling-piece, loaded with buckshot, intending upon going back to my work, to defend myself if again interfered with, and returned to Hargis's house, who had promised to accompany me, as above stated, that afternoon, with Buckley, a Pro-Slavery man, and one or two others, to assist in establishing the lines between Hargis and myself. Upon reaching Hargis's house, Buckley said that he was going to a whisky-store which stands opposite a blacksmith's shop, on the

Santa Fé trail, and which was half a mile distant from Hargis's. Buckley desired us not to wait for him, as he would meet us at my house, and left accordingly. Finding that my friends were detained longer than I had anticipated, I concluded to go out and see if I could discover anything of Buckley. In doing so, I passed by the house of William McKinney ; here I found McKinney engaged in building a chimney, and stopped to talk with him for a short time. Not seeing anything of Buckley, I started for home, and had continued on for a hundred and fifty yards, or thereabouts, when I entered the Santa Fé trail ; as I did so, I came *most unexpectedly* upon Dow, who was walking along the road, in the same direction as that in which I was going. On approaching him, he turned his head, and waited for me to come up. He was unarmed, with the exception of a wagon-skien—a piece of iron some two feet in length, and a most dangerous weapon in the hands of so powerful and determined a man as Dow is represented to have been.—Dow then entered into conversation with me about the claim difficulty, and continued to use hard language upon this subject until we had walked together as far as my house, which stands off the Santa Fé road about 75 yards. We must have gone side by side for some 400 or 500 yards. During this conversation I urged him to. compromise the matter, as I did not wish to have any trouble with my neighbors. When we got opposite to my dwelling, I moved off the road to go towards home. Dow walked on his way for a few paces, and then turned round and re-commenced quarrelling, high words passed, and Dow advanced upon me with the wagon-skien, which he was carrying in his hand, raising it as he did so, in an attitude to strike. I levelled my gun as he came on, brought it to bear upon him, and pulled the trigger ; the cap exploded but not the charge. Dow then paused, and turned as if to go away. Seeing this, I put my gun down upon the ground, which Dow had no sooner perceived than he faced towards me, and again advanced upon me with the skien, at the same time crying out, with an oath, ' You've bursted one cap at me, and you'll never live to burst another ;' hearing this, and believing that my life was in danger, I again levelled my gun and fired upon him, as he came rushing on ; the shot struck him (as I have since ascertained) in the neck and breast, and he fell—dead.

"I did not go up to the body ; but went immediately to my house, and told my wife that I had killed Dow; that I had been forced into it, having no other alternative to save my own life. I told her not to be uneasy about me ; that I was going to surrender myself up to be tried, and had no fears for the consequences, as my conscience acquitted me of any blame, I having acted only in self defence.

" Though I was not at the time aware of it, this transaction was seen by my friends Hargis and Moody, and also by a man named Wagoner, a Missourian, who happened to be in their company at the time. Wagoner is an enemy of mine. They were then on their way to ' kill a beef' in the timber not very far from my house, at which Hargis and Moody intended (as before stated), to stop, as they passed, and assist Buckley and myself in running the lines between my claim and that of Hargis in accordance with my request.

" In the evening several persons came to my house, and advised me, for fear of the Free State secret military organization—of which, as I have before mentioned, Branson, Dow's friend was one of the commanders—to leave the neighborhood. I at first declined to go, stating, as a reason for so doing, that such an act might be construed into a desire on my part to elude the officers of justice. They then suggested that I should deliver myself up to Governor Shannon, or some other fit person, at a distance from the scene of difficulty, where they believed that I would not only be in great personal danger, but have no chance to obtain an impartial hearing. I finally yielded to their entreaties, and left that night for Shawnee Mission, Governor Shannon's residence, which I reached upon the ensuing day, and immediately—in the temporary absence of the governor—delivered myself up to S. J. Jones, the sheriff of Douglas County (in which the killing took place), who happened to be in the vicinity of the Mission at the time of my arrival. Upon the return of Governor Shannon, His Excellency directed Sheriff Jones to convey me in custody to Lecompton, the county seat of Douglas, which he did. On my arrival there I was discharged upon giving bail to the amount of five hundred dollars, and am now only awaiting the assembling of a court to stand my trial."

We have read our fair copy of this paper over to Coleman, who endorses it as being entirely correct.

The so-called "murderers" statement is now before the reader, nor do we intend to add either note or comment save this.

So far as we could judge from Coleman's impartial and dispassionate manner while stating these alleged facts, we should say that he really believed what he was telling us. Whether his narrative will or will not be sustained by evidence must be proven on his trial by the testimony adduced. It will soon be settled by a judicial inquiry ;. and, in the meanwhile, we have no disposition to influence public opinion either for or against the accused.

Coleman is considered a rather good-looking man, of "genteel appearance," with dark hair and beard ; he is about five feet eleven in height ; is called amiable in his disposition, and has a wife and two children at present residing some four miles from Westport, Mo., whither they have fled for fear of the Free State party at Hickory Grove.

Governor Shannon informs us that he had commissioned

Coleman as a Justice of the Peace just previous to the killing
of Dow ; his credentials, however, although made out and
signed, had not yet been forwarded when the rencounter took
place.   Coleman has declined to receive this commission, in
accordance with the suggestion of Governor Shannon, until his
conduct in killing Dow has been judicially investigated and
decided upon.

CHAPTER XXIV

FOR LAWRENCE DIRECT.

Dec. 30.—Morning, at " old man " Harris's—breakfast over, and our travelling conveyance, a buggy with two livery-stable mules—mere rats—at the door. " Our Correspondent" *waddles* forth, equipped to encounter the cold weather in its most cutting form—that is to say, in a ride across the snow-covered and unsheltered prairies of Kansas. Let us give you an inside peep at his nether integuments. *Imprimis*—he has put on *two* pairs of woollen socks, ditto of drawers, ditto of pantaloons, item two coats, item an overcoat, item buffalo overshoes, gloves covered inside and out with fur, and a comforter whose intricate folds leave only one eye visible. As for the Major, he was so completely enveloped in buckskins—not to mention under-rigging—that he almost literally carried his wardrobe upon his back ; indeed he was *over-dressed*—a fact which he was destined to prove to his own satisfaction, as well as ours, by a tumble in the snow, where he lay kicking like a huge green turtle when you place it upon its back—until we were enabled to restrain our laughter sufficiently to rescue our friend from a predicament where he might have kicked till " the crack of doom," had no person been at hand to render assistance. Our first halt was at Shawnee Mission, where Governor Shannon wished us God-speed and a happy deliverance ; and from thence we whipped up our lazy beasts, beguiling the tediousness of the way with song and jest, and merry stories of frontier experiences, until the twilight hour brought us to Donaldson's, distant from Westport by eleven miles—for our start was a late one, and we had consumed the greater part of the day in our halt at the Mission.

Besides the usual inmates of Donaldson's house—who is himself a gruff, and not particularly prepossessing frontiersman—we found the remainder of our own party, consisting of Doctor Rodrigue, of Lecompton ; his son, a young man of some twenty years of age ; and a daughter, quite a pretty girl, who, if we guess the young lady's age correctly, was only sweet sixteen, and just about to encounter the hardships of a first trip across the Border.   There was yet another member of the Doctor's family, who merits something more than what the "Home Journal" used to call "mere mention."   He was, if report is to be credited, a man of many fortunes—a Prussian by birth, who had seen real service in European wars, where he had worn his epaulets on many a hard-fought field ; he told us, moreover, that he was present when the poet-soldier, Korner, he of "the Lyre and Sword," received his death wound, and assisted at his burial ; he says Korner was killed by a prisoner, who fired upon him from a baggage-wagon, with a musket, which had been left carelessly within his reach.

But our Prussian had laid down his military rank for ever, and taken up, instead (no uncommon change by the way) the vows and habit of a Roman Catholic priest ; indeed, it is not improbable that, as the Doctor and his family were enthusiastic followers of that persuasion, that he may have been accompanying their party as their Father confessor and spiritual guide. But we could not help thinking, as we gazed upon those strongly marked features, and that yet powerful, though now somewhat time-bowed form, that the priesthood had spoiled a good dragoon, and that the padre, like pious Friar Tuck, might still handle the quarterstaff quite as effectually as his breviary. Yet there was something touching, too—when we went to take our homely evening meal, in the fire-lighted apartment, which was both kitchen and supper-room—in the attitude of this war-worn old veteran, as he stood for a moment beside his chair, while he bent his head, and asked a silent blessing upon our food. It was, indeed, just such a picture as some of the grand old master's would have loved to paint. The man was a study in himself; and the rough cabin, with its yet more unpolished accessories, just the surroundings for a highly-finished interior of the Flemish school.

Supper was over; we had drawn our chairs nearer to the open fire-place; the winter night was dark without, and the blazing brands threw a cheerful glow upon the inmates of Donaldson's best sitting-room; the old priest had produced his short pipe, and tobacco-bag, and was now smoking placidly, with his dark eyes looking so intently the while at the glowing embers upon the hearth, that we almost fancied he must be reading some day-dream of the past in their ever-changing forms. The Major too, had divested himself of one or two courses of clothing, at least, so far as to permit of his bending his short, stout legs without outside assistance; and we, "The Correspondent," were trying vainly to get what is called a corn-cob pipe to draw, which, by the way, is a peculiarly Western institution, made by digging out the inside of a piece of cob, and then introducing a hollow reed for the stem, when the quick gallop of a horse's feet over the frozen ground, and a hallo from without, announced the arrival of another guest, who entered forthwith, in the person of a tall, athletic, and thoroughly benumbed-looking young man, who strode up to the fire-place, threw back his cloak, and extended his chilled hands towards the blazing log heap.

As he approached more closely to the fire-place, Major Clarke glanced at the new comer, and with a "How are you, Doak?"

at once grasped him by the hand. It was his brother-in-law,
who had left "House on the Prairie," the Major's residence,
that morning, and had ridden thus far on his road to Westport,
whither he was going to meet the Major ; to whom he was the
bearer of important letters, containing intelligence of an alarm-
ing and highly irritating nature. One of these epistles was
from Doctor Johnson, of whom we have already spoken as having
been shot at by some would-be-assassin, on one or two occasions,
but without effect. The other was from the Major's wife, with
whom we had the pleasure of a very brief acquaintance, during
our visit at her house, which, slight as it was, gave us a very
high opinion of the good sense and true feminine courage of our
fair hostess.

Doctor Johnson's letter, of which the Major very kindly permitted us to make a copy, reads as follows ;—

House on the Prairie, Kansas Territory, December 30, 1855.

Dear Major :

Rufus, the bearer of this letter, will inform you that matters
are fast coming to a desperate conclusion with us—a crisis which requires
both prompt and energetic action is approaching.

Your family are not safe here even for a single night. Your house is
watched as though it were a den of thieves. Your dog has disappeared ; we
presume he has been decoyed away and killed to prevent his giving an alarm.
One of your carriage horses has been poisoned, and, in addition to this, an
attempt was made to fire your house. This occurred last night, between
twelve and one o'clock A.M. It was fortunate that we discovered the fire before
it was too late ; we were but just in time to save the building. Had it been
otherwise, God only knows what would have become of your family ; for,
even supposing that they had escaped the flames, they would have been
exposed to the danger of perishing in the bitter cold of this inclement
season, ere they could have reached the nearest neighbor's house. (Major
Clarke's residence is three-quarters of a mile from any house, and the mercury at the time stood at twenty degrees below zero, and it would have
been almost a miracle, under such circumstances, if they had escaped freezing.) But to come to the point : you cannot live here ; it is risking too
much ; the very existence of your family is at stake ; your own life is

in imminent danger; you would not be safe here—no, not for a single day. If you were here it would only aggravate the evil. For God's sake, remove your family. Take them to Missouri, or up among the Pottawatomie Indians. They would be safe there. Your property, too, is in imminent danger.

Every day brings the intelligence of some new act of outrage—house-burnings, brutal threatenings, and attempted assassinations. How can we go on living thus, in God's name? Is there no law in Kansas? To whom are we to look for aid? How is all this to end? Are our lives to be menaced—is our property to be destroyed—and are women and children to be driven from their desolated homes, without the upraising of an arm to stay the perpetrators of these acts of lawless violence? Is there no power vested in our Governor—no protection to be obtained from the Executive? Or must the law-abiding citizens of Kansas be driven into the terrible alternative of defending, by Lynch law and armed violence, their homes and firesides? If we have laws why are they not enforced? Something must be done for our relief, and that speedily.

The foregoing is all which would be interesting to the reader. It is written by Dr. George W. Johnson, who is—as we have elsewhere stated—a son of Governor Johnson of Virginia. A postscript from William H. Doak, Esq., a brother-in-law of Major Clarke's—the bearer of the documents being named Rufus—endorses and corroborates the foregoing statements, and adds that they are going to get some of their neighbors to assist in defending Major Clarke's house until arrangements can be made for the removal of his family.

The letter from Mrs. Clarke is of similar import.

Major Clarke's residence is at present occupied by two families—this has been the case since the breaking out of the Kansas troubles. Among its inmates may be numbered two females and five small children. Had they been left houseless, on the bitter night of December thirtieth, to find their way through the frozen snow to the nearest dwelling (three-quarters of a mile distant), it is most probable that some of these little ones would have fallen victims to the terrible state of things which now exists in some sections of Kansas.

The facts connected with this incendiary attempt, as related to us by Mr. Rufus Doak, the bearer of the letters, are these :

Between 12 and 1 o'clock on the morning of the thirtieth of December, Mr Doak and Dr. Johnson were awakened by the appearance of smoke and a smell as if of burning tar in the room in which they were sleeping. They immediately arose, and on making examination discovered fire under one of the rooms, adjoining that in which Major Clarke's family were sleeping. They found, upon looking, that the underpinning of this portion of the house (a frame one) had been removed, and a fire of light wood sticks built underneath. To render the destruction of the house more certain, other combustibles were placed in such a position as to feed the flames. An outbuilding also filled with hay, gathered from a neighboring stack. This had been ignited, but did not burn out—probably from the hay having being wet with snow. The flames were discovered just in time to save the house.

Major Clarke and Dr. Johnson are the only persons living in the vicinity of Lawrence who signed the address to the people, recently published by the "Law and Order Convention," which assembled at Leavenworth City in November last.

MIDNIGHT.

P. S.—Information has just reached us from a reliable source, that a party of Major Clark's neighbors, well-meaning, but inconsiderate men, have it in contemplation to turn out, investigate the affair thoroughly, arrest the suspected persons, and if sufficient evidence be adduced, lynch the offenders. A man named Jones is more particularly threatened. We understood that it was in contemplation to tie him up and whip him into a confession. Major Clarke has, however, with great good sense, determined to discountenance any act on the part of the Pro-Slavery people, which might even be construed into an attempt to take the law into their own hands. He will use every exertion to bring the perpetrators of these unauthorized acts to justice, but will do so in a strictly legal way. We shall continue our journey at daybreak—he to repress any ill-judged demonstration on the part of his neighbors, whose indignation—he tells us—has been highly excited by these repeated attempts to do him injury ; and we to gather facts which will enable us to report " the truth, the whole truth, and nothing but the truth," without fear, favor, or affection. It is to be feared, however, that the Major will arrive too late.

Ere our dispatch was concluded, the four inches of candle —which our amiable host, with a shrewd eye to economy, had declared, was enough, as he reckoned, for all thar pen-work that we would want to do—were almost burned down, and as its last line was written, fairly flickered in the socket. We hesitated for a moment; listened to the deep-drawn snores of our neighbors, and then doffed our outer garments, and after groping about for a while in a sort of Egyptian darkness (though, for that matter, we never could understand why it should be darker in Egypt than anywhere else), found our way to the unoccupied half of the Major's feather-bed, where we burrowed in, so utterly wearied both in mind and body, that we were in the far-off land of dreams almost upon the instant that our tired head touched the pillow.

CHAPTER XXV.

NEW YEAR'S EVE BY A LOG-CABIN HEARTH.

DECEMBER 31st, the last day of poor old 1855.—And very early, in this Polar Region, of a winter morning to boot. But early as it is, we should have been on our way full an hour ago, had we not been delayed by the stupidity of one of Donaldson's negroes, who has been *chasse*-ing up and down half an acre of timber, in pursuit of our mule-rats, who, though lazy enough in the harness, would seem to be more than sufficiently vivacious when released from its thraldom.

Nine o'clock.—Off at last, with a freezing wind blowing keenly, and a twenty miles' ride before us to Bean's on the Wakarusa, where we expect to pass the night ; our way laid for the most part over long ridges of prairie ; the dreariest of dreary winter roads ; but the Major and myself had made up our minds to " 'joy ourselves," as the darkeys say at Christmas time ; and after our fashion, we did, for we begun singing songs most awfully out of tune, and telling all sorts of " yarns," and managed to keep even with the unpropitious weather, until within five miles of our stopping-place, and then Jack Frost got the better of us ; we grew silent ; the Major swore he was " most froze," and not another word was spoken, except to the mules, and only then in the way of admonition, until " Our Correspondent " was aroused from the half sleeping state into which he had fallen, by an imitation of a Pottawatomie war-hoop from the Major, and a cry of "Thank the Lord, there's Bean's cabin at last," as we drove up to the rail fence which formed its apology for an enclosure. We had not been housed over half an hour when Doctor Rodrigue's ambulance arrived, and reinforced our party by the addition of its hungry and half-frozen inmates.

New Year's *eve.*—We are all gathered about the fire in the already described best room of Bean's log-cabin " hotel;" and bad is the best here. There is a huge fire upon the hearth, and we draw our chairs as closely up to it as the number of the circle to be warmed will permit. It is certainly a very mixed assembly—this impromptu New Year's eve party of ours—such an one, indeed, as is only united by chance. Let us give you a few of the principal heads.

And first for the ladies, " God bless them," say we to-night, wherever they may be, by log-cabin hearths or in city chambers, whether high or low, rich or poor, matron or maid, once more we say God bless them all, for they shall be included in our toast to-night, if Bean's whisky be sufficiently drinkable to permit of our " wishing luck " in a glass of the beverage to old, dying 1855, ere he makes his midnight flitting for parts unknown.

But let's return to the ladies. Mistress Bean, a fat, middle-aged, and withal right good-natured body, occupies a cosy seat, if such a thing is to be found in an apartment which admits the wintry blast at every nook and cranny, even without counting the windows that the red cow knocked her horn through some ten days syne.

The corner opposite to our stout hostess is graced by the presence of the fair Miss Rodrigue, whose sweet, sunshiny face, shaded by a profusion of dark brown hair, and yet girlish form, would seem more in keeping with the superfluities of a metropolitan drawing-room, than with the rude furniture and very primitive residence of our landlord, Mr. Bean. Beside Miss

Rodrigue sits her father, a short, slenderly-built, keen-eyed and almost raven-haired man, with military whiskers, and an intellectual brow, whose manner is that of a polished gentleman, not the gentleman of the saloons, but that of a man who has seen the world, knows life thoroughly, and has studied mankind, until mankind has become a readable book. He is, therefore, quite at his ease, and can accommodate himself to the eccentricities of those about him, without stepping out of his own calm dignified style. To the Doctor, circumstances are slaves—not masters.

Then we have Doctor Rodrigue's son, and his father confessor, the old soldier-priest, who have already had their sittings for our pen and ink portraits. And then we must not forget our companion of the road, the Major, who sits nursing his leg—the very picture of drollery and good-heartedness—and peering into the blaze, as if he had just caught the profile of some new-born comicality which he was imaging forth among the red-eyed coals.

Then, there's "old man Bean," who was once a soldier—one of Harney's dragoons on the Indian frontier, years ago, who will tell you still that the old General can swear a little harder, and fight a little faster than any man of his feet and inches—some six feet three—whom he has ever looked upon before or since. And then last, but very far from least, there's "Our Correspondent," a long, thin, high-browed every-day specimen of New Yorker humanity—bearded—in the absence of the barberous—like a pard, of whom the least said the soonest mended.

And now, as we have somewhat minutely introduced our *dramatis personæ* to your notice, we will endeavor to increase the reader's obligation by telling him something of what they say, and as we intend to treat their talk very much in the same way as you may compliment these, our scribblings—by skimming it, don't quarrel with us if our report should come to you in a somewhat disjointed and fragmentary style. For we will venture to say that an evening's chat never took a wider range than did our fire-side conversation upon the New Year's Eve of 1856—for the subject treated, and not badly treated either in some instances, comprised the state of the country, politics, more particularly those of Kansas Territory—" the war"— from a recapitulation of which may prudence deliver us—Spiritualism—ghost stories, strange coincidences, Border life—crops Indians, and Divinity, with now and then, some sly allusions to New York modes and manners, with all their extravagance of hoops, flounces, and flirtations. So we cry place for a yarn or two, and as politics leads the van of our multiplicity of headings, we will introduce anecdote No. 1., which is a veritable yarn, by which we mean not a made-up lie—a fiction founded upon falsehood, but a dressed up truth which came to us in a home-spun garb. Are we to be blamed, then, if we should present it to you in a silken gown ? It may be called

POLITICAL ADVICE GRATIS.

We would recommend the following to politicians going West, and especially to those who are about visiting Kansas.

There was, once upon a time, a certain lieutenant in the navy of Uncle Sam, who, like a sensible man, came finally to the conclusion that " going down to the sea in ships " was a humbug, and " doing business upon the great waters " a very great bore; in short, he resigned, and as republics are proverbially ungrateful, found it necessary to seek out some new field of action, in which to mow a living for himself ; he cogitated deeply, for it was an important step ; his "bread and butter" were in the scale, and it is hardly to be wondered at that " the inexhaustible resources of the growing West " should have kicked the beam in the choice of location, the more so as there are great openings for business-hunting young men in " those diggin's," even without counting the Mammoth Cave in Kentucky. Well, our resigned lieutenant made up his mind to emigrate, and was seriously engaged in making the necessary preparations for so doing, when an old politician, a warm friend of our sailor's, dropped in to give him some farewell advice.

"My dear ——," said he, "you are going West. It is a great country—a wonderful country. You are young and enterprising ; you will enter into political life, and in all human probability be elected to Congress. Now, let me give you a few practical hints, which you will find invaluable in stumping it among the "Hoosiers," they are the result of twenty years' working in the political harness. I adopted them as my sheet anchors for the last fifteen years of that period, and my only regret is that I didn't do so during the first five. They are easy to learn and not hard to practise, for as 'brevity is the soul of wit,' I reduced the whole matter to these three simple rules :

"1. In the Western country *never tell a lie* politically, for you are sure to be found out—therefore be honest."

"2. In the Western country *never tell the truth* politically, for somebody will be ass enough to dispute with you, which leads to argument—therefore don't."

"3. In the Western country *never have anything to do with stationery* politically—meaning thereby, pen, ink and paper—for it leads to writing, which is the most irretrievable error of all, for though that which is spoken may be denied—that which is written—can't be—therefore eschew writing as you would the Devil."

Whether our resigned lieutenant followed these very excellent suggestions, and went to Congress from some border district as a *running* commentary upon their worth, we are most unfortunately not able to say—that he prospered pecuniarily we doubt not, for who does not know that Jack never fares better than when "you turn him out to grass."

Under the Theological head of our New Year's Eve log-cabin-fire chat, we remember nothing more *edifying* than the following, which its narrator, the Jolly Man, may, for aught we know to the contrary, have cribbed from the "splinters" of some obscure Far Western country newspaper ; but cribbed or not, it isn't bad, and moreover, it was related to us as being strictly true ; the reader may therefore regard it as a veritable incident in the life of a distinguished man, who united great talents with a considerable amount of eccentricity. But the Jolly Man shall tell his own story in his own way, without further preamble from us. He calls it :

FANATICISM REBUKED—AN ANECDOTE OF AARON BURR.

"It was on a bright Sabbath morning, and in a certain rural village, which, for convenience sake, shall be called Mud Hollow, that the incident occurred which I am about to relate. The 'church-going bell' had ceased ringing, and the little wooden meeting-house was already crowded to excess, for a 'revival' was going on, and all Mud Hollow was on fire with the anxiety of its people for the welfare of their souls. While things were in this truly commendable condition, the church-door opened gently, and an aged man walked noiselessly in—he paused for a moment as he entered, and looked timidly round, as if seeking for a vacant pew, but the worshippers in that immediate vicinity were all too busily engaged in listening to a 'fire and brimstone' delineation of the horrors to be expected in the *worse* world to come—which a very Methodistical-looking personage, a vinegar-faced compound of white neck-handkerchief and hymn book, was delivering in the most approved sledge-hammer style—to pay any particular attention to the advent of a new arrival. Aaron Burr, for such was the old man's celebrated name, accordingly continued on, and was walking, hat in hand, up the narrow, middle aisle, to seek out, perchance, some more charitable Christian, who might be moved by the grey-haired stranger's feeble appearance to offer him the courtesy of a resting-place. But if such were his expectation it was doomed to be disappointed, for Burr found himself obliged to continue on, and was still advancing, though the 'anxious benches' were close at hand, when the preacher paused abruptly in his harangue, extended his hand and cried out, as he pointed the fore-finger directly at his venerable hearer :

" ' Thar—thar comes a child of the Devil—a hoary-headed sinner—and ef he don't repent and turn from the error of his ways, he'll be damned—damned—damned to the lowest depths of fiery perdition, and *I shall bear witness against him* before the Judgment Seat of God.'

" The effect of this outburst seemed electrical. Burr stopped short in his tracks as if struck with a sudden paralysis. But his moment of astonishment, or it may be of speechless indignation, at the indignity which had just been offered him, was soon over, for in an instant his course of action was decided upon, as, raising his trembling right arm to enforce attention, he proceeded to rebuke the impertinence of the ill-bred fanatic, who had so gratuitously insulted him, in the following words, and it is said that you might have heard a pin fall, in the intense silence of that over-crowded building, as the startled audience listened eagerly to their delivery :

" ' Ladies and Gentlemen,' said Burr, ' with your good parson's permission, I should be pleased if you would permit me to say a very few words. You may perhaps, be aware, that my life has been one of many experiences, and I may add that in the course of those experiences, it has been my painful, although not unusual lot, to come in contact with some scoundrels, but among all the villians of whom I have ever heard, or even read

of in the calenders of human crime, I know none so base—
so unmitigated—so vile—and so utterly irreclaimable—as the
transgressor who *turns State's Evidence.'*

"Need I add, that he of the neck-handkerchief and hymn book
was 'no whar,' while the sinner was most unanimously voted unworthy of the 'doubly deep-damnation, which the reverend *gentleman* had so confidently threatened."

But our fire-side yarns have taken up too much room already,
for with such a "feast of reason and a flow of soul," as our
"Wakarusa war," wherewith to regale the reader, we can scarce
afford to tickle his literary palate with side dishes. So we must
even deny ourself the pleasure of recording good Mistress Bean's
very entertaining narrative, of the manner in which she beat off
a party of drunken Indians (who insisted on entering her cabin
by the window, after having been refused admission at the door),
with a shovel full of red hot coals, which she wielded like an
Amazon, while her younger sister lay screaming under the bed,
until the "big Ingin," who led on this riotous crew, fled, yelling,
from the scene of conflict, with his shirt on fire and an inflamma-
tion of the chest ; for our buxom hostess "upsot," to use her
own expression, not only the contents of the shovel, but the
greater portion of a tea-kettle full of scalding water into the
breast of the unlucky redskin.

There was another incident that, we regret to say, is also
"unavoidably crowded out for want of room" to do its merits
justice, and this was a wolf-fight, in which a young married
lady, who hadn't learned the etiquette of the Far Western
country, and her unfortunate husband, who was stupid enough
to discharge a gun, which, as his better half assured him, she
had loaded *so* carefully that very day, figured considerably. The
point of the story lies in the fact, that the lady had heard her
husband say that he put in just three *fingers* of powder in charging the piece ; and so, indeed, had she, the only discrepancy in

their calculations being this—that he measured *à la* hunter—by *breadth*, while she, as women are accustomed to do, calculated by *length*—which, in the end, or, to speak more properly, in the chamber, makes all the difference in the world, not only in the quantity of powder but in the severity of the recoil ; for, in this instance, our well-meaning dame could honestly boast that her husband's gun was an improvement upon any known patent, inasmuch as, under *her* supervision, it might literally be said to kill at both ends.

So much for our New Year's Eve.

We have jotted down the following conversation, which we heard to-day. It was carried on between two " Border Ruffians," and struck us as being a particularly rich, and withal noteworthy, specimen of the peculiar phraseology of the Far West.

First Borderer.—Jim, what are yeou doing now—busy, hey ?

Second Borderer.—Busy, thunder ; I'm just that busy, that I have to keep a jumping round like a toad under a harrer.

First Borderer.—How's Bob ?

Second Borderer.—Oh, Bob's flat broke, as flat as a nigger baby's head, rolled under a saw-log.

First Borderer.—Why, I thought the' ole man would have kep him up.

Second Borderer.—So. he would ; but Bob's such a no-a-count cuss that the ole man jest gin him up, and now he's so poor, that if steamboats war a dime a-piece, Bob couldn't buy a yawl.

First Borderer.—How about that fight you had tother day with Parsons ?

Second Borderer.—Wael, I allow it wasn't much of a fight, no how ; we didn't reckon nothin' on it, down our way ; it war jest a difficulty about a claim that me and some of Parsons' boys got inter ; so ole man Parsons jumped me up—but I reckon he didn't size my pile.

First Borderer.—Did you drop him ?

Second Borderer.—*Well*, I did ; but he's a mean cuss ; for I hed him down fār, and war a gougin' him, when he got this hyar right thumb of mine inter his dog-gaun ugly mouth, and I'll jest allow ole man Parsons *hes* got teeth like a bar ; for while I war a gougin' him, he kep a chawin' away, as ef my thumb war hog meat ; an' now I'll be dog-gauned ef I kin strike nary lick with it, without hollerin' like a wild Ingin, with thar pain.

First Borderer.—Wael, ole man Parsons *is* some—but come, Jim, let's licker.

Second Borderer.—Well, now ycou *air* a talkin' ; for hyar's a child that air a heap dryer nor a powder-horn. (*Exeunt omnes* to the grocery).

Apropos to groceries, an artist friend of ours, who is not, by the way, altogether "unknown to fame," tells us the following of his road-side experiences in the Far West. He had gone upon a sketching tour, and, in the course of his perambulations, "put up" at a shanty tavern, which rejoiced in a log kitchen, *one* common sleeping room, and a *bar*. Now our friend, strange as it may seem, believed that whisky, in moderation, was a healthy drink, and ought, therefore, to be patronized ; so having passed one night under his landlord's roof, he entered the bar-room, after a late breakfast, and ordered an " eye opener," by way of preparation for a hard day's study in the field. Upon tendering a dime in payment for his drink, that being the smallest coin in his possession, while the current value of the article purchased was just half that sum ; the landlord—a long, ague-shaken, hard-featured man—searched first one pocket and then the other, until breeches, coat, vest, and even an old overcoat, which hung upon a peg in the corner, had been thoroughly ransacked ; but the result was still the same—no effects. The landlord seemed bothered ; but his uncertainty soon vanished,

11*

for, having quietly faced about, and gone to smoking his corn-cob pipe, upon a low rush-bottomed chair beside the stove, he finally drawled out these words :—

"Stranger, the bar owes you half-a-dime. Bob," added he, turning to a white-headed urchin, who mixed the drinks, and managed the business of the concern in his father's absence, "Bob, do you hyar? the bar owes this hyar stranger half-a-dime."

And then, as if fully satisfied with this ingenious method of arranging the account, the landlord drew placidly at his pipe, until he may be said to have been enveloped in an atmosphere of his own. Our artist, much amused, made his exit and his sketches, and upon returning at night, quite wearied with a long ramble, he once more stepped up to the bar, and demanded a "whisky-straight ;" the compound was poured out, mixed, and swallowed, upon being assured of which, the agueish-looking vender turned solemnly to his boy, and gave utterance to this very laconic sentence :—

"Bob, the bar an' this hyar stranger hev got *squār !*"

Is not this what a mercantile man would call balancing an account by a *double entry?*

CHAPTER XXVI.

OUR NEW YEAR'S CALL.

JANUARY 1st, 1856.—New-Year's day, and no calls to be made ; what a position for a representative of the Knickerbocker State—was there ever so great a change ? no white kids—no carriage—no nice young ladies with their voluminous skirts and sunny smiles—no " compliments of the season "—no tables set out—no hot whisky-punch—no fun—no head-ache—no nothing—but in lieu of these we caught our first glimpse of New Year's morning through the chinks of a poorly-daubed log-cabin, a sort of detached chamber for two, where the snow lay almost as thick inside as it did out. And now we will beg the reader, especially if *she* be a female reader, to suppose us dressed, and then come with us to our wash-stand—it's that tin basin, in which we have just broken the ice—you can't miss it—it stands on the bench just *outside* the main cabin ; and now wait a moment until we polish ourself off with this frozen board of a towel by courtesy, and we will ask you in to the fire—but what's that ?—bang—bang—bang—why, don't you know? it's the Far Western fashion of welcoming in the New Year. Where's our revolver ? pop—pop—pop—there go five loads of powder, and now, as we have celebrated the day, let's get in to breakfast. We won't invite you to share our repast, but you may kill time profitably by watching the glorious doings of old hard-featured Jack Frost, who has decked every shrub, and tree, and creeping thing, with his silver filagree work, and fringed pendants, which glitter and sparkle like diamonds on a Northern beauty's brow, as they wave to and fro in the cold clear sunshine of this bracing winter's morning. And now a hiatus of one short hour will find us packed and ready to start. But we must first suffer a detention, for the roads are "mighty slick," as a Kansas teamster would say, and the Wakarusa creek, with its steep sides, will "bother us right smartly" within the next hundred yards; it will therefore be hardly worth while to get into our conveyances, until their respective drivers have gotten them safely over, so we will make our start upon foot, which enables us to give the pretty Miss Rodrigue an arm. We begin the descent, and had got as far in our conversation by the way, as "Take care, if you please, Miss, or *you* will certainly fall"—when suddenly we experienced a sensation (for our buffalo shoes were smooth-soled, and the hill-side yet smoother), and, as a natural consequence, our heels went up, while our head, in obedience to those unaccommodating laws of gravitation, went down, which brought us to the bottom of the "bluff," a descent of some twenty feet, in much less time than it takes to write it, where we picked ourself up as rapidly as our confusion would permit, with a sort of intuitive consciousness, which was reduced to a dead certainty, by an upward glance, that somebody was laughing at us, and that somebody, a very nice young lady, whom we had just parted from in what a Kentuckian would have styled "a most extraordinary and radiculous manner." But it's just our luck, for

> "We never had a tree or flower,
> Nor walked a slippery bit of ground,"

as the poet has it, without a catastrophe *somewhere*. Certain it is, that we didn' offer to see the "*señorita*" up the hill as well as down, though perhaps, as she had certainly seen us *down*, it would have been thing more than a fair retaliation, but we confess it, we felt, as we scrambled up the icy slope, that we would, in our unchristian frame of mind, have given all our old shoe-leather, and something else into the bargain, to have seen the damsel follow the example of her "illustrious predecessor." But we hoped in vain, for we all, alas! reached the crest of the bank in safety, where we waited for the "buggies," which had been obliged to adopt a more circuitous trail, ere they could mount the hill up which we, the pedestrians, had with so much difficulty won our way. Here we took a fresh start, and bade farewell to our fair companion, whose bright eyes looked as mischievous as only a coquettish woman's eyes can look, when she don't want to laugh at you, but can't help it, and hoisted ourself into the buggy, in which the stout Major, more *overdressed* than ever, had already stowed himself away. And then on—on—on—over the smooth, snow-covered road, through the keen nipping air, with the Ice King's' banners waving gorgeously over our heads, we sped rapidly upon our way, until the huge trunks and leafless branches of the "river bottom" were left behind, and we gained once more the open prairie-land.

The sun of January 1st was not more than three hours high, when we trotted into the main street of Franklin, and halted at its log-cabin hotel. Here we "tied up" for a few moments, and in company with Mr. Doak, entered a small frame building, labelled "Grocery," where we hoped to get a warm, even if we didn't procure a "warmer." And as such "Groceries" are common in the West, we will give the reader—*en passant*—a rough notion of its furnishing: it was a one-room affair, say, ten feet by twelve—or, if anything, smaller—with a counter—a row of rough board shelves garnished with a couple of dirty decanters, a batch of yet more uncleanly tumblers, and a box marked *Havanas*, which were but too evidently "live-oak penny-a-grabs." The stock-in-trade of the establishment, however, lay in a couple of barrels which stood in one corner, with a spigot in each, marked "Highly-rectified Whisky," with something else about "copper" upon them, which we didn't altogether understand, but afterwards determined, from a description of their contents, to be an abbreviation indicating copperas, or some similar ingredient. We have heard a shorter name for the compound, which, though inelegant, is nevertheless expressive ; this title is nothing more nor less than "rot-gut whisky," with an addenda about its "killing forty rods round a corner," which, as it is an every-day remark in Missouri, we may possibly have told you before. But let us get back to our grocery interior. The bar-tender and proprietor was what bar-tenders of his class generally are—slightly inebriated ; with no coat on—which, as his linen was far from unexceptionable, would have been rather an improvement than otherwise—and a strange knack of mixing drinks and making change. The company which graced this delectable apartment were, to do them justice, quite in keeping with the place : a *single*-eyed chap, with a very red nose, and an astonishing pair of legs, sat astride of one of the liquor barrels—he and they were evidently *proved* friends—with an old weather-beaten hat cocked knowingly over his blind eye, while the other seemed fully employed in getting up a series of winks, any one of which would have been a fortune to Burton *in ʼe* Toodles. When we entered the room, "Legs" was fiddling away—as if his very existence depended upon the accuracy of his execution—at that never-failing tune, "The Arkansaw Traveller." Next to this worthy, upon a rush-bottomed chair, which might as well have had but two legs instead of four, for any service required by its present occupant, sat a kindred spirit, who braced himself against the stove door with his right foot, while its companion swung backward and forward, or when this motion grew wearisome, varied the monotony by kicking time vigorously against the floor.

A filthy, liquor-stained table—extemporized for the occasion by placing a piece of plank across an empty barrel head—at which three bad Border specimens were playing what in Mississippi river parlance is sometimes called " a friendly game of poker," completed the filling up of this miniature pandemonium ; and when we add that those who wan't smoking, were for the most part swearing "strange oaths and barbarous to hear," we presume that we have given the reader a sufficiency of outline, which he may fill up or·not as his fancy dictates. Yet we were very polite to these fellows, for it's just possible, and highly probable, withal, that had we given ourself airs, " we mout hev got a most all-fired thrashing," but being schooled in Western ways, and knowing too, that there is no country where appearances are so deceptive as in the Far West, we did just what we should advise the reader to do in a similar "crowd" and under like circumstances. We, stepped in with a " How are you, *gentlemen* ?" declined an invitation to drink, out of respect to our interior economy, but compromised thé refusal by accepting one of the " live-oak penny-a-grab" cigars, which we endeavored to smoke until Mr Doak was ready to start, when our " Good morning, gentle men," proved us to be " a mighty well-raised young man."

Once more upon the road, Doak pressed his horse up to the side of our vehicle, and as he galloped within whipping distance, switched our lazy mule rats into something between a trot and a would-be canter, which brought the buggy over the ground at a very respectable rate, until we reached the forks of the Lawrence road, from which that renowned city is plainly to be seen. Here we halted, for it would not have been " healthy," in the then excited state of party feeling, for Major Clarke to have entered the place. So we parted with mutual good wishes, he to continue on to his residence near Lecompton, and we to achieve the real celebration of our New Year's day, by walking into the far-famed city of Lawrence--" the Athens of Kansas," to quote from the Free State people, or "the Gall Bag of the Territory," if you prefer the Pro-Slavery appellation—where we hoped to tread the classic ground, and gaze upon the impregnable fortifications of the Sebastopol of the West.

Our welcome to the *exterior* of Lawrence at least, was of the coldest, for the snow-clad prairie-slopes, the chill December blast, and the hoar-frosted woods of the Wakarusa bottom, all said mercury at zero, if no worse. Under these depressing circumstances we halted, carpet-bag in hand, at the first "improvement," as they call a house in this country. It was a shanty of the "rough and ready" sort, a composite of logs and boards, and about the size of an ordinary cow-pen : but we were anxious to see the inside of a Yankee settler's hut, so making a drink of water an apology, we knocked, was invited in, and entered, and a delightful change it was from the uninviting landscape, which impressed one so chillingly without. Let us sketch in a pleasant interior, rich in warm tints, and lit up by real heart sunshine, just such a cozy scene, in fact, as Dickens would have loved to people with his Perrybingles and Cratchits. A nice little woman with a bright-eyed baby upon her knee (we have a weakness for babies), and a tiny flaxen-haired young lady of some six years old, occupied a rude arm-chair and "home manufactured" stool, beside the old-fashioned New England cooking-stove. On the bed, which half filled the only apartment, that did duty at once, as parlor, kitchen, and bed-chamber, sat a diminutive, but clever-looking man, who smiled pleasantly as we came in, and said, "Sit down," at the same time pointing to a chair, where, as we more than half suspected, he had, when we knocked, been sitting, a good deal closer to his better-half than he was when we entered the "improvement." We say we suspected, for her dark-brown hair, which evidently *had been* most scrupulously arranged, was now disordered on the side next to *him*. Now, we don't mean to say that he had been sitting with an arm thrown round that taper waist, or that he had been kissing that almost *too* rosy cheek ; no, it *might* have been the baby, but do you know, when we think of the temptation, we are not so sure that it *was* the baby after all.

We asked for a drink, and this little woman, a very " Dot " of a wife, laid her " Dot " of a baby very gently upon the bed, with a look of motherly tenderness as she did so, that reminded us of some truly poetic lines which speak of

" A woman's crown of glory,
The blessing of a child,"

and then our New England " Dot " handed us a tin dipper full of clear, cold water—but such a dipper, " clean as hands could make it," as the old saw has it.   But it wasn't the dipper alone, for if cleanliness be contagious, it must have been so here, for, though everything bespoke a new country, everything was neat—neat even to a fault ; your eye almost longed for something out of place, just to break up the monotony.   There were plenty of books, too, that is to say, plenty for a new settlement, books that were books, none of your gilt-edged, mean-nothing sentimentalities, but hard facts, and standard fiction, with here and there a volume which bore the name of one of those

" Bards sublime
Whose distant footsteps echo,
Through the corridors of time."

And better still, the man himself was reading.   But we found him (alas) ! full of fight, though we wouldn't have you think that we don't approve of fighting, for who doesn't know that desperate diseases require desperate remedies sometimes, but then it's a *bad* business at the best, and with such a wife and baby, even without counting in the flaxen-haired little girl, a great deal *worse*.   So we are candid enough to confess that we didn't like our diminutive Yankee's pugnacity.   Yet upon this one subject he seemed perfectly rabid, for he had worked in the trenches—he had handled his Sharpe's rifle—he hated the Border Ruffians—he wouldn't be conservative—he was prepared to " do and die " in cause of Free State-ism and Kansas—in short, our friend was of that ultra type who would treat a political difficulty as an old school allopathist would prescribe for a fever, by *letting blood for it*. He was a " Deown Easter " of course—asked plenty of questions—giving guarded replies to such queries as were put to him, until he discovered that we were from " York State," and then thawed out like a snow-bank in the sun.

And this was our first, and we may as well say, in some respects, pleasantest experience of Lawrence. For we must confess that we have not yet fallen in love with this politician, or perhaps we should rather say politics-ridden town. Lawrence labors under one very serious difficulty, she needs *less talk* and *more work*. There is no cause, however good or just, which has not, since the beginning of time, been more or less afflicted by *cant*, and Free State-ism does not appear to be exempt from this universal curse. As in Missouri we heard too much of "those rascally Abolitionists," and " those infernal nigger-stealing Free State men in Kansas," so in Lawrence we were equally annoyed by the everlasting reiteration of such remarks as, " those hounds, the Border Ruffians, who would kill children and insult our women, if they were not afraid of our rifles." Now, all this is wrong, radically wrong on both sides. Give us a little less, good people, of what that much-quoted, and very sensible authority, Mr. Weller, calls, " A passin of Resolutions, and a wotin' of Supplies, and all sorts of goings on," and a little more of that honest toil which puts the sweat on the working-man's brow, and the hard dollars in his purse, and we will venture to say, that Lawrence will be none the worse politically, and considerably the better in a pecuniary point of view, for our suggestion. At present " the war " seems like charity, which " covereth a multitude of sins," for if you ask a man why he doesn't repair his uncomfortable house, he tells you he would but for the war; and the same reply will be tendered you, if a cow elope in search of better shelter than her owner's pen affords, or a pig break out of his dilapidated stye; it is ever "the war, the war," in all its moods and tenses. For know all men that the "war"—past, present and prospective—haunts Lawrence like a nightmare, until her worthy citizens are transformed into heroes of battles which might have been, while her orators season their discourses with "villainous saltpetre," and even the tailor grown familiar with "war's alarms," shoulders his yard-stick, and tells his customers how fields may yet be won.

In sober earnest, we really think that Kansas may take up the cry, "preserve me from my friends," for, even at the risk of pleasing nobody, we feel justified in saying that Southern Fillibusterism and Northern interference, have, in no respect, done Kansas any good. She has, or had, within herself elements which must, sooner or later, have produced results which would have won for her the respect, if not the admiration, of her sister States ; for we thank God that there is, even upon the Far Western border, a remnant, 'small though it be, of honest thinking, and conservative men, whose nobility of character will stand out in bolder relief in the hour of political danger and agitation, as the sky above them grows blacker and more lowering. Would that there were more such, for we should then hear less of windy vaporings with their threatenings of disunion and retaliation. But we have too much to say in the way of description, to be able to afford even a *conservative* digression here ; so let us on to Lawrence.

Upon entering the city proper, we took up our quarters at the "Cincinnati House," so called because it is literally a Cincinnati house, having been brought out in pieces from that hog-slaughtering city, to be re-united in the Territory: houses, it may be remarked, are one of the *few* "foreign importations," which unite harmoniously in Kansas.

Of this, "mine inn," we shall say nothing, for we bear in mind the proverb, of the least said the soonest mended ; it would have been a blessed thing, by the way, for those who patronized the Cincinnati's uneasy couches through those January nights, if the latter part of our quotation could have been applied practically, to its bed-room windows.

Yet, though we slight the domicil, we should be most impolite, not to say *unappreciative*, if we were to permit ourselves to forget its amiable landladies—for the " House " boasted a brace of proprietresses, which doesn't surprise us, for we hardly believe that the genius of one individual alone, could have kept up so extraordinary an establishment—but, let us assure the reader that this pair were noteworthy personages in their humble way, as much so, perhaps, as " Melissy," or even " the inconsolable widow of Deacon Bedott," who didn't "intend to git married agin." But we will do their portraits from the life, and abide by the artistic result.

And first—the elder (for age must, in this instance, take precedence of even *personal* attractions), seemed a motherly old creature, whose life was an odd mixture of silver spectacles and yarn stocking-mending, quite in the Mrs. Partington style. But these were but a tithe of this good lady's strong points, for she had large sympathies—"pitied the oppressed "—talked politics—which usually eventuated in a conglomeration of principles and parties—with some such remark, by way of finale, as " Deary me, what is the world a comin' to next?" She was, moreover, a firm believer in patent medicines, and " healin' yarbs "—had strongly methodistical proclivities, and to wind up all, wondered " what on airth we found in Lawrence to write about for the newspapers."

The younger—if forty odd *be* young—was, in every respect

save *one*, the very antipodes of the elder ; for, where her coadju-
trix was short and fat, she was tall and lean—*à la* Miss Miggs,
whose fervent attachment for "Simmums" adorns the pages of
Barnaby Rudge. In size, our junior hostess was somewhere
between five feet ten and six feet, in a pair of stockings, eter-
nally down at the heel, and if anything, rather more up than down
from the estimate first given. To complete the picture, fancy
little black eyes, set deeply into the head ; a long nose, with
what sailors term a "slight leaning to port ;" a wide mouth,
well garnished with masticators, which that droll fellow Hood
would have called

"Very large teeth for her age;"

add to these a chin, which was poked independently out, as if
it had begun life in advance of its sister features, and intended to
keep ahead or die gloriously in the attempt, and our faint outline is complete. But deary me, her good looks were the smallest singularity—she had a *tongue*. Did you ever hear, good
reader, of a tongue hung in the middle, which worked both
ways ? Didn't, hey ? Well, we have, and it's our private opinion that we came nearer to realizing that idea, in Miss Charity's
case, than we ever have before, or shall again ; and, furthermore, if that tongue rested from its labors, we are not yet aware
of the fact; we were even haunted with a terrible suspicion that
she talked in her sleep, in which case, may our good angel deliver us from being—but we won't say *that*, either. But it *was* a
tongue, that of Miss Charity's ; a tongue to be proud of ; a
tongue which would have been a mine of gold to a divine, a fortune to a lawyer, a curse to a physician, and killed any politician
dead, in six weeks from the unlucky hour in which he started it.
She had, moreover, a weakness for key-holes, which, coupled
with a most inquiring mind, led her at times into the pursuit of
information under difficulties ; but, as we wouldn't do even a

mosquito harm, unless he bit us, we will qualify this by saying, that we thought so ; for, with all these drawbacks, our juvenile landlady was an apt illustration of that sweet poetical simile, which is embodied in the quotation of

"Linked sweetness *long* drawn out."

CHAPTER XXVII.

THE BALL.

From the Cincinnati House, we started off upon a tour of inspection, which brought us finally to a narrow, half-plastered, and not over cleanly office, in the second story of a stone building, upon Massachusetts street, the main avenue as yet—unless you would consult the city as it is built upon paper—of that growing metropolis—Lawrence. Here we mounted, by special invitation, up a dilapidated wooden stairway, which ran along the outside of the house, until we reached a door, which let us into the apartment referred to. Upon entering, we almost fell into the error of the gentleman from Little Rock, who, on being elected to the Arkansas Legislature, got into the Senate chamber by mistake, and then swore that he thought the House of Representatives was a doggery ; for the room was yellow with smoke, and dingy with something not quite so easily removed. There was a stove, too—a very dirty one, in the centre of the apartment, about which we found a circle of some half-a-dozen rather rough-looking specimens of Free State humanity, tipped back in their chairs, with feet hoisted upon the hearth, into which an occasional jet of tobacco-juice was squirted. As we opened the door, everybody seemed talking at once, but more particularly a little fellow, in a rabbit-skin cap, who turned out to be an Irishman, with a brogue, and a newspaper editor, in a small way, to boot. The subject of discussion, just then upon the carpet, as near

as we could get at it, being the very interesting theme of political loaves and fishes, with the proper distribution thereof.
What wonder then, that those present, with such a bone of
contention as Kansas scrip (of which more anon), to fight about,
were like the army of Bombastes Furioso, all busily engaged in
kicking up a row? Yet this august assemblage—don't be
startled at the announcement—for remember, that this was Legis-
lation upon the Border, and even Congress itself is not always,
under similar circumstances, *quite* so dignified—was an official
meeting, for the transaction of business of the Executive Committee for the Territory of Kansas.

But they are clever fellows, these wonderful chaps of Lawrence—some of them we mean, for we brought letters to Robinson, ditto to Lane, and ditto to Lowry, and have been well
received and politely treated by all. Our being the representative of the New York Herald, may, perhaps, have stood just a
little in our way at first, but as we declared ourself ready to
make affidavit to its or anybody's else reformation, if required,
our Free State friends, at least so we flattered ourself, finally
settled down into the belief that we were, for a Newspaper Correspondent, a wonderfully *honest* sort of fellow.

Pending the adjustment of sundry Free State Editor's bills
for printing resolutions, speeches, and so forth, which were to
be liquidated in the very peculiar currency already referred to—
one of the "Executives" asked us if we were "going to the
ball ?"

What ball? Why the ball which was to take place that
night at the Free State Hotel, as a sort of house-warming for
the in-coming year, and at which all "the *rank*, beauty, and
fashion," as the English journalists express it, of Lawrence
and its vicinity would most undoubtedly appear. We had not
obtained a ticket, but would do so, as we had an earnest desire
to see the belles of Kansas Our friend stepped out and speedily

returned with a diminutive, sweet-scented, hot-pressed note-paper, gilt-edged billet-doux, printed within in italics, with a liberal allowance of capitals. Upon inspecting this very lady-like missive, we found its contents to run thus :—

" NEW YEAR'S PARTY."

"The company of yourself and lady is respectfully solicited at a Social Party, to be given at the Free State Hotel, in Lawrence, on Tuesday evening, January 1st, 1856."

Then follows a list of some half a dozen of managers, with the addenda of, tickets, $1 50

Armed with these credentials, for which our Executive friend will be pleased to accept our thanks, we inquired as to the most *fashionable* hour at which we might venture to become visible—were told eight o'clock, and accordingly entered the ball-room, an unfinished dining-hall in the Free State Hotel, at the hour indicated. We were attired for the occasion, in a suit of black, which was " built" in New York, and has been considered creditable upon Broadway ; but we might have spared ourself some trouble, for the first gentleman we met sported a short, drab overcoat, a very long red comforter, and corduroy pants, which were fitly finished at the bottom, by a pair of boots, long innocent of blacking, but bearing most unmistakable signs, to more senses than one, of being thoroughly greased; and this biped was a fair specimen, by the way, of the very free and easy manner in which the male portion of the assemblage were rigged out.

We felt out of place, but it was too late to " retrograde," so we summoned up our brass, pulled down our left collar, turned up our sleeves, deranged the set of our pants, stuck out hands into our breeches pockets, donned our hat, and then went into conversation—pending the arrival of the ladies, who were

12

holding on for the music—with our next neighbor—who turned out to be *something* from Indiana, in a blanket overcoat, and a very hoarse cold—upon that unfailing subject, " the late war " In the mean time, a Dutchman—the professor, as he is styled—who has gained a somewhat expensive immortality by giving the first concert in Kansas, which—hurrah for her musical taste!—didn't pay either himself or the printer who struck off his notices—came in with a four-legged affair that looked like a juvenile piano, not yet grown up, on which he began playing most discordantly. The arrival of the ladies, who made their appearance upon the young piano being reinforced by—judging from its execution—a still younger violin, put a stop to this thrumming, and the ball commenced.

As the room filled up, each gentleman was supplied with a diminutive paper ticket, which tickets had been previously numbered by the floor manager, from one to thirty inclusive. The object of this was to give each guest his number, so that —as the room was too small to accommodate more than four sets, for quadrilles, with variations, were the only dances attempted—each man, with his partner, got a "*fair shake*" to dance in their turn, for you were not allowed to take your place upon the floor until your number had been called. Well, to make a long story short, we danced with sundry of the Kansas belles, and saw neither lace-ruffles nor fancy undersleeves, hoops nor flounces, low-necked dresses nor embroidered handkerchiefs, but everything passed off smoothly, for all that. The dancing-hall, however, merits a more extended description. It was, as we have already stated, an unfinished room, with rough stone walls, destitute of plaster, and a broken window or two. At one side of the room a carpenter's bench was shoved up against the wall, to make way for the trippers upon the " light fantastic toe," while a cooking-stove graced either end of the apartment, and furnished a heater, which we regret to say, didn't warm the room. As for candlesticks, each window had a slip of board fastened across the sash, with nails driven in at uncertain intervals, so as to support the candles, which threw their flickering light upon this gay and festive scene. At midnight we had supper; that is to say, we ranged ourselves upon the long wooden benches, —which surrounded the room—to the number of some eighty souls or more, when, being "*all set*," at a given signal the door opened—no, we mistake, it didn't—for there was none to open—but two men entered, bearing between them a piece of plank, on which were ranged plates, containing a triangle of cold pie, some raisins, and a stick of candy each—more or less, as the lawyers say—this was followed up by a second edition of planks, and men who served everybody—*nolens volens*—with a cup of hot coffee; then came cakes, " fearfully and wonderfully " made, and then back came the plank-bearers, who removed the fragments of the feast, whereupon the dancers went to work again, and we went home to bed. We cannot, however, close our notice of the ball without recording a conversation, which we had the honor of holding with one of the prettiest, and certainly the liveliest girl in the room. It was short and sweet, and ran thus :

We.—(After a pause.) Are you fond of music ?

She.—Oh ! yes, indeed I am.

We.—(Stroking down our moustache.) Do you play on any instrument ?"

She.—Yes *sir*, I reckon I do.

We.—(Interested.) On the piano, or do you prefer the guitar ?

She.—No *sir*. But I'm great on the *wash-board*. *I've been practising all day.*

We fancied that we had listened to less *sensible* speeches in more pretentious assemblies.

CHAPTER XXVIII.

THE HEROINES OF THE WAR.

JANUARY 2d.—A clear, cold, biting day, or to speak more correctly at this present, a bitter evening, for the short twilight of winter has already given place to its long dreary, night, and even as we write, our senior hostess—the short, fat one—enters with the despairing announcement of :

" My goodness gracious ! eight o'clock, as I am alive, and Miss Charity ain't got the fust one of them dishes washed up yet. Well I never, if you men hain't gone to talkin' politics agin. I spose you'll be inductin' of another party next.   Oh ! deary-me, what *is* the world a comin' to ?"

Our motherly old hostess makes her exit, very much, if the truth be told, to our mental relief, for how *can* one journalize with any degree of personal satisfaction, not to mention truthfulness, when an old maid, and a yet older matron, aided by some half a dozen boarding-house politicians, who all agree in disagreeing, are kicking up a wordy row, within ten feet of the table at which you are scribbling, or, to be accurate, nibbling your pen, as you vainly strive to grasp the tail of some eel-like idea, which is ever slipping from you, and won't be caught.

And now for our log—let us take a retrospective view, and go back to 11 o'clock A. M., at which hour we did ourself the pleasure of calling upon Mistress W———, the *better-half* of a certain hard-working Free State politician, and an elder sister of one of our fair partners of the evening before. The W——mansion stands upon the main street (or as the good people of Lawrence delight to call it, Massachusetts Avenue); its exterior is, at the best, very far from imposing, for though it would be called a house *here*, it might be suited at the North with a less dignified appellation; as for the *interior*, it was, if we saw *all*, divided, to use a Hibernianism, into *one* room, a bed, and a cooking-stove, round which some two or three white-headed little urchins were playing noisily, while the women folks talked over that very interesting event—our last night's ball. But it was not long ere even *this* fruitful subject was exhausted, for in a country where the feminines have but one party dress, which does duty all the year round, *that* theme becomes stale, and Kansas is *almost* too new for scandal, so it is hardly to be wondered at, that the tide of words soon flowed into their natural channel, which means the Wakarusa War, for in this section of the Territory, at least, it is hard to exchange ideas with any one, without being fairly dragged into the whole *state* of Kansas, ere you have given your tongue a five minutes' run. And as this led very naturally to the personal experiences of the ladies present, who seemed quite willing to " post us up," and as these experiences were really of a very extraordinary and withal adventurous nature, we feel confident that it would be doing everybody an injustice to suppress them here. But let us preface the narration, or rather Mistress W———'s story, by the assertion that if Mistress Molly Starke was breveted to a Majority, for serving a piece upon the field, Mistress W——, (we wish we knew her own initials), should be made a Captain of Artillery, at the very least, for the very gallant manner in which she and her companion (Mrs. B——) *served* the State, in a one-horse buggy. And when we tell you this heroine's story, as we jotted it down on our note-book, from her own lips, as she sat sewing by her cooking-stove, with the urchins aforesaid playing around her feet, we presume you will not only agree with us in the recommendation to a Captaincy, but avow yourself ready to declare that Mistress B—— and her fair companion are trumps ; and a clear-grit Yankee woman quite equal, upon an emergency, to what, in vulgar parlance, is quaintly styled "a whole team, and *a dog under the wagon*" to boot. But to our tale, and we may very properly call it

THE FREE STATE HEROINE'S ENTERPRISE.

"The Kansas war was at its height—Lawrence was a Sebastopol, and the Wakarusa and Lecompton camps teemed with those barbarous hordes, the 'Border Ruffians,' when it was suddenly discovered by the stern Republicans—all black though they be—who guarded the entrenchments of this beleaguered city, that our gallant defenders lacked that *sine qua non* for legalized bloodshed, powder and ball. Here, then, was a terrible state of affairs. The enemy was at hand, the cloud of war growing darker every day, and the smoke of battle just about to be puffed into our very nostrils ; yet, from whence were we 'the unterrified' to obtain a sufficient supply of 'villainous saltpetre,'—for every road was guarded, every avenue closed, every wagon searched, and the 'Border Ruffians' had their watchful scouts upon each overlooking hill, so that no man, be he Free State, or Pro-Slavery, might come or go unquestioned. In fact, the Free State leaders were fairly bothered, but where 'the Lords of Creation' exhaust their ingenuity in vain, a woman's wit will often solve the problem, and it was so in this instance, for a certain Mistress B—— (also of Lawrence) and myself concocted a plan which, with the approval of the Free State generals, we determined to put into execution. Our scheme was simply this : We knew that both powder and lead, together with a considerable quantity of Sharpe's rifle caps and cartridges were deposited with those favorable to our cause, at two separate points upon the Santa Fé trail. It does not matter as to their particular whereabouts, but it will do nobody any harm to say that they arē to be found within ten miles of the room in which we are now seated. Now, when a woman makes up her mind to do anything, be it good or bad, it is already more than half accomplished ; so you may readily suppose that no very great space of time intervened between our determination to undertake the enterprise and our putting its into execution.

"So at eight o'clock on a bright winter morning, Mistress B——— and myself stepped into the one-horse buggy which was to transport us to the localities where these warlike supplies were awaiting an opportunity to reach the Free State camp, and then convey us back again well laden, as we trusted, with the much-desired ammunition. We were both, I can assure you, got up, so far as equipments were concerned, in a very eccenrict fashion for the trip ; as for myself, I wore *two* dresses, and a petticoat, which, though it went forth lined with wadding, came back charged with what—if I were inclined to make a pun, might be called excellent *gun*-cotton. We were, moreover, each provided with an article which, though it makes no great bustle now-a-days, was in this particular instance well fitted to increase the noise in Lawrence in the event of a premature explosion, for they had, ere we re-entered Massachusetts street, been literally stuffed with a commodity that rendered them completely water-proof, insomuch as their contents may fairly be said to have kept them as dry as *powder*. But a truce to jesting—though I have many a hearty laugh when I recall the recollections of this eventful excursion.

"We passed the picket guards of the Lawrence camp, and continued on, without meeting with any note-worthy adventure, for though we saw several parties of Missourians—the fact of our being females, and our travelling *from* the town, was probably a sufficient guarantee for our harmlessness. It was late in the morning—for we drove slowly, as we wished to save our mare's strength for the afternoon—ere we reached the dwelling of Mr, Blank, our first stopping-place, upon the Santa Fé trail. Here we received a warm welcome, coupled with many expressions of astonishment at our temerity, and, what was more to the purpose, a keg of prime rifle-powder, which I should say, for I carried it out to the buggy myself, must have contained upwards of twenty-five pounds ; this we emptied and secreted carefully about our persons, I could hardly tell you *where*. In addition to the powder, they gave us a quantity of lead ; this we also stowed away in a secret hiding-place—as for the Sharpe's rifle caps, we put those into our stockings, while the cartridges were quilted into our petticoats, under-dress, and clothing generally.   From Mr. Blank's we drove to the residence of another Free State sympathizer, who also lived on the Santa Fé trail, where we obtained not only powder and ball, but an additional supply of Sharpe's rifle cartridges, with quite a number of caps, as there were more of these latter munitions than we could conveniently dispose of—being already, as an artilleryman might say, *loaded* quite up to the muzzle —we were, though very unwillingly, compelled to entrust them to a boy, and a sturdy Free State youngster too, who, although he was not yet nine years old, was going to try and enter Lawrence—which of course involved passing the enemy's scouting parties—with an ox-team that he was driving. But we trusted, as his cart was empty, and the little fellow but a mere child, that his youth and apparent innocence would disarm the suspicions of the Pro-Slavery people, and thus permit him to pass unsearched with his dangerous cargo in safety to our lines. In this expectation, however, or, to speak more correctly, in a portion of it, we were doomed to be disappointed, as the sequel of my story will show; but I am anticipating.

"Upon completing our lading, by which time we were so con·

siderably increased in bulk, that we found the buggy rather a small pattern for two, I grasped the reins and whipped up old Sally, until she fairly broke into a run as we took the homeward road ; for it was not far from three o'clock, P. M., by the time that all our preparations for departure were completed, and we had still some ten miles to go. We continued to rattle on, although at a rather more moderate gait, for old Sally's vigorous start soon sobered down into a long, steady trot, which carried us rapidly over the smooth prairie road ; and were already within a few miles of home, when, just as I was beginning to bless my lucky stars, for what promised to be a successful termination to our adventure, an exclamation from my companion caused me to look up, and there, sure enough, were a party of ' Border-Ruffians' on horseback, whose dark figures stood out in bold relief against the wintry sky, as they dotted the summit of a distant prairie rise, where they seemed to have reined in their cattle, to observe us ; while, worst of all, two of their number—and even at that distance, they looked unprepossessing enough—were already galloping towards us at top speed, as if to cut us off. I looked at my companion, as if I meant to say, "What on earth *are* we to do now ?" and she returned my glance, in a manner that told me, as plainly as words could have spoken it, " I'm sure I do not know." For myself, I was quite at my wit's end ; I formed a dozen plans in a minute, and dismissed them with equal promptitude the next. There seemed but one course left for us to pursue, and that was to put our mare to her speed, and thereby—do what many a lady has done before—make a *runaway* match of it ; but, as we were already both married, there wouldn't have been much poetry in *that*, and even if it had been otherwise, a moment's reflection convinced me that such an escapade, under existing circumstances, would be sheer madness, as, even if old Sally could have done anything in the racing way, the heat must have been a short one, for, like that honest citizen,

12*

John Gilpin, in the song, we 'carried weight,' which would have told sadly against us ; for how *could* old Sally drag the buggy, its two inmates, and our hundred pounds of powder and ball, in a trial of speed with some twenty odd well-mounted frontiersmen, who would be able to take advantage of every cut-off in a road whose turnings we must of necessity follow. So as there was nothing for it, but to put our trust in the winding up of the chapter of accidents, with, perhaps, a little feminine diplomacy to help it out, I drew in the reins, slackened old Sally's trot to a walk, and was waiting—if the truth must be told—with my heart in my mouth, while I endeavored to look as innocent as I conveniently could, to see the upshot of this most unwelcome visitation. Judge, then, how great was my relief, when I beheld the two horsemen, who had by this time galloped up to within twenty cr thirty yards of our vehicle, tighten their bridles, and come to a sudden halt ; at the same time, lifting their hats, as they assured me, with a very killing *bow*, that they really begged our pardon for disturbing us, which, had their people only known that none but ladies were in the buggy, would never have occurred.

"To this very gratifying piece of intelligence, they added something about having thought, when they first caught sight of us, that there was a gentleman too, in which case, the very strict orders they had received, in relation to stopping and arresting every suspicious person, would have made it necessary for them to question him. To all this, we, of course, said just as much, in the way of bows, wreathed smiles, and such like courtesies, as possible, without trusting ourselves to words. I suppose we must have *looked* frightened, for the Border-Ruffians—and these certainly were very *nice* Ruffians—made their farewell salutations, wheeled their horses, and were off to rejoin their party, leaving my companion and myself, very much to our delight, to pursue our way unmolested. Upon looking back, a short time afterwards, we saw them in the distance, all busily engaged in overhauling the unlucky urchin who had charge of the ox-team and—what was to us a matter of very considerable anxiety, our additional package of rifle caps. But the Free State juvenile's detention was a short one, for we had the satisfaction to see the Missourians file off, while he of the ox-cart cracked his whip, as he urged the lazy cattle upon their road to town. He entered Lawrence that evening, and delivered his package of caps, a little rumpled to be sure, but all right, nevertheless. We have never yet, however, been able to discover in what manner he concealed them, while undergoing this inspection upon the road, for, in answer to all our questions, the younster only laughed, blushed a little, and when still more closely pressed, hung down his head and said nothing."

We afterwards discovered that the young gentleman alluded to, had deposited the package—upon first perceiving the approach of the Missourians—inside the seat of his voluminous pantaloons, which may, perhaps, very naturally, account for his diffidence when so closely questioned by the ladies.

A Western Free State man, who saw the heroines making their triumphant entry into Lawrence, upon their return from this adventurous trip, speaks thus of the personal appearance of these perambulating Free State arsenals :—

" Stranger, when I saw them wimin a comin' inter this hyar town, I jest allowed that *bustles* hed come inter fashion agin, for they wor swelled out *awful*."

CHAPTER XXIX

THE FREE STATE SIDE OF THE QUESTION.

WE had an interview this afternoon with General Charles Robinson, who is by far the most influential leader of the Free State movement in Kansas ; there were moreover two other persons present, who are also deep in the counsels of that party. Our object in seeking this interview was to notify these gentlemen formally of the purpose with which we had visited Kansas, of the duties intrusted to us, and of the manner in which we purposed (as the fairest that could be adopted), to pursue our investigations *in re* Kansas and the war. We, therefore, said plainly that we were duly accredited by the "New York Herald," as their Kansas correspondent ; in proof of which we exhibited our credentials from the editor of that paper. We then informed the General that we had already taken a peep at the Pro-Slavery version of the war, through the medium of sundry statements, official documents, affidavits, and such like, which we had obtained from his Excellency, Governor Shannon, and others of that persuasion, whom we regarded as reliable men ; in speaking of which, we very frankly admitted that the Pro-Slavery people had not only taken some little pains to post us up, but so far as we were competent to judge, had made out a very pretty case for *their* side into the bargain. We finally intimated to the General and his compatriots, that as we desired to " do justice to all men," we would spend eight days, and if necessary even more time, in Lawrence, and devote ourself, during that period, to getting up the Free State History of the Wakarusa War in as readable a form as our poor abilities would permit, and at the conclusion of our labors, give their story to the world, or if need be, in the summing up, argue their cause before the jury of Public Opinion ; not as a lawyer who has taken a fee, but as an upright judge, who permits no consideration of personal interest to " sully the purity of his ermine." But, gentlemen, added we, we cannot do this thing unaided ; we must ask, not only your co-operation but your suggestions ; for while we are willing to take down and write out your testimony, we do not feel that it is our business to obtain your witnesses ; so we notify you now, that if you have any evidence you may desire printed, we shall expect you to send those whose testimony you wish recorded, to us ; and furthermore, if we might be permitted to make the suggestion, let us have nothing but *facts*, which if denied can be sustained by proof. We want neither suppositions, rumor, personalities, nor party abuse, but simply that which is said to *lie* in the bottom of a well (and we are free to confess, by the way, that it must be a mighty deep one in Kansas), the *truth*. And now, as a last word in your ear, gentlemen, let us intimate that " two good, clean witnesses," to any one point in question, are quite as satisfactory as fifty ; the more so, as in this age of fast people, where men live, travel, eat and *read* by steam, *brevity* is most unquestionably the very *soul of wit*.

Such was our " talk," or rather the drift of it, to the Free State magnates, who, to do them justice, seemed on their part not only good-natured but very willing, so far as promises went, to aid us in our news-hunting ; and we can only say, that if they do so, we shall honestly endeavor to carry out our pledge, to give the Free State evidences, so far as they may see fit to furnish us with it, fairly to the world. We shall, therefore, introduce such papers as we may from time to time obtain, by inserting them, as received, into the pages of what is now our journal of events in Lawrence.

In presenting the Free State side of the Kansas War question, we marked out for ourself more particularly the following points :

1st. A general outline of the events which led to and attended the so-called " Wakarusa War." This we proposed to cover, by a statement from General Robinson himself, whose truthfulness, if we judge him by the testimony of his political *opponents*, is to be most implicitly relied upon.

2d. To discover whether the arrest of Jacob Branson was properly made by Sheriff Jones, and to institute inquiries into the killing of Dow by the man Coleman, with the Free State version of the difficulties which led to that most unfortunate result. To accomplish this, we intended getting the statements of Branson himself, with that of one or more of his neighbors.

[NOTE.—In this expectation we were finally disappointed, through the neglect of the Free State people to procure the presence in Lawrence of these persons ; though they had intimated that they should come in.]

3d. We desired to get at the real facts connected with the calling together, and proceedings of certain public meetings, alleged to have been holden in Lawrence, upon the day following the rescue of Branson, and which are said to have endorsed his recapture.

[NOTE.—For these matters see portions of General Robinson's narrative, as also Miller's and Bercaw's statements.]

4th. To verify or prove false the Pro-Slavery version of the circumstances attending the rescue of Jacob Branson from the Sheriff of Douglas County and his *posse*.

[NOTE.—For such Free State information as we were enabled to gather upon this subject, we must refer the reader to Bercaw's statement, and also to passages in the narrative of General Robinson.]

5th. To inquire *particularly* into the circumstances attending the killing of the Free State man, Thomas W. Barber, and if possible procure the evidence of those who were with him when the homicide took place.

[NOTE.—See statements of Robert F. Barber, the brother, and Thomas M. Peirson, the brother-in-law, of the deceased, with extract from Dr. Ainsworth attached.]

From this time forth our news-gathering work commenced in earnest, and for the difficulties under which it was prosecuted, we would refer your curiosity to the facts that we were obliged to pursue our labors in that " one common room" of the ill-regulated hotel, already alluded to ; where, with a hot stove at our back, and a Bedlam of disturbance in our ears, we scribbled up our daily gleanings, and from which, when the hour of ten P. M. came round, we were forced to retire—willing or unwilling—to our *airy* (half the windows were broken), sleeping-room above, where we slept if we could, in company with just six people ; it seems proper, by the way, to inform the reader that the seven did not, however, all occupy the same bed.

January 3d, Evening.—Scene—*that* general sitting-room—the politicians, seven in number, all assembled, two of them being provided with strong pipes, which in this *very* confined apartment, is *almost* as satisfactory as taking a smoke yourself, and so far as the perfume in your hair and clothing goes—*quite* ; the stove—a big one—is red hot, add to which that both of our hostesses are present, and both *talking*, the junior on religion, and the senior upon things in general, and then sympathize with us as we sit down to write *quietly*.

Let us see ; what is there upon our docket to-day ? Ah !

here is Mr. Albert T. Bercaw's statement in regard to the rescue of our old acquaintance upon paper, Mr. Jacob Branson—a very worthy gentleman, we doubt not. And as Mr. Albert T. Bercaw was what the dead languages call a *particeps criminis*, or what in no less *legal* English might be termed an accessory after the fact (it was not his fault that it was not before), in this recapture business, we presume that Mr. Bercaw ought to be supposed to know a great deal about the affair ; so we will, after this very *solemn* preamble, introduce that gentlemen, or what in this instance is quite as much to the point—his statement—here. It will be perceived, too, that Mr. Bercaw's narrative treats of a certain meeting at Hickory Point, and, judging from the amount of difficulty, murder, house-burnings, and such like little eccentricities, which have occurred in this thinly-settled locality, we are inclined to believe that the Hickory Pointers must be a very " rough and tumble"—not to mention pugnacious—set of gentlemen. But let us get back to Mr. Bercaw.

Note.—The following, in common with all the statements of individuals, which we have thought proper to procure, as necessary to a full understanding of the matters in question, was taken down by our own hand from the lips of the person named.

STATEMENT OF ALBERT T. BERCAW, OF LAKE COUNTY, OHIO, A FREE STATE MAN, IN RELATION TO A MEETING OF THE FREE STATE SETTLERS AT HICKORY POINT, K. T., AND EVENTS GROWING OUT OF SAID MEETING.

I was present at a meeting, which was held at Hickory Point, on or about the 26th of November, 1855. It was convened to investigate the circumstances attending the killing of C. W. Dow.

This meeting convened at noon, upon the spot where Dow was killed, and continued in session until four, P. M. Its chairman was a Free State man, named Powell. After considerable discussion, it was decided to appoint a committee of seven, whose duty it should be to select twenty-five men—whose names were to be kept secret—the persons so selected were to act as a vigilance committee. I was a member of the committee of seven.

The duties of the vigilance committee were thus expressed in one of the resolutions passed at that time, namely—

" To ferret out and bring the murderers and their accomplices to condign punishment."

When this meeting had adjourned, a few of its members, but not over fifteen in all, stepped out, and wished to call a party to burn Coleman's house. (It is proper to remark that Coleman's house was only a few rods distant from the place where the gathering was held.) This was opposed. Some one in the crowd then called out,

" All those in favor of burning Coleman's house form a line."

Against this a majority of the persons present remonstrated; among others, Abbot, a Free State man, and afterwards one of the rescuers of Branson, said, " Let us prevent them, if they should try to do it." Indeed, the opposition was so strong, that but two persons attempted it; these climbed over the fence, and approached the house, which had been deserted by Coleman and his family, who had fled and taken the most of their furniture with them. Upon reaching the building, one of the men clubbed his Sharpe's rifle, and burst open the door; they then set fire to some articles inside, what, I do not know, as I did not enter the house, but remained with the crowd. In a short time the smoke began to issue from the building, upon seeing which, those who were opposed to the burning of the dwelling, entered, and extinguished the flames before they had done any very great damage. I have since learned that the house was burnt down that night, but know nothing of the matter myself. The crowd then dispersed.

As I was returning home from this meeting, I saw a party of mounted men, whom I supposed to be Pro-Slavery men, riding in a body towards Hickory Point. My suspicions were aroused as to their intentions; I went therefore, and took counsel with two Free State men, named Abbot and S. N. Wood; while thus engaged, a person, named Tappan—who is also a Free State man—informed us that the party which I had seen were Sheriff Jones's *posse*, who were then on their way to arrest one Jacob Branson, a Free State settler, at Hickory Point. Upon learning this, S. N. Wood and Abbot obtained horses, mounted, and rode up to Hickory Point, to notify Branson that the Pro-Slavery sheriff was in pursuit of him, and that he would certainly be arrested if he did not make his escape. Upon reaching Branson's residence, however, they discovered that they had come too late to effect the object which brought them there, as Branson had already been taken. They then instituted inquiries, but were unable to ascertain in what direction Sheriff Jones's *posse* had gone. Messengers were immediately dispatched to alarm the Free State settlers, and rally men for the rescue of Branson. In the meanwhile, Wood and Abbot had returned to Abbot's house, where the party were to meet, who intended to effect a re-capture. I was on my way to join this party at the place appointed, when I heard a couple of shots and hastened forward. Upon reaching Abbot's, where I did not enter, but remained near the dwelling upon the outside, I was told that Branson had been rescued, and was then in the house. When I came up, Sheriff Jones was remonstrating with our people, and saying that he wished to get possession of Branson, whom he claimed as his prisoner; he stated, moreover, that he (Jones) was the Sheriff of Douglas County, and that he would send an express to Governor Shannon for men to aid him in carrying out the law.

We had, upon this occasion, about *twenty* men; I don't know the exact number; there might have been *more*. Our people were all armed with Sharpe's rifles. After the rescue, I accompanied Branson to Lawrence, and was present at a public meeting, which was held at that place, upon the ensuing day. This meeting *endorsed* the *Hickory Point Resolutions*.

Here follow the Hickory Point Resolutions referred to :—

PREAMBLE AND RESOLUTIONS ADOPTED BY A MEETING OF CITIZENS AT HICKORY POINT, K. T., NOVEMBER 26TH, 1855.

Whereas, Charles W. Dow, a citizen of this place, was murdered on Wednesday afternoon last, and whereas, evidence, by admission and otherwise, fastens the guilt of said murder on one F. M. Coleman, and whereas, facts further indicate that other parties—namely—Buckley, Wagoner, Reynolds, Hargis, Moody and others, were implicated in said murder, and whereas, facts further indicate that said individuals and parties are combining for the purpose of harassing and even murdering unoffending citizens, and whereas, we are now destitute of law, even for the punishment of crime, in this Territory, and whereas, the aforesaid individuals have fled to Missouri, therefore—

Resolved, That we deeply sympathize with the family and relations of the deceased.

Resolved, That we regard F. M. Coleman, and those connected with him, as wilful murderers, who should be treated as such by all good citizens.

Resolved, That we are ready to stand by and defend any and all of our fellow-citizens, in protecting their lives and property; and consider it our duty to spare neither time nor expense in ferreting out, and bringing to condign punishment, all connected with this infamous crime.

Resolved, That a vigilance committee of twenty-five be appointed, whose duty it shall be to bring the above-named individuals, as well as those connected with them in this affair, to justice.

Resolved, That we stamp with disapprobation, the actions of those persons, who knowingly permitted the body of the deceased to lay by the roadside, without giving information in regard to it.

JANUARY 4th.—We have spent the greater portion of to-day in the prosecution of our Kansas news-hunt, in pursuing which, we wandered into the "preserve" of a certain Mr. Christian, we dont mean a *hard* Christian by the way, but a *good* Christian, who, being naturally a jovial little fellow, with a good-humored face, laughing eye, and keen appreciation of the ridiculous, suited us at first sight, so we have fraternized wonderfully, as the reader may suppose.

We had not been very long in our little friend's somewhat diminutive office—which was indeed so small, that it quite realized our idea of that cockneyism, " a box in the country "—ere we discovered that he not only handled the pen of a ready writer, but indulged it at times in scribbling for the newspapers. So we complimented his style, and finally managed to overcome his diffidence, for we all know that the *genus* Author is but human at the best, until at length we had persuaded him to give us a peep into the manuscript, and as our peep convinced us that it was *worth* reading, we will write him a *preface* first, and then give you Mr. Christian's very *fair* explanation of the " Kansas embroglio," for which—Christian's account we mean, and not the embroglio—*multum in parvo* would be no bad heading.

The following is a letter addressed to a member of the Kentucky State Legislature, in answer to one requesting information as regarded the state of affairs in Kansas. Its writer, James Christian, Esq., is a citizen of Lawrence, and we are disposed to call particular attention to his statements from these circum-stances :

Mr. Christian holds an appointment under the Territorial government, as County Clerk, of Douglas County, K. T.   He is of the Pro-Slavery party, but withal a strong *union* and *conservative* man.   We hear of him from the Free State people, as a person much respected by both parties.   He has been retained by Coleman as his counsel in the Dow matter—is in favor of making Kansas a Slave State—has lived in Lawrence since the middle of March last—has his family with him and intends to remain in the Territory—is spoken of as being a straightfor-ward, and strictly honorable man—is an Irishman by birth, with, to use his own expression, " a slight touch of the brogue, and a considerable taste of the blarney," and finally, Mr. Christian has resided in the State of Kentucky for fifteen years, has never had the good fortune to " own a darkey," but would like a couple if he could afford that luxury, as he thinks they might be made useful.

MR. JAMES CHRISTIAN'S HISTORY OF THE KANSAS DISTURBANCES

LAWRENCE, K. T., *Jan. 1st*, 1855.

MY DEAR —— :

          " I suppose you have heard of the troubles in Kansas, and read, perhaps, some of the many falsehoods which have been scattered broadcast over the land.   I have, as yet, seen *nothing* in the public prints, which may be regarded as strictly true, on either side of this question, for editors and letter-writers are like lawyers, very apt to tell but one part of the story, and that in their own way; indeed, like the Jews of old, they can never dis-cover the ' beam in their own eye,' but seek rather to pull out the mote from their brother's.

          " The true cause of these Kansas troubles was not an arrest by the Sheriff under the Territorial law; it had its origin far back in the halls of Congress, when the Nebraska and Kansas bills were passed, when the Missouri Compromise was declared null and void, and ultra men boasted in our Legislative Assemblies, that if they could not defeat these bills in one way they would in another, and returned to their homes to organize 'Emigrant Aid Societies,' and 'Kansas Leagues,' with the avowed intention of defeating the objects of the *Kansas* Bill, by Abolitionizing the Territory. This was the *first wrong*, and it aroused the indignation of the 'Fire Eaters' of Western Missouri, whom Benton, in his *peculiar* manner, styles nullifiers, scamps, and rottens; these were headed by such men as Atchinson, B. F. Stringfellow, C. F. Jackson, Col. S. A. Young, with others of lesser note, but all tried soldiers of the Anti-Benton campaigns, from 1849 to 1855, when Atchinson was beaten as Senator.

"When the first election in Kansas (for delegate) came on, these gentlemen called out the Pro-Slavery forces, and marched their men into the Territory to cast their votes for *Whitfield.* This was done to counteract the influence of the Boston Aid Societies and Kansas Leagues, already alluded to. This might have been all well or ill enough, if the evil had stopped here, as the Free Soilers, when they came in, ruled it with a high hand ; in many instances treating the Pro-Slavery and Western settlers with the grossest injustice, by driving them from their improvements, or cutting their timber before their eyes, at the same time bidding them defiance, as they (the Yankees) 'had the power, and meant to take the country.' This it was that prompted the Pro-Slavery and Western men to seek protection from their friends in Missouri, who, to do them justice, were as zealous in giving assistance as they were prompt to ask it. Things were in this condition when the spring elections came on for members of the Council and House of Representatives. This took place on the 30th of March, 1855, and the people of Missouri, delighted with their success at the fall election, came in with renewed vigor to the Kansas ballot-boxes, bringing with them an ample supply of their favorite institutions—*bowie-knifes, pistols* and *whisky*—to the great terror of the Yankees—not to mention the trepidation of the liege subjects of Her Majesty Queen Victoria. But to continue, the Ides of March came on, and the 30th of that month is a day long to be remembered in the history of this Territory. Missouri poured in her citizens to the number of some *five or six thousand* men, who carried the election, and returned every Pro-Slavery candidate in the field by overwhelming majorities ; thus securing every member of both houses of the Kansas Legislature. To effect this, they in some instances replaced the judges of election, appointed by Governor Reeder, by substituting men of their own principles. It is but just, however, to state that they chose for this purpose *bona fide* residents of Kansas, which the Governor's proclamation permitted, inasmuch as it gave authority to the electors, in case any judge should refuse to serve, to elect another to fill his place. The judges alluded to were N. B. Blanton and James B. Abbot, of the 1st District. (See Governor Reeder's proclamation of the 8th March, 1855.) The judges, so substituted, *disregarded* the instructions of the Executive, in striking out the word 'legal' from their certificates of election. This was *their* first great wrong."

Note.—Though not embraced in this letter, our informant has given your correspondent so graphic a description of this election and its attendings, as it was carried on in the Lawrence District, that we have requested him to describe it for the amusement, and it may be instruction of our New York politicians. I mean those of the hard shell rough-and ready order.

Mr. Christian's account runs thus :

" Upon the morning of the 30th of March, a clear sunshiny day, the voters of Lawrence District began assembling about the door of the polls, which was held in a small log shanty, quite a one-horse affair, situated upon the outskirts of the city of . Lawrence. In the mean time, the invading army of Missouri voters, who had arrived the day before, to the number of some eight or nine hundred men, were encamped in the vicinity of the polls. At 9 A. M., the hour appointed for the opening of the polls, the Missourians, well armed, walked down to the one-horse shanty, before alluded to. Their leader, Young, then took the oath required by the judges of election. To *avoid the rush*, and prevent *unnecessary* crowding, the Missourians then formed a line some hundred yards in length, on either side of the shanty window, in which the voters were to deposit their ballots. Through this alley-way the voters passed in ; but as the living stream was for some time continuous, and a retreat through the lane impossible, it became necessary to adopt some plan by which to get rid of the voter after he had been polled. This was no easy matter ; but, as a happy expedient, it was at length determined to hoist each polled man upon the roof of the shanty, where he seized- hold of the shingles and thus assisted himself over until he had gained the other side, from whence a second jump brought him in safety to the ground, leaving him at liberty to supply the place of some friend who had not *yet voted*. The vote thus polled in the Lawrence District was upwards of one thousand, of which two hundred and twenty-five were Free Soil and the balance Pro-Slavery.

" The Free Soilers were so utterly confounded by this very *energetic* action on the part of the Missourians, that they *neglected*—except in some three or four instances—to send in their protests in proper time, that is to say, before the Governor (Reeder) had given certificates to the persons so elected. The Pro-Slavery party had therefore a majority of two-thirds in each House of the Legislature, where they could, and *did*, do as they pleased with the members returned at the *second* election, which was held in May, in accordance with the Governor's (Reeder's) proclamation, and, as was anticipated, ousted the Free Soil members from their seats. This was *another outrage.*

"This Legislature—styled Bogus, by the Free Soil party—met, in accordance with the Governor's proclamation, at *Pawnee*, a *paper city* on the extreme verge of civilization, with no house to shelter them from the inclemency of the weather. I was present, and shall never forget the first meeting of the Kansas Legislature; for to me, at least, it was a most novel sight to see grave council-men and brilliant orators of the House of Representatives cooking their food by the side of a log, or sleeping on a buffalo-robe in the open air, with the broad canopy of heaven for a covering.

"During this meeting of the Legislature at Pawnee, we had several severe showers, and it was amusing enough to behold these Romuluses of Kansas, as they scampered, with their beds upon their backs—like an Irish pedlar—to some new houses which boasted neither window nor door, and kept out but illy the pelting storm. There were but two things in abundance at Pawnee—rocky mounds and highly-rectified whisky.

"Being fairly drowned out, the Legislature at length adjourned to Shawnee Mission, whereupon the Governor vetoed the Bill ; this was the *final* rupture between the Governor and the Legislature; then came the tug of war. Both parties from this moment broke out into open hostility. The Governor and his Free-Soil friends repudiated the Legislature and its acts, and bid defiance to both ; they spoke of it as the Missouri Bogus Legislature. The Legislature, on their part, were not slow to retaliate; they racked their ingenuity to insult and aggravate the Free Soil party, and if possible widen the breach already existing between the two contending *factions*, for I can scarcely dignify with the name of party those who condescend to such a petty warfare as exists between the Kansas agitators. The Legislature, in the first place, memorialized President Pierce to remove Governor Reeder, which was done, but avowedly for another office, the Kaw Land speculation. They then attempted to padlock the mouths of the Free Soilers by preventing their expressing an opinion as to the right of individuals to hold slaves in Kansas Territory. Their next move was to appoint officers to put this padlock on, or in other words to execute *their* laws, and as most of the members lived in Missouri, it was no very singular thing that they had friends to reward in that State, who were patriotic enough to "move into Kansas" if they could get an office there; this several of them did, and accordingly came into the Territory with their commissions in their pockets. In due time the Legislature closed this, their labor of love, and returned to the bosom of their families, with their well-earned pay in their pockets, with which to improve their farms in Jackson and other counties of Missouri.

"The Free Soilers now took the field in earnest, by holding conventions, passing resolutions, and listening to inflammatory appeals to the worst passions of their nature, to resist even unto death the enactments of the Kansas *quasi* Legislature. Things went on thus until the 26th of November, 1855, when a warrant was issued by a justice of the peace, and put into the hands of the sheriff of Douglas County, for service. The sheriff was met by a body of armed men and his prisoner—one Jacob Branson—rescued. The rescuers then brought Branson into the town of Lawrence, during the night, where their drum beat to arms, and by eight next morning a town meeting was called, and a committee of safety appointed, to take measures accordingly. From this moment our troubles began in earnest—Sheriff Jones sent an express to Governor Shannon for aid to protect him in carrying out the laws.   In the mean time the Governor issued his proclamation calling out the militia to enforce the laws. Others sent runners into Missouri, for assistance to aid the militia, and by Saturday, Dec. 1st, the forces on both sides began to arrive in great numbers.   The Free Soilers flocked to Lawrence, the militia to Lecompton, and the Missourians to the Wakarusa camp.   The Free Soilers were occupied from the 1st to the 8th of Dec. in throwing up breastworks to defend the place.   All work and business was suspended, and martial law ruled supreme.

"Picket guards were sent out every night to observe the army of invasion.   Prisoners were taken on both sides—the allied, or Pro-Slavery army, examined and pressed whatever came in their way; even the United States mail was detained and stopped upon the road ; in fact, all communication with Lawrence was cut off on the side nearest the State Line.   On Friday evening, Dec. 7th, an express was sent to Governor Shannon, who visited our town and inquired into the state of affairs, and acknowledged that he had been greatly deceived as to the position of the citizens of Lawrence.   His Excellency finally concluded a treaty of peace with the officers of the Free Soil army, by which it was understood that there was to be no more forcible resistance to the law, but all should have their legal remedy through the courts.   Thus ended the Kansas war. The sheriff, Jones, has made several arrests since the compromise without interruption, and a better feeling seems to prevail. So mote it be.

"Now, in justice to the people of Lawrence, I must say that a large and respectable portion of this community did not endorse the acts of the rescuers of Branson, nor did they countenance an armed resistance to the law.   This spirit of lawlessness came from the rabble as a general thing—or the most notorious Abolitionists.   I have lived among these people for the last ten months, aud have heard most of their speakers, and have listened to but *two* who advocated an *armed* resistance, and neither of those were *here* upon the day of the disturbance. I do not *say* that they were frightened, but they *had business* which unfortunately took them away *just at that time.*

"Though the Free State men deny the legality of the acts of the so-called Bogus Legislature, and are determined to resist them to the death, they are not prepared to adopt the ridiculous alternative of preventing the execution of their enactments—unless by a legal process through some regularly established Court of Justice. *It was the threats of the Missourians* which induced the people of Lawrence to fortify their town, and organize themselves as a military force:—they did not, therefore, desire to bid defiance to the law, but to *defend their lives and property from anticipated violence.*"

And so endeth the narrative of this Pro-Slavery Christian. We have read it over to several of our Lawrence Free State friends, who seem to consider it a very impartial document—the only passage excepted to being that in relation to the want of accommodations for the Kansas Legislature, while in session at *Pawnee*, in regard to which our Free State informants affirm that there were *some* houses there, and that if the Kansas Legislature, or to speak more correctly, its components, had really wished to obtain "board and lodging," they could have found both, either at *Pawnee*, or within a very short distance of that place; but it is alleged that the "Missouri Bogus Legislature," as the good people here delight to designate that august body, rather *preferred* to play at camping out, until the "severe showers" came, with "healing in their wings," to give these Romuluses of Kansas, as Christian calls them, a reasonable excuse for transferring the scene of their deliberations from *Pawnee* to *Shawnee* Mission, which, as the reader will perceive, was, so far as the names of the places are concerned, a mere matter of moonshine, insomuch as there is only a difference of *two letters*.   Having never seen *Pawnee* ourselves—though if it be less endurable than the Mission, it must be comfortless indeed—we are rejoiced to say that we cannot throw any light upon the matter in dispute.   Nor would we if we could—for we haven't made up our mind upon the Kansas question yet, and don't intend to—at least upon paper; for our object in writing this book—besides its purely selfish ones—is to give the facts, and then leave that sagacious individual, the reader, whoever he may be, to form *opinions* for himself.   So " pitch in" either way, gentlemen politicians, Pro-Slavery or Free Soil, as your fancy leads you, and may the printers' devil, or whatever other saint watches over the destinies of scribblers, forbid that we—the author—should pen one line that might bias your inclinations—" av' they be *vartuous*."

CHAPTER XXX.

THE FREE STATE COMMANDER-IN-CHIEF.

JANUARY.—We have been favored by a long conversation upon Kansas matters to-day, with Major General Charles Robinson, the Commander-in-Chief of the Free State army—or Kansas Volunteers, to call them by their legitimate appellation—and as this gentleman has very kindly furnished us with a history—the Free State version of course—of these unhappy disturbances between our fellow-citizens of Kansas and Missouri, we will introduce it here, premising, as we do so, that we believe this statement to be well worthy of attention, for we have written it down word for word from the General's own lips, and we are free to confess, that there is no politician, upon either side, in the Territory, who bears a higher reputation, among both friends and foes, for personal integrity, and undoubted veracity, than does Major General Charles Robinson.

MAJOR GENERAL ROBINSON'S HISTORY OF THE WAR.

" In the month of November last, a rumor reached Lawrence that a man named Dow, a settler at Hickory Point, some ten miles distant from that place, had been killed by one Coleman, without provocation on the part of Dow. It was also reported that no attempt had been made, nor would be made, to arrest the murderer; and, moreover, that a number of the settlers at

Hickory Point had called a meeting to take the matter into consideration—at which, one or more citizens of Lawrence were present. Certain resolutions were passed, in reference to bringing Coleman to justice. After this meeting was dissolved, and as the Hickory Point settlers were returning to their homes in the evening, it was discovered that a party were in pursuit of one Jacob Branson, a resident of that neighborhood, with whom Dow had lived. Fearing that he would be 'lynched,' the Hickory Point settlers determined to ascertain the real purpose of this intended arrest. While engaged in taking council upon this subject, a party of some fifteen men, who had assembled near the house of Mr. Abbot, at Blanton's, saw an equal number, or thereabouts, of horsemen advancing towards them, whereupon they hailed this party, who had halted, and inquired if one Branson was with them, to which Branson replied that he was, and a prisoner. The Free State or Hickory Point men then directed Branson to leave those whom he was with, and come over to them, which he accordingly did. The rescuing party then came with Branson to Lawrence, arriving in the night. The drum was beaten, and a gathering held, without formal notice, in School House hall, at about eight o'clock A. M. of the day following Branson's arrest. Here the incidents as they occurred were related by Branson and others of the rescuing party. I was not aware of this assemblage being held (Dr. Robinson resides upon the bluff, which is nearly half a mile distant from the main body of the town), and did not, therefore, attend until near its close. After hearing the speakers, the meeting appointed a committee of *ten* persons, of which I was one, to examine into the matter, and report the course which, under the circumstances, was most proper to be pursued. Another committee of *three* was also appointed to wait upon Judge Cameron, then residing in Lawrence, who had issued the warrant upon which Branson had been arrested, and inquire by what authority he had done so.   At the close of the meeting I was called upon to speak, and accordingly made some remarks to the effect that we should not array ourselves against the laws of the United States in anything that we might do.   I counselled prudence generally.   The meeting continued in session until noon, and then adjourned to re-convene at two o'clock, P. M., and receive the reports of the committees.   Upon rendering these, the Committee of *ten* stated, that the citizens of Lawrence and its vicinity were without the protection of law, and in view of this circumstance, proposed the immediate enrollment of all such persons as were willing to arm themselves in the defence of law and order; they furthermore recommended the appointment of a standing Committee of *ten*, to be styled the Committee of Public Safety.   This report was adopted, and the Committee of *ten*, already selected, were accordingly appointed members of this standing committee.   The committee of *three* reported that they had obtained an interview with Judge Cameron, who stated that he acted in the matter of Branson's arrest by virtue of authority vested in him by the Territorial Legislature.   This closed the acts of the meeting. The Committee of Public Safety then organized, by selecting one of their number—myself—to act as the Military Commander of the Free State army, in case of an attack, which was then confidently expected, for it was currently reported that the town of Lawrence had been threatened with demolition by the Missourians.   I was the presiding officer of the committee, but not the chairman.   The committee then proceeded to take action by enrolling such persons—citizens of Lawrence and its vicinity—as were willing to serve.   I cannot recollect the number, whose names were given in at that time.   We finally enrolled *eight hundred*, and could have brought *one thousand* fighting men into the field, in case of an attack.   These enrolled men were all armed with Sharpe's rifles, or shot guns, and were well supplied with ammunition—many had pistols—those not enrolled were for the most part armed with some kind of weapon.   We had, moreover, cannon."

(Meaning, as we have since learned from another source, a mounted howitzer, with one hundred rounds of Shrapnell shot. The first organization of these men, as we have been informed, by G. P. Lowrey, Esq., the chairman of the Committee on Public Safety, was into squads of fifteen or twenty men, under the command of captains; these were afterwards changed, as recruits came in, into companies, and organized into a regiment of infantry, under the command of Col. J. H. Lane, who finally, when another regiment was added, was made a Brigadier General, and placed in command—under Major General Robinson—of the 1st Brigade of Kansas Volunteers.   Mr. Lowrey also states, that the number at present enrolled is between eight hundred and one thousand men, of whom eight hundred are armed with Sharpe's rifles, the remainder being provided with western rifles, or double-barrelled shot-guns; there is also a company of mounted men, 70 in all, armed with revolvers and sabres, or in lieu of these, pikes with scythe or sabre-blades attached, which were carefully sharpened).

" From the time of the formation of this Committee of Public Safety, the Pro-Slavery forces began to accumulate from Missouri and other quarters—their numbers being variously estimated at different times, from two hundred to two thousand men.

" When the people of Lawrence finally learned that a large force was collected both above and below this place, and that an attack might be speedily expected, we commenced fortifying the place; these fortifications were earth-works, thrown up by our volunteers under the superintendence of Col. Lane.   Nor did we, in the meanwhile, neglect to set forth our condition, and seek aid from every official source from whence it could be hoped for.   We sent people into the Territory to represent the condition of the people of Lawrence.   We applied to the commanders of the United States military posts in Kansas, for the means with which to repel these Missourian marauders, who were even then threatening our town with destruction. We also dispatched a communication to Governor Shannon, to inquire if these so-called militia were menacing us by his order, and if so, calling upon him either to restrain or remove them from our vicinity, or we should be compelled to seek aid from higher authority— referring to the Chief Executive of the nation, General Pierce, to whom we sent a telegraphic dispatch of similar import. A memorial was moreover drawn up and signed, and a messenger sent to lay it before Congress, and request an investigation by that body of our acts, and the causes which prompted them. In the meantime, the Pro-Slavery forces continued to augment, and committed depredations upon travellers and the country generally, by robbing wagons, taking prisoners, interfering with peaceable travellers upon the public highway, and even stopping the United States mail. And in addition to these unprovoked outrages, they showed an evident disposition to excite our people to acts of hostility, in firing nightly upon our picket guards, by which, however, as it fortunately happened, no one was hurt. In the meanwhile the Governor's proclamation made its appearance for the *first* time in Lawrence, *how*, or in what manner, I am unable to say. *No copies were ever sent to us in an official way,* nor had any communication been held with us up to this time, as a community, either by Governor Shannon, Sheriff Jones, or any other Territorial officer, in his official capacity. Nor was any attempt made to arrest the rescuers of Branson, or any other person in Lawrence. While our people were in this state of ignorance as regarded the objects and intentions of the Pro-Slavery army, one of our citizens, a man named Thomas W. Barber, while on his way to his home, some five miles distant from this place, was mortally wounded by two of the sheriff's *posse.* This increased the excitement among our volunteers to such an extent, that it required the utmost exertions on the part of their officers to restrain them from attacking the offending parties. It was about this time that Governor Shannon first communicated with us, by a letter dated from the Executive office at Shawnee Mission." ·

[NOTE.—-We have endeavored to obtain a copy of this epistle but were unable to do so.]

" He added a verbal message to the effect that he would talk with us in person *soon*. This had an influence in allaying the excitement, for our people were determined to forbear, so long as there was any reasonable hope of coming to an amicable understanding with the hostile forces.   Our next advices from Governor Shannon came through a verbal message from the Wakarusa camp, whither his Excellency had gone to take the command of his army. It simply informed us of the time when he purposed visiting Lawrence.   We accordingly sent out an escort who met him at Franklin, and accompanied him into our town ; several of his Pro-Slavery friends came with him. Upon his arrival here, the Governor was introduced to some of our citizens, and then had a private interview with General Lane, and myself, as representatives of the citizens of Lawrence ; in the course of which he admitted that there had been a misunderstanding, and appeared anxious to get out of the difficulty.   He acknowledged, moreover, that *he saw nothing out of the way*, thus far, in the course pursued by the citizens of Lawrence in arming themselves for their defence. In fact, so perfectly satisfied was Governor Shannon of the justice of our position, that there was at this time no obstacle in the way of an immediate cessation of hostilities, save this: that he feared he would be unable to control his men, and therefore desired to await the arrival of the United States troops, then momentarily expected from Fort Leavenworth.   His Excellency furthermore declared, that if he were to inform his command, that he (the Governor) had concluded peace with the citizens of

Lawrence, without demanding an unconditional surrender of their arms, they would at once raise the ' Black Flag,' and march upon the town.

" After the termination of this interview, Governor Shannon and his friends remained with us as our guests until late in the afternoon, when they departed, the Governor promising to return the following day at 8 o'clock A. M. He accordingly reëntered Lawrence on the ensuing day, at a somewhat later hour than he had designated. A statement mutually agreeable to both parties was then drawn up and signed by Governor Shannon, as the chief Executive of Kansas Territory, on the one side, and Brigadier General J. H. Lane and myself, as the Commanders-in-chief of the patriots of Kansas, on the other. This consumed the day until 4 o'clock P. M. General Lane and myself, at the request of Governor Shannon, then accompanied him to Franklin, to meet a committee of thirteen captains of the Pro-Slavery army. This was done, to satisfy the Governor's *posse*, who, as before intimated, were disposed to demand an unconditional surrender of our arms, as a *sine qua non* in the terms of our treaty. Upon uniting with this committee, the Governor made a lengthy speech, without apparently satisfying the Missouri captains that he had done his duty in coming to an uder·standing with the citizens of Lawrence, which should leave them in possession of their arms, or in a position for defence. After a prolonged and somewhat excited debate, the stipulations, as set forth in our paper of agreement, were recited, and a majority of the captains decided that they had, under the circumstances, no right to demand our weapons, and would, therefore, retire peaceably with their men. This was on Saturday night, (Dec. 8th.) General Lane and myself then invited the captains to visit Lawrence, see the town, and become acquainted with our people : to which we added the assurance that if they knew us better they would esteem us more.

"On the ensuing day, Governor Shannon visited us, dined with a party of our citizens, and was introduced to several of our ladies. This was at the Free State Hotel, in an upper chamber some 12 by 18 feet in size, which was then occupied by a committee of twelve ladies of Lawrence, who had met there to arrange a social gathering, to take place on the following day (Monday, Dec. 10). This festivity was gotten up as a sort of general peace-demonstration, to be attended without distinction of party. While the Governor was thus pleasantly engaged in conversation with the ladies, it was reported to me that the disbanded Pro-Slavery forces were reorganizing for an attack upon the town. This came from the officer of the guard. I immediately sought the Governor and informed him of this rumor, and also of the fact that we were acting without authority, and if a collision should ensue and any one be killed, we would be liable to be tried for murder. I therefore suggested to him the propriety of giving us a written authority to protect ourselves and the town. To this he readily assented, by saying that if I would draw up such a paper he would sign it, which was accordingly done."

And now, General, said we, there is yet another matter, and we trust that your modesty will not refuse us a request which we are about to make ; you are a public character, and as such, may in some measure be regarded as public property; the world will soon ask, if it is not already doing so, "Who is General Robinson ?" enable us, then, if you please, to answer this question, by informing "all whom it may concern" who General Robinson *is;* or, in other words, give us the necessary data to write out an outline, if nothing more, of your *previous* self, and we will try and manage your *present* without assistance:

Now, it is only right,—for we like *diffidence* in a great man, though *brass* is, as a general thing, much more highly appreciated,—to state that this Free State soldier and politi cian, yielded with considerable reluctance to our request, and then only when it was repeated urgently. But as we *did* obtain the desired data from this distinguished individual we will introduce by way of a finale to the present chapter a

BIOGRAPHICAL SKETCH OF MAJOR GENERAL CHARLES ROBINSON.

Charles Robinson was born in Worcester County, Mass., on the 21st of July, 1818; was educated at Amherst College, but did not, we believe, graduate at that institution ; studied medicine at the Medical College in Pittsfield, Mass., where he received his diploma as an M. D., in 1843; practised his profession at Belchertown and Fitchburg, in the same State, until his removal to California in 1849, by way of the Rocky Mountains. Upon arriving in the El Dorado of the West, Dr. Robinson settled at Sacramento, where he played a prominent part in the " squatter riots " of 1850, in which, as the reader may perhaps remember, the Mayor of Sacramento, and some eight or ten others, lost their lives. Upon this occasion, Dr. Robinson fought upon the side of " squatter sovereignty," and was seriously wounded—it was asserted, mortally, at the time. For his alleged conduct upon this occasion, and while still suffering from a desperate hurt, Dr. Robinson was indicted for murder, assault with intent to kill, and for conspiracy; tried before the District Court of Sacramento—and acquitted. While still in. confinement, on board the prison-ship, he was nominated and elected to the Legislature of California, from Sacramento district. This was in 1851. In July of the same year, he sailed from California in the steamship Union, which was wrecked on her passage to the Isthmus ; in the difficulties which followed this disaster, Robinson is said to have borne an active and conservative part. After many delays, he finally managed to reach New York city, in September of 1851 ; was at Havana at the time of the Lopez execution, and a witness to that cold-blooded murder. Upon his return to the East, Dr. R. recommenced the practice of medicine, in Fitchburg, where he remained until June of 1854, when he emigrated with his family to Kansas. Here, he settled himself at Lawrence, where he still resides upon his "claim," some half a mile distant from the main body of the town. Unlike his compatriot, General Lane, Dr. Robinson— or, as we should now begin to call him, General Robinson—does not call himself a man of property; he says he is simply "a poor man whose business prospects have been sadly damaged by the war."

In Kansas politics, Gen. Robinson was a member of the State Constitutional Convention—is chairman of the Free State Executive Committee, and in addition to this, holds the military rank of Major-General and Commander-in-Chief, of the Kansas Volunteers —as the Free State army of Kansas style themselves. He may be regarded as the real head—the thinking one, we mean—and mainspring of the Free State party; or, to speak more correctly, of all that party who are worth anything. We believe him to be a keen, shrewd, far-seeing man, who would permit nothing to stand in the way of the end which he desired to gain. He is, moreover, cool and determined, and appears to be endowed with immense firmness; we should call him a conservative man, *now ;* but conservative rather from policy than from principle. He seems to have strong common sense, and a good ordinary brain, but no brilliancy of talent. In fact, to sum Gen. Robinson up in a single sentence, we consider him the most dangerous enemy which the Pro-Slavery party have to encounter in Kansas.

In person he is tall, well made, and more than ordinarily handsome; gentlemanly, but by no means winning in his manners, with one of those cold, keen blue eyes that seem to look you through.

CHAPTER XXXI.

THE HEROES OF THE WAR.

THE following anecdote, which we find noted down upon our journal for to-day, may well be styled the most brilliant incident of that renowned struggle, " the Wakarusa War," at least upon the Free-State side of the question. We don't vouch for its truthfulness, but as it comes from "high authority," as a *bona fide* event of the campaign, we feel bound to chronicle it here, the more so as it is really a very readable story :

It would seem that a certain Major Blank—we have a fondness for Blanks, for who ever heard of a Mister Blank, or even a Major Blank bringing an action for libel—we really don't know that we give our soldier rank enough, for in good truth, he ought to be a General of Brigade, if a most impudent, but withal cunningly-devised stratagem, can brevet a Kansas volunteer. But to get on with our narrative, the stronghold of Free State-ism was besieged, and the excitement upon both sides, as the newspapers say, tremendous. Old muskets were in demand, rifles at a premium, and six-shooters worth their weight in gold, but though these were to be had, there was yet a desideratum in the way of fighting-tools, which had of late become a matter of serious perplexity to the military chiefs in Lawrence—they lacked artillery. Nor did their want seem likely to be supplied, when— as luck would have it, a messenger trotted into town with the gratifying intelligence, that some sympathizing New Yorker had sent a six or twelve-pounder (we have forgotten which), with ammunition to match, to assist their troops in killing off the "Border Ruffians," and moreover, that this "material aid" was now lying all snugly boxed and safely stowed away, in the warehouse of a Kansas City commission merchant. But Kansas City was one of "the enemy's" strongholds—Pro-Slavery up to the hub—and how to get the piece into Lawrence, over guarded roads, and in troublous times, without exciting a suspicion, which would have undoubtedly changed the destination of this "peace maker," was a problem which might well have puzzled the ingenuity of that very acute practitioner, a "Philadelphia lawyer." But, as our Free State warriors *had* a sprinkling, of the real wooden-nutmeg, calculating, *Deown East Yankee* breed among their counsellors, it was not very long, before they laid their sagacious heads together and hammered out a plan for its deliverance.

As the reader may readily suppose, there were but few to whom the particulars of this notable scheme were communicated, at least at the time, so it excited but little curiosity, when Major Blank, of the Quarter-Master's department, accompanied by two or three travelling friends, rolled out of Massachusetts street one winter morning, in a stout Pennsylvania wagon, drawn by a couple of active mules, and took the road for Kansas City, which, as everybody knows, is located on the Missouri river, near the frontier line of the territory.

Upon reaching their place of destination, our Major—who had, with very unusual modesty, dropped his title for the time being, thereby reducing his appellation to plain Mister Blank, who was presumed to be a citizen of Lawrence, journeying to Kansas City on business of his own—lost no time in waiting upon the commission merchant, and accordingly repaired to his storehouse, where he sauntered in with a very nonchalant air, at the same time remarking "that as he was going back to town with a wagon that was most empty, he guessed he might as well take a box or tew along with him," which he understood had been stored there for a friend of his, one Mr. John Smith of Lawrence, who had requested him, if he could do so conveniently, to bring them along with him upon his return trip. Now as Mr. Blank was an accommodating sort of chap, and moreover, wanted to oblige his very good friend, "Mr. John Smith, of Lawrence," he "calculated that it wouldn't put him out of his way, and so he'd take 'em, and run the risk of gettin' pay for his trouble."

Now our commission merchant was a red-hot Pro-Slavery man, who would as soon thought of taking the wages of the foul fiend himself, as of assisting " those rascally abolitionists in Lawrence," by either word or deed. But as the thing looked all right, he was fain to point out the boxes—there were but two, one of them containing the gun and the other its carriage—which the Major receipted for, and was about getting into his wagon with such speed as their weight would permit, when the Pro-Slavery man—made suspicious, it may be, by some peculiarity in their appearance—objected, and the following dialogue ensued ;

Pro-Slavery Merchant.—Look hyar, stranger, thar's somethin' mighty dubersome about them boxes. They say you Lawrence folks air gitting all manner of curious traps up thar, to wipe out our boys with, and I'll jest allow to hev a squint inter them goods afore they roll out of Kansas City.

Free State Major.—Wäal I guess, Mister, there ain't nothin' extra in 'em no how. I don't know for certin, but John Smith says he's expectin' a buggy-wagon, along with some other notions, which his folks are a sendin' out from York State, and I shouldn't wonder if it wan't them. But I guess they might hev bought it a tarnation sight cheaper in Saint Louie, and saved payin' freight, beside, don't yeou ?

Pro-Slavery Merchant.—I don't kear nothin' fur that, but I'll be dog-gauned ef I don't think it's about reasonable to hist a lid off of them thar boxes, and see what's inside fur myself. Well I do, stranger.

Free State Merchant.—Wāal, I kinder sorter expect that ef ycou'r willin' tu take the risk, it won't make no *great* difference to Mister Smith, any way, ef ycou du, so here goes; hand us that axe, will ycou, Sam?

At this stage of the conversation, Mister Blank seized the axe and knocked up one side of the lid of the larger receptacle, which, as he well knew, contained *the wheels*, and then threw down the instrument, at the same time calling out triumphantly,

"There, Mister, didn't I tell yeou, jest look for yeourself. Guess you'll say I'm right another time; ef that ain't a buggy-wagon it ain't nothin' at all. Don't yeou see the wheels?"

Being thus urged, our Pro-Slavery merchant peeped in, saw what he supposed, in the uncertain light of the building, to be a pair of wheels, and feeling, perhaps, a little crest-fallen at this "lame and impotent conclusion" of his suspicious scrutiny, "acknowledged the corn" by saying,

"Well, I'll jest allow I *wor* a spot too particular this time; so hist them inter your wagon, boys, and roll out as lively as you choose. Jim, you infernal nigga, whar air you; come hyar, and help these gentlemen pack thar plunder. Stranger," added he, turning to the Major, "mout I ask you to step inter the office and take a drink? I've a powerful far article of corn whisky in thar."

While the "stranger" stepped in to drink, the gentlemen, assisted by "that infernal lazy nigga, Jim," made good use of their hands; for by the time the Major and his Pro-Slavery friend had finished "imbibing," and exchanging their parting assurances of very distinguished consideration, the boxes, with their concealed munitions of war, were all ready, in one sense, to go off, having been securely stowed upon the bottom of the conveyance, with an upper covering, most ingeniously arranged, of tin pails, wicker-work, wooden ware, and such like "Yankee notions," which formed an excellent screen for the real valuables of the load, and at the same time gave an air of greater innocence to this masked flying battery.

So being all right, they rolled out of Kansas City, and went on their way rejoicing. But our Free State Major's anxieties were not yet over, for they had barely reached a point upon the Lawrence trail, known as Wyandotte Hill, when the mules "stalled," and their wagon stuck fast in the mud. What was to be done? One thing was evident, that it would never do to unload their cargo, while every avenue which led to Lawrence was fairly alive with those terrible fellows, the Border Ruffians, who would, in all human probability, have "made no bones," that is to say, left not a whole bone in the skins of our Major and his party, if they had caught them with their "contraband of war." It "*was* a fix," as the Major afterwards expressed it, "of the darndest kind." In the mean while time was passing, and things began to look desperate. But Major Blank was a small Napoleon in such dilemmas ; so after scratching his perplexed pate silently, as if he had an idea under the hair, and might get it out by friction, for at least five minutes, he turned suddenly towards his men, while a quiet smile crept over his face, like sunshine after shade, and exclaimed, " I've hit it, boys. I calkulate we've played these Missouri Pukes *one* real Yankee trick ; and now tarnation seize 'em, we'll treat them to *another*, and, if they only knew it, a darned sight the smartest of the tew. Jest wait awhile till some of them nigger-drivin' fellers come this way, and see if we don't git all the help we want."

And having thus delivered himself, our Major picked a dry seat by the side of the road, where he squatted down upon his haunches, and struck up Yankee Doodle to kill time.   But he had got no further than

> " Yankee Doodle keep it up,
>   Yankee Doodle dandy ;
>   When all yeour lasses biles away,
>   Yeou can't expect much candy,"

when the "nigger-drivin' fellers," who were to furnish the expected aid, made their appearance in the shape of a detachment of " Border Ruffians," all armed and equipped, and *en route* to reinforce the Pro-Slavery encampment upon the Wakarusa bottom.   Nor was their march either a silent or an orderly one, for they came, cursing the Abolitionists at every stride, until, like Saul of old, they might fairly be accused of " breathing out threatenings and slaughter " as they went.

But for all this our Yankee Major knew right well that to help a man's wagon out of the mud is but an every-day western courtesy, and even Missouri " Pukes " are much too well " raised " to permit even a political prejudice to interfere with their good breeding.   So when our Free State officer straightened himself up, and hailed their leader—who looked as if he had kept on " a chillen' " until the ague had shook all the flesh off his bones— by drawling out,

" Waal, neow, Kernel, guess yeou'd let some of yeour men lend a feller in trouble a helpin' hand, wouldn't yeou ; for I'm stalled down yeou see ?"

The response was a hearty one, for " the enemy " not only hitched on a couple of their own horses to assist the efforts of the well-nigh exhausted mules, but even put their sturdy shoulders to the wheel, and thus extricated the Free State Artillery from that most unrelenting of detainers, a Kansas mud hole, where it might have stuck, but for their volunteer exertions, until the " *crack* of doom," without making a *report*, no— not even in the newspapers.

Being thus happily relieved from his *embroglio*, Major Blank said his "good day to yeou, gentlemen," and "I'm railley obleeged to yeou ;" and then, having first pretended to employ himself about his wagon until his late benefactors were fairly out of sight, our military chieftain took a long squint ahead, cocked his starboard eye knowingly at his companions, told the driver to start up his team, and then proceeded with the strain of

"Yankee Doodle 'tis a tune
Americans delight in,"

as if he hadn't a care, or even the shadow of one, west of the Alleghany Mountains.

From this point, says our informant, the Free State soldiers and their cannon journeyed prosperously on until they were within some ten or fifteen miles of their destination, when their leader (the Major) left the party and rode ahead, after agreeing with his men upon certain signs, such as dropping cards by the wayside, which would forewarn them in case he discovered any danger of interruption upon the road. But our Free State commander was evidently not only shrewd, but lucky, for he found none to molest nor make him afraid ; so in due course of time, the "pacificator" and its guardians entered the main street of Lawrence to add their valuable aid to the earth-work defences of that beleaguered city.

It is furthermore reported that on the ensuing day, when the *modus operandi* of this affair (which was almost too good to keep quiet—the more so as there was no longer any need for secrecy), had reached the Pro-Slavery camp, not even a barrel of flour was permitted to pass "the enemy's" lines without being opened and thoroughly searched. But, alas for the "Border Ruffians!" all their precautions were but a repetition of that oft-practised prudence, which takes excellent care to "shut the stable door when the steed *is gone*."

If this be not what a Virginian would call a "darned mean Yankee trick," and one of the real, original, no-connection-with-any-other-establishment sort into the bargain, we should be pleased to know what is?

And now, for another bit of documentary Free State testimony, which we shall present here in the shape of "a statement of facts connected with certain meetings, which were held in the town of Lawrence, on the day following the rescue of Branson from Sheriff Jones." For this information, we are indebted to the courtesy of Mr. Josiah Miller, the editor of the "Free State," and a citizen of Lawrence, in which place the journal alluded to is published.

MR. MILLER'S STATEMENT.

"On the day following the rescue of Branson from Sheriff Jones's *posse*, there was a meeting held at Lawrence, where the party who had effected his rescue had arrived, with Branson in company, at about four o'clock, A. M. Upon entering the town, the rescuers beat a drum about the streets, going through regular military evolutions, with arms shouldered, etc. There was considerable excitement; between eight and nine o'clock, A. M., a meeting was convened in 'Union Hall,' which, we understand, is called Union Hall, School House Hall, and by some, Robinson Hall. This meeting was got up by the rescuers of Branson, as all wished to hear a statement of the facts. About one hundred persons were present; it was as fully attended as our town meetings generally are; the assemblage nearly filled the house. S. N. Wood, the leader of the rescuing party, was present, with a sword buckled round him; he was unanimously appointed chairman; and, on taking his seat, made some vague and ambiguous remarks in regard to the rescue of Branson. He would not call it a rescue, but said they had simply ordered Branson to come out from Sheriff Jones's party and join theirs. He intimated that one of their number (Abbot), who gave this order, was the commander of the military company to which Branson belonged (the Wakarusa Co.), and had, therefore, a right to exercise his military authority, by giving Branson a command, which he (Branson), as a military man, was bound to obey. Wood stated further, that, when Jones's people threatened to shoot Branson if he stirred, his men (the rescuers) cocked their Sharpe's rifles, and would, in the event of the sheriff's party firing, have annihilated every man of them, as each of his people had picked his man.

"Branson followed Wood, and gave an account of the circumstances attending his arrest and rescue. He said that Sheriff Jones's party excited his suspicions by not taking a direct road (after leaving his house), but going from one Pro-Slavery settlement to another, in the vicinity of Hickory Point. He added that Jones never showed any writ on making the arrest. Branson said, that he was sleeping at the time of the sheriff's visit, and on being awakened by their knocking at the door, arose and opened it, when Jones rushed in, with a pistol in either hand, followed by his party, and informed Branson that he was his prisoner. Jones did not state where he was to be taken, or for what purpose ; but he afterwards learned (though not from Jones), that he was going to Lawrence, to be examined upon a peace-warrant ; they provided him with an animal to ride. Branson did not appear to have been uncivilly treated while on the road. He further stated, that they proceeded on until they met the rescuing party ; when the rescuers commanded Jones to halt, the parties were about eighty yards apart. Some of the rescuers then called out, "Is Branson there?" He answered, "Yes," whereupon they directed .him to leave Jones's party and *fall in* with theirs.

"Upon the conclusion of Branson's statement, a committee of *ten* was appointed, to take the matter into consideration, and, if necessary, prepare for the defence of Lawrence. This committee was styled the Committee of Public Safety. They were all citizens of Lawrence. The 'Ten' retired to consult, and concluded for the time, to act entirely upon the defensive, and, if Sheriff Jones came to arrest the rescuers, to permit it to be done.

"I have omitted to state that, after the conclusion of Branson's remarks, it was

"*Resolved*, That this meeting *approves the conduct of the men who rescued Branson*.

"After some discussion, this motion, through the influence of General Robinson and others, was withdrawn.

"Violent speeches were then made by Anson H. Mallory, of Lawrence, the Quarter-master General to the Kansas Volunteers, during the 'late war,' who wound up his remarks by moving, that a committee of three be appointed, to wait upon Hugh Cameron, Esq., a Justice of the Peace, under the Territorial Legislature, and inquire by what authority he issued the writ to arrest Branson. This was adopted, and a committee visited Judge Cameron accordingly, but with no better result than the information that he, Cameron, was acting under a commission from Governor Shannon, and issued the writ in accordance with the authority thus vested in him, and on an affidavit filed by one Buckley.

"The meeting then adjourned at noon, to re-commence at two, P. M., to receive the reports of its committees, at which time it met, when the reports were rendered, and adopted, as above stated."

Our informant adds, that the Sharpe's rifles are, as he believes, furnished to the Kansas Volunteers at twelve dollars, in Kansas scrip, which has been quoted—in Kansas—at a discount of fifty cents on the dollar.

CHAPTER XXXII.

HIS HONOR JUDGE PORTLY.

January 6th.—At a cabin upon the prairie, known as "Barber's claim."

We are sitting in company with a Free State settler's family, consisting of himself, his wife, sister, little ones, and friend, in the warmest apartment of the *two* which our young frontiersman calls *home.* A wild winter storm howls drearily without, while the cold increases hourly—and although the table at which we are seated stands close to the stove, the chill air that finds its way through every nook and cranny of this comfortless—foul-weather residence—benumbs our stiffening fingers, which are striving, but in vain, to hold "the pen of a ready writer," as they jot down these inklings of adventure for to-day.

We left Lawrence at an early hour this morning, in company with our friends, G. P. Lowry, Esq., of Free State celebrity, and a certain Mr. Eldridge, the proprietor of the "Eldridge House,"—late Free State Hotel, that is to be, in Lawrence, and of whose establishment we shall speak more fully elsewhere. Our journey of to-day, if a matter of ten miles can be called a journey, was quite an impromptu affair, for when we settled ourselves to journalize at the "Cincinnati," between seven and eight o'clock, A. M., we had not the remotest intention of leaving Lawrence to-day; but as our friends were driving out upon the

road which passes Squire Portly's—we will give him that name
for want of a better—who, as everybody ought to know, is a
gentleman with "a most capacious stomach," and high-strung
Free Soil principles, we determined to accompany them, at
least so far as his Honor's dwelling—for our friend Portly had
"squatted" within a mile or so of the residences of Barber's
brother, widow, and brother-in-law, from whom we hoped to
obtain a narrative of facts, connected with the shooting of Thomas
W. Barber, who was, as the reader may already know, the only
victim of the Free State Wakarusa war.

A somewhat less than two hours of travel, over one of the
bleakest of all bleak prairie roads, brought us through in a half
frozen state to old Portly's "improvement"—a very snug, well
chinked, Siamese—twin-like pair of log cabins, in one of which
we found the fat Squire himself, looking the very picture of lazy
contentment, as he sat with his. short legs cocked comfortably
up against the stove, while a long-stemmed, smoke-blackened,
cob pipe protruded from its resting-place, between his few remaining teeth, at which his Honor kept sucking away as placidly as
what he was pleased to term "a powerful smart spell of the
phthisic" would permit. Upon our entrance, old Portly, whom
we had met before, noticed the fact by grunting out a short-
winded welcome, as he motioned us to a vacant rush-bottomed
chair, which we had barely taken possession of, when the door
opened, and the Judge's good lady added herself to the party
already assembled, in the person of a keen-eyed, hard-featured
little dame, the very antipodes, in externals at least, of her
unctuous lord, for while the Judge was literally "a man of
weight," who would have played but a sorry part either in a
marching regiment, or a foot-race, his spouse was thin, even to
a fault; indeed she was to all appearances but a mere rack of
bones, over whose unpicturesque outline nature had condescended
to draw an angular wrinkling of skin, which, between "the ager,"

exposure to the sun, and downright hard work, had finally become embrowned to an extent that quite carried out the idea of a well-dressed hide. In fact, Portly's "*lesser* half" was really a wonder in her way; for though you might have been inclined at first sight to have said that this antiquated matron stood upon her last *limbs*—yet it was only necessary to face her battery of words to convince even the examiner of a Life Insurance Company, that the old girl was, "barrin' accidents," good for twenty years to come, for we will venture to say, that Madam Portly's powers of volubility were second to those of no other woman in the Territory; our long hostess, Miss Charity, always excepted. And didn't she give it to the Border Ruffians—and didn't she pitch into the Missourians—not to mention the Pro-Slavery side of the Wakarusa war in general, with a special addenda in favor of "Atchinson and his crew?" To "all of which" questions "and singular," candor compels us to make answer —*well* she did.

But let us give the reader an extract—a random one withal —from a wonderful chapter of this good old lady's frontier experiences—which she poured out thick and fast—as his Honor Judge Portly was strapping on his buffalo overshoes to show us the way to "Barber's claim," which, as we have already hinted, was what Kansas men would call "near by," which—being translated—would in this instance signify a mile or so off; and now for a specimen of his "*lesser* half's" volubility:

"Waal, stranger, yeou see it wor in thar fust part of thar evenin'—but not so dark as it mout be. Waal, I wor a settin' by thar store, when thar come a knock to thar door, so I riz an' opened it, an' I'll jest allow that thar wor forty men in all a settin' on thar hosses around thar house. To be sure me and my old man the Squire thar, *ave* hed a few words about thar bein' that many, but I jest *know* I'm right; for thar's my darter Wetumpky, she that's thar married one—for yeou see she got a man in Ingianny afore we moved to Kansas—an' she's a right peart woman, I kin tell yeou, stranger; more pearter, I reckon, than any gal of her raisin' that yeou ever sot yeour eyes on, I do expect. And Wetumpky jest up an' told thar old man, the other day, that he wor a gettin' so blind· that he didn't know a hawk from a handsaw; and what wor more, that she seen them men herself, and she war jest willin' to swār, that if thar warn't a powerful sight on em, thar warn't nary one. So the Judge hes a kinder gin in lately, an' concluded that I wor right.

" Wael, stranger, as I wor informin' on yeou, I riz, an' opened thar door, an' when I noticed who wor thar, I jest allowed that we wor all murdered ; fur yeou see, thar Judge wor away— though, to be sure, he's got to be considerably no account at fightin' since he's had the phthisic so powerful bad ; an' what wor more, got his thumb chawed up in a whisky scrape down in Ingiany. ; and as fur thar boys, they wor done gone to a speech-ifying down to Lawrence ; so I kinder skeared—John Portly, whar's your manners ? Why don't yeou invite thar stranger to take a drink, instead of standin' thar, a-lookin' at us like a sick coon ? and he a goin' out inter that prairie, and thar Lord knows, that whisky never hurt no man when it air so powerful cold. Wael, as I wor a-tellin' yeou, stranger, I wor *some* skeared ; and I allow, that badly skeared, that I didn't say nary word fur nigh onto a minit ; but I got over it, stranger, fur yeou see, bein' Hoosier raised, I kin ginerally allow to take my own part right smartly ; so says I, Whar mout yeou come from, gentlemen ? and with that, they jest went on a-tellin' me a long rigmarole of stuff about how they wor from Iowa, and—Judge, I *air* astonished at yeou ! why don't yeou ask thar stranger to sugar ? Don't sugar, hey ? Wael, that *air* radiculous ! it air curous, too, fur I always allowed that thar Yorkers used a heap of sugar. But whar wor I?—oh, I wor a-tellin' yeou that thar men wor a savin' that they hed come from Iowa to help thar Free

State folks down in Lawrence to whip thar Missouri nigger-drivers that wor a-comin' to burn thar town ; an' they talked like they wor the men that our folks wor expectin' down ; fur we hed hearn, stranger, that thar wor help a-comin from up in Iowa ; but I jest *knowed* that these fellers wor a-lyin' to me from thar start ; an' I wor right, for directly one on 'em speaks up— for yeou see, stranger, some on 'em hed got off and hitched thar hosses ; an' says he, ' Madam, I mout as well tell yeou that our boys air Missourians, and almighty flat-footed down onto thar Free State men to the back of it ; and as fur what brings us hyar to-night, it's jest this : thar's a report goin' round, that yeour old man, thar Judge—an' hangin' wouldn't be unhealthy fur him—hes got a power of Sharpe's rifles cashed hyar in thar house ; and as our boys air bound to have 'em, thar air a few questions we would be pleased to hev yeou a-replyin' to.' Wael, when I hearn that, stranger, I jest allowed that I couldn't hold in any longer ; fur though I'm dreadful easy to please, I ain't a-goin' to be rode over ; so as I wor all-createdly riled, I jest up an' let 'em hev it. You may question all yeou want, says I, an' answer too, for all thar good that yeou'll git from it, for I consider yeou a swārin', drinkin', keard-playin' lot of thieves an' no account cusses. I wor a-goin' to hev told 'em a heap more, but they jest sidled by me inter the buildin', an' in a minit, they wor all over it. Wael, yeou see, thar wor a man a-stoppin' with us —a stranger that wor drivin' a settler's team—and so thar Missourians, when they found it out, went straight up to his bed— fur bein' powerful tired he wor a-sleepin' up in the loft ; and when they got whar his bed wor, they didn't say a word, but one on 'em wakened him up, while t'other one cocks a pistol and sets it to his year. An' so they kept on askin' him questions about who he wor, an' whar he wor from ; and about what he hed in his wagon : an' every answer he'd make the feller that held the pistol kinder made a motion with it, till thar poor man wor that skeared that his eyes seemed nigh onto 'stickin' out' of his head ; an' then, as ef they hadn't done enough already, the man with thar pistol lets it go off, as he allowed by accident, but I jest expect it wor done a-purpose, an' thar ball went through thar floor an' down inter thar room below, whar my married darter, Wetumpky—the peart gal I wor tellin' yeou on, stranger—wor a-standing underneath, and.—But yeou ain't a-goin, air yeou, stranger, fur I've only jest got started onto what I war a-tellin' yeou ; but ef yeou must go, stop in when yeou're a-trav'lin' this hyar road agin ; the Judge will be powerful glad to see yeou, and then I'll jest tell yeou all about it ; fur it's curous, stranger, an' jest shows up them Border Ruffians to be what they air."

Here old Portly *slipped* out, and we followed him, leaving the garrulous dame to continue her interminable narrative, or reserve it as she saw fit, until the arrival of some more Job-like victim. We remarked, by the way, that the Judge heaved a gentle sigh as he got into the open air, which may have proceeded from that " powerful hard spell of the phthisic," or it is just possible, from a sense of mental relief ; but if you asked us which, we could only refer you to " his Honor," and say, ¿ Quien sabe ?

As the weather was cold—the foot-path slippery—and our short-winded companion greatly troubled with " the heaves," our walk to Barber's claim was of the longest, and even upon reaching it we were again delayed by the absence of Barber himself, who did not make his appearance, until a white-headed little youngster had been sent to tell him that " a gentleman from York State was up at the house and wanted to see him."

We found this Mr. Barber a quiet, plain, inoffensive seeming sort of man. Upon explaining to him the nature of our business in Kansas, as also our desire to obtain a reliable statement of the facts connected with his brother's death, he very kindly promised to give us an account of this tragical affair, in which he himself, in company with his brother-in-law, Mr. Peirson, had been a prominent actor.

So we produced our note-book, while the settler's wife hunted up the ink, which was at length discovered at the bottom of as heterogeneous a mass of " plunder" as was ever gathered together, even beneath the rafters of a Far-Western log-cabin. And now we would call the attention of the reader to the following :

STATEMENT OF ROBERT F. BARBER, IN RELATION TO THE CIRCUMSTANCES ATTENDING THE SHOOTING OF HIS BROTHER, THOMAS W. BARBER, BY A PARTY OF THE PRO-SLAVERY FORCES, IN THE MONTH OF DECEMBER, 1855.

NOTE.—Robert F. Barber, late of Preble County, Ohio, and now a resident of Kansas Territory, makes the following statement, which has been read over to him, and to which he is willing to make affidavit when legally required.

On or about the 6th of December, 1855, at 1 o'clock, P. M., I left Lawrence (K. T.), in company with my brother, Thomas W. Barber, and my brother-in-law, Thomas M. Peirson ; we were all mounted ; I was provided with a Colt's Navy Revolver, and Peirson had a small (5 inch) Colt's Revolver, but Thomas W. Barber was entirely unarmed. We were on our way to our homes, distant about seven miles from Lawrence, and had ridden some three and a half miles, when we observed a party of from twelve to fifteen mounted men to the right of the California road, in which we were travelling. This party was apparently making directly for it. They were over half a mile from us when we first saw them. We then left the California trail, to take a cross road, to the left, which was the shorter one to our residences; this was immediately after we discovered the horsemen. We had at this time no idea that they intended to interrupt us, nor did we quit the highway for the purpose of avoiding them. We had left the main road by some half a mile, when we saw two of these mounted men advancing before the rest, as if to cut us off; this they did by approaching us on our right, and placing themselves in front of us, or nearly so. They came up at a trot, while we were walking our horses. The remainder of the approaching party had in the meanwhile halted in full sight of us, but at a distance of from two to four hundred yards.

One of the men who rode up to us was mounted upon a grey horse; he was heavily built, with a broad face, and I believe whiskers. The other seemed a tall, well-made person, dressed, if I remember right, in dark clothing, and mounted upon a sorrel horse.

I think that the man on the grey horse acted as their spokesman; when they came up and halted, the man on the sorrel stood a little off the road, but close to it, and to the left of his companion who had checked his animal in the road, not more than a couple of yards from our horses' heads, and directly in front of us. The man on the grey horse then ordered us to halt, and we did so immediately. Upon coming to a stand, the position of our party was as follows :—

My brother Thomas W. Barber was beside me, and on my right, while my brother-in-law, Peirson, was a little to my left, and in our rear; we were all in the road.

After halting us, the rider of the grey horse asked, "Where are you going?" My brother Thomas W. Barber—who answered for our party—replied, "We are going home." He then asked us, "Where are you from?" my brother answered, "We are from Lawrence." "What is going on in Lawrence?" was the next question. "Nothing in particular," said my brother. "Nothing in particular, hey?" replied the man. He then added, "We have orders from the Governor to see the laws executed in Kansas." Thomas W. Barber then asked, "What laws have we disobeyed?" Upon hearing this, the rider of the grey horse raised his hand and pointed towards his party, at the same time exclaiming, "Then, turn your horse's heads and go with us." My brother then said, "We won't do it." "You won't, hey?" said their spokesman, at the same time starting off with his horse so as to bring him on the right side of my brother —who moved his horse's head slightly towards him, as he did so. The man drew his pistol as he started, but halted on reaching his new position to the right of my brother—I can't say what the rider of the sorrel was doing in the meanwhile, for their spokesman rode between him and my brother, and my attention was at that moment taken up with drawing my own pistol, which was belted on behind my back, in such a manner that I was obliged to seize it with my left hand; this I did under the belief that we were about to be attacked. As I was changing it into my right hand to fire, I saw their spokesman—the man on the grey horse—discharge his pistol at my brother. I did not think at the time that my brother was hit. This man, after firing at my brother, rode right round into the road, and halted some ten paces in our rear. I wheeled my horse and shot at him, but missed; I cannot say that he returned my fire, but on changing my position I saw the smoke of the pistol of the man on the sorrel, who was still in his old postion. I then fired a second barrel at him, but missed, as I had done before.

After I had fired at the man on the sorrel horse, he rode up to his companion, and on reaching him they exchanged a word or two which I could not distinctly hear, and then galloped off towards their party. As they started I fired at them again, for the third time, but with no better success. We still stood firm in our tracks, not having moved our horses except to wheel them, from the beginning to the end of the affray.

The main body of horsemen was still halted, but full in sight. Thomas W. Barber then turned to us and said, "Boys, let us be off;" we started accordingly, at a gallop, on our road. At this time, the two men were still galloping towards their party. My brother and myself rode side by side; my brother-in-law, Peirson, who had a slower horse, following in our rear. After riding in this manner for about a hundred yards, my brother said to me, "That fellow shot me;" he smiled as he said so. I asked him, "Where are you shot?" He pointed to his right side. I then remarked, "It is not possible, Thomas?" To this he replied, "It is," at the same time smiling again. I do not think that he realized how badly he was hurt. After uttering these—his last words—he dropped his rein, and reeled in his saddle; seeing that he was about to fall, I caught hold of him by the left shoulder, grasping the loose overcoat which he wore. I held him thus for nearly a hundred yards; I could then hold him no longer, and he fell to the ground; as he did so, I slipped from my horse, at the same time calling out "Whoa;" both horses stopped immediately; I bent over my brother, and found that he was dead, and felt that we could do nothing for him. As Peirson and myself stood in the road consulting, we saw the other party riding towards us, and thinking that we could accomplish nothing by remaining where we were, I said to Peirson, "We had better be off." He objected, saying, "If we ride away, they may overtake and kill us; we had better stay where we are, and let them take us prisoners." I replied, "I will die before they shall take me prisoner." He then agreed to go, saying, "Let us be off as fast as we can." We galloped on accordingly. After riding nearly a mile, Peirson asked me if I saw any one coming? I looked back, and discovered two men galloping in pursuit. Peirson turned his head, and perceived them also. This was the last I saw of them. I am confident that some of the pursuing party must have discovered my brother's body, as they were riding upon

14*

the hill where it lay.   This transaction took place, from beginning to end, in an open prairie country, where there was no timber to shut out the view.

Peirson had his revolver in his pantaloons pocket, on the right side. He says that he could not get it out in time to shoot.   He certainly did not fire during the affair.   He lost his pistol, however, and overcoat; the pistol he has never seen since, as he tells me.

After riding about three miles, and finding that my horse was "giving out," I dismounted, feeling confident that the animal had been wounded in the affray; I did not stop to examine him at the time, but supposing that I was still pursued, left him standing in the road, and continued my way homewards on foot.   I afterwards learned that the horse had been shot low down behind the fore-shoulder, on the right side.   The horse died that night.   I do not know the size of the ball which killed the animal; I did not look for it.   The carcass has been dragged away and eaten by the wolves.

I think that the man on the grey horse, who shot at my brother, used a small (5 inch) Colt's revolver.

CHAPTER XXXIII.

A VISIT TO THE WIDOW BARBER.,

ONE or two persons who made a superficial examination of Thomas W. Barber's body, say that the ball which killed him entered his right side, just above the hip. There was little or no external bleeding—there being but a very small spot of blood visible on his shirt, and that just opposite the wound. The hemorrhage was internal. We presume that this was the immediate cause of his death ; it may also account for the apparent absence of any pain, for we are told that the unfortunate man uttered not a groan—a smile was on his face to the last, and still lingered round the clay-cold lips when they had been sealed for ever.

It is to be regretted that no thorough post-mortem examination of the body was made, for the size of the ball, which yet remains in the corpse—or if shattered, its weight—will, doubtless, prove which of the attacking parties gave the death-wound, as Major Clarke, one of their opponents, was armed with a small Colt's five inch revolver, while Col. Burns, of Weston, Mo., his companion, is stated to have used a Colt's navy revolver, which carries a ball of about two-eights and three thirty-seconds of an inch in diameter—the barrel being seven and a half inches in length. The orifice of the wound is described by eye witnesses as being very small ; one person states not larger than a buck shot-wound ; another informant says, "a small pistol ball."

The importance of this testimony is, however, lessened, if not made worthless from the fact that the mouth of the wound would naturally close somewhat, and perhaps entirely, after death. It must be remembered also, that no examination of the body took place until twenty-four hours after the affray. It will be perceived too that there is some discrepancy in the statements of Barber and Peirson, as to the size of the pistol used by the man on the grey horse (which would appear to have been Major Clarke, who answers to the description of a heavily-built, broad-faced man). Barber thinks that the man who shot his brother had a small "five inch" pistol—such as Clarke is reported to have used—while Peirson seems equally confident that his brother-in-law was killed by a ball fired from a navy revolver. Peirson and the two Barbers were, at the time of this affray, regularly enrolled as privates of the Bloomington Company (D), of the 1st Regiment Kansas Volunteers, then serving in Lawrence, to defend that place against the so-called "Army of Invasion," under Governor Shannon ; they were absent on leave at the time.

We presume that the whole matter—so far as the result of any judicial inquiry is concerned—will hinge upon the *authority* of Clarke and Burns to *demand* and *compel* the surrender of Barber and his companions, and the *liability* of the parties interfered with to such an arrest.

Since writing the foregoing, we have been favored with the following extract from a letter written R. M. Ainsworth, M.D., of Wyandot, K. T., a regularly educated physician, who made a superficial post-mortem examination of Barber's body. The letter is addressed to G. P. Lowry, Esq., a prominent Free State man of Lawrence. Dr. Ainsworth being of the same persuasion :

" WYANDOT CITY, K. T. Dec. 23d, 1855.

*   *   *   *   *   *   *   *

"While I write I will mention that I lately heard a discussion as to the cause of the death of Barber. It was stated that he died from the effect

of the *fall from his horse* and *not* from the shot. I have had considerable
experience of gun-shot wounds in the Pennsylvania Hospital, and elsewhere. I examinedthe body of Barber, and I pronounced his wound fatal,
the missile having passed through a vital part.

(Signed,)   "R. M. Ainsworth."

Having taken down Barber's testimony, we inquired for the
residence of his brother-in-law, Peirson, which, as we had been
told, was situated upon the prairie, at a distance of some half
or three quarters of a mile from the "Barber Claim." On being
informed that we contemplated going there, the settler, very good
naturedly, remarked that he would walk with us. Upon hearing
this, our short-winded friend Squire Portly, hoisted himself
out of the hide-bottomed arm-chair, in which he had been puffing like a high-pressure engine from the moment of our arrival,
and "allowed" that, as "it war gitting considerable late, he'd
better be a movin' towards home, for it aggravated his phthisic
powerfully to stop out after night ; an Doctor Squills had enjined
on him to be dreadful kearful of catchin' cold, till thar warm
weather come agin." So we made our farewell salutations to His
Honor, and then prepared to accompany our new acquaintance
(Barber), who—with a friend of his, one Jack Quarter,
a Captain of Artillery, in the Free State Army—had, as we
have already hinted, very kindly offered to direct us in the path
which led to Peirson's " Claim " (the word " Claim," by the way,
is generally used in Kansas in referring to a settler's residence,
that being the title by which he holds his land).

And now let us put before the reader the statement of Peirson, which we took down in the same manner as that of Barber,
by writing it out, sentence by sentence, from the narrator's dic-
tation. Having done this, we will ask the reader to accom
pany us upon our visit to the cabin, where the Widow Barber
has taken up her abode since the acting out of that terrible

tragedy, which so suddenly rendered desolate this now afflicted woman's once happy home.

STATEMENT OF THOMAS M. PEIRSON, LATE A RESIDENT OF HENRY COUNTY, INDIANA, AND NOW A CITIZEN OF KANSAS TERRITORY, AS TO THE FACTS CONNECTED WITH THE SHOOTING OF HIS BROTHER IN LAW, THOMAS W. BARBER, BY A PARTY OF THE PRO-SLAVERY ARMY, ON THE 6TH OF DEC., 1855.

ON the 6th of Dec., 1855, at about 1 o'clock, P. M., I left Lawrence in company with my brothers-in-law, Thomas W. and Robert F. Barber. We were all mounted and on our way to our homes, some seven miles distant from Lawrence. I was armed with a small Colt's revolver, which I carried in my right pantaloons pocket. Robert F. Barber had a Colt's Navy revolver. Thomas W. Barber had no arms of any kind.

We followed the California road for three miles or more, when we turned off the highway to take a cross-road which led to the left, towards our homes. Just before doing so, and while still in the California road, I saw a party of from 12 to 15 mounted men to the right of the trail, and some half a mile or mile distant, they appeared to be coming towards the California road. In a few minutes I saw two men detach themselves from the main body and ride forward at a quicker gait, as if to cut us off. We were riding fast at the time, but immediately slackened our speed to a walk, so as to give these people no excuse for interfering with us. We had no idea at that time, that they intended to molest us. We had ridden about a mile in the cross-road, when these, two men who had taken a shorter cut, got ahead of us, and came in from the right, at a trot. They rode side by side. One of them halted directly in front of us in the road, and within a few feet of our horses' heads. He was a stout, thick-set man. I don't think he was tall, believe he had a moustache, but can't say certainly. He was riding a grey horse. His companion took his position to the right, and a little in our rear, near the edge of the road. Don't remember anything of his appearance, except that he was riding a sorrel horse.

The man on the grey horse did all the talking on their side, and Thomas W. Barber answered every question except one, on ours. The man on the grey horse ordered us to halt; we did so. He asked, "Where are you going?" T. W. Barber answered, "Home." "Where were we from?" Barber replied, "From Lawrence." "What was going on there?" was their next question. I think two of us replied to this. They then asked some questions in regard to the Kansas difficulties. Thomas W. Barber stated in reply, that he did not think that either we or the people of Lawrence had violated any laws. The thick-set man then ordered us to "turn back." Thomas W. Barber said, "We can't go back, we want to go home." Our position at this time was as follows: I think that I was a little in the rear of the Barbers, and to their left, my brothers in law were side by side, Thomas W. Barber being on the right.

I did not see the main body of our opponents until after we had ridden half a mile on the cross road; they were then advancing at a trot.

Upon our refusing to go with them, the man on the grey immediately wheeled his horse towards us, rather facing Thomas W. Barber, drew his pistol, and, taking a deliberate aim, as I judged, from the way in which he held his weapon, fired at Thomas. I *think the pistol was a navy revolver.* I saw Thomas settle down in his saddle as the pistol was discharged. I thought he was hit. The man on the sorrel horse fired immediately, the reports of the two pistols were almost simultaneous. We had not fired at that time. As they drew their weapons, Robert F. Barber drew his pistol and fired three times without success. I was trying, but without success, to draw my pistol. I did not attempt to draw it until I saw our opponents drawing theirs, when I finally got it out, our opponents had wheeled and were galloping off towards their party. Thomas then said "Let us be off." We started accordingly at the top of our horses' speed, the Barbers riding almost in front of me, and I following in their rear. We rode on thus for some two hundred yards or more, when Thomas W. Barber fell from his horse. I had noticed before he fell that his brother was supporting him in his saddle, in which he seemed unable to sit, as he had dropped his rein. Robert F. Barber stopped the horses and dismounted, as his brother fell; he went and looked at him. I did not dismount. Barber said "He is dead." We consulted as to what we should do. I said, Perhaps we can take him before us on the horse. I had barely uttered the words, when I saw the party advancing upon us again, that is to say, that portion of them who had got over the hill. We supposed it to be the same party which we had just seen; they were some two hundred yards distant. We then mounted our horses, and, supposing that we should be murdered if over taken, left Barber's body and started off on a gallop towards home.

I supposed that I had replaced my pistol in my pantaloons pocket, but afterwards discovered that I had lost it. I have not seen it since.

Robert F. Barber's horse was mortally wounded in the affray, and died that night.

We have now put the reader, very minutely, in possession of the circumstances attending this tragical affair, as they are stated by Barber and Peirson, whose account is, of course, adopted by the Free State party, and we have taken great pains in procuring this testimony—for the killing of Barber is in every one's mouth—has been *garbled* by the local press on both sides, and, we regret to add, made a source of *political* capital against the Pro-Slavery faction. It cannot, however, be denied, that there is, in this matter, no mean, between the extremes of *murder* and *justifiable homicide*. It was either an *assassination*, or a legalized or military taking away of life, growing out of the unfortunate man's refusal to obey the stern require ments of martial law, in which latter case, the agents of that law must be held blameless. With this question, and its vast field of evidence, we shall have *nothing* to do ; we are not called upon to decide. It must finally be settled by a judicial inquiry, which, if we mistake not, will be obliged to carry its investigation *far back* of the *mere actors* in this lamentable affair. *Who* brought on this war ? *who* raised these opposing armies ? *who* furnished men and *arms* ? *who* authorized them to act, and from whence did *they* derive *their* authority ? These are all questions which will be *asked*, and must be *met* by the *responsible parties*. Public sentiment will demand it, and then, *let those who are innocent clear their skirts*.

But come—let us change the scene ; forget, for a time, the mere party interest in this matter, and gaze with us upon that darker picture, which, alas ! for poor Humanity, so seldom struggles out into the light ; bear with us then, for a moment, while we tell you of our visit to *the widow's desolated* home.

It stands upon the bleak prairie ; a shelter—for it merits no better tit'e—of two rooms. We entered it in company with the brother of the deceased, just as the darkness of a stormy winter evening was gathering over the snow-clad slopes of the long, treeless prairie rolls. The room into which we were shown seemed comfortlessly furnished, not from any lack of means, but from the difficulty of procuring such matters in a newly-settled country ; two or three females and children were crowding up to the stove, for the night was bitter cold, and even a large wood fire scarce heated an apartment so slightly walled. Between a heavy pine table, on which a flaring tallow candle stood flickering and sweltering in its socket, and the half-curtained window, against which the sleet and biting winter wind beat drearily, sat a woman of some forty years of age, plainly clad in a dress of coarse dark stuff ; she was leaning forward as we entered, and seemed unmindful of all about her. It needed no introduction to tell us that this was the widow of Thomas W. Barber, the sole victim of the otherwise bloodless "Kansas War." No, the thin hand which supported the aching head, and half shielded the tear-dimmed eyes, as well as the silent drops that came trickling slowly down those wasted cheeks, had already told the story. What could *we* say in the way of consolation ? What was the cause of "Kansas and liberty" to her ? Could the success of a party, or the advancement of a principle, dry those burning tears ? Could *they* soothe the sorrows of what she herself has called "a poor heart-broken creature ?" Oh, ye demagogues ! ye peace-breakers ! ye incendiary orators, of both North and South, whose aim it is to urge on a strife, that you yourselves, are not slow to avoid ! could you but have stood beside us, in her once happy home, and have listened to the broken sentences, uttered with all that unstudied pathos, which an agonized and grief-torn spirit alone can give, we hope, for the sake of our common humanity, that the lesson would have sunk deep into your hearts. Hear what she says :—

" *They* have left me a poor forsaken creature, to mourn all my days. Oh, my husband ! they have taken from me all that

I held dear—one that I loved better than I loved my own life."

These are her very words. We have added nothing to them, nor have we taken aught from them.

There are circumstances connected with the life and character of the man Barber, which make his death more particularly to be deplored. He adds another to the long list of victims who have been sacrificed to the demon of political excitement. Barber is spoken of as a quiet, inoffensive, and amiable man ; domestic and unexceptionable in his habits, and deeply attached to his wife, to whom he had been married between nine and ten years. He was, moreover, the leading man among the agriculturists in his neighborhood ; a lover of fine stock ; and a careful, pains-taking farmer ; such at least is the reputation which he bore in Ohio, the State from whence he emigrated. He was unarmed when he received his death-wound, and on his way to his home. His wife, to whom he had written to inform her of his coming, was expecting him. She is said to have loved her husband with more than ordinary devotion. Her sister-in-law tells us that they used to rally her, upon her almost girlish affection and solicitude for Thomas. It was her habit, when she saw him coming back from his work, to leave the house, and go forth to meet him on his way. If he failed to return at the time indicated, she grew anxious ; and if his stay was prolonged, oftentimes passed the night in tears ; when ill—the same informant tells us—she would hang over his bed, with all the anxiety of a mother for her child. She would seem, too, to have had a presentiment of some impending evil, for after exhausting every argument to prevent her husband from going to join the Free State forces in Lawrence, she said, " Oh, Thomas, if you should be shot, I should be all alone indeed ; remember I have no child—nothing in the wide world to fill your place." And *this* was their *last* parting. The intelligence of his death was kept from her—in mercy—through the kindness of her friends, but only to be announced, without the slightest preparation, by a young man, who had been sent out from Lawrence, with a carriage, to bring her in to the Free State Hotel, where her husband's body had been laid. Upon arriving at the house where Mrs. Barber was, he rode up, most unthinkingly, and shouted, "Thomas Barber is killed." His widow heard the dreadful tidings, rushed to the door, cried, "Oh, God! what do I hear?" and then filled the room with her shrieks. We have heard, too, a description of the heart-rending scene, which took place when they brought her into the apartment where her husband's body lay; of her throwing herself upon his corpse, and kissing the dead man's face; of the fearful imprecations, which, in her madness, she called down upon the heads of those who had separated her from all that she held dear; and these things were related to us by men, who turned shudderingly away, from the exhibition of a sorrow which no earthly power could assuage. It is, moreover, stated that her companions were obliged to hold her forcibly down in the carriage, from whence her frantic exclamations rang out along the prairie, as they conveyed her from her home, to the chamber of the dead.

CHAPTER XXXIV.

A SNOWY NIGHT IN A SETTLER'S CABIN.

January 7th, Evening.—We are back again in our accustomed seat, at the "best hotel" in Lawrence, having arrived by our own private conveyance (Shank's mare), some two hours ago. We find matters and things at the "Cincinnati" in very much the same condition as they were when we left here yesterday morning to make our "hegira" to Judge Portly's. The old lady has grown no stouter ; the long-tongued damsel no less talkative, while the red hot stove at our back, the wrangling of the political disputants at our side, and the stifling air of this over-heated sitting-room are, we regret to say, quite as annoying as they ever were. Add to these, that "Our Correspondent" has a first-class nervous headache, and, then, for sweet charity's sake, if not for ours, make all due allowances for the shortcomings of this day's log. So, having written our preamble, let us "go back to the beginning," and take up the thread of our interrupted narrative.

We were, if we mistake not, at "Peirson's Claim," from whence we sallied forth, after completing our note-taking, with our friends Barber and Captain Jack Quarter, as guides, to find our way across the prairie, back to the residence of the first named individual, at whose cabin we had been invited to spend the night. Nor was our walk thither either a pleasant, or for that matter, a very safe excursion ; for in the three hours which had elapsed since our arrival at Peirson's, there had been, what

the " clerk of the weather " might have called, a " perturbation "
in the atmosphere ; in fact, a sombre winter evening had gone
from bad to worse, by transforming itself into a boisterous
January night, whose intense darkness, would have rendered it
sufficiently difficult to find our way, through the accumulated
drifts which had obliterated every vestige of a trail across the
prairie, even without the additional disadvantage of a driving
snow-storm, which beat blindingly in our faces, and made us
fairly bow our heads as we turned to face its fury upon our
homeward track. Fortunately for us, however, we had an
excellent guide in Captain Jack Quarter, who being an old
sailor, piloted us by the direction of the wind, which was blowing a gale from the north-west, in which direction, or nearly so,
our true course lay. But notwithstanding the feeling of security
which was engendered by the Captain's assurance, that " though
it blew great guns, and had a dirty look to windward, he'd
bring us safely into harbor for all that," it was with no little
pleasure—not to mention a certain feeling of relief—that we
caught the first glimpse of the ruddy light which gleamed forth
into the darkness, like a messenger of welcome, from the low case-
ment of Barber's solitary cabin. A few minutes later, found us
thawing out over the cooking-stove, where a hot supper was in
process of preparation, under the supervision of the settler's
wife, a clever little body, who bustled about cheerfully, as she
did what tidy hands could do, to render her frontier home comfortable, at least so far as its rude accommodations would permit,
to her husband's unexpected guests.

" What would you have done," said we to the Captain, when
we were once more safely housed, " if we had lost our way upon
the prairie ?"

" Done," replied the Captain, after a moment's thought ;
" why I should have got into a hollow, and if possible found the
lee-side of a hill ; and then I would have picked me out a path

fifteen or twenty yards long, where I could have had the wind at my side, and walked it back and forth, like a skipper on his quarter-deck, till morning. And now that I have answered your questions, do *you* know what I would have done if, having lost our way, you should have tried to go to sleep?"

"Why, as for that I could scarcely say. Wake me up, perhaps."

"Wake you up," cried the Captain. "Yes, I'de have abused you, picked a quarrel with you, pitched into you, and then kept you *warm*, and myself, too, by thrashing you until we had light enough to find a shelter by."

We thanked our friend for his kind intentions ; but expressed a hope that we might, on everybody's account, never be under the necessity of putting him to the trouble of so fatiguing an exercise.

And now, good pen, whip up ; increase your pace, or we shall be " most froze," and for aught we know to the contrary, " winter" *upon paper* at some settler's cabin on the prairie. So let us knock out the adjuncts and shorten our sentences.

Ten o'clock, P. M.—Supper over—storm worse than ever—everybody very cold. Half an hour later—storm doing badly, and everybody much colder. Midnight—storm terrific—fire gone out—wood ditto, and no more to be had until morning. Somebody proposes " going to bed." Everybody embraces somebody's idea. Settler's wife disappears into " the other half of the house," for its single board partition makes a very impartial division of this two room establishment. Settler's wife bustles about, is evidently " setting things to rights"—returns—presents us with a tallow dip in a log-cabin candlestick, and having done so, intimates that " our" room is ready—which by the way, includes the Captain, who is to be our bed-fellow. We " take the hint," and make our *buenas noches* accordingly. We open the partition door, and pop into a chamber,

whose temperature suggests the idea of Parry and the Poles.
We could, without any particular tax upon our imagination,
fancy ourself an Esquimaux, who feels really quite at home.
For there is—no exaggeration by the way, Mr. Reader—
about an inch of snow upon the floor, not to mention "a
right smart sprinkling" over the bed, where it has drifted in
through the badly-built walls. In fact, the snow-storm, which
is at this moment doing its work, *inside* our sleeping apartments,
is quite a pocket edition, or, perhaps, one might better call it an
uncorrected abridgment of that which is even now "making night
horrible" without—as the wintry winds blow and roar, and scream
and call gustily to each other, as they brush the white flakes
from the hurrying wings which bear them howling across the
unsheltered plain. In view of these circumstances we gaze round
us as we enter, in silent consternation—it is too late to retreat
—the settler and his wife have already "bunked in" on the floor,
from whence their long-drawn snores already give notice that
there *are* those who *can* go to. sleep, the warfare of disagreeing
elements to the contrary, notwithstanding, the instant their
heads touch the pillow. But one cannot meditate with any
mental satisfaction—or for that matter, bodily either, when the
mercury says, eighteen below zero—and the fire is *non est* to
boot. So we made up our mind, pulled off our boots, and
then followed the example of our illustrious predecessor, the
Captain, by plunging headforemost into bed, with everything
on—as we hope to be lucky—except the articles aforesaid.
Mem.—we are not quite so confident that our bed-fellow took
off *his*, but as he didn't wear spurs, and as we are of an easy disposition, and by no means disposed to make a fuss about *trifles*,
at least while sojourning upon the frontiers of Kansas—we concluded not to allude to the fact, but keep carefully out of range,
lest our friend, if ridden by the nightmare, should be inclined to
fancy himself a horse, in which latter case, our chances of being

kicked to death before morning, seemed even more than moderately good. And being thus uncomfortably in bed, we turned our attention toward making an effort to sleep—in short, we endeavored to compose ourself, but it was not to be done; no, "not at any price." The snow-storm inside bothered us—turn as we please —twist as we would—it was still the same. If we laid upon our back, the freezing particles watched their opportunity, and whenever we closed our eyes, descended in a trice, to build little suspension bridges across the lashes, or settle themselves to thaw upon the tip of our weather-beaten nose. Nor was our position improved by a change to either side, for our ears would be immediately attacked—while, if we gave up and retreated—as we finally did—by fairly turning our back to the enemy—they took us in the rear, and dropped flakes into our hair, where they got up sliding parties, from the top of our organ of veneration—a mighty small one by the way—down to the nape of our neck, which gave them a clear run of at least eight inches—we have just been measured so as to be sure of the distance—and, at the same time, furnished us with the innocent, but withal somewhat nervous amusement, of keeping tally as they went. At length we could stand it no longer, and were about giving up our slumber in despair, when a blessed apparition caught our weary eye, which, though it came in a somewhat questionable shape— don't be frightened—was neither sheeted ghost, nor goblin grim, for though undoubtedly but " a thing of bone," 'twas nothing more than an old blue cotton umbrella—a sort of family umbrella, built to shelter three of the real old-fashioned practical common sense kind. But, what had we to do with the umbrella— be it big or little? Ah! that's just it—for we assure you that we regarded that umbrella, to quote from our fat hostess of the Cincinnati, as " a clean dispersion of Providence." But how? Well, listen and we will tell you. To return—we gazed sleepily at the apparition—suddenly a thought struck us—we sprang out of bed—we seized upon this commodious, albeit somewhat dilapidated shelter—we regained our place among the blankets— we opened our prize, and spread its blue cotton canopy, with the holes most judiciously arranged, above our head, and then fell asleep, like a virtuous Correspondent as we were, to dream—

> " Of covered pits, unfathomably deep,
> A dire descent! beyond the power of frost;
> Of faithless logs; of precipices huge,
> Smoothed up with snow."

into which we were constantly tumbling, with an umbrella a mile or two in diameter, by way of a saving parachute.

January 7th.—Up very early *per force*, with a snow-bank upon our legs, and our beard frozen fast to the Mackinaw blanket, which had formed an upper coverlet to the pile of robes, over-coats, etc., that we had heaped upon the bed. Our patent tent, by the way, had given out during the night, owing to an accumulation of snow, and the general airiness of its texture. We dress—breakfast—write, and finally dine, at the very primitive hour of noon, at Barber's. We linger a while to chat with our good-natured hostess, and then say good bye. We don our buffalo overshoes, and foot it through the drifts of last night's storm—which has now passed away, leaving the winter sky " cold but clear"—to Judge Portly's—we approach the Squire's improvement—we contemplate entering—we see Dame Portly at the only window which hasn't got an old hat in it, and our courage fails us—the fire would be pleasant—a little something warm equally so—but then there's the " other half of that story.', We ponder —second thoughts are best—our first intention has a round or two with the second—result, the first thought is knocked, as a Yankee might say, " into everlasting fits," *alias* a cocked hat. It is but eight miles to Lawrence—we step out—two hours elapse—the sun is going down—we are once more within " the lines"—militarily speaking—which have in this instance " fallen in *unpleasant* places"—of the Sebastopol of the West. We were quite out of breath, but, *gracias á Dios*, back again—and for the other matters which should be chronicled upon our log-book for to-day, are they not written in the following chapter ?

CHAPTER XXXV.

FREE STATE FACTS.

January the 7th, in continuation.—We have obtained from General Lane the necessary *data* with which to gratify the curiosity of those, who may desire to know something of this Free State leader's antecedents.

James H. Lane was born in Boone County, Kentucky, on the twenty-second of June, 1822. He is a son of Amos Lane, a Western lawyer of considerable celebrity, who figured in the politics of his day as Speaker of the first Legislature of Indiana, and member of Congress during the Presidency of General Jackson, where he proved himself one of the warmest supporters of " Old Hickory's " administration.

Young Lane was educated at Lawrenceburg, Indiana, where he afterwards studied law in the office of his father, and was admitted to the bar at an early age. In July, 1846, he raised a company of volunteers for the Mexican war at Lawrenceburg, Indiana, was elected captain, and marched with it to New Albany, in the same State. Here, he was elected colonel of the Third Indiana Volunteers (not the Indiana regiment that was a little hurried at Buena Vista), and accompanied it to the seat of war. Upon his first visit to Mexico, Colonel Lane served under General Taylor for a year, and commanded (as he tells us) one-third of the troops engaged, at Buena Vista. In July of 1847, he returned to Indiana, but not to rest upon his laurels, for we find him actively engaged in recruiting the Fifth Indiana regiment, which he organized and brought out to Mexico. Of this regiment he was colonel, under the command of Gen. Butler—was under fire with it in various skirmishes, and joined Scott in the city of Mexico ; but after the capture of that place.   Upon the declaration of peace, Lane's regiment was disbanded, and in July of 1848, we find the colonel laying aside his military rank, but only to be crowned with the civil honors which were awarded him in the following year by his adopted State.   He was nominated in 1849 as Lieut. Governor of Indiana, and elected by ten thousand majority.   Before the expiration of his term of office he was selected as one of the electors for the State at large, and cast the vote of Indiana for President Pierce : was nominated and elected to Congress, by a majority of one thousand, in a district where his predecessor had gone in by a majority of but sixty votes ; was a member of the Thirty-second Congress ; voted for the Kansas and Nebraska bills, under instructions ; came to Kansas immediately after the adjournment of Congress, and settled near Lawrence, in which vicinity, the General informs us he has invested to the amount of seven thousand dollars, for the most part in real estate.   He intends to remain in the Territory.

In Kansas politics, General Lane claims to have been among the first to bring forward the necessity of a State organization, and to have draughted the national platform at the Big Spring Convention.   General Lane is the chairman of the Executive Committee for the provisional government of Kansas, and was President of the Constitutional Convention.

These facts may be relied upon, as we have obtained them from General Lane himself.   The General says nothing of his military services in Kansas—but the intrenchments which encircle Lawrence, and which he himself planned, are still to be seen —a temporary monument at least to his talents as a military engineer, and in addition to these, a " well-drilled brigade," assures the beholder that the Brigadier-General has not yet forgotten the tactics learned in Mexico under Scott and Taylor.

General Lane is talked of as a candidate for office, when Kansas gets to be a State—a Senator, we believe. We presume that his very distinguished party services would, in such an event, secure him at least that amount of promotion, if not more.

In person, we do not consider General Lane good-looking ; he is too much in the rough and ready style—nor is he prepossessing in his manners. But for all that, unless that lying jade, Dame Rumor, does him injustice, he is a great ladies' man, and wonderfully successful with the "soft sex," as Mr. Weller, senior, calls them.

In his speeches and general political course, Lane is the very antipodes of Robinson, for where Robinson would throw on cold water, Lane would apply the fire-brand. He is fluent enough, but over strong in his expressions, and too incendiary in his suggestions to please a conservative man.

But of these matters judge for yourselves, good people, for Lane goes East to lecture upon Kansas and "the War," past present, and to come.

And now for a medley of Free State information, all jumbled together, as they have been noted down (first come, first served), in that repository of *facts*—our much-blotted note-book.

So let us "write up" Kansas scrip to begin with.

Kansas scrip, is a peculiar currency whose market value is about as difficult to quote as a Brazilian "millrea," which is, as every sailor who has put into Rio Harbor well knows, a fluctuating representative of an uncertain number of "dumps," and "dams," the latter being copper coins, of huge dimensions and exceedingly unclean exteriors. This scrip was the child of many discussions, but was finally brought forth by the Territorial Executive Committee; when that august body authorized its issue to the amount of twenty-five thousand dollars. This *paper* may in some respects be considered valuable, insomuch as it pays the expenses of those who suck government pap, if there be any such in Kansas, or in other words, makes the political Free State Kansas mare go. It is not, however, to be confounded with the " war scrip," which is, as we learn, issued by the Territorial Executive Committee on their own responsibility. The last-named scrip furnishes the sinews of war, digs entrenchments, buys rifles, and for aught we know to the contrary, fires them off to boot. The Free State that is to be, is supposed to foot the bill. The Free State Treasury has, however, another string to its bow, in the shape of an expectation to get these documents cashed by Uncle Sam, through the influence of Governor Shannon. But we have good reason to suppose, that so far as such a recommendation would avail them, His Excellency the Governor would see the Free State party, scrip and all, in that extremity first, and *then* wouldn't endorse it.

As a " true copy " of this precious paper may be interesting to our Wall street and other financial operators, we will append the following sample, of Simon Pure Kansas scrip.

KANSAS SCRIP.

Wood cut: woman holding scales, supposed to be blind to her own interests.

No. 62.　TOPEKA.　　　　Nov. 26, 1855.　$20.

This is to certify that CYRUS K. HOLLIDAY, or bearer, is entitled, on presentation, to receive from the Treasurer of the

STATE OF KANSAS

Twenty Dollars, with interest at ten per cent per annum, for account as per bill on file, for the payment of which the faith of the State is pledged.

Attest—J. K. GOODWIN, Sec'y.

　　　　J. H. LANE, Ch'n Ex. Com., Kansas.

[*The Kansas Freeman Print, Topeko, Kansas.*]

Proclaim liberty throughout the land, and to all the inhabitants thereof.

We cannot say that we should care to invest very largely in either "wild cat banks" or Kansas scrip.

Apropos to official Free State Kansas documents, the following "circular" will come in very properly here. We have been requested to circulate it, and take this method, as the best calculated to comply with the desire of these propagandists. It certainly proves that the good citizens of Lawrence are fully alive to the necessity of "tickling the ears of the dear people."

OFFICE EXECUTIVE COMMITTEE,
KANSAS TERRITORY, Jan. 4, 1856.

SIR: A deputation, consisting of Messrs. Lane, Emery, Hunt, Goodin, Dickey, Holliday and Sampson, have been this day appointed to visit the United States, to plead before the people the cause of Kansas, and to convey and lay before Congress the constitution of the State, recently adopted by our fellow-citizens. We respectfully bespeak from the friends of freedom such attention for them as the importance of their mission demands.

They are instructed to visit and address, early in February, the people at Burlington, Iowa city, and Dubuque, Iowa; Springfield and Chicago, Illinois; Lafayette, Indianapolis and Richmond, Indiana; Dayton, Cincinnati, Columbus and Cleveland, Ohio; Detroit, Michigan; Milwaukie and Madison, Wisconsin; Buffalo, Rochester, New York city and Albany, New York; Worcester, Lowell, Springfield, Salem and Boston, Massachusetts; Hartford and New Haven, Connecticut; Providence, Rhode Island; Portland, Augusta and Bangor, Maine; Concord, New Hampshire; Burlington, Vermont; Philadelphia, Harrisburgh and Pittsburg, Pennsylvania.

Done at the office of the Executive Committee, Kansas Territory, the day and year above written.

J. K. GOODIN, Secretary.　　　　　J. H. LANE, Chairman.

And here follow two documents which, though less pacific in their nature, are still historical facts, which even in the absence of any other testimony, would most conclusively prove that the Free State people of Kansas did have an army. We presume that the originals of these War Office forms will be treasured in the securest receptacle of many a Kansas Volunteer, who will at some future day, in the pride of his heart, cause them to be framed and glazed, and hung upon his cabin wall, as an abiding remembrance, for his little ones at home, of that tremendous struggle—the famous Wakarusa war, which is—as yet —like the Q. E. D. of the Irishman's proposition, "which was to be demonstrated."

The first is a copy of a Captain's Commission in the Free State Artillery :

[Patriotic woodcut—An Eagle looking very fierce.]

JAMES H. LANE,

General Commanding the First Brigade of Kansas Volunteers.

To all who shall see these Presents—greeting :

Whereas, it has been certified to me by the proper authorities, that Thomas B. has been duly elected to the office of Captain of the Kansas Artillery, of Kansas Volunteers, raised in the said Territory, by authority of the people of Kansas, to defend the city of Lawrence from threatened destruction by foreign invaders,

Therefore, know ye, that in the name and by the authority of the said Territory, I do commission the said Thomas B., as aforesaid, in the said company, to serve from the date hereof until the said force retires from said Territory.

In testimony whereof, I have hereunto set my hand at Lawrence City, the twenty-seventh day of November, A. D. 1855.

J. H. LANE,
General Commanding First Brigade Kansas Volunteers.
M. G. ROBERTS, *Aid, 1st Regiment Kansas Volunteers.*
[Herald of Freedom, Print.]

And here follows the form of a private soldier's discharge, which will, in the good time coming, be valuable, if only for its autographs :

<table>
<tr><td>{ Wood cut—}
{ a cannon. }</td><td>HEADQUARTERS KANSAS VOLUNTEERS, }
LAWRENCE CITY, *Dec.* 12*th*, 1855. }</td></tr>
</table>

This is to certify that Richard Roe faithfully and gallantly served as private in the Lawrence Cadet Company (E) Kansas Volunteers, from the

27th day of November, 1855, to the 12th day of December, 1855, in defending the City of Lawrence, in Kansas Territory, from demolition by foreign invaders, when he was honorably discharged from said service.

SOLOMON WILDES, *Capt.*

MORRIS HUNT, *Col. Commanding 3d Regiment Kansas Volunteers.*
J. H. LANE, *Gen. 1st Brigade Kansas Volunteers.*
C. ROBINSON, *Major-General.*

For the present prospects of the Free State party, at least in the City of Lawrence, we cannot augur favorably. They appear to be disorganized, quarrelling among themselves, talking about "loaves and fishes," as the heading of the annexed circular abundantly proves, and conducting themselves generally in such a suicidal way, as to excite a doubt in the mind of an impartial looker-on, as to the disinterestedness of some, and the zeal of others.

"A house divided against itself shall not stand," saith the Scriptures, and so, we fancy, it may prove with the Free State party in Kansas. For they even now agree in disagreeing, in evidence of which, we may remark that the *regular* "Free State ticket," has already been followed by another, styled the "Free State *Anti-Abolition* ticket," the words "*Anti-Abolition*" being its strong point, for it is intended to insinuate the idea, that if their principles be opposed to Abolitionism, those of the regular ticket men must *à fortiori*, be in favor of its ultra views. And, as many of the Free State men have seemed anxious to define their position, and at the same time purge themselves from the charge of Abolition proclivities, which the Missourians and Pro-Slavery men of Kansas have been heaping upon their heads, it is not improbable that this latter ticket may be elected, even if Anti-Abolition Free State-ism should be compelled, for policy's sake, to make a *marriage de convenance*, with "moderate Pro-Slavery." Such a course, indeed, was actually hinted at in a conversation which we held, during our stay in

15*

Lawrence, with one of the candidates and prime movers of the new ticket. Certain it is, that they are raising heaven and earth, after their own fashion, to secure success; which means, driving about the country, talking, making speeches, distributing hand-bills, and abusing their opponents generally. There is *one* omen, however, against the "Anti-Abolition" ticket; it is said to have been concocted on a Sunday, in regard to which, one of our landladies of the Cincinnati—the fat and antiquated one—speaks as follows :

"Oh ! deary me, well I never, ef them sacradotal men hain't a gone and bin inductin' of a party on the Sabber day; a flyin', as yeou might say, right smack in the face of the Commandments. Well, you needn't laugh, Mister, there won't no good come on it, I kin tell yeou. If yeou jest knowed, but ef course yeou don't, for it was afore yeou was a baby, I guess, but when I was being courted, and Seth Smalltree was a cumin' arter me, I know he and Bill Haddock inducted a party to go a slayin' with us gals, on a Sabber day evenin', and the slay got upsot, and, to be sure, nobody was hurt, but parson Johnson said it was a clear dispersion of Providence, that nobody wan't killed, and put it inter his sermon; he had a powerful gift in sermonizing, had parson Johnson next Sunday. So yeou see, Mister, ef what I say won't come true, for them misgiven men won't git no office at all, and all on account of breaking the Lord's day, as a body might say, right inter pieces. Well, deary me, what's the world a comin' to next, I wonder."

Here the old lady got her knitting under way again, and as we saw her rocking-chair resume its pendulum-like vibrations, we turned quietly round to continue our interrupted journalizing.

But here are the tickets—so pick and choose for yourselves, Kansas Free State gentlemen voters:

Office.	FREE STATE ABOLITION TICKET.	FREE STATE REGULAR TICKET.
Governor	W. Y. Roberts.	Charles Robinson.
Lieut. Governor	M. J. Parrott.	W. Y. Roberts.
Secretary of State	C. K. Holliday.	P. C. Schuyler.
Auditor	W. R. Griffith.	J. A Cutler.
Treasurer	E. C. K. Garvey.	J. A. Wakefield.
Attorney General	H. Miles Moore.	H. Miles Moore.
Judges Sup. Court	Geo. W. Smith.	S. Latte.
" " "	S. W. Johnson.	W. Conway.
" " "	J. A. Wakefield.	Morris Hunt.
Rep. Sup. Court	S. B. McKenzie.	—— Thurston.
Clerk Sup. Court	S. B. Floyd.	S. B. Floyd.
State Printer	R. G. Elliott.	John Speer.
Rep. to Congress	M. W. Delahay.	M. W. Delahay.

We have introduced the "circular" annexed as bearing upon these rival tickets and their backers. The James Redpath, who signs the letter, in relation to Judge Wakefield, is the present correspondent of the St. Louis Democrat, and for other papers. We have heard him bitterly condemned by the Pro-Slavery party, for alleged misrepresentations of Kansas difficulties, but as an offset to this, Mr. Redpath is spoken of in the highest terms by the leading men of his own party, who certainly *should* know him best. E. C. K. Garvey, is probably the most active worker among the bolters, who are interested in the election of the *Anti-Abolition* ticket. The circular reads thus :

"THE LOAVES AND FISHES TICKET.

"The correspondence given below indicates that William Y. Roberts, Esq., does not sympathize very fully in the movement of certain disaffected politicians to get up a new ticket for the forthcoming election.

" We learn that Judge Wakefield has been nominated as a candidate for the supreme bench by the same faction, with Judge

Johnston, and G. W. Smith, Esq.   E. C. K. Garvey is the nominee for Treasurer, and Elliot, of the Free State, for State printer; in short, we believe, nearly the whole horde of disappointed political aspirants have been looked after on this ticket, and yet, with two or three exceptions, every nominee expresses no sympathy for the movement.

LAWRENCE, K. T., *Dec. 26th*, 1855.

DEAR SIR:

The undersigned, delegates to the late Free State Nominating Convention, hearing that certain disaffected parties have, in private caucus, changed the nominations made by that Convention, so far as to substitute the name of Charles Robinson for your own for Lieutenant Governor, and your name for his as Governor—and are now engaged in circulating this action as the action of the legitimate Convention, desire to know if you are aware of these facts, and if so, whether you approve of, or will countenance such a course.

Very respectfully yours,

W. M. McCLURE, *7th Sen. Dis.*
E. R. ZIMMERMAN, 11*th.* "   "
G. P. LOWRY,   1*st.* "   "

HON. W. Y. ROBERTS.

LAWRENCE, K. T., *Dec.* 26*th*, 1855.

GENTLEMEN:

Your note of this date is to hand, and in reply I have to say, that I have heard the report to which you refer, and that I have no connection or sympathy therewith; but, on the other hand, have opposed the movement from beginning to end, as disorganizing and opposed to the interests of the Free State party of Kansas, and shall continue to discountenance the movement should it be persisted in.

Very truly your obedient servant,

W. Y. ROBERTS.

Messrs. McCLURE, LOWRY, and ZIMMERMAN.

"Since the above was in type we have received the following note from Mr. Redpath:

LAWRENCE, *Dec. 29th*, 1855.

SIR:

I am authorized by Mr. J. A. Wakefield to state that HE WILL NOT ACCEPT any nomination on the opposition ticket. Mr. Parrot requested me to say in his name that he would not accept ANY State office under any circumstances; and Judge Johnson, also, gave the Leavenworth delegation similar and equally positive instructions.

JAMES REDPATH.

EDITOR OF THE HERALD OF FREEDOM.

"We are glad to learn that Col. Lane, also, opposes the loaves and fishes ticket. He justly says that he would not consider himself worthy the confidence of the party if he failed to support the regular nomination; and adds, further, that the regular ticket is *not*, as the disappointed office-seekers allege, an 'Abolition affair.'"

CHAPTER XXXVI.

THE SEBASTOPOL OF THE WEST.

WE have headed this chapter " the Sebastopol of the West," meaning thereby—if so obvious a title need an explanation—the town of Lawrence and its defences, or as the Yankees in these parts would term it in their vernacular, " Lawrence and its forts."   And Lawrence is a great place—or what will come to the same thing in the end—is going to be ; indeed, it already boasts a main street—a *real* one, we mean—for streets and (for aught we know to the contrary), parks, public edifices and squares beside, are as "plentiful as blackberries" upon those paper maps which speculators in city lots so much delight in ; and Lawrence, to do her justice, is quite as grand *upon paper*, as any ideal metropolis that was ever laid out in a Far-Western swamp, during the land fever of what the song calls some

"Twenty years ago."

But as our business, as a faithful historian, is with that which *is*, rather than that which Old Father Time may see fit to make or mar in his ceaseless flight, we shall confine ourself to things as they exist, and leave those matters, which " might, could, would, or should be "—as Murray has it—to the coming years— and perchance to that coming man, who shall seek to build upon our foundation, by writing up some future " Iliad " of the Wakarusa War.   And now to our description.

The *real* main street, of which we have spoken, has been christened by the good citizens of Lawrence after the fostering-mother of this abiding-place in the wilderness, insomuch as they have called it after the Old Bay State, by giving it the name of Massachusetts street.   This thoroughfare has a circular earth-work at each extremity, and houses, good, bad, and indifferent—from the substantial three-story stone building, down to the settler's temporary, mud-daubed, one-room log-cabin—upon either side of it.   It is, moreover—as newly-planned streets usually are, and always ought to be—of very liberal dimensions, as regards the allowance which has been made for present road-way, and a prospective side-walk.   Upon this street stands, the Cincinnati House—already alluded to—the Executive Office—of which we have also spoken—with sundry " stores," dwelling-houses, &c. (the " stores," by the way, would be creditable to the enterprise of any rising town); and last, but by no means least :

THE ELDRIDGE HOUSE *late* FREE STATE HOTEL—which merits a separate paragraph ; for Lawrence will soon be entitled to boast that she has within her entrenchments the finest hotel in Kansas Territory, or for that matter, upon her side of St. Louis.   This edifice has been in course of erection for some six months past, and will probably be opened for the reception of guests by the first of March (1856).   It is a three-story stone building, seventy feet long by fifty wide, with an addition or wing of twenty-four by forty-five feet.   When finished, it will contain in all, no less than seventy-five rooms.   The proprietors, Messrs. S. W. and T. B. Eldridge, have also contracted for a barn, eighty by thirty feet, which will afford ample stabling.   The interior finish and furnishing will be equal—at least so says the proprietor—to that of any hotel out of New York city.   We hear of private

parlor-sets, costing $350—of chairs worth $40 a-piece, &c
This establishment—as we have already hinted—has been
re-named the Eldridge House, but it has almost (from its intimate connection with the times that tried men's souls, during
the Kansas War), become "classic ground"—so we presume
that its old appellation of the "Free State" or "Emigrant Aid
Society's Hotel" will cling to it still—or, if it be preferred, it
might be called the Hotel of the Port-Holes, from those much
talked-of embrasures, which so few have *seen*, and so many talked
about, that are *said* to exist in its parapets.

Apropos to the Eldridge House. A letter was received here
a few days ago—directed, as we were told, to General Robinson
—its writer is a Mr. Williams (a moneyed man, of Boston, and a
partner, we believe, in a wealthy firm in that hard-to-find-your-
way-about city), who, in the kindness of his heart, "wants to do
something for Lawrence," and therefore inquires the exact size
of the new Hotel's best parlor, which he evidently intends furnishing at his own expense—all free gratis—for nothing. Well,
it is a much better way—to our fancy—of investing "given
money" in Kansas, than by putting it into Sharpe's rifles and
revolvers, even with a possible *quid pro quo* in the shape of Kansas scrip.

And now, having favored the reader with an *apropos* to the
Eldridge House, we will have an *apropos* to *Eldridge*, to please
ourself. This gentleman—or the one which we had the pleasure
of being acquainted with—has been engaged in "the hotel business" in Kansas City (Mo.) ; where, if report speaks true, there
is quite as much liquor drank, and quite as much card-playing
done, as at any other frontier town—"Natchez under the Hill,"
as it used to be—or Little Rock in Arkansas, not excepted.
[Remember, we speak from Free State reports, now.] But to
our story. Eldridge was keeping hotel, and somebody "kicked
up a row" in Eldridge's house, which was knocking things gene-

rally into what Paddy calls "a holy show of smithereens," when Eldridge—seeing that the fun was likely to be expensive—interfered, and—as is not unusual in such cases—had the combatants unite and turn upon him for his pains—one of whom drew his pistol, and pointed it at Eldridge's breast, at the same time intimating that he intended to shoot our landlord—who, as it happened, was entirely unarmed. It is said by those who were eye-witnesses to the affair, that even under these "depressing circumstances," Eldridge didn't "back down;" on the contrary, he "showed his courage," and at the same time proved, to the entire satisfaction of all concerned, that a man *may* be born East of the Allegany mountains, and still have quite as much "pluck" as even a Far-Western "fire-eater," by quietly picking up a chair, which he brandished above his head with this very pithy observation :

"Shoot, you cowardly rascal ; but if you *do* shoot, take good aim ; for if you don't kill *me*, I shall kill *you with this chair.*"

And since we have touched upon this subject, we will, even at the risk of adding yet another, "aside" to our already too numerous digressions from the Kansas highway, spin a yarn or two which we have picked up, we can scarce say how, during our sojourn in the Far West, and we shall do so the more confidently, as a lesson is to be gained from their perusal ; for they go to prove two facts : Firstly, That even a "Border Ruffian" don't like to shoot when you have "got the draw upon him ;" and Secondly, That there is a *moral* courage which acknowledges no position so bad, that a cool head and firm heart cannot find an honorable road to an extrication, or at least, point out a course which, if persisted in, will, in nine cases out of ten, cow the bully, and enable its possessor to come off conqueror.

We shall begin, therefore, with an occurrence, the scene of which, we are pleased to say—for it gives us an immense amount of latitude in its narration—is laid in the once almost uncivilized Territory of Arkansas ; and when we say Arkansas, we mean the Arkansas of the long past, as it used to be in those "good old times" (to quote from thoroughbred frontier's men), "of pistol and bowie-knife sovereignty," when every man carried his own life, and not unfrequently the lives of a few of his neighbors, in his coat back or breast pocket, and the "regulators" had a funny way of hanging an unpopular individual *first*, and then trying him *afterwards*.

It was therefore during the existence of this highly commendable state of things that a certain young officer of the army, who had recently joined his regiment—and whom we shall, therefore, for convenience sake, call Lieutenant Newcome—arrived, at the close of a very fatiguing day's travel in the spring—when, as the reader may know, an Arkansas bottom road is a happy compound of "corduroy" and "hog wallow"—at a log-cabin hotel, or to call it by its more appropriate appellation, "doggery," in a certain little town which shall be nameless. Now it so happened at the time of our young Lieutenant's visit—for the "doggery" was "Hobson's choice," there being no other place within twelve or fifteen miles which could furnish horse feed and shelter—that this tavern of bad repute was favored by the presence of some half a dozen Border men, who, to do them justice, could hardly have been improved upon in their very peculiar way. And as one at least of these worthies will play a prominent part in the characteristic incident which we are about to relate, we may as well sketch him in as a fair sample of the lot.

Mr. Jake Chowler was an accomplished, but withal, somewhat eccentric rascal. He could cheat his companion at a "friendly game of poker," and shoot him afterwards—if he had the audacity to object to the procedure—with as little remorse as he would have brought down a "painter" or "drawn a bead upon a bar." In person, he was a tall, lank, fever-and-ague-shaken specimen of humanity, with unkempt, towy hair, and a most pro·

digious beard, which looked as if it might have been permitted to grow from the date of its first appearance; he had, moreover, keen eyes, deeply sunken, and as restless as an Indian's ; add sharply cut features, high cheek bones, a low, receding forehead, and a sensual mouth—and you will have the portrait of one of the worst men who ever made laws to suit himself upon the Arkansas frontier.

As for his dress, if you be curious in externals, imagine a coon-skin cap worn nearly upon the back of the head, a loose, tobacco-stained old overcoat, much the worse for wear, in whose side pocket the butt of a horse-pistol was distinctly visible, a pair of mud soiled pants with riding leathers, and buffalo overshoes—and you have completed an inventory of garments which argued quite as unfavorably for their wearer as did the reckless, dissipated expression of the man himself. In fact, to sum up Mr. Jake Chowler, or as he preferred calling himself, Pine Knot Jake, in the fewest possible words, he was the terror of the country round ; for with him to "jump a man up," with reason or without reason, for it mattered little as to the amount of provocation with Jake, was "good sport," and to shoot him afterwards, the consummation of a rather amusing affair.

With so peace-breaking a disposition, it is hardly to be wondered at that "Pine Knot Chowler" should have made a mental note of our young officer's quiet entry into the cabin where, at that particular moment, Mr. Chowler was enjoying himself, by indulging in the innocent relaxations of alternate whisky-drinking, gambling, and dancing, or as the individual in question would have termed it, "breakin' down ;" for there was a white-headed old darkey present, who was aiding the revel by the execution of

"That good old tune"

which he rattled off upon his violin, with a facility of execution which betokened a practised hand.

In the mean time our Lieutenant, who was still suffering from the effects of a recent illness, had taken an out of the way seat near the stove, where he evinced a strong disposition to avoid any intercourse with the Borderers. It may be, too, that the young man laid himself open to the charge of "putting on airs," by neglecting, upon his entrance, to salute the company, either by the customary "good evening, gentlemen," or the yet more *Western* polite greeting of asking "the crowd" to "step up and liquor" at "his expense."

None of which, as we have already intimated, had escaped the keen eye of Mr. Jake Chowler. "He didn't like it. He allowed that thar dog-gauned city raised *thing* in thar brass buttons, war a puttin' on mighty high falutin' ways, an' crowdin' thar boys a heap."

But Pine Knot Jake was not the man to confine his indignation to mere words ; so after " standin' it" as he said, " until a human couldn't bar it no longer," he walked up to the stranger, and the following dialogue ensued :

Chowler.—(At the same time slapping the Lieutenant familiarly upon the back)—Step up, hoss, an' liquor.

Lieutenant.—I thank you, sir, but I don't feel like drinking.

Chowler.—Yes, yeou do : so jest step up, stranger, an' kinder move yourself too; don't yeou see that thar crowd air a waitin' ?

Lieutenant.—But I don't wish to drink, sir.

Chowler.—I don't kear ef yeou don't. I want you to drink with *me.* My name air Jake Chowler : Pine Knot Jake they call me whar I come from, all on account of my bein' so dreadful easy to whip. Will you drink with *me now* ?

Lieutenant.—No, sir.

Chowler.—Ef yeour a goin' to crowd a man that thar way, I jest tell you, stranger that yeou *shall* drink with me.

Lieutenant.—And I tell *you,* sir, that I will not.

Chowler.—Wael, stranger, ef you *will* hev it so—here Mr.

Chowler drew a horse-pistol, which he cocked and pointed at the Lieutenant's head—I'll jest let yeou know, that ef yeou don't take a drink with this hyar child, and be right sudden a doin' it, I'll raise the top off your head with this hyar tool, and ef *that* don't settle yeou, I allow to gather yeou by your hār, an' shake yeou till your dog-ganned toe-nails drop off.

Upon receiving this mild intimation, a close observer might have noticed the sudden change that passed like a cloud shadow over the young soldier's face; for his eye flashed, the lip was compressed, and the thin nostril dilated ; but these signs of indignation, if such they were, lasted but for a moment, and as the pale features settled back into their wonted repose, there was almost a smile, though some would have called it a *meaning* one, upon Lieutenant Newcome's face, who, nevertheless, appeared subdued, for he rose to his feet, as if to comply with this very pressing invitation.

"Mr. Chowler," said our Lieutenant, as they approached the filthy pen of liquor-stained boards, which enclosed the, if possible, still dirtier "bar," "Mr. Chowler, I know your character ; I am entirely unarmed ; I have told you that I did not wish to drink, and should not do so now, except upon compulsion ; at the same time, I prefer drinking *even with you*, to being shot down in cold blood."

To this, the bully made no verbal reply, but laughed insultingly ; ordered "drinks for two," laid his pistol upon the counter, and, at the same time, turned his head slightly round, to exchange telegraphic congratulations with a companion, upon the ease with which he, the accomplished Pine Knot Chowler, had "backed down one of Uncle Sam's highfalutin pets."

But Mr. Chowler's moment of triumph was destined to be short-lived—indeed, its end was already at hand—for young Newcome, who had an eye like a hawk, had been watching his unceremonious acquaintance's movements keenly. He saw the pistol laid down; a thought flashed across his mind; to execute it was the work of an instant. He edged quietly towards the bar, and extended his right arm, as if to take up the tumbler, in which the whisky, brown sugar, etc., had already been mingled for his benefit, but instead of doing so, he leant forward, shoved his persecutor aside with one vigorous push of his left hand, and, at the same time, grasped the weapon, which, fortunately for him, was still cocked, and then, with one spring, placed his back against the wall, and, as they say out West, drew a bead upon Mr. Jake Chowler's left breast, who, in utter amazement at this most unexpected change in the position of affairs, was, at the moment, regarding him with distended eyes, and open mouth, not to dwell upon certain indications of bodily trepidation, which had suddenly appeared upon the crest-fallen bully's now anxious face.

"Mr. Chowler," said our Lieutenant, whose voice was even calmer than it was when he declined the first invitation to step up and drink, "Mr. Chowler, you had, or thought you had, matters all your own way, but a moment ago ; then, you were armed, and I was not ; now, however, the tables are turned, so, as I have the superiority at present, you will very much oblige me, as there is a fiddler present, by stepping out upon the floor, and favoring this good company with a specimen of your dancing."

Mr. Chowler.—But I don't *feel* like dancin', stranger.

Lieutenant.—Exactly what I said to you, Mr. Chowler, a short time ago, when you requested me to drink ; but though you *do* look as if you didn't *feel* like dancing, I must really insist upon your favoring us, the more so, as your friends seem to be anxious for you to begin.

Mr. Chowler.—But I don't *want* to dance, stranger.

Lieutenant.—My own words again, sir ; but you must permit me to answer your objection in the same manner that you replied to mine; I don't care whether you do or not; I wish you to dance for *me*; *my* name is Harry Newcome, and when at my post, they call me, although not considered easy to whip, a person who won't be imposed upon. *Now*, sir, will you dance for me, or shall I be under the painful necessity of carrying out this parallel to our recent conversation, by promising to shoot you in case of a refusal?

Mr. Pine Knot Chowler looked into the Lieutenant's eye, which was fixed intently upon his own, and, for a moment, there was something in the almost fiend-like expression of the baffled ruffian's face, which bespoke a tiger foiled, but nerving himself for some desperate leap; a second glance, however, at the steady hand, whose fore-finger rested upon the trigger of a weapon, which, as nobody knew better than Mr. Jake Chowler, had never yet missed fire, had its restraining effect; so, with something that sounded marvellously like a smothered growl, Mr. Chowler stepped out upon the floor, and made a sign to the terrified darkey, who had, since the bully's discomfiture, sat staring with protruding eyes at the brass-buttoned stranger, to "strike up somethin' about right," and then began shuffling away, like a bear upon a hot iron plate; but though his movements were awkward enough at first, there was something either in the tune or in the necessity of making the best of a bad matter, which seemed to operate soothingly upon the Borderer, for as the negro bent to his instrument, and rolled out the according notes, Mr. Chowler's grim features relaxed, expanded, and finally widened out into a really hearty laugh, as he finished up a hoe-down, with a sort of first-class, back-action double-shuffle, and cut-the-pigeon-wing step in the most approved Arkansas style.

"Stop, Mr. Chowler," cried the Lieutenant.

Mr. Chowler stood firm in his tracks as if glued to the floor, the music ceased, and a dead silence reigned in the cabin.

"Mr. Chowler," said the young officer, "I came here to-night a stranger to you all; I neither interfered with you, nor did I do anything to provoke the treatment which I have received. You insisted upon my drinking with you. I declined, not from any desire to give offence, or because I believed that I should incur any degradation by so doing, but simply for the reason given in my reply to your invitation, that I did not feel like it. A little good luck, Mr. Chowler, coupled with some management upon my part, has enabled me to prevent, as well as *punish* your attempt to force me into doing what I had already positively declined. And now, sir, I can only say, as I have told you before, that I have not even a pen-knife, with which to defend myself—for I am about to return your pistol—and if either you or your friends should see fit to murder an unarmed man, I can do nothing to deter you."

"But, Mr. Chowler," added the Lieutenant, as he laid down the weapon and turned to resume his seat, "I shall not drink with you or any other man upon compulsion."

It is reported that Mr. Pine Knot Chowler gathered himself up, stared first at the pistol, and then at the "stranger," who had now returned to his low chair by the stove, where he sat, to all appearances, as if utterly unconscious of the existence of such a being as his late antagonist, in the world. Mr. Chowler grasped the pistol, let down the hammer, then took it up and played with the trigger, as if undecided as to how he *ought* to act. In fact. Mr. Chowler was meditating upon his late defeat; he, the "Pine Knot" had been "backed down," he "felt bad," he "would hev given thar best hoss he ever rode," as he afterwards expressed it, "to get even." But the lesson he had learned was too recent and too strong for him. He accordingly forced a smile—swallowed his share of the old Monongahela at a gulp— paid for *both* drinks, of which one still remained untasted upon the board, pocketed his pistol, "allowed that thar stranger fur an Eastern-raised man, wor a hoss," and finally remarked, that

" as it war a gettin' powerful late, he reckoned it about time for him to be a travellin'."

The second incident which we promised the reader, took place upon that equally favorable locality for the acting out of such affairs as these—a down-river Mississippi steamboat. The circumstances are briefly as follows :

The table was laid for dinner in the spacious upper-cabin of what in those days—for the occurrence which we are about to relate took place many years ago—was considered a first-class river-boat. The passengers were seated at their meal, when a swaggering, devil-may-care fellow—who had spent his time since coming on board at " Natchez-under-the-hill," between corn-whisky and cards—came sauntering in from the " social hall," and took his place at the board, at the same time drawing forth a brace of hair-triggered duelling pistols, which he cocked, and laid upon either side of his plate, in 'such a manner that the muzzles of the loaded weapons were pointed directly at the breast of a grey-headed merchant from New Orleans, a very quiet, unobtrusive sort of person, who sat opposite the gambler.

" Sir," said the old man, " will you do me the favor to remove those pistols, for it is impossible to eat my dinner comfortably when my life is endangered by the very careless manner in which you have thrown down your weapons."

To this mild remonstrance, the person addressed vouchsafed no farther reply than an oath, coupled with the intimation, that " if the old fellow didn't like it, he might leave the cabin ; but as for himself he would not move his fire-arms, to please the best man that ever walked."

Upon receiving this discourteous reply the old merchant uttered not a word, but resumed his chair, from which he had partly risen, with the air of a man who had made up his mind to endure an annoyance which he cannot prevent. In a few moments, however, he raised his head, made a signal to the negro-man, a pri-

16

vate servant of his own who was attending upon him, and gave some whispered order; the negro disappeared, entered the merchant's state-room by its outer door, but immediately returned to his place beside his master's chair, where he stooped down, produced something from behind his back, and placed the articles, whatever they were, in the merchant's hands, as the old man put them quietly back to grasp what he had sent for. A moment more and all present were electrified by seeing the old gentleman straighten himself up, with a cocked pistol in either hand, which he levelled full at the gambler's head, at the same instant calling out,

"If you stir, or dare to move a finger, sir, you are a dead man."

He then motioned to the negro who stood grinning at his side.

"Tom," said he, "go round and take up that person's pistols, remove the caps, and lay them in the berth in his state-room; he won't need them, at least, until after dinner."

"As for you, sir," added he, turning to the discomfited swaggerer, as Tom literally carried out his master's instructions, "I fancy you will not be disposed to bully even an *old* man in future."

When the Screamer No. 3 stopped to "wood up," some two hours afterwards, the "gambling man" was, "by particular request," one of those who landed, and remained upon shore.

And now, after this long, but, as we trust, not altogether uninteresting digression, let us return to the consideration of "Lar-ence" and its "forts," which will—as this chapter has already outrun its intended limits, be treated of in a military point of view in the next.

CHAPTER XXXVII.

LAWRENCE IN A MILITARY POINT OF VIEW.

WE have already hazarded the opinion that the town of Lawrence could be taken, her earth-work trenches, Sharpe's rifles, Kansas brigades, and "circular forts" to the contrary notwithstanding, in something less than two hours by the watch, and we will now endeavor to give our reasons for this belief.

Imprimis—We should fancy that the idea of "a war," or even of being called upon to put their town in a position for defence, could never have occurred to those who selected the site of this "city," that is to be; for, in a military point of view, we could hardly fancy a location which would be naturally more open to an attack, or less susceptible of being successfully defended, at least, by any hastily erected temporary work, than this political "bone of contention, the Athens of Free State Kansas." But let us give the reader a rough idea of its situation and surroundings, and then, if he do not concur with us in our opinion, we shall feel inclined to pronounce him a most unmilitary man, and "agree in disagreeing."

Lawrence stands upon a plain, or to speak more correctly, upon that portion of the open prairie which slopes gently toward the belt of timber that marks the course of the Caw River— a stream, which flows, if we remember rightly, within a couple of hundred yards, or less, of the town itself. There is also a ravine, deep enough to cover the approach of troops for a night attack, that leads almost, or quite, into the town.   But the unfavorable peculiarities of country just alluded to, are by no means the most important of the natural disadvantages which might militate against the Free State soldiers in case of an attack; for a huge "bluff" lifts its treeless brow above the otherwise almost level landscape, and stands sufficiently near to command the town.   In fact, a portion of its crest is within five hundred yards—a very neat distance for artillery practice—of the "circular forts," and earth-works that it overlooks.   This "bluff" is, moreover, extensive, and easier of access from the far side than on that nearest the town, which is somewhat precipitous.   Now what, let us ask, is there to prevent an enemy, if provided with artillery, from gaining this elevation with his pieces during the night, and crowning the heights with a battery, which could be prepared to open its fire, ere daylight should betray its presence to the besieged.   True it is that the Free State Volunteers boast that they have, on several occasional proved the efficiency of their Sharpe's rifles, by discharging them with effect from the "circular fort" nearest the "bluff," at a board placed upon that point of the elevation which an enemy would be most likely to occupy.   But who does not know that *target* firing is *one* thing, and *real* practice, with a return of your favors—and it may be with interest—quite a different affair.

There is yet another manner in which Lawrence might, with nothing more than volunteer sentinels upon the look-out, be successfully surprised, and that is, by marching men down, under cover of night, upon the opposite side of the Caw River, and then crossing them to the timber which shades the Lawrence margin of the stream, by boats or rafts previously prepared.   These rafts might be launched above, and dropped down almost noiselessly with the current, from whence, upon effecting a landing, a very short run would bring the assailants within striking distance of the defenders of the place, and thus enable them, by a hand to hand fight, to gain possession of the town.

It was, as we are informed, the intention of the "Border Ruffians" to have taken Lawrence, had the late difficulties actually ended in a fight, by a cavalry charge; in such a case, the storming party expected to receive but one or two volleys from the Free State Sharpe's rifles, before they would have been enabled to rush in, close man to man, draw their pistols and bowie knives, and thus gain the day. It appears that these worthies trusted not a little to their—as a general thing—superior personal strength, activity, and expertness in using their weapons. On the other hand, the Free State Volunteers are equally confident that they could have kept up so withering a fire from the repeating arms-with which they were provided, that no Missourian could have lived to get within pistol-shot of their entrenchments. But in regard to these matters, who shall decide, where conflicting factions disagree, as to what *might* have been the *modus operandi* and *ultimatum* of a fight which we rejoice to say, did not take place, and we sincerely trust, *never will.*

As regards the details of the defences at Lawrence, we should certainly have been "better posted" than we are. As it is, we can but plead the intense cold, which reigned supreme during our visit to this Sebastopol of the Far West, and interfered so sadly with our study of *exposed* fortifications, as to prevent an intended examination into the results of General Lane's Free State military engineering. There is, however, an addenda in our favor, to this apology, in the shape of a desperate endeavor made one January afternoon, when we sallied forth, note-book in hand, to take measurements and dimensions. This ended in our gaining the edge of a slippery ditch, into which, as we were busily engaged in pacing off the front, we tumbled most inglori ously, thereby proving, to our own satisfaction at least, that the

Free State entrenchments were certainly dangerous to absent-minded Yankees, whatever they *might* be to the "Border Ruffians."

And now as our latest Lawrence intelligence dates back to January the 9th, we will crib the following from a Free State correspondent's letter, dated at that place on the 25th of the same month ; it might very properly be headed, "sixteen days later from the seat of war." The writer, by the way, seems to be quite as fully impressed with the "cold weather" as we were—but read what he says.

LAWRENCE, K. T., *Friday, January 25th,* 1856.

*　　*　　*　　*　　*　　*　　*

One man, who started on foot to come here last Monday, was badly frozen, and barely escaped with his life, by swinging his hat for aid, after becoming unable to walk—and the Samaritan who first came to his assistance was the Pro-Slavery Sheriff Jones, who was riding about one mile distant at the time. He found him shockingly frozen, and put him upon his own horse, in which manner he carried him about three miles to the house of an Indian, where he was well cared for—but it is doubtful whether he will ever be able to walk again, for I have heard to-day that his feet are so badly swollen as to crack open. Indeed, I may say that I never saw so many people suffering with chilled feet and hands before in my life, as there are now in Lawrence. Full one half of those who walk our streets limp as they go, and are obliged to wear buffalo over-shoes, or something very loose upon their feet. I know of some women who are obliged to use crutches for a similar reason. This is called the coldest winter known here for twenty years.

*　　*　　*　　*　　*　　*　　*

Cold weather is the only fortuitous event for the Free State party I have to mention. I believe it is that alone which keeps our opponents from pouncing upon us. It would be impossible to conduct a campaign successfully while the cold is so severe. We know they have an underground organization which probably extends through all the Southern States, and that all who are connected with it are pledged to *fight in any case, right or wrong,* and never to return till the Free State party is extinct. They drill every day at Westport and other prominent towns along the border, but are totally silent upon the *object* of their movements when questioned by strangers. We learn, to-night, that everything is extremely quiet at Kansas and other places, just now. It is a common subject of remark among our Free State friends there ; they are puzzled to account for it. Persons who appear to be in authority, are seen riding from town to town, holding conference with prominent Pro-Slavery men, but not one word of their designs can be drawn from them. Letters from our friends, yesterday, from Leavenworth and Kansas, state that there is something threatening in the undercurrent, and their advice to us is to prepare for the worst. We are fast doing so. A week ago, one hundred well-armed men could have stormed our town, but our condition was not known in "Pukedom." We had no powder, shot, or lead, and but few provisions; but yesterday half a ton of lead arrived, and nearly as much powder. Two other teams are on the way with the same "material aid." Provisions are also coming in, so that we shall soon be in good condition for defence. Last night about sixty men were detailed from the different companies, and a party set at work upon each of our five fortifications. Cabins were hastily thrown up within the entrenchments, stoves prepared, and they are now boarding themselves in soldier-like order. The fort at the foot of Massachusetts street is circular, about one hundred feet in diameter, made of earth and timbers thrown up about seven feet high, with a walk of some four feet in width upon the top. Upon this circle we have a soldier in full uniform, walking night and day, giving our town something of a military appearance. Generals Robinson and Lane are constantly in the Council Chamber with other subordinate officers.

We are not so well prepared for a campaign now as we were in December. Then, our harvest was just over, the weather mild, and men could leave their families for a few days without uneasiness on their account. Now, provisions, money and wood are scarce, and many who came before to our aid could not be urged to do so again without paying them in advance, so that their families might not suffer in their absence. We have started men to-day to different parts of the Territory, to give notice of our danger, and warn our friends to be ready at an hour's notice.

Many are of the opinion that we shall not be attacked till the new Legislature meets, or until we attempt to move the wheels of our State organization on the 4th of March. This may be true, and it may also be true, if large forces from the East, North and West do not reach us before that time, that the Legislature will immediately adjourn after organizing, until the 1st of May, when we shall be sure of a great accession to our military as well as our industrial strength.

*   *   *   *   *   *   *

As regards the opinion expressed in the foregoing communication, in relation to the Kansas difficulties reaching their crisis upon the 4th of March, we are disposed to believe that its writer is most probably correct, for though but little inclined to play the part of prophet upon any political stage, or even to claim, in such matters, the old Scottish gift of "second sight," we are willing to predict, that the Ides of March are pregnant, either with good or evil for "the Territory" and its future. That the Free State people will carry their new State Government into effect, by assembling their Legislature, and swearing in their officers elect, we cannot for a moment doubt ; while we have, at the same time, good reason to feel confident, that Governor Shannon, as the Territorial Executive, will, in such an event, cause the parties concerned to be arrested, not for *treason*, as has been currently reported, but under a law passed by the so-called Kansas " Bogus Legislature," which provides, that any person who shall take upon himself any trust or office, without being duly elected, and appointed to such trust or office, shall be judged guilty of a misdemeanor, and punished by a certain amount of fine or imprisonment, which is specified in " the Act."

And since we have entered upon the consideration of events, which *may* take place in Kansas, it will be well, at this stage of our erratic " History," to lay before the reader such official documents, as have recently been issued from the ·highest authority at Washington, for the guidance of the Territorial Executive and all parties concerned, in the event of any further disturbances, which might lead to a violation of law and order in the region indicated.

It will be perceived from the following letters, that this inter-ference of the President in Kansas affairs has been in some measure called forth by the solicitations of General Robinson—the so-called Free State Governor elect, and others of that party.

LAWRENCE, K. T. Jan. 21, 1856.

THE FREE STATE LEADERS—TO FRANKLIN PIERCE, PRESIDENT OF THE UNITED STATES.

SIR:

We have authentic information that an overwhelming force of the citizens of Missouri are organizing upon our border, amply supplied with artillery, for the avowed purpose of invading this Territory, demoralizing our towns and butchering our unoffending Free State citizens. We respectfully demand, on behalf of the citizens of Kansas, that the commandant of the United States troops in this vicinity, be immediately instructed to interfere to prevent such an inhuman outrage.

Respectfully,

J. H. LANE, *Chairman Ex. Committee K. T.*

C. ROBINSON, *Chairman Ex. Committee of Safety.*

J. R. GOODIN, *Secretary Ex. Committee K. T.*

GEORGE W. DEITZER, *Secretary Committee of Safety.*

LAWRENCE, CITY, Jan. 23, 1856.

THE FREE STATE LEADERS—TO THE PRESIDENT OF THE UNITED STATES.

SIR:

We notified you that an overwhelming force, supplied with artillery, was organizing upon our borders for the avowed purpose of invading Kansas, demoralizing the towns and butchering the unoffending Free State citizens, they constituting fourteen-twentieths of the entire population. In addition to the relief respectfully demanded in that notice, we earnestly request you to issue your proclamation immediately, forbidding the invasion. We trust there may be no delay in taking so important a step to prevent an outrage which, if carried out as planned, will stand forth without a parallel in the world's history.

Yours respectfully,

J. H. LANE, *Chairman Ex. Committee K. T.*

C. ROBINSON, *Chairman Committee of Safety.*

16*

The President has accordingly issued the following proclamation :

PROCLAMATION OF THE PRESIDENT.

Whereas, indications exist that public tranquillity and the supremacy of law in the Territory of Kansas are endangered by the reprehensible acts or purposes of persons, both within and without the same, who propose to direct and control its political organizations by force; it appearing that combinations have been formed therein to resist the execution of the Territorial laws, and thus, in effect subvert by violence all present constitutional and legal authority; it also appearing that persons residing without the Territory, but near its borders, contemplate armed intervention in the affairs thereof; it also appearing that other persons, inhabitants of remote States, are collecting money, engaging men, and providing arms for the same purpose; and it further appearing that combinations within the Territory are endeavoring, by the agency of emissaries and otherwise, to induce individual States of the Union to interfere in the affairs thereof, in violation of the Constitution of the United States. And, whereas, all such plans for the determination of the future institutions of the Territory, if carried into action from within the same, will constitute the fact of insurrection, and, if from without, that of invasive aggression, and will, in either case, justify and require the forcible interposition of the whole power of the general government, as well to maintain the laws of the territory as those of the Union.

Now, therefore, I, Franklin Pierce, President of the United States, do issue this my proclamation to command all persons engaged in unlawful combinations against the constituted authority of the Territory of Kansas or of the United States to disperse and retire peaceably to their respective abodes, and to warn all such persons that an attempted insurrection in said Territory, or aggressive intrusion into the same, will be resisted not only by the employment of the local militia, but also by that of any available forces of the United States; to the end of assuring immunity from violence and full protection to the persons, property and civil rights of all peaceful and law-abiding inhabitants of the Territory.

If, in any part of the Union, the fury of faction or fanaticism, inflamed into disregard of the great principles of popular sovereignty, which, under the Constitution, are fundamental in the whole structure of our institutions, is to bring on the country the dire calamity of an arbitrament of arms in that Territory, it shall be between lawless violence on the one side and conservative force on the other, wielded by legal authority of the general government.

I call on the citizens, both of adjoining and of distant States, to abstain from unauthorized intermeddling in the local concerns of the Territory, admonishing them that its organic law is to be executed with impartial justice; that all individual acts of illegal interference will incur condign punishment; and that any endeavor to interfere by organized force will be firmly withstood.

I invoke all good citizens to promote order by rendering obedience to the law; to seek remedy for temporary evils by peaceful means; to discountenance and repulse the counsels and the instigations of agitators and disorganizers; and to testify their attachment to their country, their pride in its greatness, their appreciation of the blessings they enjoy, and their determination that republican institutions shall not fail in their hands, by co-operating to uphold the majesty of the laws and to vindicate the sanctity of the Constitution.

In testimony whereof, I have hereunto set my hand, and caused the seal of the United States to be affixed to these presents.

Done at the city of Washington, the eleventh day of February, in the year of our Lord one thousand eight hundred and fifty-six, and of the independence of the United States the eightieth.

FRANKLIN PIERCE.

By the President: W. L. MARCY, *Secretary of State.*

Here follow the Secretary of State's instructions to Governor Shannon.

MR. MARCY TO GOVERNOR SHANNON.

DEPARTMENT OF STATE, WASHINGTON, *Feb.* 16, 1856.

SIR:

I herewith enclose to you a copy of a proclamation by the President, dated the 11th inst., duly authenticated, and also a copy of orders issued from the Department of War to Colonel Sumner and Brevet Colonel Cooke, of the United States Army.

The President is unwilling to believe that, in executing your duties as Governor of the Territory of Kansas, there will be any occasion to call in the aid of the United States troops for that purpose, and it is enjoined upon you to do all that can possibly be done before resorting to that measure; yet if it becomes indispensably necessary to do so, in order to execute the laws, and preserve the peace, you are hereby authorized by the President to make requisition upon the officers commanding the United States military forces at Fort Leavenworth and Fort Riley, for such assistance as may be needed for the above specified purpose. While confiding in the respect of our citizens for the laws, and the efficiency of the ordinary means provided for protecting their rights and property, he deems it, however, not improper, considering the peculiar situation of affairs in the Territory of Kansas, that you should be authorized to have the power herein conferred, with a view to meet any extraordinary emergency that may arise, trusting that it will not be used until you shall find a resort to it unavoidable, in order to insure the due execution of the laws and to preserve the public peace.

Before actual interposition of the military force on any occasion, you will cause the proclamation of the President, with which you are herewith furnished, to be publicly read.

I am, sir, very respectfully, your obedient servant,

W. L. MARCY.

Hon. WILSON SHANNON, *Governor of the Territory of Kansas.*

The following communication is addressed to Governor Shannon, as the Chief Executive of Kansas Territory, by the Secretary of War. It covers a copy of the orders issued from his department to Colonels Sumner and Cooke, the military commandants, who are directed, under certain contingencies, to lend their aid in putting down any future disturbance which may arise in Kansas.

THE SECRETARY OF WAR TO COLONELS SUMNER AND COOKE.

WAR DEPARTMENT, WASHINGTON, *Feb.* 15, 1856.

SIR:

The President has, by proclamation, warned all persons, combined for insurrection or invasive aggression against the organized government of the Territory of Kansas, or associated to resist the due execution of the laws therein, to abstain from such revolutionary and lawless proceedings, and has commanded them to disperse, and retire peaceably to their respective abodes, on pain of being resisted by his whole constitutional power. If, therefore, the Governor of the Territory, finding the ordinary course of judicial proceedings and the powers vested in the United States Marshals inadequate for the suppression of insurrectionary combinations or armed resistance to the execution of the law, should make requisition upon you to furnish a military force to aid him in the performance of that official duty, you are hereby directed to employ for that purpose, such part of your command as may, in your judgment, consistently be detached from their ordinary duty.

In executing this delicate function of the military power of the United States, you will exercise much caution, to avoid, if possible, collision with even insurgent citizens, and will endeavor to suppress resistance to the laws and constituted authorities, by that moral force, which happily, in our country, is ordinarily sufficient to secure respect to the laws of the land, and the regularly constituted authorities of the government. You will use a sound discretion as to the moment at which the further employment of the military force may be discontinued, and avail yourself of the first opportunity to return with your command to the more grateful and prouder service of the soldier—that of common defence.

For your guidance in the premises, you are referred to the acts of 28th of February, 1795, and 3d of March, 1807 [see Military Laws, pages 301 and 123], and to the proclamation of the President, a copy of which is herewith transmitted.

Should you need further and more specific instructions, or should, in the progress of events, doubts arise in your mind as to the course which it may be proper for you to pursue, you will communicate directly with this Department, stating the points upon which you wish to be informed.

Very respectfully, your obedient servant,

JEFFERSON DAVIS,
Secretary of War.

WAR DEPARTMENT, Feb. 15, 1856.

SIR:

The foregoing is a copy of the letters addressed to Colonel E. V. Sumner, United States Army, commanding at Fort Leavenworth, and to Brevet Colonel P. St. G. Cooke, commanding at Fort Ripley, and is furnished for your information.

I have the honor to be, very respectfully, your obedient servant,

JEFFERSON DAVIS,
Secretary of War.

Hon. WILSON SHANNON, Governor of Kansas Territory.

Among the various answers which have been addressed to the Kansas Free State party—appeal for aid—we have seen no document so unexceptionable, both in its tone, and in the very high ground which it takes, upon the subject of "State interference," as the following communication from Governor Wright of Indiana.

REPLY OF THE GOVERNOR OF INDIANA TO THE KANSAS APPEAL FOR AID.

In answer to the appeal for aid signed by J. H. Lane, Chairman of the Executive Committee, and C. Robinson, Governor-elect of Kansas Territory, Governor Wright, of Indiana, has written the following letter:

Executive Department, Indiana,
Indianapolis, Feb. 12, 1856.

Gentlemen:

Your communication of the 31st of January, addressed to me in an official capacity, and asking that steps may be taken to protect your people from the violence of the citizens of Missouri, is now before me.

If the Legislature were in session, I should lay your communication before them, not with the most remote idea that Indiana would deviate from her well-known opinion, upon the principle involved, but out of respect to you as citizens.

I shall certainly not interfere in the domestic institutions of your Territory, nor recommend that our people should take any part therein.

The conduct of the Missourians, as well as of those from the Free States, who have gone into your Territory, with the view of controlling your elections, and not to become *bona fide* citizens, is alike reprehensible, and liable to the severest censure and punishment.

But the remedy for these evils is properly and constitutionally lodged with the legal and sovereign power of the Territory; and if this is not sufficient, it is most wisely left to the action of the Executive of the Nation, and to that of Congress.

Our form of Government never contemplated, for a moment, that, in the domestic troubles so frequently arising in the different States and Territories of the Union, sister States in the confederacy should take any part

Whenever this doctrine is assumed and carried out, we shall find ourselves approaching a state of things that will sweep away all the safe bonds and ties that bind us together as one people.

We must live faithfully up to all our contracts—not only discharging the duties we owe to our own State or Territory, but those we owe to the National Government. And this can be done most effectually by guarding against the slightest encroachment upon the great bond of our Union, which makes us a united people. In the furtherance of this object we should act toward every member of the confederacy alike—to each as equal to equal. While we enjoy the right to make our own form of Government as to all our domestic institutions, we should freely accord the same right to others.

There is a spirit of propagandism, which seems to be increasing in the South and the North, to which even the law-making powers is invoked. This must not be countenanced or encouraged. The whole force of the legal power of the State or Territory, must be brought into vigorous action to arrest it.

When this fails, the ample power vested by the Constitution in the Executive, and Congress of the nation, must be sought. Should all this prove ineffectual, we shall be not only on the verge of anarchy and rebellion, but ready for the worst of all evils—intestine war with all the calamities that must follow the hostile array of neighbor against neighbor, brother against brother, son against sire—war among those of the same race, the same name, the same blood.

As a State, we are surrounded by our sisters in the confederacy, differing in many domestic institutions. In some of them have occurred mobs, riots, and destruction of human life; in others the sanctuary of the elective franchise has been invaded; but the thought has never occurred to our peaceable and law-abiding citizens that the sovereign power in these respective States, in connection with the strong national arms, was insufficient to bring about the observance of law and order.

So long as our people recognize this principle, and fully carry it out, we shall have respect for the supremacy of law, and for its administrators. If we depart from it in the higher and more delicate relation that we sustain to the different members of the confederacy, we shall find that, in the same proportion, citizens of the counties and townships will be engaged in open violation of law—trampling upon those in authority, in the smaller communities, and there will be no safety for property, liberty, or life.

The want of confidence, North and South, in the ability of the people of

Kansas to mould their own institutions to suit themselves, and the con-sequent aggressive spirit of interference for the purpose of influencing their elections, seem to originate in a sort of egotism, both in parties and individual citizens, who, while they doubt the integrity and capacity of the people of Kansas, are ready to assert their own honesty and ability to regulate their institutions for them.

Indiana, as a State, has wisely selected her own domestic policy. She is willing to give her neighbors the same right, and to suppose them capable of choosing and deciding for themselves. She has never given any cause of complaint to any of her sister States or Territories. And I do most sincerely hope that none of her citizens will so far forget the relation they sustain to their neighbors, and the national compact, as to take any part in the strifes and contentions of others who are openly violating the laws of the land.

Notwithstanding it was telegraphed from your Territory to New York that I was willing and ready to offer the assistance of citizens of this State, in your controversy, let me assure you that while I have the honor to be her Executive officer, I will not in any manner attempt to bring her down from her present high position, and have her in any way mingling in the domestic strife of her sister States or Territories. The sentiment of our people is to leave the settlement of these questions to the people of Kansas, who are the actual citizens of the Territory. If this cannot be brought about—if influences are at work which render this impossible—the remedy is not to be found by others unlawfully interfering, but, by the Constitution and laws, is most properly lodged in the hands of those who have the power and ability to restore order and peace.

Appeals are frequently made to our sympathies, to redress grievances and outrages, which occur in many of the relations of life, and in many instances, these influences command our services. But in the higher and more important relations we sustain to each other, as members of our happy form of government, the Constitution and the laws should alone be the rule of our action.

There are those who indulge in the use of hard names and sectional phrases, such as subserviency to Southern interest, doughfaces, and the like, in order to influence the public mind, and to arouse our people to the violation of law. All this, however, I ardently hope, will not lead our people away from the great principle that underlies all our institutions— the absolute right of each State and Territory to make its own institutions, without the influence of others.

Upon this principle we can stand and maintain the peace and harmony of the Union with safety and honor. It is the corner stone upon which the security and perpetuity of the Union rests.

Having the utmost confidence that the people of Indiana will not, under any circumstances, abandon this high position, I frankly say to you, no efforts will be made by this department to induce a solitary citizen to enter upon a crusade against any portion of the people of the Union or their institutions. If others do wrong, we will do right.

I have the honor to be, yours most respectfully,

JOSEPH A. WRIGHT.

JAMES II. LANE, C. ROBINSON, AND GEORGE W. DEITZER, *Lawrence City*, K. T.

We feel constrained to add the following note. While in Lawrence, we heard it spoken of as a matter of public notoriety, that Governor Wright, of Indiana, was one of the strongest and most active sympathizers with the Free State party in Kansas, in proof of which, General Lane, on one occasion, exhibited to us a letter, which he informed us had been received by himself, from Governor Wright, of Indiana, but a day or two before. We read this letter. It was, if we remember aright, dated at Indianapolis, and was certainly signed by Joseph A. Wright. The writer, in this communication, *approves* in the strongest terms of the course pursued by the Free State leaders in Kansas—advises Lane to go on as he had begun—assures him of sympathy, and promises "material aid" in the following, or nearly, the following words ·

"I have money, and can raise men, and if necessary, will furnish five hundred as good boys as are to be found upon the Wabash valley."

Now, we should be pleased to know, how we are to reconcile this *plain* spoken letter, which preaches " war to the knife," with his Excellency of Indiana's very pacific reply to his *soi-disan* Correspondent's appeal for help, when it comes before him in his official capacity, and in which he vindicates doctrines, which would do credit to William Penn, or Mr. Bright himself? There is evidently a trifling mistake somewhere.

We may as well add the *finale* to our documentary information, by closing this chapter with an abstract from the official catalogue of the members and officers of both houses of the First Legislative Assembly of Kansas Territory, which convened on the 2d day of July, 1855.   This is what the Free State party call the "Missouri Bogus Legislature."

MEMBERS AND OFFICERS OF THE COUNCIL.

Names.	Age.	Occupation.	Nativity.	How long in the Territory.	Quotations from their speeches.
T. Johnson, President, Supt. of Shawnee Mis.	53 yr's.	Farmer,	Va.,	18 Years,	Justice to all.
R. R. Reese, Pres't. pro tem.,	43 "	Lawyer,	Ohio,	10 months,	Just laws and rigid execution.
John W. Forman,	36 "	Merchant,	Ky.,	12 years,	The Organic Act—our Charter of Liberty.
A. M. Coffey,	51 "	Farmer,	Ky.,	4 "	"The Union, it must be preserved."
D. Lykins,	34 "	Physician.	Ia.,	12 "	Cuba must be annexed.
W. P. Richardson, Maj. Gen. Com'g. K. M.,	53 "	Farmer,	Ky.,	9 "	Hemp for negro-stealers.
H. J. Strickler, Brig'r. Gen. K. M.,	24 "	Survey'r & Civ. Eng.	Va.,	6 months,	The South and her Institutions.
L. J. Eastin, do., Ed. Leavenw'th City He'd.	40 "	Printer,	Ky.,	9 "	Negro Slavery for Kansas. "Good."
D. A. N. Grover,	26 "	Lawyer,	Ky.,	10 years,	Homestead for the Squatters.
Wm. Barbee,	29 "	Lawyer,	Ky.,	1 "	Majority shall rule.
Jno. Donaldson,	25 "	Merchant,	Ky.,	6 months,	The cause I advocate must succeed. It is right, it is just.
A. McDonald,	37 "	Lawyer,	Va.,	10 "	"United we stand."
E. Chapman,	27 "	Lawyer,	La.,	10 "	As an American, I reverence the Constitution, now and forever.
Jno. A. Halderman, Ch. Clk.	24 "	Lawyer,	Mo.,	14 "	
Ch. H. Grover, As. Clk.	24 "	Lawyer,	Ky.,	11 years,	A new treaty with the Delawares.
T. C. Hughes, En'g. Clk.	37 "	Farmer,	Md.,	5 months,	Down with the National Democracy in Kansas.
S. J. Waful, En'g. Clk.	28 "	Farmer,	N. Y.,	14 "	Kansas—May her virgin soil be unpolluted by the foul stain of free-soilism.
O. B. Whitehead, Sgt.-at-arms,	41 "	Farmer,	Va.,	2 years.	

MEMBERS AND OFFICERS OF THE HOUSE OF REPRESENTATIVES.

Names.	Age.	Occupation.	Nativity.	How long in the territory.	Quotations from their speeches.
J. M. Banks,	36 yr's.	Farmer,	Penn.,	1 Year,	"Justice and truth."
J. P. Blair,	47 "	Farmer,	Tenn.,	6 months,	
O. H. Browne,	84 "	Farmer,	Md.,	1 year,	"Be just and fear not."
D. L. Croysdale,	26 "	Physician,	Mo.,	1 "	
H. B. C. Harris,	30 "	Physician,	Va.,	9 months,	Act justly but fearlessly.
W. A. Heiskill,	47 "	Merchant,	Va.,	6 years,	"The South—her rights and interests."
Samuel D. Houston,	36 "	Farmer,	Ohio,		
Alex. S. Johnson,	23 "	Farmer,	K. T.,	23 "	Peaceably if we can—forcibly if we must.
R. L. Kirk,	37 "	Farmer,	Ky.,	9 months,	"My country, my whole country."
Frank J. Marshall,	38 "	Merchant,	Va.,	4 years,	"Be sure you're right, then go-ahead."
Wm. G. Mathias,	29 "	Lawyer,	Md.,	10 months,	No disorganization—no fanaticism.
M. W. McGee,	36 "	Merchant,	Ky.,	1 year,	Kansas with Southern institutions.
H. D. McMeekin,	33 "	Merchant,	Ky.,	5 "	"We fight to conquer."
A. Payne,	36 "	Farmer,	Ky.,	1 "	Union first—South all the time.
Samuel Scott,	52 "	Farmer,	Ky.,	7 months,	Onward march to victory.
W. H. Tebbs,	32 "	Physician,	Va.,	1 year,	Non-intercourse and Southern rights.
A. B. Wade,	26 "	Farmer,	Mo.,	1 "	
G. W. Ward,	55 "	Farmer,	Ky.,	1 "	Justice and the South.
T. W. Waterson,	44 "	Farmer,	Penn.,	18 months,	Kansas for the South, now and forever.
Jonah Weddle	28 "	Teacher,	Va.,	1 year,	"Kansas, the South and the Union."
Jas. Whitlock,	37 "	Farmer,	Mo.,	10 months,	My country's flag.
Samuel A. Williams,	85 "	Farmer,	Ky.,	6 ".	"Kansas and the Union."
Allen Wilkinson,	85 "	Farmer,	Tenn.,	8 "	
H. W. Younger,	43 "	Farmer,	Mo.,	8 "	Order and liberty.
J. H. Stringfellow, Sp'kr Ed. of "Squatter Sovereign,"	85 "	Physician,	Va.,	1 year,	Squatter rights.
J. C. Anderson, Sp'ker, pro tem,	25 "	Lawyer,	Ky.,	10 months,	Vox populi, vox Dei.
J. M. Lyle, Chief Clerk.	22 "	Lawyer,	S. C.,	6 "	Civil and religious liberty.
Jno. Martin, As't. Cl'k.	21 "	Lawyer,	Tenn.,	6 "	Strict construction of the Constitution.
J. C. Thompson, Engros. Clerk,	25 "	Lawyer,	Ohio,	1 year,	To the victors belong the spoils.
B. F. Simmons, Enrolling Clerk,	29 "	Lawyer,	N. C.,	6 months,	Union only when it protects our interests.
T. J. B. Cramer, Serg't-at-Arms,	38 "	Farmer,	Va.,	1 year,	
B. P. Campbell, Door-Keeper,	23 "	Farmer,	N. Y.,	10 months,	"Kansas to be the brightest star of all."
John T. Peery, Chaplain,	38 "	Minister,	Va.,	12 years,	Religion—the corner-stone of civilization.
John T. Brady, Pub. Pr.	24 "	Lawyer,	Md.,	16 months.	The Constitution.
S. A. Lowe, Cong. Clk.	35 "	Lawyer,	Md.,	2 years,	Money makes the mare go.

NOTE.—The members were all *Pro-Slavery* in their politics, except Samuel D. Houston —a Free Soiler—who, finding himself in a strong minority, resigned his seat.

If the foregoing be correct, it certainly goes far towards dis·proving the allegations which have been made as to the members of the so-called Missouri Bogus Legislature being citizens of Missouri. For it will be perceived, by reference to these tables —which are accurate extracts from the official record—that eleven Members of the Council had been residents of the Territory for over a year, six of whom had been ten years in Kansas ; while of the members of the House of Representatives, twenty individuals had resided in the Territory for one year, of whom five were residents of over four years' standing: the total of officers and members of both houses being fifty-three. Of the quotations from their speeches, we like those the best of Messrs. Coffey and Chapman in the Council, and Martin and Brady in the House. They are evidently Union men of the right stamp

JUSTICE TO GOVERNOR WRIGHT.

NOTE.—Since writing the foregoing, we have learned from a gentleman who left Lawrence on the 29th of January, that the letter referred to—which Gen. Lane supposed to have been penned by His Excellency the Governor of Indiana—was really written by Judge John W. Wright, of that State; the epistle being signed J. W. Wright, and being, moreover, very hastily written, the initial of the middle name, W., was mistaken for A., which is the second initial of Governor Wright's name—hence the mistake. Judge Wright's letter, as we have been informed, was published in the New York Tribune; it says, if we remember the words, " I have *sons* and money, and will raise five hundred as good boys," &c. As His Excellency the Governor has been blessed with but one *daughter*, and no boys at all, it has afforded no little amusement to the good people of Indiana that their Governor should have been accused of volunteering to send his *sons* to fight a possible Free State battle in Kansas. Judge Wright, by the way, is reported to stand by his belligerent communication. We sincerely hope that the Governor will be equally strenuous in carrying out to the letter, the irreproachable sentiments contained in his reply.

CHAPTER. XXXVIII.

FREE STATE ODDS AND ENDS.

To return to the consideration of Lawrence, or rather, to contrast the place with other frontier settlements, we should say, that if Free-State-ism be an element of respectability, the town of Lawrence is certainly a proof of its salutary effect, for in many respects, it will compare favorably with any Far Western, or, for that matter, almost any New England village, as regards the moral and intellectual tone of its inhabitants. We must allow that while we remained there, we saw neither card-playing, gambling, nor drinking; which is more, we fancy, than even the most enthusiastic admirer of "Southern institutions," can say truthfully, of any Pro-Slavery town in Kansas. And this commendation of Lawrence may, if we be correctly informed, apply to most of the *Free State* settlements in the Territory. The same thing may also be alleged in the majority of individual cases.

"I can tell," said a Pro-Slavery man to us, during our sojourn in Kansas, "I can tell a *Free State* settler's claim from a Pro-Slavery man's—particularly, if the latter owns negroes, as far as I can see it; for while the slave-owner's dwelling is, as a general thing, in bad repair, and his land shiftlessly cultivated, the Free Soiler's farm is not only well cared for, but exhibits, in all its appointments, the orderly results of a superintending *head* as well as a working *arm*.

We must confess that this very candid admission, on the part of our Pro-Slavery friend, has been abundantly endorsed by our own personal observations, both in Kansas and elsewhere. There is a difference, and a most unmistakable one, between the surroundings and conveniences of life, which are, even upon the frontier, a *sine qua non* with the Free State emigrant ; and the " dead-and-alive," " get-along-any-how " system, which but too frequently renders comfortless the Pro-Slavery man's "improvement." Were we to analyze the causes which lead to, and continue this strongly-marked contrast, we should say, that it proceeded not from any physical or natural advantages on the part of the more thrifty proprietor, but simply from the fact, that in the one case, the agriculturist *does his own* work, and has it *well* done in consequence; while in the other, the planter trusts to chance, and a lazy " nigger " or two, which usually ends in things being only half done, or, as sometimes happens, in their being neglected altogether.

As an evidence of the very dissimilar working out of the two systems just referred to, we will give the reader a *brief* outline—with the proviso, that " there are *exceptions* to all general rules " —of a " squatter's improvement " in either case : and first for the *Pro-Slavery* man's.

More land than its owner can cultivate *properly* " at present," or probably ever will; an ill-daubed cabin; a tumble-down chimney; a filthy yard; hogs and poultry running at large, where they ought *not* to be; the fences down; the gate, if there be one, off the hinges; the doors too short for the spaces they are intended to fill; the windows stuffed with old hats and cast off clothing, to make up for their deficiencies in glass; timberland half cleared ; and then left to grow up again; no shelter for the cattle; more than a sufficiency of snarling worthless curs. So much for *exterior*.   Within :—A dirty floor, and tobacco-stained hearth; broken, or worse still, half-mended furniture; no books;

ink hard to find; writing-paper laid away since the "old man writ out a receipt for Sam Harris's nigger about six months ago;" pens in some un-come-at-able locality; whisky plenty; a "pack of keards" in the house; the females look care-worn, sickly, and overworked; the children would be the better for a little "Deown East" *common* schooling; the man himself seems rough, uncouth—and in political matters, where his peculiar prejudices come in play, is narrow-minded, ignorant, and uncompromising. His best hope in life is to "get along" in a happy-go-lucky sort of way, which he calls "a-doin'-right-peartly"; and his sole policy, as an agriculturist, is expressed in a firm determination, which he is constantly coming to, but never carries out—*not* to raise hogs and corn upon his farm, another year, because he did so last season, which resulted, as he "allows" in "thar hogs eatin' up all thar corn, an' thar niggars eatin' up all thar hogs," a procedure that left him at the end of the year, with a balance "of nary red cent to buy store goods with." "And so he plays his part."

But how is it with the *Free Soiler's* "location?"

Timber-land yielding slowly, but surely, to an axe, that leaves no unfinished work behind it; cultivated fields, which are witnesses in themselves, that no effort has been spared to make the recently virgin soil do its utmost as a producer. A rough cabin, it is true, but as comfortable within, as mud plastering and solid logs can make it. The fences are in good order; the gate turns easily upon its home-made hinges, and is kept closed by a weight, which does what careless people sometimes forget to do, by shutting it. The windows, like an old lady with the rheumatism, are full of panes; the "unclean beast" keeps his place, and the chickens have a coop; there is enough and to spare in the store-room, and food for the brain upon the shelf. The woman is something more than a domestic drudge; there

are fifty things that tell of her feminine taste, as well as pains-
taking neatness in the little adornments of this frontier home.
The children "get their lessons" and "say them to mamma
every day." The man himself is keen, shrewd, and calculating; he determines what ought to be *done*, and then goes and
does it. He will, if circumstances favor, grow rich.

And now, we would appeal confidently to any common sense,
and impartial Pro-Slavery man, to know whether these two
every-day pictures are, or are not, "sketches from the life,"
which could be verified, if need be, by ten miles of travel, in
almost any one of the border counties of our far-western slaveholding States ?

The amusements—if so warlike a people have time for such fri-
volities—of the good citizens of Lawrence, would appear to be
confined to the excitement of talking politics, getting up meetings,
passing resolutions, listening to speeches, and discussing Kansas
matters generally ; unless, indeed, when they see fit to vary
these pastimes by the lighter relaxations of "playing soldier,"
digging trenches, and building mud forts, or it may be, by dancing, until the grey dawn peeps rebukingly in upon their revels,
at such social gatherings as that which we have endeavored
to describe, under the head of the "New Year's Night party."

There is yet another peculiarity about these "Lawrence
folks," which is decidedly in their favor—they are a reading people, and here again, as a faithful delineator, we are constrained
to admit, that this seems a *Free State* singularity, also, for on
the Border, "niggers" and brains, do not, alas ! always go
hand in hand. They are, moreover, if the postmasters are to be
credited—a writing people—at least, so far as their correspondence is concerned—for those having charge of Uncle Sam's mails,
say, that the Lawrence letter-bags both go and come more
heavily laden, than those of any other town in the Territory

As another evidence of her literary proclivities, Lawrence is soon to have a " circulating library," for an enterprising Rhode Islander—and who does not know that " Little Rhody's " children go far and wide, and in many instances fulfill the Scriptural injunction by being " wise as serpents," though not always " as harmless as the dove "—has opened a little shop, bookstore, and what-not, upon Massachusetts street, and intends adding a perambulating collection of standard works within the year. The person alluded to, is a certain Mr. Wilmarth, of Providence, who will—we doubt not—prove " a credit to thar diggins "—all stony though they be—" that gave him birth."

And now, let us resume our journalizing, for our time in Free State Kansas grows short, and our visit to the " seat of war " is drawing to its close. Yes, we have argued the matter both *pro* and *con*—to go or not to go, being the question—but after an hour's consideration of the many reasons why we should, and the few why we should not, return to the civilized East, with its home comforts, and excellent *reputation* for steady habits, we were about adjourning the case to another sitting, when the entrance of our friend, Eldridge, interrupted our cogitations, and turned the scale in favor of *to go*. For it appeared that he was about starting upon the morrow, in his own conveyance, for Kansas City, Mo., the road to which passes through Westport —our first halting-place upon the home-trail—and was even then looking for us, to invite " Our Correspondent " to accompany him upon the journey as far as he desired to go. And since peace was concluded, and tranquillity restored, we could see nothing to detain us, as a newspaper correspondent, in a region where startling events and interesting items were already like angel's visits, becoming few and far between. So we said amen to Eldridge's proposition, packed our leathern hold-all, and then sat down to write, under the caption of January 8th, such last lines as the following :

Jauuary 8th.—Our last evening at the " Cincinnati House."— The tallow candle is lighted—the stove red hot—the political disputants all assembled—our fat landlady bends over her everlasting stocking-mending, and " Long Sweetening " gabbles away as if her tongue was an express train, and considerably behind time at that.

" Our Correspondent " occupies his accustomed chair, but his usual allowance of elbow-room has been docked down, by a " circumstance," to half a table, and " the circumstance," my curious friend, is a short, duck-legged, and broad-shouldered individual, with an unwholesome complexion, fiery red hair, coarse hands, and glassy, weak eyes, which keep blinking under their faint eyelashes, like a night owl's in the sun. This " circumstance," too, was a somewhat notorious but withal amusing character in his way. In fine, he was a person—if his own account may be credited—of terrible experience—a Free-Soil Politician martyr of class A, No. 1, who had fought, suffered and bled—'twas at the nose —for the advancement of Popular Sovereignty, Black Republicanism, and such like, in Kansas ; for all of which he had been rewarded—oh ! most ungrateful world !—by becoming the butt for

" People's wicked jokes."

Yea, even among the " faithful " of his own party. But as there was really some fun in the animal—his grotesque outside to the contrary, notwithstanding—we determined to " trot him out :" so with this praiseworthy object in view, we entered into conversation with the Circumstance, who was a Colonel, withal, having been breveted to that rank by some mischievous wag, for his distinguished services—as his funny friend expressed it— in annoying the Border Ruffians while a prisoner in their camp, until his unbounded loquacity had fairly bored those worthy people into granting the martyr an unconditional parole.

" Colonel," said we, after a conversational opener, upon that nnfailing theme, the weather, " you seem to be quite a literary man, if one might judge from the closely-written sheets which you are so busily adding to."

The Colonel admits the soft impeachment, and proceeds to inform us that " it was a kinder history like of what he'd bin a-goin' through, while under guard among the Pro-Slavery soldiers in the Wakarusē "—as he pronounced it—" Camp."

" If it's a fair question, Colonel, might we inquire what you intend doing with your ' history,' when it is completed ? Is it to be published, or do you merely propose to circulate it in its present form among your political friends ?"

" Wael, neow, I guess it is a-goin' tew be printed, Mister ; I'm a-ritin' it out tew send tew the Editor of the Nigger Sufferin', Sympathizin' Thunderbolt of Freedom.—This name will do as well as any other.—" I'm a-doin' it up amazin' slick, tew, and a-fixin' off them Border Ruffians just about right. I shouldn't wonder ef it made considerable of a stir when it gits published. I did think when I fust thought of putting my persecutions all down on paper, of sendin' it tew the Editor of Mr. Harper's Magazine, which maybe you've hearn tell on ; but I calculated, after considerin' a spell, that the Thunderbolt would pitch intew those all-fired mean scamps—the Missourians—a nation sight stronger."

We intimated that we concurred fully in the Colonel's sentiments, and expressed an opinion that the " history would make considerable of a stir." We, moreover, insinuated, as flatteringly as we could, that " Our Correspondent " would be delighted if its talented author could favor us with a perusal of his manuscript ; to which our friend, " The Circumstance," obligingly consents, and after a very slight display of diffidence, hands over the first fifteen pages, being all, as he says, that he has " yet got finished up right slick, and copied off ready for the editur." It is, moreover, written upon foolscap—quite an appropriate selection of stationery—which goes to prove that

'' The Circumstance " has an innate knowledge of the fitness of
things, or, as Mr. Somebody says, " goes in for a most refreshing
preservation of the unities."

We unfold the manuscript—we settle ourself to read—the
contents are *peppery* and AMUSING withal—the style knocks Murray and the writers on Composition into fits—the spelling is an
improvement upon Webster's " biggest," insomuch as " The Circumstance " goes entirely by sound, or, in other words, spells
with a Deown Eastern accent. We get deeper into the story—
our face expands—we have arrived at the most solemn part of
" his sufferin's "—he is choked—he is reduced to a solitary shirt
—he endeavors to eat, not only his own words, but somebody's
else, but his irritated stomach rejects the indignity, and vomits
forth the written word, even as the whale of old did Jonah—we
go on with our reading—we smile—we can't help it—we bury
our face in the sheets to conceal our mirth, for we are perusing
that part of the martyr's narrative, which sets forth his thrilling
adventures in the town of Franklin, where—so says his history---
he was taken to a grocery—it may, perchance, be the same that
we have elsewhere described—by his captors, the renowned Sheriff Jones being at their head, and then and there compelled to sit
by and look on patiently, while his Border Ruffian guards whiled
away the night by playing sundry games of euchre, with a due
observance of the Far Western rule of " anti up or leave the
board," " until," says the martyr, " Sheriff Jones lost forty-five
dollars, and then, bein' busted up himself, turned round and
asked me if I didn't want tew take a hand, which I guessed was
intended to be a addin' of injury to insult, as Mr. Boz's parrot
said, when they carried him away from his native country, and
made him study the English language afterwards."

At this point of " The Circumstance's " narrative, we tried
one of Mr. Weller's easy inside laughs, which proved a failure
—we could restrain our mirth no longer—we " snickered right

out "—"The Circumstance" looked astonished—so we made a bad joke to cover our breach of etiquette, and tried to look sorry and sentimental as we once more bent over the manuscript ; but it wouldn't do, " Natur' would have her way "—we read a line or two—relapsed again—apologized—burst into another roar, and finally, with a hasty good night, seized a tallow candle, and fairly rushed off to bed, muttering something as we went, about packing up and an early start, but, in reality, to escape the storm of wrath, which our ill-timed merriment had called forth; for the unwholesome hue of our bandy-legged " Circumstance's " angry face was already rivalling the intensity of his fiery red hair, as the worthy Colonel strove in vain to stammer out his indignation.

And now, let us add another medley of useful information, ere we say farewell to Kansas, and take the homeward road.

The following is an abstract of a letter addressed to the editor of the " Missouri Democrat," by a—Free State—Kansas Correspondent.   It may very properly be headed

A BORDER RUFFIAN NOTICE TO LEAVE, ETC.

KANSAS, *Monday, Feb.* 18, 1856.

The Kickapoo Rangers, who are reported to be collecting in the vicinity of Eastin, have sent the following letter to Mr. Sparks, advising him to leave :—

TO STEPHEN SPARKS.

The undersigned, as you are aware, are citizens of this neighborhood. Many of us have come here with our families, intending to make Kansas our permanent home.   It is our interests and desire that peace and good will prevail among us, and whatever may conduce to this desirable end will meet our hearty approval.

The local excitements that have occurred in this vicinity have been principally attributed to you, and, as we believe, justly.   You have figured in them conspicuously, and in the affair at Eastin, more reprehensibly than ever.

Believing, therefore, that your further residence among us is incompatible with the peace and welfare of this community, we advise you to leave as soon as you can conveniently do so.

[Here follow the signatures of thirty-seven persons.]

I have copied the above from the original letter sent to this city by Mr. Sparks, who says he knows several of those whose names appear affixed to the letter. The letter is written in a plain, legible hand, and neither of the signatures correspond with it, showing that the document was prepared with some care, and by one not on hand to sign it at the time it was sent.

Mr. Sparks, you will doubtless remember, was taken prisoner at the election at Eastin, on the 17th of February last, by the Rangers, and afterwards rescued by Brown with fifteen men.

NOTE.—For this act, Brown—according to Free State letter-writers—was subsequently taken prisoner by a party of the Rangers, and put to death.

WHAT IS IN THE WIND?

The "Independence Dispatch' states that the militia of the border counties in Missouri, are to rendezvous at Fort Scott, in this Territory, on the 29th of February. What business has the military forces of Missouri in Kansas? and why do they concentrate their strength at Fort Scott at that particular juncture?

It is a fact, that military organizations have been forming everywhere along the border in Missouri, consisting generally of mounted riflemen. We have observed these demonstrations for some time, and now comes a notice to invade the Territory on the 29th inst.

Senator Atchison, in his speech at Platte City, a few days ago, told his friends to hold themselves in readiness against the 4th of March, when they would be called upon to march into the Territory.

NEWSPAPERS IN KANSAS.

Leavenworth Herald.—Democratic and Pro-Slavery in its politics—published weekly at Leavenworth City. This was the first newspaper established in the Territory—on the 23rd of Dec. 1855, it had reached the 15th No. of its second volume. It is edited by Brig. Gen. Lucien J. Eastin—Reeves Pollard, a relation of the Hon. William C. Reeves, acts as its corresponding editor at Washington City. Its subscription list is estimated at 2,500. It is furnished at $2 00 per annum in advance ; this is, we believe, the uniform price of all newspapers in Kansas— there being as yet, no *Daily* printed in the Territory. Eastin and Adams are the proprietors of the *Leavenworth Herald*.

Squatter Sovereign.—Published at Atchison, on Nov. 6th, had reached the 39th No. of the first volume. Democratic and Pro-Slavery—subscription list estimated at 2,200. Edited by Stringfellow and Reby, who are also its proprietors.

Kansas Pioneer.—Published at Kickapoo, Leavenworth Co., Pro-Slavery and Know Nothing. On 9th Dec. had reached 6th No. of 2d volume, edited by A. B. Hazzard, Wm. P. Berry, its assistant editor, is said to own the paper.

Herald of Freedom.—Published at Lawrence. Edited by William G. Brown. The Kansas Correspondent of the St Louis Democrat, a Free Soil sheet, writes, as we are informed, to that paper—that this journal lost $6,000 during the first year. Is ultra Free State.

The *Lawrence Tribune* was formerly published at Lawrence, and was edited by S. N. Wood and Spear, but is now either defunct or removed to some other part of the Territory. It was Free State in its politics.

Kansas Free State, published at Lawrence. Free State in its politics. Miller and Elliot editors and proprietors.

Kansas Freeman, Free State ; published at Topeka, Shawnee Co., edited by E. C. K. Garvey, an Irishman. This journal was the organ of the Free State Convention at Topeka, during its session, to report whose proceedings it published a daily until the adjournment.

Territorial Register, owned and edited by Mark W. Delahaye, the Free State candidate for Delegate to Congress, an ultra Free State sheet ; the press and type of this journal were thrown into the Missouri river by a mob, last month ; the cause of complaint *alleged* being certain slanderous attacks upon the moral character of the Kickapoo Volunteers.

The *prospectuses* of several new papers on *both sides* are out, but we shall content ourself with giving a list of those now in existence.

CHAPTER XXXIX.

LAST LINES.

AND now we must be brief; suffice it to say then, that we left Lawrence at an early hour upon the 9th, reached Westport, Mo., upon the evening of that day, where we booked ourself, *per force*, by Smashup's line for Jefferson City, where we arrived with, wonderful to relate, only one serious upset upon the 14th. Here, as we are very independent, we gave Smashup and Co the cold shoulder, by taking our own conveyance—our trustworthy Shank's mare, for the Gasconade, a distance of some five and forty miles, which we walked upon the railroed ties in two days. Then came Herman, from whence we travelled by the Pacific railroad to St. Louis, where we put up at Barnum's, one of the few hotels in the Western country, which we have any knowledge of, that is *not* a *Barnum* in more senses than one. Here we tarried one night, and in the morning pursued our way eastward ; but as we have already given the reader a somewhat lengthy sketch of our journey westward *to* St. Louis, we will bid him good-bye so far as our incidents of travel go at this point, for railroading is very much the same thing, whether you go or come.

And finally, for a grand display of rhetorical fireworks, by way of finish to our history of the Wakarusa war ; we would respectfully request that we may be permitted to introduce the following.

We are about to say a long farewell to Kansas, unless, indeed, her good citizens should graciously condescend to get up another war, in which case we shall be on hand with all convenient speed to *see* the fray. and it may be, " write up " its history.   But for the present, good-bye to the Territory—a sad farewell withal, for—political rows, and this bitter winter weather, always excepted—we are disposed to like Kansas; moreover, we believe in Kansas, for she will, at some future day, accomplish much greater things than party quarrels, or Wakarusa wars.   Her strength is within herself—she has natural advantages which nothing but the Almighty's arm can wrest from her grasp—a fertile soil—a healthy climate—a wide expanse of territory—the want of timber being her only indwelling drawback.   Give her these, and—we care not whether they come from the North or from the South—for we have in this matter no sectional prejudices—give her, we say, but a sufficiency of true-hearted, and able-bodied Anglo-Saxon men and women, every-day working-people, not fine ladies and gentlemen, not broken-down politicians, or pot-house-ranting fillibusters, and we will venture to predict that the moral atmosphere of the Territory would clear itself from its impurities within six months time, but above all things, let the men who are to till those yet unbroken acres, and ere long make the laws of the State, which is soon to take her glorious place among the proud sisterhood of the Republic, be *conservatives*.   For it is a well-established fact, that as Radicalism is the disorganizer, so is Conservatism not only the pacificator but the absolute preserver of the frontier.   And we feel assured that if those who claim to be the best friends of Kansas—and in saying this we reiterate our disclaimer of any sectional leanings—would but be satisfied to attend to their own affairs, and let border disturbances alone, it would be infinitely better for the Territory and a real blessing to its inhabitants.   Nations, like individuals, derive but little benefit from officious outside interference, however well intended it may be.

When we started for Kansas, we expected to see a fight, a "free-fight" at that, but we have been disappointed. For though we found her political lions quite ready to growl, and not unwilling to show their teeth ; yet, when it came to using them, they—as a Western man would quaintly express it—"want thar," and we don't believe that many of them would have been "thar" if the struggle had come. This is, therefore, to our mind, another reason—as we would be denied even the poor consolation of knowing that a conflict might rid us of some bad men—for deprecating most strenuously either incendiary speeches or inflammatory publications, for all these things can tend to but one result, and that is, to arouse the worst passions of the most brutal and least reflecting people ; and believe us, that there are none who appreciate more fully than *some* of the lead-ing agitators *in* Kansas the truth of the assertion—that it is far easier to excite a mob, than to restrain that mob, when evil counsels have done their irritating work. And furthermore, do not every-day occurrences prove that those who are readiest to

"Cry havoc and let loose the dogs of war,"

are not always the first to be *in at the death*?

But we are not prepared to admit that a reasonable amount of "blood-letting," might not, *at one time*, have done the future Kansas a world of good, that is to say, if the bleeding could have been confined to her own "body politic." But when Kansas bleeds, Georgia must open her veins, and Massachusetts too, for when this comes to pass it requires no prophet to foretell a struggle which will crimson alike the Missouri and the Hudson. Were it otherwise, we would declare ourself an upholder of the doctrine that "a little *fighting* saves a deal of *quarrelling*." But of one thing we feel confident, Kansas Territory has already been the theatre of too many *windy* battles, in which words—words—words—bad words—harsh words—devilish words—have been rattled down like hail-stones, night after night, and day after day, by interested *talkers* upon *either* side, who didn't care a brass farthing whether the true interests of the people went to *Pandemonium* or not, so long as they—Messrs. A B and C, the chief strikers upon the political anvil—got an office. Would to God that this great, and *at present* happy country, had some vast *lunatic asylum*, located, if you please, amid the wilds of the Rocky Mountains, where tried and convicted demagogues from all quarters of the Union, could find a home, be supported at the public expense, and punished by a forced perusal of their own mischief-making speeches, and verily, if this book could but accomplish the establishment of so laudable an institution, we, its author, should feel more than compensated for our labor and our time.   Finally then,

"Farewell, and if forever, still farewell"

to Kansas and her children.   We have, if we mistake not, left behind us, among our newly-formed friends of both the Free State and Pro-Slavery parties, many sincere well-wishers, whose kind regards will accompany us to our far Eastern home, and to whom our heart goes out, across the weary miles which separate us, and we flatter ourself, too, that for a New Yorker, and a newspaper correspondent, we have been wonderfully successful in our fraternizing with the so-called "Border Ruffians," a title, by the way, in which the residents of the frontier counties of Missouri take no little pride.   We have even told you of a lady who, at a Kansas "sociable," refused to accept the hand of a Free State gentleman in the dance, because *she* was a "Border Ruffian." The epithet is therefore not one of reproach, save in the mouths of their political opponents.   And since we have touched upon the subject, permit us, before closing this paragraph, to remark that a "Border Ruffian" is not always, as many would have you to suppose, necessarily either a villian, a low-bred fellow, or a cold-blooded assassin, and yet were you to credit all that you hear, and we regret to add, much that you read, you might easily imagine that the Border Ruffian was a horrible compound of the three; in fact, a man so utterly degraded as to be unworthy of the Bible, and an outlaw, not only in the eyes of Christian men, but even to those who tell us weekly from their pulpits, of the blessings accorded to the peace-makers, who shall be called the children of God.

Let us, then—who have seen with our own eyes, and heard these matters with our personal ears, which are, we assure you, quite as long, *but no longer* than those of other people—sketch the inner and mental, as we have already done the outer and physical man of this much abused class of our Native American brotherhood.

The Border Ruffian, as the *better* half of his *sobriquet* indicates, is born and, as he himself would express it, "raised" upon the Border. He is generally a person of great endurance, strong limbs, iron constitution, and undoubted personal courage ; he is, however, subjected to all the intellectual disadvantages and deprivations of bodily comforts, which are the inseparable accompaniments of a life upon the frontier. But, if some things have been denied, others have been granted ; he can do that, my city friend, which you cannot ; we would back him against you, and take long odds upon the issue, in a "rough and tumble" fight ; where you would fail in hitting a barn-door with your rifle, he would draw the same weapon upon a squirrel, and turn coolly round, with his fore-finger upon the trigger, to ask you " where you would have him shot ? in the right eye, or did you allow to prefer the other ?" If you can flourish a yard stick, my nice young man, he understands the bowie knife ; and though he couldn't do much at a "polka redowa"—"first time off"—he'd trouble you at a foot-race, and ride the scariest horse that ever put you in fear of your life, between Brooklyn

Ferry and John Eyes. Be candid, then, and admit that in *physical* accomplishments at least, he is your *equal*. But stay, we haven't done with you yet; we want you to acknowledge something *more*. Would *you* have done better had you been in *his* place? Allow a little latitude then, for a difference in tastes, pursuits, circumstances, and above all in training. He sees the world in his way, not in yours; habit has taught him to consider a "bar fight" good fun, and a well-chinked log-cabin a "right smart house." You might consider the one a very terrible sort of amusement, and the other hardly fit for a cow-shed. What wonder, then, if our Border Ruffian *be* a little rough? Try it for yourself; spend six months in his shanty, and we will venture to say that, at the end of your probation, your dear friend, who *used* to know you very well upon Broadway, wouldn't be able to "tell tother from which," no, not even with the assistance of his best eye-glass. But does it necessarily follow that our "outsider" must, therefore, degenerate into a beast, or even be lacking in those finer qualifications of head and heart, which, after all, make or mar the man? We answer, most emphatically, *no*. For *as a general thing*, and we speak from a very large personal experience of American frontiersmen, as they really are, we firmly believe that, in *these respects*, they will compare—considering their educational defects —favorably with the inhabitants of any of our sea-board States, and we defy any man or any set of men to prove the contrary. Nay, we will even go further, and declare that, were you to test this thing, and in so doing, place the man of the log-cabin beside the man of our metropolitan mansions, we would, in nine cases out of ten, back the Border Ruffian for natural intelligence, sterling integrity, and true worth, not to mention *honor*, against the smooth tongued, accurately-attired citizen, and trust confidently to the result to uphold our decision. Strike out the names of our self-made and rudely-nurtured men from the records of American genius, literature, enterprise, and patriotism, and then tell us, if you please, how much would there be left upon the page, which History might find worthy of recording? We cry shame, therefore, upon the wholesale defamation of our own Far Western citizens, which has, of late, been scattered broad-cast through the land. If the shell be rough, does it then follow that there is no sweetness in its kernel? or must the diamond be deemed valueless, because there is no polish upon the stone?

And now, a word or two on the other side. Ultra Pro-Slavery men generally, and more particularly the *Missourians*, are but too much in the habit of denouncing every one with whom they come in contact—who is known to be a native, or even a resident of a Free State—as a fanatic, an Abolitionist, a negrostealer, or, for that matter, almost anything which is bad, low, vile, and irreclaimable. They make the question of Slavery, in season and out of season, a *sine qua non*—an all-proving touchstone—by which every man's moral and political character must, in their estimation, either stand or fall, as his belief inclines to the one side or the other. There is, in fact, but one question asked, and that is, " Do you endorse the peculiar institutions of the South ?" or, as they define it, " Are you all right on the goose ?" If you, being Free State born, answer *yea*, you may be believed, or, as frequently happens, be charged openly or in secret, with approving a doctrine by words, which you really do not endorse at heart. If, on the contrary. you should answer *nay*, then look out for squalls ; you may simply be insulted, but in some parts of the country, you might be tarred and feathered, and that too, without benefit of clergy. All this, of course, applies to a certain class, who are as great fanatics in their way, as the most incendiary Eastern Abolitionists, and we regret to add that this fillibustering class, under the influence of an ill-judged outside pressure, is increasing daily ; indeed, it would almost seem that the South was really striving to see the North in its worst possible light, until, in their legislative assemblies, and public meetings, as well as in the editorials of their journals, we hear naught but disunion—Southern rights—war to the knife—and such like phrases, which must sound badly *abroad*, and ought to be regarded as a national disgrace *at home*.

And now, farewell ! Take care of yourselves, good people, and if you will go to Kansas, go there as conservative and law-abiding men. They feel the want of such persons there now, and will, it may be, need them still more in the stormy times to come ; for, let the citizens of the United States take it to heart, that this disturbance in Kansas means something. At present, two thousand conservative men would do more to save Kansas and the Union than you

> " Good easy men, who think full surely that
> Your greatness is a ripening,"

may ever condescend to realize until it is too late.

And now finally, farewell.

THE END.

DERBY & JACKSON'S

STANDARD BRITISH CLASSICS

IN FIFTY VOLUMES, COMPRISING:

BOSWELL'S JOHNSON,	Four Volumes.
ADDISON'S WORKS,	Six Volumes.
GOLDSMITH'S WORKS,	Four Volumes.
FIELDING'S WORKS,	Four Volumes.
SMOLLETT'S WORKS,	Six Volumes.
STERNE'S WORKS,	Two Volumes.
DEAN SWIFT'S WORKS,	Six Volumes.
JOHNSON'S WORKS,	Two Volumes.
DEFOE'S WORKS,	Two Volumes.
LAMB'S WORKS,	Five Volumes
HAZLITT'S WORKS,	Five Volumes
LEIGH HUNT'S WORKS,	Four Volumes

Pronounced the most valuable and handsome set of books ever intro duced into the American market. Put up in two elegant cases, bound in half calf antique, or half calf gilt. Price $2 25 per volume, or, per set, $112 50.

We also have the same works, bound in neat cloth, for $1 25 per volume; or sheep, library style for $1 50 per vol.

*** **Either or all of the above will be sent by mail, post-paid on receipt of price.**

W. H. Tinson, Printer and Stereotyper 43 & 45 Centre St., N. Y.

THE STANDARD FRENCH CLASSICS.

NEW AMERICAN EDITIONS.

(*Uniform with* DERBY & JACKSON'S *Standard British Classics.*)

EDITED BY O. W. WIGHT, A.M.

TRANSLATOR OF M. COUSIN'S PHILOSOPHY, AND EDITOR OF SIR WILLIAM HAMILTON'S
PHILOSOPHICAL WORKS.

THERE having long been felt among book-buyers and scholars generally, the need of library editions—convenient in size and reasonable in price—of the greatest and best FRENCH AUTHORS, Derby & Jackson have undertaken to supply this desideratum, by the publication, in uniform style of print, paper and binding, translations of the works of those celebrated French Writers, which have become classic in the History of Literature. Fifteen volumes are now ready, as follows:

MONTAIGNE'S COMPLETE WORKS.
In 4 vols., 12mo., Cloth, $5; Sheep, library style, $6; Half calf, gilt or antique, $9.

FENELON'S ADVENTURES OF TELEMACHUS.
12mo., Cloth, $1 25; Sheep, $1 50; Half calf, gilt or antique, $2 25.

PASCAL'S PROVINCIAL LETTERS.
12mo., Cloth, $1 25; Sheep, $1 50; Half calf, gilt or antique, $2 25.

VOLTAIRE'S CHARLES TWELFTH.
12mo., Cloth, $1 25; Sheep, $1 50; Half calf, gilt or antique, $2 25.

MADAME DE STAËL'S GERMANY.
In 2 vols., Cloth, $2 50; Sheep, 3 00; Half calf, gilt or antique, $4 50.

VOLTAIRE'S LA HENRIADE AND OTHER POEMS.
12mo., Cloth, $1 25; Sheep, $1 50; Half calf gilt or antique, $2 25.

PASCAL'S THOUGHTS.
12mo., Cloth, $1 25; Sheep, $1 50; Half calf, gilt or antique, $2 25.

CHATEAUBRIAND'S MARTYRS.
12mo., Cloth, $1 25; Sheep, $1 50; Half calf, gilt or antique, $2 25.

LA FONTAINE'S FABLES.
Two vols., 12mo., Cloth, $2 50; Sheep, $3 00; Half calf, gilt, or antique, $4 50.

MADAME DE STAËL'S CORINNE.
12mo., Cloth, $1 25; Sheep, $1 50; Half calf, gilt, or antique, $2 25.

THE STANDARD FRENCH CLASSICAL LIBRARY.

Embracing the preceding 15 volumes, in a neat case, cloth, $18 75
Same—Sheep, library style, ... 22 50
Same—Half calf, gilt, ... 33 75
Same—half calf, antique, ... 33 75

" The best Painter of Sea Characters since Smollett."
Edinburgh Review.

MARRYAT'S NOVELS.

First complete American edition, printed from new stereotype plates, long primer leaded, matching in size the popular 12mo. edition of Irving, Cooper, Dickens, etc.   Containing :—

JACOB FAITHFUL.	PETER SIMPLE.
KING'S OWN.	MIDSHIPMAN EASY.
SNARLEYYOW.	NEWTON FORSTER.
NAVAL OFFICER.	THE POACHER.
JAPHET in Search of a Father.	THE PHANTOM SHIP.
PACHA OF MANY TALES.	PERCIVAL KEENE.

Price in Cloth, ...	$12 00
" Sheep, library style, ...	15 00
" Half calf, extra, ...	24 00
" Half calf, antique, ...	24 00

" Captain Marryat's writings depict life at sea with the same fidelity, and with far more spirit, than any of the fashionable novels portray a rout, a ball, or a breakfast, and we much prefer the subject as well as the talent of the nautical novels ; a storm at sea is more animating than a crash at St. James' ; we prefer a shipwreck to a ruin at Crockford's ; the sly humor of the old sailor is more amusing than the exclusive slang of Bond street, and a frigate action calls up higher feelings and qualities than a hostile meeting in Battersea Fields.   Captain Marryat's productions are happy in more senses than one : he employs neither the effort nor the prolixity of Cooper ; his conception of character is so facile and felicitous, that his personages immediately become our intimate acquaintance, and astonish us by their faithful resemblance to whole classes of beings similarly situated.   Captain Marryat's humor is genuine, it flows naturally, and insensibly communicates to the reader the gaiety the author seems himself animated with."— *Westminster Review.*

*** The above will be sent by mail, post-paid, on receipt of price.

BOOKS WRITTEN BY A. S. ROE.

THERE is no writer of the present day who excels this charming author in the natural and home-like simplicity of his style, and the natural interest and truthfulness of his narrative. In thousands of families and Sabbath Schools his books are read and re-read with ever-increasing delight. The young and old, the quiet and gay, are alike fascinated by his pages. Rival editions of all his books have been published in England, edited by the Rev. Dr. TAYLOR, where they have already reached the enormous sale of 120,000 volumes—a sure indication that his pen is one whose "touch of nature makes the whole world kin."

IV'E BEEN THINKING ; or, The Secret of Success. 12mo., clo., $1 00
TO LOVE AND TO BE LOVED ; or, Strive and Win. 12mo., clo., . 1 25
A LONG LOOK AHEAD ; or, The First Stroke and the Last. 12mo, clo., 1 25
THE STAR AND THE CLOUD ; or, A Daughter's Love. 12mo., clo., 1 25
TRUE TO THE LAST ; or, Alone, on a Wide Wide Sea. 12mo., clo., 1 25
HOW COULD HE HELP IT ? or The Heart Triumphant. 12mo., clo., 1 25

From the London Critic.

" Mr. Roe is one of the most successful of American writers. He has originality of thought, and natural powers of invention."

From the New York Christian Intelligencer

" Mr. Roe evidently knows how to touch the heart-strings ; indeed, he sweeps them with a master's hand. At one time we find it impossible to restrain a gushing tear ; at another every risible nerve is in full exercise."

From the United States Magazine.

" Hogarth not more surely touches life with his wizard spell. It is transfixed and permanent. ' A Long Look Ahead ' is the crystallization of his genius, and, like Goldsmith's ' Vicar of Wakefield,' should be placed upon the shelf to show what American views and manners reveal, just as that simple tale tells of what comes from English institutions. He is an American truly and heartily : American in thought and feeling, American in tone and language. His books will live as graphic pictures of the times he delineates. Rather of the old school in Church and social privileges, he is sufficiently universal to make his delineation national. There is about him a complacency, a wholesome cheerfulness, a fertility of resource, a hopefulness, a glow and persistency wholly Yankee."

₊ The above will be sent by mail, post-paid, on receipt of price.

MARION HARLAND'S WORKS.

ALONE, ...	12mo., $1 25
THE HIDDEN PATH, . .	12mo., 1 25
MOSS-SIDE, ...	12mo., 1 25
NEMESIS, ...	12mo., 1 25

OF the success of MARION HARLAND'S "ALONE," "HIDDEN PATH," and "MOSS-SIDE," in this country, it is hardly necessary to speak. Nearly

500,000 READERS

testify to their wonderful popularity. In the language of the *New York Observer*—"There is genius, pathos, humor, and moral in her charming pages; much knowledge of human nature, and power to delineate character;" And of the *New York Evangelist*—"Home, sincerity and truth are invested with most attractive charms. While engaging the imagination she makes all submit to its moral impression, and enlists the reader's approbation exclusively with the virtuous and true."

The *New York Evening Post*, in a review of the "HIDDEN PATH," says:

"The following notice of this work, which we find in the *Richmond Enquirer*, is from the generous pen of Mrs. ANNA CORA RITCHIE, and contains a just tribute to the literary talents of the most successful female writer Virginia has yet produced:

"'Let this *noble* production (we use the adjective in its fullest sense) lie upon the table, enliven the hearth, be the household companion of every true-hearted Virginian. Foster this gifted daughter of the South with the expanding sunshine of appreciation, the refreshing dews of praise—stimulate undeveloped genius, which has never yet "penned its inspiration," to walk in her steps, emulate her achievements, and share her honors—let Virginia produce a few more such writers, and the cry that the South has no literature of its own is silenced forever! The "HIDDEN PATH" is a work that North or South, East or West, may point to with the finger of honest pride, and say "*Our daughter*" sends this message to the world—pours this balm into the wounded hearts—traces for wavering, erring feet this "HIDDEN PATH," which leads to the great goal of eternal peace.'"

As much, or more, can be said in praise of

"ALONE," "MOSS-SIDE," AND "NEMESIS."

₊ The above will be sent by mail, post paid, on receipt of prices.

DERBY & JACKSON, PUBLISHERS,

498 Broadway, New York.

THE WORKS OF JANE AUSTEN.

Comprising "Pride and Prejudice," "Sense and Sensibility," "Mansfield Park," "Northanger Abbey," "Emma," and "Persuasion." First American Edition, with steel vignettes, complete in 4 vols., 12mo.

Price in Cloth, · · · · · · $4 00
"   Sheep, library style, · · · 5 00
"   Half calf, gilt or antique,· · 8 00

Miss Austen is emphatically the novelist of Home. The truth, spirit, ease, and re fined humor of her style, have rarely been equalled. She will always retain a leading position in literature, as the representative of the domestic school of novels, of which she was the founder, the great charm of which is truth and simplicity; and notwithstanding the brilliant successes of many recent imitators, she still remains undisputed mistress of this class of composition.

THE WORKS OF HANNAH MORE.

Two vols. now ready.

Comprising "Cœlebs in Search of a Wife," her Tales and Allegories. With portrait on steel. 12mo.

Price in Cloth, · · · · · · $2 00
"   Sheep, library style, · · · 2 50
"   Half calf, gilt or antique, · · 4 00

"How many have thanked God for the hour that first made them acquainted with the Writings of Hannah More. She did, perhaps, as much real good in her generation as any woman that ever held the pen. It would be idle for us to dwell here on works so well known. They have established her name as a great moral writer, possessing a masterly command over the resources of our language, and devoting a keen wit and a lively fancy to the best and noblest of purposes."—*Quarterly Review.*

*** The above will be sent by mail, post-paid, on receipt of price

W. H. Tinson, Printer and Stereotyper, 43 & 45 Centre St., N. Y.

THE WORKS OF CHARLOTTE BRONTE

(CURRER BELL.)

Comprising "Jane Eyre," "Shirley," and "Villette."   Complete in 3
Vols., 12mo.

Price in Cloth, ... $3 00
"   Sheep, library style, ... 3 75
"   Half calf, gilt or antique, ... 6 00

EVELINA;
OR,
𝔗he 𝔥istory of a 𝔜oung 𝔏ady's 𝔍ntroduction to the 𝔚orld.

BY FRANCES BURNEY, (*MADAME D'ARBLAY.*)

With a Life of the Author by T. B. Macaulay.   12mo.

Price in Cloth, ... $1 00
"   Sheep, library style, ... 1 25
"   Half calf, gilt or antique, ... 2 00

"Frances Burney was the wonder and delight of the generation of novel readers
succeeding that of Fielding and Smollett, and she has maintained her popularity better
than most secondary writers of fiction.   In painting the characters in a drawing-room,
or catching the follies and absurdities that float on the surface of fashionable society,
she has rarely been equalled."—*Cyclo. of English Literature.*

CORINNE; or, Italy.

BY MADAME DE STAEL.

TRANSLATED BY ISABEL HILL.

With Metrical Versions of the Odes by L. E. Landon.   12mo.

Price in Cloth, ... $1 00
"   Sheep, library style, . . 1 25
"   Half calf, gilt or antique, . 2 00

"It (Corinne) possesses the highest merit as a work delineating character, and de-
scriptive of scenery, and inculcates a pure morality.   Its eloquent rhapsodies upon
love, religion, virtue, nature, history, and poetry, have given it an enduring place in
literature."—*Goodrich.*

*** * The above will be sent by mail, post-paid, on receipt of price**

W. H. Tinson, Printer and Stereotyper, 43 & 45 Centre St., N. Y.

THE WORKS OF ANNE RADCLIFFE.

Two vols., now ready.

Comprising "The Mysteries of Udolpho," and "Romance of the Forest"
With steel portrait.   12mo.

Price in Cloth, ... $2 00
"   Sheep, library style,   .   .   2 50
"   Half calf, gilt or antique,   .   4 00

Like the great painter with whom she has been compared, Mrs. Radcliffe loves to sport with the romantic and terrible—with the striking images of the mountain forests, the cloud and storm, wild banditti, ruined castles, half-discovered glimpses of visionary shadows of the invisible world which seem at times to cross our path, and which still haunt and thrill the imagination.

THE WORKS OF JANE PORTER.

Two vols., now ready.

Comprising "The Scottish Chiefs," and "Thaddeus of Warsaw."   With
steel portrait.   12mo.

Price in Cloth, ... $2 00
"   Sheep, library style,   .   .   2 50
"   Half calf, gilt or antique,   .   4 00

" 'Thaddeus of Warsaw,' 'which in our youth beguiled us of our tears,' is a favorite. It is to Miss Porter's fame that she began the system of historical novel-writing, which attained the climax of its renown in the hands of Sir Walter Scott.   And no light praise it is that she has thus pioneered the way for the greatest exhibition of the greatest genius of our time.   She may parody Bishop Hall, and tell Sir Walter :

'I first adventured—follow me who list,
And be *second* Scottish novelist.' "
Fraser's Magazine.

***** The above will be sent by mail, post-paid, on receipt of price.**